Tejas Desai was born, raised and currently lives in New York City where he works as a supervising librarian for Queens Public Library. He is a graduate of Wesleyan University and holds a MFA in Creative Writing and Literary Translation from CUNY-Queens College. He is the author of the international crime series *The Brotherhood Chronicle* and *The Human Tragedy* literary series. In 2012, he founded The New Wei literary movement which seeks to promote provocative and meaningful narrative artists. His articles on literature have been published in *HuffPost* and other publications.

Praise for *The Run and Hide*

"At once timely and exciting, Tejas Desai's *The Brotherhood Chronicle* is a must-read and will keep you guessing."—*Queens Courier*

"Tejas Desai nailed the underworld grit of Queens in *The Brotherhood.* With book two of the trilogy, *The Run and the Hide,* the story of Indian-American Niral goes international in scope. From debt, he enters a crime world that takes him to Thailand and India. The well-crafted settings and swift dialogue take the reader on an unforgettable journey. There are dark themes, but it contains hope for redemption for Niral, his family, and the Hindu Brotherhood organization."—Matthew Allison, http://the-mallison.com

"This book is truly enjoyable. You should read it to learn more about different cultures and countries. It's a ticket to fun and suspense!"—Kacper Jarecki, author of *The Depression of The Blue Rainbow Sprinkle* (2014)

Other Books Released by The New Wei

The Brotherhood Chronicle

The Brotherhood by Tejas Desai (2012)

The Brotherhood by Tejas Desai (Second Edition) (2018)

The Human Tragedy

Good Americans by Tejas Desai (2013)

Independent Books and Blogs Recommended by The New Wei

A Brie Grows in Brooklyn by Brienne Walsh (online blog, http://abriegrowsinbrooklyn.com)

Waiting for the Bomb by Richard Livsey (2013)

The Other Son by Allan Avidano (2014)

The Depression of The Blue Rainbow Sprinkle by Kacper Jarecki (2014)

Escape from Samsara: Poems by Vijay R. Nathan (2016)

Celebrity Sadhana: Or How to Meditate With a Hammer (The Paparazzo Poet Meditations) by Vijay R. Nathan (2018)

THE RUN AND HIDE

*

THE BROTHERHOOD CHRONICLE

VOLUME 2

*

TEJAS DESAI

NW
THE NEW WEI

New York

The Run and Hide by Tejas Desai

Published by The New Wei LLC in Fresh Meadows, New York, September 2019

ISBN-13 # 978-0-9883519-9-8
Library of Congress Control Number: 2019909521

Cover Design by Fena Lee

Table of Contents

Book Two

“We cannot hope to escape karma by refraining from our duties:
even to survive in the world, we must act.”

— Veda Vyasa, the *Bhagavad Gita*

“Embrace nothing: If you meet the Buddha, kill the Buddha.
If you meet your father, kill your father. Only live your life as it is,
not bound to anything.”

— Gautama Siddhartha

Preface by the Author

This second volume of *The Brotherhood Chronicle* expands the narrative universe first introduced in *The Brotherhood.* A plethora of new characters, some of whom were mentioned in the first book, are thrown into the narrative landscape, and old ones return. In addition, the settings are international and vast, and the narrative seesaws between the stories of many characters.

Chronicle, I think, is the correct description for this series, for it is an accounting of a fictional world that one might imagine may be, in some strange way, related to our own. No time has called for a factual accounting of our world more than this one, with its fake news and fake media, but no time has also demanded that it be documented in fictional form more than this one, for no one believes the "factual" accounts of our time anyway.

I hope you will enjoy this story as "entertainment," as Graham Greene once called his thrillers, but also as an examination of the conflicts and crises of our time. It is an international crime epic, a meditation on Hinduism and Buddhism, as well as a multicultural and multinational stew of decadence and corruption, filled with unique characters, humor, philosophy, mystery, and action. Perhaps one might even consider this akin to "God's plenty," as Dryden once described *The Canterbury Tales,* if one is willing to believe in such a concept. I hope you enjoy it.

Tejas Desai

Orientation

After the cataclysmic events in New York City, Niral Solanke, scarred both internally and externally, was banished to the other side of the world to the country of Thailand, where he began working for an international criminal gang called the Dragons. He had incurred a debt after his friend Wan, a Dragon associate, saved his life and helped him find the Italian-American mobster Roberto Tragliani. The amount of the debt was unclear and seemed to increase endlessly, but Niral did not care. For the next few years, he was a broken shell of a man, discarding morality, sex, religion, and anything else but the simplest pleasures, surviving day to day in a world that had grown increasingly violent and inhumane.

While he welcomed death as much as life, luck shined upon him. Despite the wishes of some fellow Dragons, his weak demeanor and hesitancy to commit violence did not result in a death sentence. Rather, he was given to a diamond merchant, a fellow American named Duncan Smith, a legitimate business partner of the local Dragon boss, Fan Hong. But soon they were betrayed, and the criminal world asked him to conform, just as many organizations and ideologies had asked for his loyalty in the past. Then others, both old and new, were ready to pounce on him, too, just as men and women in his orbit continued their dance toward death, liberation, or something in between, forced to survive in a violent, oppressive, chaotic universe.

The following volume describes what occurred several years after the previous volume. Let there be mercy on earth.

Book One

PART I

†

Bangkok, Thailand; Kanchanaburi, Thailand

1

The sun shone down on Bob's head as he snapped pictures of the Thai mythology murals: pierced pigs drowning in rivers, demons with eyes like raccoons staring out below depictions of mass slaughter, deities making their occasional appearance as ape-humans.

Bob wiped his brow under his cap brim and turned to the touch-up artist next to him. "It ain't even this hot in El Paso," he exclaimed to an uncomprehending, "cool heart" smile in response.

"Time to move on," Bob said to himself, stuffing his smartphone back into his pocket. He was glad that Linda hadn't accompanied him. Her bitching about the heat was worse than in Texas. The hotel suited her well enough.

At the gate of the Grand Palace, Bob turned to the ceremonial soldier. "Korp khun krap!" he exclaimed.

"Sawat dee khap, sir," another man stated, correcting him. "That is the correct phrase. May I introduce myself? I am Porn, a government official."

The man was skinny. He was dressed in a crisply ironed gray shirt and smiled broadly at Bob.

"Howdy," Bob said, trying to keep the accent right. "Thought that was goodbye."

"Same, same," the official responded. "It is the same, sir. Let me guess. You are from Houston?"

"El Paso. But yeah, Texas," he said, touching his cap brim.

"Very good. I love Texas. I have a cousin studying there. Let me ask you: have you seen the other wats? Your ticket gives you admission to three attractions."

"Didn't know about no other wats," Bob replied, taking out a folded map from his pocket.

"Yes, sir. Do you have your map? Let me show you."

Bob offered his map. Porn unfolded it, took a pen from his shirt pocket, and circled two other wats on the map of the Grand Palace. "I can take you there. Only fifty baht for roundtrip on a tuk-tuk. Compliments of the Thai government, sir. Here is our ride now."

Bob turned and saw a tuk-tuk pull up. An enthusiastic driver gave him a thumbs up.

"The government?" Bob questioned.

"Yes, sir. Special price."

2

Porn gave Bob a thorough tour of Wat Pho, a large temple complex south of The Grand Palace. The tour included general histories of the Reclining Buddha, the stone panels depicting the Ramakien and many other Buddha statues and his Arahant disciples. Bob enjoyed the tour, but he was tired when he got back to the tuk-tuk and declined to see the other wat.

"I understand," Porn said. "It is hot, sir, even for us. But I have another option for you, if you will consider it. The government does many things. We enforce the law, for one. When we raid illegal operations, sometimes we seize merchandise. Often, this merchandise is forgotten and stored away for years. After a while, a special task force sells this merchandise for cheap prices because they do not want to put it back on the general market, but they also do not want to get nothing for it...."

"If you're trying to sell me drugs, forget it," Bob said sharply, losing his accent a bit. "I know what they do to drug dealers and users here."

"No, sir! We are the government, sir. I am talking about diamonds."

"Diamonds?"

"Yes, sir. We sell them for sixty percent off. You will make a fortune reselling them in America."

"Thought you were showing me a temple?" Bob asked, still suspicious.

"This is a side operation, sir. Tell me, are you retired? Do you get social security? Is it enough for you there, in Texas?"

Bob thought about his response. "My situation is none of your business. My wife is waiting..."

"Your wife! Your wife will love it. Think of how many rings you can make for her. Come, I only want to show you. If you do not want to buy anything, no one can force you. This is Thailand. We are the true land of the free."

Bob stared at Porn as he smiled. Then Bob shook his head and smirked. "You do know how to talk, huh?" He hesitated, then, staring up at the sun, said, "All right, I guess it won't hurt to take a look."

3

"Tell me, Bob, does your wife treat you well?" Porn asked him as they drove through some narrow streets.

"She's a wife," Bob said. "She led me to the promised land, then tugged me under, and pulled me up again. She's been a good wife, but she's a wife."

"I know what you mean, Bob. You will meet my wife, Duanphen, at the shop. She is a government official, too, who works with me. She is a sweet woman with good Thai values, Chiang Mai values, but sometimes I wonder if I treat her right. She doesn't know about the other women, my mia noi and the giks. Do you know what those are?"

"Yep, Porn, I do. Used to have plenty of those in the States. Actually started here. I fought in the Vietnam War. I was stationed in Khorat and got used to young Thai girls. When I went back, I wasn't nothing but working-class scum, but Linda, she got me to start investing my money. I got to working in finance, and soon enough, I was a millionaire."

Bob realized he had said too much. He started to mutter. Porn's eyes had gone wide.

"A millionaire?"

"Not no more," Bob backtracked. "I lost it all."

"Ah," Porn said, smiling slyly, "then this deal will be perfect for you. Come."

They entered a dead-end street and pulled up to a single shack. Painted a dull green with a red door, it stood in an isolated corner. Soon, the door opened. A beautiful young Thai woman dressed in a traditional, red and gold pha nung emerged. She performed a wai—a Thai greeting and sign of respect—and gestured for Bob to come inside. Bob followed her lead, smiling at the beautiful girl.

Inside was a small, cramped room, followed by a slight passageway that led to a bathroom. On the right side of the room was a counter behind which a single, humorless man stood at attention, his arms to his sides. Porn followed Bob, smiling at Duanphen as he entered. Then Duanphen closed and bolted the door, waiting beside it.

Porn spoke to the humorless man in Thai. The man nodded, ducked below the counter, and rose, holding a briefcase. He lay it on the counter. When he opened it, Bob's eyes widened.

A pile of diamonds lay inside, shiny and crisp.

"Easy $10,000, Bob," Porn said. "All you need to pay is $4,000, and it is yours. We can ship it to Texas, no problem."

He picked up one tiny stone and examined it. "And you're selling it for that much, why?"

"It is all profit to us. But we don't want the public to know we are selling impounded merchandise. Don't worry, we will use it to fight sex trafficking and child exploitation."

Bob swallowed. "How do I know they're worth that much? I don't have no one to check 'em."

"You will have to trust us, Bob. We are offering you a good deal."

"But I don't have that kind of cash on me."

"We take credit," the woman by the door said, smiling and nodding respectfully.

Bob looked at Porn, then Duanphen, then the unsmiling man, unsure.

"Come on, Bob, do it for Linda," Porn said, punching him lightly on the shoulder.

Bob heard a knock on the door. Porn scowled and turned. Bob saw Duanphen unbolting the door.

"Duanphen..." Porn yelled out, but the door had opened. Bob saw the tuk-tuk driver pushed inside. His hands were in the air. After him, two men followed. One was white with long, dirty blond dreads. The other was Indian. He had distinctive white blotches on his face, like clouds in a sweetened cup of coffee. Both held guns with silencers on their tips.

Duanphen shut the door and bolted it.

Porn cursed Duanphen in Thai, but it was too late. The white man shot the tuk-tuk driver in the back. He fell on Bob, who pushed him away frantically. The man behind the counter tried to duck, but the white man was too quick, hitting him with a shot to the head, which exploded like a watermelon, spraying blood and brains on Bob's cap as he held his hands up and closed his eyes, screaming.

"Shut up!" the white man shouted, and Bob went silent. "What's your name, mate?" the white man asked.

"Bob," he answered timidly, opening his eyes. He saw a gun pointed at his head.

"Bob, I'm Rob. Rhyme time, isn't it? Don't get ideas and don't have no worries, and you'll get out of this easy. No more screaming."

Bob nodded. Ignoring the briefcase, Rob went around the counter and ducked under it.

For the first time, Bob recognized Niral as the Indian man with the burn marks on his face. Niral pointed his gun at Porn, who had his hands up, but Niral's hands were shaking. Duanphen was behind Niral, waiting attentively.

"You bitch!" Porn exclaimed in English after saying what Bob imagined was the same thing in Thai. "You heartless, gold-digging..."

"Shut up, Thanat, or Porn, or whatever you're calling yourself," Niral said. "You know what we want. Tell us where it is."

"I don't have it anymore. I spent it. That was long time ago."

"You owe us what you stole. Plus interest. If you didn't want to owe us, you shouldn't have cheated us."

Porn sunk to his knees, putting his palms together.

"Tell Duncan I'm sorry. I didn't mean to. I didn't know..."

"You double-crossed us, selling us that worthless crap. Sir, you're lucky we came—," Niral started to tell Bob, but then he recognized it was Bob Macaday, and he shut up.

"I will get you your money back," Porn insisted. "I work for Sumantapat. He can pay."

"We're not interested in Sumantapat," Niral responded. "We want the money you stole. Period."

Rob stood up. "It's not here. We checked your apartment too, you cunt. Tell us where the moolah's at."

Porn glanced at Duanphen and whispered something to her in Thai. Rob raised his gun to him.

"Tell us, you wanker," he commanded.

Porn spit at Niral's feet. "You kill me now, if you must. But I know you can't."

"We don't care about you," Niral said. "If you don't tell us where the money is, we'll find it another way."

"I mean you are a coward, you Indian filth."

Porn leaped at Niral and grabbed his gun, trying to turn him around. Niral almost toppled over, but he stood his ground, struggling with Porn. Bob noticed Duanphen's face go red. She placed her palms on her cheeks. Rob didn't move, aiming at Porn's back.

Bob heard a shot. He could hear someone gurgling, then hard, desperate breathing. Porn fell backwards to the floor, holding his stomach. Niral held the gun in his hands, staring at it. His shirt was bloody.

Porn coughed blood. Rob still held him in his sights.

"Cowards," Porn muttered. He got up again and tried to lunge toward Niral, who was frozen in place, but Rob shot him three times in the back. Porn fell on his hands and knees, then sideways. He curled up and stopped moving.

"That's how you kill a cunt," Rob stated. Duanphen's eyes were closed.

Niral stared at the body and wiped away a tear with the back of his hand, blood smudging his face.

Rob came up behind Bob and put the gun to his head. Niral emerged from his trance.

"No!" Niral yelled. "Leave him."

"He knows my name. Knows Duncan's name too," Rob said.

Bob turned slowly, noticed the gun, and realized he was about to get shot.

"He won't say anything. I can tell," Niral said.

Rob locked eyes with Niral. He seemed to understand him.

"A missing American won't be good," Duanphen added.

Rob acknowledged Duanphen and put down his gun.

"You're lucky, mate," Rob said to Bob. "First not getting ripped off, now getting a second chance at life. But there's a price to pay. You're gonna help me clean up. And then you're never gonna mention this shit again to nobody. Got it?"

Bob nodded fiercely.

"Good. Niral, chop this wanker's head off and take it to Duncan. I'll finish cutting the body, and our new buddy here will help me."

From a duffel bag on his back, Rob took out a long machete. Duanphen put her hands on Niral's shoulders.

"There's a change of clothes in the back room," she told him. "For the blood."

Then she approached Rob and kissed him on the lips.

"He probably spent the money," she said. "I'll go with Niral so Duncan can understand that."

Rob smirked. "Apsara, sweetie," he said, using the name he knew her by, "you are convincing." They kissed again.

Niral appeared upset. Rob handed him the machete, handle out.

4

Niral drove his motorcycle up through Banglamphu, swerving through the cars and tuk-tuks, battling the other motorcycles for position. Apsara rode side-saddle, her hands gripping Niral's shoulders. He held the head, wrapped in several layers of cloth, between his legs.

Near the Chao Phraya river, they entered an old, unmanned gate and approached a deserted lot next to a warehouse. Niral parked the motorcycle. He felt Apsara's hands grip his shoulders firmly before she kneaded his tight muscles. She giggled and leaped off the bike.

"Kob-khun-kha!" she shouted. "Thank you!"

Niral moved his legs wide so he could get off the motorcycle, holding the head firmly so it wouldn't drop. His hands were shaking.

"Duncan will be happy," she said.

He gave her a sharp look. "How can you be so cheery? We just killed three people."

"Rob did. You don't shoot well, shaky."

"You would be happy. You seduced Thanat like it was nothing."

She turned serious. "He stole from Duncan. From you. He knew what could happen."

"Yes. Just don't think I'll fall for your tricks. I have plenty of experience with that."

"You wish, shadow face! I have many boyfriends. Do I need another?"

"I know you do. You're already Duncan's mia noi. So why are you screwing Rob?"

"Just because I am mia noi doesn't mean I cannot be wife to someone else. You think I just want to be mia noi..."

"Wife? You'll never be like Lamai."

She slapped his face. "Don't say that Chiang Mai cunt name to me," she snapped, snatching the head from Niral's hands and running toward the warehouse. Niral rubbed his cheek, then wiped his brow. It was still hot, and his mouth was dry. He needed some fruit soon. Water wasn't enough to satisfy his thirst.

He climbed the stairs to the fifth level, crossed the dilapidated floor filled with old crates and boxes, finally entering a large office decorated with green carpet and red walls. Duncan, his blond, wavy hair dipping over his ears and his eye twitching like usual, embraced and chuckled with his mia noi while sitting on his desk carved from Monkey Pod and featuring ornate designs of various Buddhas.

Apsara rubbed his penis through his pants, but Duncan stopped her and stood up. Niral saw the head on the front of the desk.

"Mission accomplished. Congratulations," Duncan said, holding out his hand. Niral shook it.

Duncan gave Niral a hesitant smile, then turned to Apsara.

"Give us a few minutes, honey. I need to speak to Niral alone."

Apsara smiled wryly and left the room, closing the door behind her.

Duncan moved behind the desk and gestured for Niral to sit. He did.

"I know this hasn't been easy for you," Duncan said. "I didn't want it to come to this, but it did. As Americans, we don't understand it, but losing face isn't something any Thai can stand, let alone a gangster."

"But we aren't gangsters, Duncan."

Duncan breathed, his eye twitching. "As long as I am Mr. Hong's poo noy, and as long as you're my poo noy, we are. We look weak if we don't respond to disrespect. And if we look weak, Mr. Hong looks weak. Then the Dragons look weak. And weakness is cut out of the body, like a gangrened limb."

"I guess I've been spoiled."

"Believe me, I didn't want this. I tried to get out of it, but there was no way. Remember when Nam recommended Mr. Hong get rid of you? He said you were worthless, spineless, but I saw something in you. I said I'd take you for my business. And even if they had kept you, you'd have killed a lot more people by now to prove your worth. So consider yourself lucky."

"You know I appreciate what you did for me. What you've done. You've treated me like a brother, like a best friend, rather than a worker or a slave."

"I'm glad you recognize it, and believe me, I appreciate what you've done for me too. Thanks for killing this scumbag. But we still don't have the money he stole."

"He probably spent it."

"It seems unlikely he could have spent so much in a short time. Unless he gave it to somebody or sent it back home, wherever that is. But whatever. We'll never get it now. If he gave it to Sumantapat, we definitely won't."

"I know Mr. Hong doesn't want to mess with him."

"He wants to lay low, work in peace. We had no choice but to kill his people, too, since Thanat decided to get into bed with them. Make sure Rob cleans up the scene and leaves no trace. What about the tourist?"

"He won't talk."

"You let him live?"

"Rob will take care of it. We don't need a missing American on the news."

"True." Duncan seemed to think, his eye twitching again. "Okay. Listen, Mr. Hong's in town. He flew in from Hong Kong this morning, and he's chilling at Same Same. Bring the head to him. It's tribute. He'll appreciate it, maybe even reward you by cutting your debt."

Niral became nervous. "Will Nam be there?"

"Probably. Don't worry about his dumb ass. Maybe he'll even pay you some respect now."

"That's what I'm worried about."

Duncan stood, taking the head in his hands, staring at the clothed dome.

"We're both in the same boat now, buddy," he said.

5

Niral stopped his motorcycle in front of a Muay Thai boxing school and bought a fruit shake. He watched the vendor, a man named Kan, drop the saline solution into the blender, followed by papaya, banana, and guava.

"You look tired," Kan said as he fixed the cover. The blender whirled. "You take Muay Thai lessons and you feel better. You get girls, like that girl I see on bike with you."

"I don't want that girl. She's poison," Niral responded.

"Girl good for you, my friend. You need girl, I can tell. You take lesson, you make muscle, they forget about Indian face with blah white stupid."

The blender stopped whirling. Kan took off the cover and poured the juice inside a glass and put a straw inside it.

"Yeah," Niral said, taking the drink in his right hand. He sucked hard on the straw while he held the head in the crook of his left arm, using it to shield the bulge of his gun inside the holster on his hip.

"You know I joke, Khun Niral. I know you not cheat me like other Indians. Your face beautiful, have balance like Hanuman."

"Balance, between man and animal?" Niral asked, handing back an empty glass and fishing in his pocket for money.

"Balance, like Hanuman," Kan repeated. "Hanuman have balance."

6

Niral sped through the heart of Bangkok and toward the Sukhumvit district. Once there, he parked his motorcycle next to the stairs leading up to the Skytrain. A boy with no legs sat by it, holding out a cup.

Niral ignored him as he proceeded across the sidewalk toward another staircase which would take him up to the Same Same bar. To its left, in front of a different bar, two Indians flirted with a ladyboy. Niral stared at them angrily as he passed them and ascended the staircase, the walls of which were graffitied with funny statements and drawings of sex acts.

Upstairs, he passed through door beads into a well-lit waiting area with a bar tended, as usual, by a Dragon henchman named Mok.

"Niral! Welcome!" he exclaimed. Then he noticed the head. "You finished the job?"

"How do you know?"

"We gossip. You know us."

"I heard Mr. Hong is in town. Is he here?"

"Duncan sent you?" Mok asked, laughing. "I know you would not come on your own. Let me tell Nam you are here."

He walked through a lavish blue curtain. Niral waited for a few minutes. He regarded the head as his hands continued to shake but for a different reason than before. Mok re-emerged from the curtain, followed by a shorter, wiry fellow with a long Dragon tattoo down both his arms.

Nam slapped Niral on the back. "Long time, Khun Niral. You brought a present. Mr. Hong will be happy. Come."

Niral was shocked by Nam's congeniality. He followed his former harasser through the dark tunnel of the club, toward a table where Mr.

Hong sat, drinking some Johnnie Walker Red Label in a shot glass. Mr. Hong smiled at Niral, who tried to wai to him with his hands full. Mr. Hong stood, tall and handsome in his beige suit, and took the head.

He removed the cloth and stared at Thanat's face.

Mr. Hong nodded at Niral.

"Good. Sit."

Niral did as ordered. Mr. Hong turned the head so it faced Niral. The shocked expression that still lasted past Thanat's final breath made Niral shudder.

Nam pulled up a chair and placed two more shot glasses on the table. He took the bottle of Johnnie Walker and began to pour, but Mr. Hong put his hand over the glass.

"Let the youngest pour," Mr. Hong said, "the poo noy."

Nam appeared angry, but he deferred to his boss. He performed his wai to Mr. Hong as earnestly as possible, holding his hands high above his head. Niral's hands were still shaking as he took the bottle and spilled some over Nam's glass and onto Nam's pants.

Nam glared at Niral sharply, but Mr. Hong laughed, diffusing the situation as Thais did. Nam had no choice but to practice the custom of "cool heart" and imitate his laugh.

"I'm sorry," Niral said nevertheless, out of force of habit.

"You've proven yourself a Dragon," Nam forced himself to say. "We should tattoo your back."

"He is scarred already," Mr. Hong said, laughing. "He has done well. He is not a Dragon yet, but he can become one."

"True, we can't have a gay Dragon," Nam reminded him.

"We will cure him yet," Mr. Hong said. He raised his glass. "To honor and respect. To saving face from sia naa."

They drank. Niral felt the sting down his throat and coughed.

"I love Thailand. Do you love Thailand?" Mr. Hong asked Niral.

Niral nodded.

"It is Candyland," Mr. Hong continued. "It is my home. I go to Hong Kong, Singapore, Shanghai, Seoul. The Chinese there try to tell me I am home, but my home is Thailand. This place is sanuk, all the time." He held his glass up. "I am glad Duncan took you. You have grown. But you are still too dark in the mind. Come to Scandal tonight. You, Duncan, Rob. Apsara will be there too. We will celebrate our victory over evil with sanuk mai krap."

"I don't know..." Niral began to say.

"Don't worry, man," Nam interrupted, slapping Niral on the back. "We'll have some ladyboys for you."

"Or some boys," Mr. Hong said, laughing.

Niral's phone buzzed, and he sighed. He saw a text from Rob.

"I have to go, Mr. Hong," he said. "I have a pickup to make."

"Of what?"

"Diamonds. From our supplier."

"Make sure it is not glass," Mr. Hong said.

"We do every time."

"The time you didn't wasn't good," Nam reminded him.

Niral got up. "I hope we won't have to do this again."

"Me too," Mr. Hong replied, rising too. "I don't want a war with Sumantapat. He must not find out."

"He won't. Rob cleaned up the mess."

"Good."

Niral made a deep wai to him, and Mr. Hong nodded back. Nam acknowledged him warily.

"See you tonight," Mr. Hong said.

7

Niral sped back across Bangkok, past colorful wats, swarming European tourists, and a Hindu ceremony for Ganesh, breathing in the gasoline exhaust as he snaked through Silom, down Charoen Krung, then south along the Chao Phraya river.

He passed through a hole in a chain-link fence and stopped near a warehouse on the shore. Rob's motorcycle was parked outside. Inside he was at the table, magnifier in his eye, examining a diamond he had just unwrapped.

Shekhat, the merchant, was standing near the doorway. His brothers were eating some rotli-shak dal-bhat at the far end of the warehouse.

"Niralbhai," Shekhat said in Gujarati, "you are late."

"I was on the other side of Bangkok."

"Your partner is good. Watch out for your job."

"Are you raising the price again?" he asked, ignoring Shekhat's comment.

"You must understand, my shipment costs are increasing. Even under Modi, the government is not good. Taxes, regulation. I have been giving Duncan a break. But I have no choice now."

"You've already raised the price twice. You will force us to find another merchant. Or buy it online. Or go to the source."

"The source?" Shekhat laughed. "You will fly to India to buy it there? You know online has shipping costs, too. Understand, I am a reasonable businessman."

"We'll do what it takes. We've been loyal customers. We don't need to give an excuse."

Shekhat's face turned grim. "Niralbhai, I have asked around about you to my family in Surat. They have contacts in Yam Gam. You were a Brotherhood follower."

Shekhat had tried to befriend Niral through their mutual Gujarati background, but he had never before brought up The Brotherhood or Niral's past.

"I was a Brotherhood follower, that's true," Niral replied. "What business is it of yours?"

"You must understand, while I was not a Brotherhood member, I loved Bhen. I know Bhai has been different, but I did love Bhen when she was alive. And following her teachings, I try to be fair in my business. So if I did not have to raise prices, I would not. But I will tell you this: because you are a brother, if you want to go into business with me, independent of Duncan, I am willing to listen."

Niral shook his head. "I think I'll go help Rob," he said. Niral took out his magnifier and went to work, unwrapping each diamond and making sure the specifications were met regarding clarity, cut, weight, and color. Even one scratch would result in rejection. They separated the stones that were damaged or didn't seem to match the dimensions. Then, of the ones they selected, they determined which were worth purchasing based on the price. Finally, they matched each stone against a list Duncan had emailed them.

"You'll take off twenty percent for the batch like usual, mate?" Rob asked. "We'll take more then."

"This time I can take off fifteen percent," Shekhat replied.

"That's highway robbery, mate."

"Call it what you want. You can decide."

Rob smirked. He took out wads of baht and slapped them on the table. Then he slipped the diamonds, rewrapped now, into the bag.

"You won't believe what I had in this bag before," Rob said. "Don't guess."

"Your friend is strange," Shekhat said to Niral in Gujarati. "But he is smart."

Niral figured this jab was due to his rejection of Shekhat's suggestion. He wasn't sure what either of them would gain out of collaborating; it was probably just a business tactic used to gain favor. He hadn't heard The Brotherhood mentioned in years, and he doubted Shekhat had ever followed Bhen.

8

They dropped the diamonds off at Mr. Hong's factory, getting a receipt that stated a time to pick up the jewelry. Once they delivered the finished product to Duncan, he would mail the jewelry to his vendor in New York, receiving his payment by money transfer and giving Mr. Hong his slice.

They drove to Khao San Road where they shared a studio apartment in a guesthouse occupied mostly by backpackers. Upstairs, Rob collapsed on the bed while Niral stood around nervously, thinking about the day's events.

"What'd that leech go on about, mate?" Rob asked.

"How he's raising the price."

"Fucking wanker," he said, making a hand gesture that imitated jerking off. "No wonder Duncan wanted to do business with that Thanat, Porn, or whatever the fuck his name was."

"That was a mistake. We should have checked the stones before the exchange. Then, he wouldn't have been able to run."

"Threw that glass in his grave, bro. But what was Duncan thinking, getting them through Burma? What a fucking idea. Next thing we'll be running guns."

"Thanat made us look like idiots. But we did him in, right?"

Rob laughed. "Not you, shaky. Don't worry, your secret's safe with me."

"I shot him," Niral said softly.

"Yeah, but ya didn't kill him. No worries, Duncan and Mr. Hong can think that. It's fine with me. They already know I'm a bloody killer."

"You didn't kill that tourist, did you?"

"Who, good 'ol Bob?" he said, trying to imitate an American hick accent. "No worries, I made him part of the crime, told him if he yabbered, I'd be visiting him again."

Niral nodded. "Good. You know where he's staying?"

"Why, you wanna say hello? You know this guy from the States or something?"

"Of course not. Just wanna make sure..."

"I wouldn't lie to you, mate. He's alive. Your goodie-tootie ass can relax."

Niral swallowed. "Mr. Hong invited us to Scandal tonight. To celebrate."

"All right. I'm game. Been rooting the same cunts of late."

"Apsara's working tonight."

"She knows I got giks."

"You do it in front of her?"

"She knows it's a fair go. She roots plenty of blokes in that place."

"She's trouble. What if Duncan finds out you're banging his mia noi?"

"He's got Lamai. What does he care? Anyway, he's not going to find out—unless you tell him."

"What about Sveta?"

"She's in Phuket whenever I need her. But it's not like in Pattaya, when I could just go over."

"What happened there anyway?"

"Long story, mate. Russian bloke named Boris gave her trouble, so I bought her out and put her far away."

"You did that for her?"

"Unlike you, I'm an independent contractor. I can."

"Remember who brought you in, that's all."

"I'm liking Candyland. Isn't that what Hong calls it?"

"Yeah. He still thinks I'm gay."

"And he's bringing some ladyboys for you?"

"What do I do?"

"Tell him you've changed. Root a girl tonight."

"I don't want to."

"Don't know what's wrong with you, bro. You got a dick, right?"

"I look like two-face. Or some pockmarked freak."

"These are cum dumpsters, mate. They're paid to not care."

"You know what happened."

"What that has to do with this, I don't get it."

Niral shook his head in frustration.

"Let's go over to McMurphy's," Rob suggested. "Hang out with some Norwegians and Brits. That always does the trick, ya?"

9

Later that night, Rob motorcycled to Patpong, Niral on the back. They parked near a bar filled with tourists and ladyboys, then cruised through the crowd under the tents of men and women selling pirated DVDs, watches, t-shirts, and fake jewelry, past girls dressed like flight attendants and cowboys, trying to hawk men into their clubs, and staircases that led up to pussy pong shows. They stopped at a doorway that lead to a large, two floor club with a neon sign emblazoned: Scandal. It was Mr. Hong's club, his favorite in Asia, and it showed.

Outside, a girl dressed like a sailor parted a red curtain for them after Rob gave her a knowing look. Above a circular bar, girls danced lazily in camouflage bikinis. Some customers looked far up, as through the ceiling they could analyze the pussies of schoolgirls dancing on the second floor through a transparent stage.

Next to the bar, at one of many plush booths, Apsara sat in her camouflage bikini with two drunk white guys, trying to talk them into a private room for "boom boom." They had bought her a lady drink, it seemed, but were hesitant to take the ultimate plunge.

Rob ignored her, and Niral followed him up the stairs. They acknowledged the madam, an experienced, retired prostitute named Lek, and she took them past the schoolgirl stage, where men stood behind the steel handrails, encouraging the women on. She turned right, past a curtain, to a private area where Mr. Hong, Nam, and Duncan sat, drinking Johnnie Walker, Mai Tais, and Singha beers.

"My soldiers," Mr. Hong called. He was clearly drunk. "My heroes. Come, sit by me."

They both pulled up a seat. This time, Nam was quick to take out the shot glasses and pour the whiskey for them.

"Very good. Good soldier," Mr. Hong said to Nam in Thai, who deferred with a head nod.

"We will drink to a successful operation," Mr. Hong said in English, raising his glass.

All five downed their shots. Only Niral coughed. Nam smiled at him.

"We have presents for you," Mr. Hong said. "But first, where is Apsara?"

Lek was still standing behind them. "Ploy is with farang," she responded, using Apsara's stage name at Scandal. "She is making money."

"She was key," Mr. Hong said. "I can't believe I found her at the auction."

"Yes. Usually we buy forty-year-old heifers," Nam said in Thai.

"She's a good girl. I hope you will reward her," Duncan said.

"Of course we will reward her. Do you think we don't appreciate?" Mr. Hong asked.

"It was my mistake," Duncan said. "I will pay her. But I also thought..."

"Duncan, you are my poo noy. Your mistake is my mistake. And your correction is my correction."

"Yes, Mr. Hong."

"You don't worry. I will pay down her debt, a bit."

Duncan performed a wai to him. "I thank you, Mr. Hong."

Niral became nervous. He stared at Duncan, expecting him to mention Niral's debt, but Duncan didn't.

"Remember, Duncan, no more mistakes," Mr. Hong said. "No more loose ends. We must be careful. We have a good relationship with the police, we pay our bribes, but Sumantapat has more contacts. He cannot know we killed his men. I have told you about my experience. This is why I stick to prostitution, gambling, and jewelry. As long as we pay our tribute to Mr. Chang in New York and to the Chinese bosses in Shanghai, we will be good. We don't need extra trouble. Let Sumantapat deal in ya ba and this other garbage. Let him take the risks. If I found out one of my men was dabbling in ya ba, I'd kill them before the yellow shirts got them."

"Ya ba is shit," Rob said. "Fucks up your mind."

"Yeah, stick to Johnnie Walker," Nam retorted.

"Here they are," Mr. Hong exclaimed, when five women dressed in bikinis approached. "My gifts to you."

"Bloody hell," Rob said.

Niral noticed the fifth girl was taller. Her face had manlier features. He looked at Duncan.

"Mr. Hong," Duncan said, after noticing Niral's stare, "remember Niral is gay. He doesn't like ladyboys either."

Mr. Hong said something in Thai to Nam, then he laughed and stood up.

"We don't have a Boyztown here, but I'll see what I can find for you at the gay clubs, Niral." But as he started to leave, he was stopped by another girl in a camouflage bikini. It was Apsara.

"Don't worry, Nam, I will take care of my Indian friend. He needs to be cured," she said, rubbing his shoulders.

"I can get you a boy, no problem," Nam said to Niral.

Niral glanced at Duncan, who nodded at him.

"That's okay, I think I need to be cured," Niral said. "I don't want to be gay anymore."

Nam smiled. "Are you sure?"

Niral stood up and let Apsara take his hand.

"Good job, Ploy," Nam said to Apsara. Then he slapped Niral on the back. "We'll make you into a Dragon yet."

Apsara led him past the stage, where Niral saw a fat white man dancing with a skinny Thai girl, the crowd cheering him on as his stomach fat jiggled uncontrollably.

They entered a bland room with blank, cracked walls and a single bed. Apsara closed the door, then pinned Niral against it.

"Aren't you going to thank me for saving you?" she asked.

"Thank you," Niral replied.

"Why don't you like me, Niral?" she asked, rubbing his penis through his pants.

"Why do you like me?"

She smiled. "I like everybody, Niral."

"That's why I'm skeptical."

"You are not healthy, my friend. Cumming is good for you. Let me take it out and suck it."

She lowered herself down to her knees and unzipped his pants. She took out his penis and began to suck it, but he wiggled away and covered himself again.

"What is your problem?" she asked, wiping some pre-cum from her lip. "You don't want release?"

"I've had enough in my life," he said.

"Really? Do I remind you of someone?" she asked, standing and approaching him.

"Please, just tell them we did it," he requested, backing up.

"How many times can I save you, Niral? You owe me."

"Did Thanat owe you too?"

"Forget about him. You don't know how to relax."

"Look, I'll pay you for it. Just tell them we did it."

Apsara nodded and smiled. "Maybe you are gay," she said, holding out her hand. Niral counted 2,000 baht and put it in her hand.

"No bar fine? That's 600 baht."

Niral took out another 1,000 baht and put in her hand.

"Very good doing business, sir," she said. "You want to fuck me, I am here."

Niral moved aside as she turned, opened the door and left. He was hyperventilating as he wiped tears from his cheeks.

10

Outside, Niral ignored the tame lesbian show on stage and walked briskly back to the private area, where he hoped to locate Rob so they could leave. But he found Duncan alone, drinking a Mai Tai, a Johnny Walker bottle next to him.

"Had a good time?" Duncan asked.

"I didn't fuck her," Niral said. "I paid her to say I did."

Duncan laughed. "She's good at that. Look, she's a hooker, I'm not saying you can't."

"I don't want to. Anyway, she's your mia noi."

"Yeah, but I've got giks up the wazoo. You should try it."

"Does Lamai know?" Niral asked, even though he knew the answer.

"She's gotta wonder where I am half the night. But she never says anything. Thai women know what goes on. You know it's standard here."

Niral sat down. Duncan pushed a Chang beer toward him.

"Drink up."

"Think I'll leave once Rob's finished."

"How'd the deal with Shekhat go?"

"Didn't give us the full discount. Says he's raising prices again. Shipping costs."

Duncan shook his head. "Not surprised. Trying to run a legit operation is tough work. A lot of guys just smuggle it. But Mr. Hong wants us legit. Whatever. I think we'll have to try Plan B though."

"Really?"

"Yeah. I've got a contact. I already set it up."

Niral swallowed. "You didn't tell me."

"We've discussed it before. Remember that weekend in Ko Samet when we talked about India?"

"I remember, but that was theory."

"Well, it's becoming a reality. You leave tomorrow night."

"Tomorrow?"

"I got the person-of-origin card for you, ticket, money in the bank in India, even a cell phone with an Indian SIM card and an Indian ID, man. You're set. Only thing you need is transportation and a place to stay. But you've got family there, right?"

"I haven't talked to them in years."

"You could always get a hotel. Sorry, I didn't bother with that part, figured you could cope. You're coming back the next day, though, with the merchandise."

"Hold on, Duncan. After that bullshit with Thanat, we're just going to jump in with another huckster?"

"I've done my research. He's legit. Guy named Talim."

"A Muslim?"

"You got a problem with that?"

Niral shook his head. "Rob coming too?"

"No, I need him here."

"For what?"

"Business. Not your concern."

"Not my concern? I brought his ass here."

Duncan glared at Niral. "He's an independent contractor. I think you forget our relations. My business with him is none of yours. And vice versa. Where you converge, sure, you can co-relate."

"I just wished you had told me earlier. Going back to India after..."

"Yes, I'm aware of your history. You've told me the whole boo-hoo story. But it's been years now. You do this for me, I'll cut you in more and more. We'll both be rich, and eventually I'll free you from the Dragons."

"That's what you said about this job. But you didn't say anything to Mr. Hong when..."

"I've spoken to him about it privately. Don't you trust me?"

Niral licked his dry lip. "Yes."

"Good. Now have some fun."

"Will I have a gun?"

Duncan didn't respond; he drank from his Mai Tai. "You'll get further instructions tomorrow," he said.

Rob returned. By then, Niral had chugged down the Chang beer and three shots of Johnny Walker Duncan had poured for him.

"How ya going, mate?"

Niral stood up and almost stumbled. "Let's go."

"Ya'll right?"

Niral headed down the stairs. Rob shrugged his shoulders, said goodbye to Duncan, and followed. Outside, they ran into Mr. Hong and Nam.

Mr. Hong was drunk and happy. He smiled and put his arms around both of them.

"We're going to a club in Soi Cowboy, then late night to an auction," Nam explained. "Hopefully not too many heifers."

Rob examined Niral. "I think he's had enough. I'll take him back." Rob patted Mr. Hong on the back, then got himself out of the embrace, and waved to Niral. Niral began to stumble forward.

"You've got to work hard and play hard, Niral," Nam said. "Isn't that what they say?"

Niral stumbled around, bumping into tourists and pushing others away, until finally he bent over and vomited next to a stall selling DVDs.

"Looks like he's cured," Nam commented, laughing.

"Yeah, it's the aftereffect, mate," Rob said. "I'll take care of it."

The owner of the stall was having a fit, but Rob grabbed him by the throat.

"Calm down, mate. Clean this up, or we'll have a problem. I've got backing."

The owner glanced at Nam, who showed off his tattoos.

He nodded furiously. Rob released him, and he backed off. His son, working beside him, pretended not to notice.

Rob slapped Niral on the back and pulled him by the shoulders.

"Let's get you back, chunder-fuck," he said.

11

Niral awoke to the Gayatri mantra ringing in his ears. He often did. He'd never investigated the origins of the chant, just assumed a temple was nearby.

When he turned, he saw Apsara in this bed, naked, staring at him.

Startled, he turned away and fell off the bed.

He heard laughter, both male and female. When he got up, rubbing his head that hurt from both the fall and a hangover, he saw Rob beside Apsara, naked too.

He realized he was also naked.

"What the fuck did you do to me?" Niral asked.

"You fucked me last night, Niral," Apsara said. "You fucked Rob, too."

Niral coughed hard. Rob laughed.

"You'll believe anything, mate, won't you?"

"Why am I naked?"

"You threw up all over your clothes. I wasn't gonna let you sleep in them. Or soil our bed."

"And how'd she get here?"

"Motorcycle," Apsara replied, shifting her body and opening her legs so that her pussy faced Niral. She began rubbing it and moaning. Niral shielded his face with his hand and turned away.

"I went back to get Apsara after the club closed. We ended up heading to the auction with Mr. Hong and Nam. Lot of heifers, it's true."

"You surprised I went, Niral?" Apsara asked.

"No. I know you're at home there."

"I had no choice that time. No money. I support my sick mother and daughter, remember?"

Rob pushed Apsara. "Get your clothes on, ya cunt. Niral can see your pussy another time. Everyone else sees it. Nothing new."

Apsara smiled mischievously and hopped off the bed.

"I didn't fuck her, Rob," Niral said. "I just paid her..."

"Yeah, I know. You should give him his money back," he suggested to Apsara.

"You know I need money," she responded, slipping on a t-shirt that said, "I Want Dick" featuring a woman with a thumbs up.

"You're a greedy bitch," Rob said.

"Fuck, I've gotta see Duncan this morning," Niral shouted, remembering their conversation the night before. "And I need a fucking fruit shake."

"He'd split by the time I got back to the club," Rob informed him.

"But he gave me directions," Apsara noted.

"What directions?" Niral asked.

"You're going to India today, right?" she said.

Niral looked flabbergasted. "How'd you know?"

"He wants me to give you the papers."

"You?"

"Sure, I am part of the team now. Remember Thanat?"

Niral shook his head. "I can't believe this shit. First Rob, now you?"

"What do you mean, mate?" Rob asked.

"You know he wants me to buy diamonds in India and bring them back because Shekhat's raising the prices again? Except I'm going without a gun and without you. What the fuck are you doing here that's so important?"

"Nothing, mate. Guess he just trusts you more."

"You're such a liar."

Rob stood up. He was naked, his numerous multicolored tattoos blazing on his hard, muscular chest. His penis, large and half-engorged, hung menacingly.

"We go back a long way, Niral, but don't ever call me a bloody liar. I've risked a lot for you, even lied for you about this Thanat thing. I know it was just you and Duncan before, but things change. I reckon it's changed for the better."

"Whatever. Just give me the papers if you have them."

"That's her job," Rob said, kissing Apsara's cheek as she slapped him playfully. "I'm getting dressed and going down for breakfast. See ya later."

12

Downstairs at the guesthouse restaurant, Niral ate an English breakfast of scrambled eggs, sausages, baked beans, and an English muffin, along with a fruit shake of lychee, jackfruit, and papaya as he pondered what to do. He took a short walk, watching the backpackers sitting around or trekking aimlessly, the hungover stragglers who had just ditched their bar girls from the night before trying to get over their weaknesses.

He took out his smartphone and stared at it. He'd heard international calls would be cheap, but he'd never bothered making one. Just a few basic emails, months apart, the first year he'd been there. First to his parents, then texts to Rob while he was in Malaysia, requesting he come over because his boss needed muscle.

He dialed the international code for the US and then the number. He put the phone to his ear and held it, listening to the rings endlessly buzz, his heart thumping. Then, he heard a voice.

"Deddy?"

A pause on the other side. "Niral?"

"Yes, Deddy," he responded, his voice shaking. "It's me."

"Oh my God, Niral. You're alive."

"Did you think I was dead?" he asked, tears flowing down his cheek. "Did you call for an investigation?"

His father paused. "No. Savard said you were probably alive. You would contact us when..."

"I'm ready now. But I need something."

"Of course. What, money?"

"No. I need Val's phone number in Surat."

"Why? You are visiting?"

"Yes. I have business. I deal diamonds now."

"You are not teaching English anymore? Your mother was afraid..."

"Do you have it?"

"Niral, have you been praying? Have you forgotten Bhen?"

"Bhen's dead. I thought Bhai was in charge now. No, I haven't been praying. I've forgotten praying. Do you have the damn number?"

His father gave him the number but said he would call Niral's cousin Valmiki to set up a pickup from the Mumbai airport, a ride to Surat, and a stay overnight. It was easier because Niral hadn't seen Val since they were children.

"Please, Niral, do not let years go by again."

"Thank you, Deddy. I'll be in touch when I can."

He hung up. Then he headed to McMurphy's bar.

Rob was inside, watching a recorded soccer match with some Brits. He waved him over.

"How ya goin', mate? Calmed down a bit?"

"Sure. Listen, I'm sorry I called you a liar."

"No worries, mate, I can be a liar. Look, I know Apsara can be tricky. Thanks for not fucking my girl, though ya could have and it would've been all right, too."

"Guess I'm just jealous. Duncan and me had some good times. He's my poo yai, you know," Niral said.

"Duncan's a right guy. You'll still have it. We've been partying since Brooklyn, I ain't gonna forget that. You, Jeremy, Chloe—you were my friends when I didn't know no one except the cunts I worked for. And when those buggers forgot me, you still came to see me in Westchester. I ain't forgettin' that."

"Listen, that tourist Bob. You know where he's staying? His hotel, I mean."

"Told me he was shipping off to Kanchanaburi this morning. His wife's been bugging him about seeing the bridge on the River Kwai or something. Says he might stay on the rafts. Remember that?"

"Yeah, those loud karaoke boats at night."

"Good times. That hot Thai chick drinking shots like nothing at the club, still singing her guts out. You going over or something?"

"No, just curious that's all. I've got to do some errands before I head to India tonight. I'll see you later."

13

He drove two hours out to Kanchanaburi on his motorcycle on the off-chance he might spot Bob Macaday. The thought of Bob staying in a raft house seemed absurd, but then again, running into him in Thailand in the middle of their hit was strange enough.

He cycled up the quiet streets of Mae Nam Khwae, scanning the occasional tourists and backpackers. The river and raft houses were to his left, the death railway bridge farther up. The only high-end hotel he recalled that wasn't several kilometers up the river was the River Kwai Resort, which offered luxury rooms with views of the river and easy access to the bridge and the WWII museum. Niral pulled up into its parking lot and went inside the lobby.

He thought he might have to bribe the desk clerk for a name and a room number. He didn't have to bother. Bob and Linda Macaday were sitting in the lobby, studying a map and bickering over their destination. When they saw Niral, their skin paled.

"Oh my God," Linda said, shuddering and turning red. She wore a simple white dress, and Niral saw no pearls. She stood up. "Please, don't fetch him."

"Who?" Niral asked.

"The black man. I'm sorry about before. I love my husband. I won't..."

"We're not associated anymore," Niral responded. "I want to talk to your husband, if you don't mind."

She turned to Bob. "I told you, honey, they said he went to Thailand. Why did we come here?"

"I won't hurt you," Niral said. "I just want to speak to Bob."

Linda's hand was shaking. "Bob, I think I'm getting an attack again. Please..."

He stood and rubbed her shoulders. He no longer affected a Texas accent. "I'll take her to her room. She gets these panic attacks sometimes. Then I'll come back down, and we can talk."

14

Niral followed Bob just in case he decided to slip away. When he emerged from the room, Niral put a gun to his back and told him to walk.

They trekked down the river to a field, where two sets of shrubs shielded them from the river and the road. A small spirit house stood by one of the shrubs, filled with a miniature Buddha and various other Thai Gods as if someone came to worship here.

"Please don't kill me," Bob pleaded, holding his hands up. "I won't talk. Niral, you know me."

"What are you doing here?" Niral asked.

"It's a long story. You won't believe it."

"Try me."

"Look, we were in witness protection, okay? After Vishal disappeared with the money, they arrested some Lucchese family members for the land fraud. They needed a witness, so I agreed to testify in return for no charges for my involvement in Coleman. I told them what I knew about Vishal, and I also testified that he told me about his involvement with Roberto Tragliani, which was a lie, but I knew that's what they wanted to hear. Their lawyers tripped me up on cross, but they had enough forensic and digital evidence, and anyway, the jury wanted to believe it, so they got their conviction. The Feds told me that Roberto's daughter, Alicia, took over the family business and swore revenge against me and Vishal, so they relocated us to El Paso, Texas and gave us new identities—I kept my first name but I got the last name Murphy and Linda became Patricia. We even learned the local accent and phrases.

"Linda got paranoid though, always thinking the Italians would show up one day and kill us. She started getting these panic attacks. We thought of disappearing across the border into Mexico, where no one would find us, but Linda got paranoid about the Mexican drug gangs, too; they caused enough trouble on our side of the border. So I thought back to my days in Vietnam and hanging out on the base in Khorat. Thailand became a real possibility, plus it had cheap medical care in case Linda kept having her panic attacks. We figured the calm Buddhist culture would soothe us. That's what we were arguing about, whether we'd visit a temple after the bridge. We want some solace, too."

"Yeah, and the young girls here aren't bad either, right?"

Macaday grinned sheepishly, but he hid it just as fast.

"I'm human, Niral, but I love my wife."

"Seems like you've had to put up with a lot."

"She stuck with me after the cheating and stayed with me in witness protection. She's a different woman now, and I'm a different man. I've been honorable."

"She could still change her identity back at any time, divorce you, and take half your money."

"What money? The Feds seized most of my assets. They haven't given it back, and coming out to challenge it would mean certain death.

Linda's not coming out; she'd be dead too. We're stuck together in this new reality."

"So you don't have any money?"

"I had some savings apart from my investments that the Marshals let us put in our new accounts. It's not nothing, but it's not what I was used to. That's why I fell for that gem scam, I guess."

"Yeah, you fell for that pretty easily, it seems like," Niral said.

"Look, I won't say anything, but why don't you clear things up for me? Why'd you kill that guy Porn? And why'd you call him Thanat?"

"Rob didn't tell you? It seemed pretty obvious anyway."

"He stole something from your boss. Who's your boss?"

"You don't need to know all that. I believed you wouldn't talk, otherwise I wouldn't have told Rob to let you live. Then again, you did talk against the Lucchese and Vishal."

Bob put his palms together. "You think I want to be in witness protection again, this time in Thailand? I've learned my lesson from this experience. I'm not getting involved. My eyes are closed. Just a peaceful life, nothing else."

"Yeah, with gem resales."

"Look, Niral, I'm sorry about happened to you. I'm sorry about Lauren. That guy Amrat must have been a real nutjob. And Vishal, wherever he is, I hope he's feeling guilty about everything he did."

"You think he's still alive?"

Bob shrugged his shoulders. "I assume so. Who else could have stolen all that money? Maybe he's in the Caribbean or in Switzerland or Africa or India. I don't know. But if he ever shows his face, the Feds will nab him. He's not safe anywhere."

"So you haven't heard from him?"

"No, Niral, I haven't."

Niral shoved the gun back in its holster.

"Okay. I believe you, so far. If you want a Buddhist temple, there's one a few kilometers down a road going right past the night market and down the opposite river bank. It's up on a hill, you might have to climb it. I tried going for some salvation or something, but it didn't stick. It never does. But if you want to try it for yourself, go right ahead."

PART II

†

Mumbai, India;
In and Near Surat, India

15

Customs was a breeze. Niral didn't remember it that way. Last time he and his parents had gone through customs, his parents had to open their bags and talk their way out of a bribe. Outside in the arrivals lounge, dragging his bag, he searched for his cousin, Valmiki, who he hadn't seen in many years. He saw his name on a sign, but the man holding it was darker than Valmiki.

"Val?" Niral asked, approaching.

"Your cousin sent me, Niralbhai. My name is Manu."

Niral trusted him, for some reason, but knew he should be careful. He followed the man to the parking lot, where he placed his bag inside the trunk of a black car and got into the passenger's seat.

"Why didn't Val come?"

"He must work tomorrow morning. India is not like before. People must work."

"We're heading to Surat?"

"Of course, Niralbhai. Please, sleep. I will wake you when we get there."

Niral stayed awake long enough to see the barrel fires and the Dubla squatting and shitting along the road, the shantytowns that continued to pervade the new India. He saw a couple of bonfires too but fell asleep before he could process them. When he awoke, Manu was gesturing toward a restaurant with a Veg sign.

"You must be hungry. Let's eat some of the best dosa in Gujarat."

"We're here."

"In Gujarat. Surat is still farther."

They pulled inside the lot. Niral could see the stars bright in the night sky, and he felt the cool air that he had never associated with India because he had previously come during the monsoon season. Two truckers chewed and spit paan onto the road as they chatted to pass the time.

Inside the restaurant, a single worker wearing a clean white apron took their order, which Manu gave with a quick flourish of Gujarati.

"Do they have different types of dosas?" Niral asked.

"They have many dosas, good dosas. Eat it with your hands, you will see. Also, amazing chai! We might even have bhajiya."

They did. Niral was impressed. The dosa was simple and oily, but it was delicious, even though he passed on the chutney. The bhajiya was spicy but refreshing. He could taste the chickpeas and the potatoes. He hadn't eaten Indian food in a long time. He always avoided the Indian restaurants in Bangkok.

The chai reminded him of his mother's, but he tried to repress the memory, even as it arrived. He was so busy fighting his past that he didn't notice two burly men wearing chandlos approach the table.

"A friend wants to speak to you," one of the men with a slight beard told him gruffly.

Niral glanced at Manu. "Only a brief moment," Manu stated.

"You know these people?" he asked.

"Don't worry. They won't hurt you. Just a brief..."

Niral tried to rise and run, but the bearded man grabbed him by the neck and shoved him down. Then, Niral saw a gun come out and rest against his heart.

He was led to the back, past the kitchen, and toward the outhouse, until he was stopped and forced down a secret, creaky staircase, past some old boilers and into a plain room, carpeted with an unimaginative and dull red carpet. A mandir featuring the Trinity of Gods was displayed on a slightly elevated platform. Niral also saw a large picture of Bhen next to some folded chairs.

Two more burly men stood by the platform. Between them sat a skinny man wearing owl glasses and dressed in a white dhoti. He concentrated on an open book.

When Niral was stationary, flanked by the burly men, Manu awkwardly behind him, the skinny man raised his head, smiled, and closed the book.

"Niral," he stated, tapping the carpet. "I have waited to see you for years. Come, sit."

"Who are you?" Niral asked as he felt a brutal push on his back. He stumbled forward, then sat down, his feet behind him in the Buddhist manner.

"You don't know me? Why, I am your teacher. I am Bhai."

"You're not my teacher."

Bhai smiled. "Your father told me you had lost your faith. I do not blame you. The actions of a few apples had poisoned, temporarily, our organization. But we have recovered, and The Brotherhood is better than ever. No corruption, no violence, only love, commitment to knowledge, truth, self-study, self-betterment, and social justice."

"I just had a gun to my heart."

"That is a practical necessity. You see, there are elements that wish to poison us again. Or more frankly, to destroy us. This is why I needed to see you. I understand you are headed to see a man named Talim."

"Yes. He's a diamond merchant. I'm here to buy diamonds for my boss."

"He claims to be a diamond merchant. I have no doubt he sells some diamonds, likely smuggled or stolen. But he is also a terrorist. Yes, he has ties to the most heinous Islamic extremists in India and beyond. Even in Thailand."

"My father told you I was buying diamonds here. But how'd you know..."

"Niral, we have grown as an organization. We have our ways; we hear things. But we don't know all things. This is why we need you. Once we discovered you were visiting Talim, we knew that you were our best mole inside his plot."

"What plot?"

"We don't know. We have our annual Shri Holi event tomorrow night in Dwarka. They may strike there, but we aren't sure. We only know he is planning something."

Niral recalled Holi was around this time of the year. He hadn't thought about it before and didn't want to now, either, because it would bring back memories from the past.

"How will I learn anything?" he asked. "I'm just going to buy some diamonds from him."

"This is where technology comes into play," Bhai said. One of the guards, apparently a Sikh and who wore a turban on his head, handed Bhai what looked like a black chip. He held it up to Niral.

"If you place this inside their lair, on any metal surface, we will be able to hear them."

Niral swallowed. "Why would I? I'm just a diamond merchant now."

Bhai snickered. "You have become a Buddhist, haven't you? Like Siddhartha, you have run away from your duty to escape suffering. But Niral, you are not an island. You are a man and an Indian. If you do not act, people will die. Many people. Your people. Do not take this lightly."

"I don't know anything you are saying is true. I don't need this."

He got up and faced the bearded guard, who held the gun up to him. Bhai rose behind him.

"What are you going to do, kill me?" Niral asked. "Go ahead. I'm already dead."

"I don't want to kill you, Niral," Bhai said. "We don't kill people. Leave that to the Muslims. But I do want to convince you. If you won't listen to me, listen to an old friend."

The Sikh guard turned and opened a door next to the folded chairs that Niral had not noticed before. A frail, dark man came out, wearing a stained, white kafni pajama. Niral felt tears in his eyes that he failed to suppress. As he approached, the old man held his hand up, and Niral instinctively placed his palms together and bowed.

"Bless you, my son," Narendrakaka said, tapping Niral's head. "Bless you."

16

After they had embraced, Narendrakaka explained his position.

"Niral, I have been living a peaceful life in your mother's village of Yam Gam, doing my penance for my crime. Since my own family disowned me, your parents took pity and allowed Kauntiaunti and me to live in your mother's old house, since your Motimasi had died. I had intended to live a peaceful existence, helping the Dubla or the Halpati, as they are often called, cultivate your parents' mango farm when the seasons arrived, and meditate the rest of the time. But events have forced me to become more socially aware.

"Niral, I would not say this if the situation was not dire. The Brotherhood, under Bhai's leadership, has spread our doctrine of self-study, equality, and peace more efficiently than Bhen, I must admit. He has consolidated much of the older, more individual, superstitious beliefs into a coherent, rational core. This has done much good in many of the communities, where the Dubla have become better educated and the injustices of the caste system have dissipated a bit. This was fundamental to Bhen's vision, as you recall. But in other communities, and Yam Gam is one, the opposite has occurred. I am afraid that many young men are ripe for radicalization that Muslims and other extremists, including Hindus, can exploit.

"You see, Yam Gam is currently run by a Dubla mayor named Prameshbhai, who controls both the Brahmin and Dubla vote through divide and conquer tactics. He continuously plays them off each other, to make conflict, and then uses his own power to resolve them and enrich himself. The recent spikes in land prices and sales, the building of larger homes, and the increased materialism has only exacerbated this trend. As the Brahmins get richer, the Dubla become jealous. Some educated Dubla, using the OBC benefits, can compete, but even they are often victimized because their power is not as great.

"It is too complicated to explain, but I will tell you that in other villages, where this dynamic has played out, Muslim clerics have moved in, pointed out the inequities of the caste system and the falseness of their Gods, and converted the Dubla to Islam. They have used violence and intimidation to then forcefully convert Brahmins, Vaishya, and others. The Brotherhood has been able to move in first at times, but often it has failed. Still, we are the force that the radical Islamists fear the most, and a strike upon us, particularly at a big festival, will be seen as a major victory for them, not to mention cost many lives. Please, Niral, Bhai and I have had our differences, but he is not wrong about this."

Niral remembered shooting Vishal, Narendrakaka's son, in the groin. He said, "What do want me to do? I am a different person now. I have different obligations."

"You are the same man, Niral. You have simply been hurt, as I have. You have walked along a path of indifference to get over it. Now you must engage yourself and fulfill your duty."

"My duty is buying and selling diamonds," he said, turning his back on Narendrakaka.

Bhai commanded his guards to put down their weapons. "We cannot keep you, Niral. We have reminded you of your duty, but we will not force you."

Niral turned back to him. "How is it my duty? You don't own me! I'm Thai now. You don't own me."

Bhai stared at him, as if trying to read him.

"Does someone else own you?" he asked. "Or are you free?"

Bhai approached him and put the chip in his palm.

"It is your choice. Manu will take you to your appointment. You can plant it or throw it away."

Niral looked at Narendrakaka. "It's good to see you, Narendrakaka. I'm sorry about what happened, but it's not my problem."

17

Manu drove Niral toward Surat. Niral had thought of hailing a rickshaw, but he didn't know whether that would be wise either, considering some of the stories he had heard. He cursed Duncan for not arming him.

Manu didn't speak to him. He was clearly offended that Niral had rejected Bhai's command. Niral, for his part, asked Manu why he worked for Bhai.

"He saved my life, Niralbhai," he finally revealed after a long pause. "Spiritually. I was lost before The Brotherhood came into my life. And they gave my family a good home, away from the Dubla slums. You see, I am a Dubla, Niralbhai. I am the lost soul who has been saved by The Brotherhood."

Niral didn't reply. He saw high-rises and skyscrapers as they entered Surat, dwarfing more shantytowns under their blue tarps.

"Plenty of building," Niral said.

"Yes, Niralbhai. India is not like before. These buildings have helipads, swimming pools on the roofs. They cost many crore rupees. The land is booming, the farmers are selling."

"Are you taking me to Val's house?"

"I am taking you to your appointment with the Muslim terrorist, Niralbhai. Unless you want me to go somewhere else."

"I prefer it if you drop me off at Val's house."

"Why?"

"I think it's obvious."

"Your cousin's house is in Rampura, not near Rander, where I assume the Muslim terrorist is. But very well."

They drove through curving roads and honking rickshaws, dust swirls and fearless pedestrians. They avoided an ox in the middle of the street, tamed by his handler, and turned into a driveway.

"Your cousin Valmiki, Niralbhai," Manu said. Niral emerged from the car. Manu helped him get his bag out of the trunk. An old man stood in the doorway, smiling.

"Your Vikasmama," Manu explained.

"I know," Niral said. "Thanks for driving me. I appreciate that part."

"Your father is a good man, Niralbhai," Manu said. "I hope you follow in his path."

Niral turned away and approached Vikasmama. He bowed to him.

Vikasmama blessed him. He was thrilled at Niral's arrival and welcomed him inside with profuse gratitude.

"We are so happy you are here, Niral. Your mother has not come to India in a long time."

"I'm glad too, Vikasmama. But I must get to..."

A little girl about ten years old came downstairs. Her eyes were crossed, and she wobbled when she walked. She asked Niral who he was. He knew this was his afflicted niece Amrita.

"I'm your uncle, Amrita," he said. "Niralkaka."

"Niralkaka, why is your face like that?" she asked in Gujarati. Niral was taken aback.

"Amrita!" Vikasmama said. "Is that a nice thing to ask?"

"That's okay," Niral said, smiling. "Amrita, I was burned in a fire."

"On Holi?"

Niral stopped smiling. "Yes, on Holi, Amrita."

"I'm sorry," she said, then turned and ran back.

"Amrita is a character," Vikasmama said. "You will get used to her. You have picked a good day to come, Niral. We are having a bonfire on the roof tonight. Sobha's family is coming too."

"Where is Val?"

"He is at work, at the bank. Sobha, his wife, is also at work. Now we must work, even on Phalguna Purnima, the day before Holi."

Niral found out the bank where Val worked was where Duncan has set up the account.

"Can you get a rickshaw to take me there?"

"Of course. I will go, too."

"No need. I don't want you to leave Amrita alone."

"Nonsense. I don't want you to get lost."

"If Val is there, how can I get lost?" Eventually, he convinced Vikas to stay put. He put his stuff in a guest room and carried what he needed in his pockets and a duffel bag. Vikas summoned a rickshaw and told the driver in Gujarati where to take Niral. They haggled over the price, as Indians do, until they reached agreement. Vikas told Niral the price and not to take any shit from the driver if he budged on it. Then Vikas gave Niral some rupees to hold him over. Niral reluctantly accepted.

The driver didn't speak to Niral. He drove him around the streets and the roundabouts. Niral saw people lined up with trays in their hands.

Others were starting large fires. Niral closed his eyes when he saw them or shielded his face.

The driver stopped next to a building guarded by a soldier holding a rifle. He said something in Gujarati, but in an accent Niral couldn't understand.

Niral got out and gave the driver some rupees. The driver frowned and drove away.

Inside, Niral confronted a banker at a desk who didn't seem eager to help him and simply pointed toward a line to the teller. But when Niral asked for Val, he guided him to an office where his cousin, light-skinned as in his youth and looking similar with apple-shaped cheeks and a large forehead, sat studying accounts.

Val was elated to see him. They shook hands and Niral sat. They exchanged pleasantries and Niral told him about his parents and his residence in Thailand. Val apologized for not picking him up but said Niral's father had insisted he would hire the driver. Then Niral asked Val about his account.

"You have an account in an Indian bank?" Val asked.

"My boss created it for me so I wouldn't have to carry the money here. I need to buy some diamonds."

"I see. Can I see your passport or an ID?"

Niral didn't want to take out his fake Indian ID, so he used his passport.

"This might take some paperwork, since you are a foreign national."

"I have a PIO card."

"I will ask my boss."

Val went away, then came back. "My mistake, that was the old policy. Now it is easy. You can even go to the teller."

"I want to take out a large amount." Niral told him the amount. Val nodded and handed Niral a slip. Val disappeared, then reappeared, holding the rupees in wads of bills.

Niral took them and dumped them into his duffel bag.

"Niralbhai, be careful. A rickshaw driver may see that, drive you to an isolated spot, and rob you. Do you want me to drive you to your meeting?"

Niral checked his watch. It wasn't even ten o'clock yet.

"You can just leave?"

"I will ask my boss. It is not as casual as before, but we still have privileges you Americans do not. Plus, today is the Phalguna Purnima, the day before Holi."

Niral's heart beat faster. "Right, I've heard."

"Yes," Val said smiling. "Sobha and I started work early, so we could leave early and prepare for the bonfire tonight on our roof. You have picked a good day to come."

Niral swallowed, remembering what had transpired during the last Holi he had celebrated a few years before. He stood up.

"I don't want to bother you."

"It is no bother, Niralbhai. We are family, and I want you to be safe."

"Okay, but I need to make a phone call first."

While Val talked to his boss, Niral stepped outside the bank. He switched the SIM card in his phone to one Apsara had given him, then dialed the number for Talim. The number rang several times. Finally, a gruff voice answered.

"Talim? It is Duncan's associate," Niral said.

"Who?" the voice asked. Then another voice answered.

"Duncan's man," Niral repeated. "For Talim."

"I am Talim," a third voice answered, followed by a fourth voice.

"Is this a joke?" Niral asked, almost hanging up. But then a fifth voice ordered, "Drive to Rander." He gave specific directions, past a new, ornate building called the Golden Mosque. Then, he hung up.

Niral tried to memorize the directions. As he did, he peered across the street and spotted a car similar to Manu's. He couldn't see the driver but thought it possible Manu was following him.

Once Val came out, he stopped caring.

18

The road to Rander passed a fort and arched over the Nehru bridge, crossing the Tapi River. Val swerved his motorcycle through the narrow streets, past hawkers and boys who wore topis and salwar kameez. Niral, on the back, noticed the anorexic dogs here, unlike in Thailand, limped along and did not hustle after motorcycles.

They entered a large square and took a right at a clothing market. Ahead, he saw the Golden Mosque with its shiny gold dome.

Val stopped suddenly. The bike tipped over. Niral caught the ground with his foot.

"Your meeting is in the mosque?" Val asked, turning to Niral.

"I don't know," he answered. "I need to call them again."

He called again. A sixth voice answered. Niral told him he would hang up if it was another trick.

"If you are at the Golden Mosque, walk down the alley next to it until you reach a door without a handle. Come alone."

Niral tried to ask another question, but the other line went dead.

"I have to go alone. Can you wait for me?" Niral asked.

"Are you sure you don't want me to come?"

Niral knew he should have help, especially while carrying all this money. In fact, he should have asked Val if he had access to a weapon. But if he didn't go alone, he could have more trouble. He considered calling Duncan, but he didn't want to seem indecisive. So he decided to risk it.

"I'll be right here," Val told him. "I will give you my cell number. Call me if you need assistance."

Niral punched Val's number into his phone, then approached the alley next to the mosque. The path became skinnier and curved to the left. Two boys played cricket at the far end of the alley, but that was a long way down. He didn't notice any doors. He progressed about thirty meters. Then he saw three doors in succession. The first two were made of wood. The third door, made of metal, didn't have a handle.

Niral stood in front of it. He knocked and waited. He considered calling Talim's number again, then thought better of it. He felt uneasy. He decided to return to the mosque and call Duncan. But then the door opened. A large figure swooped down on him and pulled him inside.

The door shut behind him. In the darkness, he was groped ferociously by many hands. He fought back, but he was punched in the stomach, hard enough that he started seeing flashes and gasped in tremendous pain as he held his stomach and crumpled to the ground.

His face pressed against what felt like a grate. His hands were tied behind him. Suddenly lights appeared. He saw the grate now, and through it, he stared down on a basement level where two garrisons of men lined up by a desk, all looking up at him.

Niral was pulled up by his arms. He was kneed in the back, then allowed to scissor his legs and ultimately regain his balance. With a flashlight illuminating the path, he was pushed forward and forced to march down a flight of metal stairs, the stairs pounding and resonating with each step.

Downstairs, he was brought to the desk. The man pushing him had a long beard and wore a white robe. The other men were clean-shaven and wore camouflage.

A man sat behind the desk. One of his eyes was lazy. The other penetrated Niral's consciousness with a persistent stare.

"Mr. Solanke, I am very glad to meet you."

The bearded man stepped forward. He placed the bag of money on the desk, along with the contents of Niral's pockets. Then, he handed the man the bug Bhai had given to Niral.

"What is this? A gift from the Gods?" the man asked, examining it.

"Are you Talim?" Niral inquired. He was nervous and sweaty yet his anxiety liberated him enough to speak. He felt sure he would not leave the building alive.

"You can call me Talim, sir. To what do I owe the pleasure?"

"I thought I was here to purchase diamonds. Instead I'm being robbed."

"On the contrary," Talim said, examining the bug with Niral's magnifier. "You are being saved."

"How is that?" Niral asked.

Talim placed the bug on the table. Using the magnifier, he crushed it.

"I wonder if Bhai will hear us now?" he asked.

Niral's sweat dipped down to his mouth. He tasted the salt.

"Don't worry, you are not in danger, Niral Solanke. We needed to make sure you were not armed, bugged, or followed. We might have the latter problem, but it is irrelevant. We can move with enough time. But the persistent issue of Bhai remains. Tell me, what do you think of Bhai?"

"How do you know that I know him?"

Talim stood. He wore a crisply ironed, white shirt.

"We have done our research, sir. And your boss was able to inform us of the rest."

"My boss?"

"Well, yes. Duncan Smith. He is your boss, yes?"

Niral felt weak. His knees buckled, and he fell on them. But the bearded man pulled him up again by his arms and held him up.

"Duncan said you were stronger than what I see. But fortunately, it is not your strength that we value. It is your cunning."

"Sorry to disappoint you," Niral said, regaining his senses. "But I don't have that either."

"Nonsense. I can tell you do. I'm sure you feel betrayed by Duncan right now, but don't worry, he has made a good deal for you."

"What deal?"

"Maybe you should ask him."

Talim took Niral's cell phone and played with it.

"I need your passcode. Then you can speak to Duncan as long as you desire."

Niral hesitated, but then reluctantly, Niral told him the code. Talim dialed Duncan's number, introduced himself, then gave the bearded man the phone, who put it to Niral's ear.

"What the fuck, Duncan?" Niral asked.

"I'm sorry to surprise you like this, Niral, but I couldn't afford to tell you in Thailand. Plus, Talim needed to check you out."

"For what?"

"Niral, don't worry, this is going to work out well for us. After this is over, we'll be rich and free. I'm going to pay your debt to Mr. Hong. We'll move to Chiang Mai and drink Mai Tais together forever. All you have to do is kill Bhai."

"Sorry, Duncan, but I don't get it."

"Talim wants Bhai dead. He can tell you his reasons. I know you hate him, too, for his part in what happened in New York. That's why I thought of you and why I made this deal. Now you can obtain your revenge. And we'll get paid well. You'll be free. Best of all worlds."

"Why'd you lie to me? You're my poo yai. That's not the way it should work. And I understand a poo yai expects his poo noy to do his bidding, but you expect me to kill somebody?"

"You killed Thanat, didn't you?"

"I had to. This is different."

"Is it? This is a continuation of the Thanat problem. Losing money to Thanat has hurt us financially. It's lost us face, too. Talim will pay handsomely for this service. This will help us get back on our feet and then some. We can extricate ourselves from the Dragons, the Thai social structure. We'll have the good of Thailand without the bad of Thailand."

Niral didn't respond.

"Look," Duncan continued, "I would have sent Rob, but he doesn't have this 'in' with The Brotherhood. Bhai's guarded all the time. You have to figure out how to kill him. It'll take more than brute force."

"I still can't believe you would do this to me, Duncan. I thought I knew you."

"Stop with the bullshit, man. I saved your ass from extermination, remember? I treated you like a bro even though I didn't have to. This'll free us both. I'm doing you a favor."

Niral hesitated. "How am I going to kill him? I've got to go back to Thailand tomorrow."

"That's okay. That's on purpose. Right now, you just have to gain his trust. I'll send you back for another delivery soon enough. Pretend like you are spying on Talim, even though you're doing the exact opposite."

Duncan spoke to him more about the plan. Then, he asked to speak to Talim.

Niral had to urinate, but he held it in. He licked his dry lips. He wanted a fruit shake and the peace of Thailand.

Talim hung up the phone. "You kill Bhai, you'll be free of your gangster friends. It's a win-win, as you Americans say."

"Why do you want Bhai dead?" Niral asked.

Talim sighed. He sat down. He gestured to the bearded man, who untied Niral's hands. Another man placed a chair in front of the desk. Niral was pushed down by his shoulders and forced to sit.

"I'm sorry for the lack of hospitality, but we have to be careful, you understand. It is a long story, Bhai and I, but let me tell you the frank truth. He is responsible for the murder of my entire family. Is that reason enough for revenge?"

"Your whole family?"

"Remember what happened in New York? It was the result of Bhai's manipulations of the monetary fund. As the man in charge, he is responsible for so much suffering. We have a shared history, Niral Solanke, a tragic history. But my tragedy was more direct. Do you know the Babri Mosque in Ayodhya? How it was destroyed by Hindu zealots who preached hatred of Islam?"

"I know the basics, yes."

"Before he became Bhen's husband and right-hand man, Bhai, then named Rajesh Rana, was a Hindutva agitator, a member of Shiv Sena. For years, he gave speeches against the Babri Mosque and was one of the speakers who instigated the riots that destroyed the mosque in 1992 and killed many people. One of those people was my mother."

"She lived in Ayodhya?"

"Yes. We lived in Godhra, in Gujarat, but my mother had moved to Ayodhya to attend Saket College on a scholarship. You see, my parents were poor, but they had dreams. They were not strict adherents of Islam. No, they did not understand its true nature, or the nature of Hinduism, for that matter. They even, in some sense, considered themselves Hindustanis. But then the Babri masjid was attacked, and riots followed. My mother disappeared and was never seen again. She lived in the Muslim district because she felt comfortable there and the rent was cheap. We believe she was burned alive so badly that no one could identify her, and the locals discarded her ashes without a proper investigation. So many people were killed."

"I'm sorry to hear that. But why Bhai specifically? There were many agitators, I'm sure."

"I will get to that, Niral Solanke. But first let me continue my story. My father moved on. He was a tailor, a simple man, not as educated as my mother. He remarried for a short time, but then his new wife ran away with another man. We were poor, but we were happy, my brother, my sister, and I.

"Ten years passed. I was only sixteen then, on the cusp of manhood, but still a boy. My brother was fourteen, and my sister was twelve. I attended the local high school. I had many Hindu friends. I was in love with a Hindu girl. But then the train was burned a short distance away, and the riots began. It is like you have heard and worse. Vans of Hindu thugs, wearing bandanas and shouting 'Jai Rama' and other slogans began driving into our neighborhoods, carrying machetes and cans of kerosene.

"They stabbed my pregnant neighbor in the stomach, then cut out her baby and burned it in public as she watched, dying. They raped women on the street while they tortured and killed their husbands. My sister had been playing outside when the gangs moved in. I tried to save her, but my father grabbed me, pulled me inside, and forced my brother and I to the roof, barricading the entrance to the stairway. From the roof, we watched helplessly as a Hindutva follower held my sister and a kerosene can over her head. He told us he would make her drink it, douse her in it, then light her on fire if we did not come down and meet our fates. We could not. I've regretted it every day. We watched my own sister burned alive as the assailant shouted 'Shri Holi!' I can still hear her screams."

Niral shuddered and closed his eyes as he listened. Tears escaped from his eyelids and ran down his cheeks.

"I know you have been through the same thing, Niral. You have the scars to prove it. You have the memories inside you, no matter how much you have repressed them, of the horrors of Hindu fundamentalism. Now look. I do not remember much after. They burned my house, they continued to taunt us and sustained their atrocities for as long as I can remember. We seemed to stay up there for days. We didn't trust anyone who asked us to come down, not even the police. Only when fellow Muslims told us that it was safe did we finally descend.

"My father wept over my sister's body. I could not stop shaking. Later, the police arrived. They told my father that he could make a statement.

They put him in the police car and drove him away. I never saw him again. I believe he was murdered by the Hindu police.

"My brother Tanveer and I tried to rebuild our lives. I quit school to work so I could take care of him and make sure Tanveer could attend school. But I remembered what the assailant had shouted, and I learned that it was a slogan used by The Brotherhood. Rajesh Rana, after his days as a Hindutva agitator, joined Bhen's organization, and despite, or perhaps because of his past reputation, he became her right-hand man and ultimately her husband. Without her knowledge, or perhaps with her tacit support, he continued to agitate. He believed his speeches would convert right wing Hindus to The Brotherhood cause, increasing the organization's numbers and donations, whether these funders truly believed in the ideology or not. I believe this was his intent when the train was burned. Other scarred Muslims I befriended told me Bhai had met with Hindu gangs he had been courting and encouraged them to seek revenge after the train incident, so that The Brotherhood would be well-represented in the minds of people sympathetic to the Hindutva cause. You see, Bhai was directly responsible for the deaths of my sister and my father, and most likely my mother, too.

"We wanted revenge, my Muslim brothers and I, but despite years of plotting, we could never get close to him. He always had bodyguards, and in open settings, the crowds were organized so that even armed with a pistol you could not get close enough for a shot. One man tried and was gunned down himself.

"We tried another plot where we had a man wear a bomb strong enough to blow up the crowd and the stage. We bribed someone high up in The Brotherhood who would allow him access to the front of the crowd, but when we attempted the bombing, the bribed official must have tipped off the bodyguards, who shot the bomber before he could reach the crowd. The bomb went off, but only a few people nearby were killed. One of them was my dear brother, Tanveer, who had been waiting in the car the suicide bomber had exited.

"When Bhen died and Bhai succeeded him, the attempts became more difficult, even as my lust for revenge became greater after my brother's death, and my contacts and power increased among my fellow

Muslims. Bhai moved The Brotherhood's headquarters to Dwarka, on the coast of Gujarat, many kilometers from here or Ayodhya. He built a temple complex there with much security. Rarely does he have open events now. Rather, he slithers about underground. I tried to engage Pakistani agents of Lashkar-e-Taiba to cross the border with Gujarat and assassinate Bhai at the complex before escaping to Pakistan, but it did not work out. The Holi event tomorrow at the temple complex was an option, but we decided we could not crack security. It's better to have an inside man."

Niral wiped his tears. "I was carrying a bug for Bhai. Why do you think I would help you?"

"I know how Bhai's mind works. He is paranoid, and he has contacts. If he knew you were coming, certainly he would speak to you and encourage you to work against us. So that is not surprising. I trusted Duncan's account of your bitterness toward Bhai. I hope that has not changed."

Niral cleared his throat. "I rejected Bhai's offer to spy on you. He gave me the bug anyway, so I put it in my pocket. I didn't intend to plant it. Do you believe me?"

"You would be dead if I did not. But you will follow Bhai's command. Say you planted the bug. He will believe it simply malfunctioned. Say you will keep in touch with us, befriend us, but work with us to kill him. When you make your next trip here, you will inform him of our false plans so he can waste his time on security for that while you work on getting alone with him to kill him."

"If I kill him, they'll kill me."

"You will have to figure out how to escape. Believe me, Duncan's reward will be substantial, and so will yours."

"What if Duncan tries to cheat me?" Niral asked.

"That is between him and you. But I hope you will not let us down, Niral Solanke. We both have a personal stake in this, remember that."

Niral recalled the events in New York. Bhai wasn't directly involved in Amrat's actions, but certainly his audit of the fund had led to Vishal's actions. Niral was not sure whether he hated Bhai, but he had no faith in The Brotherhood, and he was angry at Hindu fundamentalists.

"Okay, I will do what you say," Niral responded. "But you have to trust me and my methods."

"We will trust as far as it makes sense to trust. Now you must excuse us, as we need to escape this place through our tunnels. Bhai's men may have tracked you here and might descend at any time. We will be in touch again, but reaching me by phone may be difficult. I will speak with Duncan."

The bearded man put his hand on Niral's shoulder. Niral shrugged him off.

"Ali will take you up and show you out the proper door," Talim explained. "And take these."

He handed Niral back his papers, money, and magnifier, along the duffel bag which now contained a pouch. Niral stuck his hand in the bag and massaged the pouch. He guessed they were diamonds. Whether they were real or fake, he didn't know.

"For your deception," Talim said, smiling. "Good luck, Niral Solanke."

PART III

†

Phuket, Thailand; Phang-nga, Thailand; Krabi, Thailand

19

Rob drove all night and reached Phuket by morning. Normally, he would have flown. He loved the view from an airplane as he descended, the crags, appearing as if they emerged from the clouds themselves, made him feel he was entering a heavenly place, though he didn't believe in heaven or hell or anything in between. No, as he had explained to Sveta on his last trip to Phuket, lying in bed in her flat, the view was an illusion but one he welcomed. It made him certain that Thailand was the place for him and anyone who believed that they could be a god, regardless of their past, that they could possess what they wanted within the bounds of pleasure. Australia or America need not apply.

"Not America?" Sveta had inquired. "I understand Australia. We barely get out alive."

"America's a dumpster, too. You're a fucking slave until you die. Everything's rigged for the top one percent."

"That is what they say about America in Russia, too. But you do not think the president has rigged things there? And you see the red shirts and the yellow shirts here..."

"Fuck politics. That's all show. I'm yabbering about the nature of shit. Here even politics is a party. Everything's fucking sanuk. You get up every day and you wanna enjoy. Over there, you get up every day, and you wanna die. Sure, no one produces shit here, but who cares? It's all about the sanuk."

"I am not having sanuk."

"What's wrong with you, sweetie? You didn't have sanuk in Pattaya either. I got you away from Boris. Now you're unhappy here. It's in that Russian blood, I reckon."

"You move me from one slavery to another slavery. And you talk about sanuk?"

"You wanna compare this shit with Oz? Remember what I got you out of there."

"You worked for them."

"I didn't realize. The extent of it, I mean. I didn't know."

"Tell me, Rob," she said, snuggling up to him closely. "Why did you want to get out? I know for me, I was slave in Melbourne. But for you, you were free."

Rob hadn't answered. He hadn't wanted to think about it. He had dressed and left, drank at a number of bars on Th Bangla, got a massage, banged a girl tight, had another round, banged a bar girl, then went back home to Sveta, lying next to her in the dark, trying to forget the past. But sometimes it came to him, in flashes, and that's what happened on his drive down, all twelve hours or so, driving down Route 4 through random rains and fogs, even as he witnessed the beauty of Thailand's eastern coastline. In the darkness, he thought perhaps he had overestimated Thailand's pull, its seductive aura, just as he had once overestimated Queensland's. Nothing is anything but a contrasting accident of nature, a stimulated illusion meant to rise your expectations until the rug is pulled out under you and you plunge into the dung underneath.

He'd escaped before. He was Australian; he could. He had lived in Europe, America, Hong Kong, Malaysia, Indonesia. Odd jobs, dead-end jobs, and occasionally muscle. Eventually, he found something wrong, causing his departure. But he never forgot the people who had helped him or those who had sponsored him. When Niral had texted him about an opportunity in Thailand, he'd risen to the occasion. And he'd finally found a country he didn't want to leave. There were so many fruits here that he could never exhaust them. And for more than a year, he hadn't doubted this—until now.

Yet, as the sun rose and he approached Phang-nga, seeing those magnificent limestone crags perched against the clouds contrasted against the white sand and crystal blue water of the beach and the run-down town next to it, he realized his doubts had been silly. Even with the ugliness of his actions, the fruits of the land and the people made his adventure—and his life—worth it.

He parked in front of a restaurant. He was driving Duncan's car, a black sedan. He sat down at a table outside.

A skinny man approached him, carrying a menu.

"Hello, Mr. Rob," the man said.

"Pasat, how ya goin'? You got that menu for me?"

"Yes, sir," Pasat said, handing it to him. Inside he found a slip of paper, folded up. He put in his pocket, looked over the menu, then ordered a southern dish, gaeng sohm and roti, along with some Thai coffee.

A few tourists led by a guide entered the restaurant next door. It was while on a tour of Phang-nga from Phuket that Rob had met Pasat months ago.

"That was some good tucker. I really bogged in on that, mate," Rob said, after he had eaten his food quickly.

"I am glad you have enjoyed, Mr. Rob," Pasat answered. Rob threw down some baht, drank the remaining coffee in one gulp, and got back into the car. A few kilometers down the road, he pulled over, took the paper out, and unfolded it.

The directions had him go farther south. That was closer to Muslim territory, of course. He left Phang-nga and continued to drive down Route 4 toward Krabi. Feeling sleepy, he was glad he had slurped down that coffee, as it kept his eyes open. Maybe he should have dozed off with Sveta before going on this journey, he thought, but it was too late now. And anyway, he was expected.

After an hour, he took a detour, as the instructions explained, toward the coast. Then he made some turns down deserted roads, wondering if he was going the right way, as no street signs could guide him, only one turn after another.

He drove into an alcove where he saw a few houses build on stilts, followed by several houses on ground level. The end of the road was a dead end of forest.

He heard a door open. Next thing he knew, the car was surrounded by three men dressed like soldiers, holding AK-47s. Rob braked and stopped his car.

They yelled at him in a language that wasn't Thai. Rob had learned some Thai by now, and he could tell the difference. He raised his hands, hoping they wouldn't shoot. His gun was in its holster on his waist, but he knew he was no match for AK-47s.

A skinny man wearing a salwar kameez and topi approached the car. He was smiling.

"What is your name?" he asked in English through the open window.

"Rob Johnson."

"Your real name, sir."

Rob wasn't sure what to say. "Rob Johnson."

"Show me your passport. You were told to bring it."

Rob took it out of his duffel bag, shielding the machete also inside. He handed it over. The man opened and examined it with a sly smile. Then, he flicked it into the back seat of the car. "Mr. Borisslava Maric. Why do you say you are Rob Johnson?"

"I never changed it. I hate that name."

"It is a nice name. Better than Rob, no?"

"My old man was a wog. He abandoned my mum."

"A wog?"

"Fucking Crote. Yeah. She left too and my grandma raised me in the bush, at least for a few years."

"So you are bitter at your father?"

"Wouldn't you be? I bet you knew your old man."

Rahmat stood up straight, like a Buckingham Palace soldier. "My father is Allah, Mr. Rob. We do not need biological fathers."

"Can I get out of this hot tub?" Rob asked.

Rahmat gestured for him to come. Rob half-intended to take out his gun and start blasting, but his rational side told him to be cautious.

He was right. As soon as stepped out of the car, he was thoroughly padded down. One of the soldiers grabbed his gun from his holster. Another soldier searched his car and found his machete, then handed it to Rahmat.

"What did you bring this for, Mr. Maric?" he asked, brandishing it.

"To cut off your hands and feed them to Allah, what the fuck do you think?" he replied.

Rob laughed as Rahmat's mouth dropped.

Rahmat backed up and twirled the machete in his hands. "A comedian. I think we may get along. Tell me, what do you hope to bring back with you to Bangkok?"

"Whatever Duncan wants. It's his car."

Rahmat nodded toward a building. "We have the inventory here. Come."

A soldier pushed him roughly. Rob turned his head, angry, but he controlled himself and entered the building. The soldiers followed, then the door closed. A few lamps hung down from the ceiling. From their light he could see a few crates.

"Until we see the ultimate result, the load we give is light, but it is a solid amount, the first of three installments, equivalent to the cash paid by Mr. Solanke minus the diamonds and with a slight advance on the mission. Is this clear?" Rahmat asked.

Rob nodded. "I reckon so. Duncan told me we're not getting diamonds this time."

"No, you are not."

Rahmat opened the crate. Rob saw a bunch of children's dolls.

"You gammin with me?"

Rahmat didn't understand Rob's words, but he seemed to understand their meaning.

"Look closer," he said. Rahmat moved the dolls aside. Then Rob saw the mint containers.

"You've seen the police stop certain vehicles or buses, trying to find Malaysian or Burmese immigrants? We cannot make it easy for them to hang us."

"Can't believe it. Really is ya ba?"

Rahmat picked up a container. Rob saw the red pills shaped like Tums.

"Do you want to try one?"

"Never get high on your own supply," Rob narrated nervously.

"What?" Rahmat asked.

"American phrase. Nothing. Look, don't wanna go crazy right now. Hear it fucks up the mind."

"It alters the senses of those who are weak. Those who have not seen the right path of Allah or read the word of Mohammed. No, they are not so lucky, but perhaps it will steer them toward that course. Eventually."

"Yeah, you guys are so righteous."

"Mr. Rob, Mr. Maric, whatever your name is, when I look at you, I see not a man but a relic of a man, with two halves split down the middle. You will never see that in a Muslim. He is a rock, a solid whole. But the Buddhist, the atheist, the Christian, the deist, he is like you, perpetually divided. He cannot walk straight when he is not on solid ground. We will work as hard as we can to make the ground solid. Whether he walks straight is his business."

Rob nodded. "I see your point, mate."

Rahmat put the container back in the crate. "Would you like to survey the inventory? I have heard you do that with the diamonds."

"Sure," Rob said, putting his hand into his pocket. "Duncan did give me an estimate of the amount of product."

"Let me tell you what each crate contains. Below these containers are wrapped rectangular plastic holders containing bags of heroin that are meant to appear like gifted shirts. Below that are straws stuffed with ya ba tablets, and below that again are bags of heroin, but this time meant to look like packets of flour. You see, we like a good mix of the obvious and the concealed. Do your inspection, Mr. Maric."

Rahmat moved aside and stood respectfully with his hands folded against his groin, the machete still in his hands. Rob glanced at one of the soldiers, who had a slight scar on his face and was grinning viciously. Rob's heart started beating, thinking it might be a trap. But then, he had no cash or value of his own, and if they wanted him dead, they could have already killed him.

He checked the crates. The amount of containers seemed roughly equivalent to what Duncan had estimated. Duncan had never told Rob they would be picking up drugs in so many words, but Rob had guessed correctly, since Duncan had told him he could back out and go back to

Malaysia if he had wished. He'd be close enough to cross the border. But he didn't want to back out.

"We have a deal, Mr. Rob?" Rahmat asked.

"Deal," Rob confirmed, holding out his hand. To Rob's surprise, Rahmat performed a wai, palms together, and stated, "As-salam alekum, Mr. Rob."

20

Duncan sat in his office, watching Apsara do a strip show for him. When he tired of it, he slammed his hand against the desk. She ceased the show and dressed quickly.

"Let's talk about Rob," Duncan said. "I told you to get close to him, not fall in love with him."

"I'm not in love with him," Apsara pouted.

"But he's in love with you."

"That's what you wanted. I am good at that."

"You are. I almost fell for it, too. Good thing I have Lamai."

Apsara frowned. "I don't know why you insult me like this, Duncan. After all I..."

"Yes, you've done a lot for me. And you'll keep on doing it. Until the debt is paid."

"Why do you want to know about Rob? He has been very good. Better than that Niral."

"He's hiding something. I can't put my finger on it. I'm not saying he's going to drive to Malaysia with the merchandise, but there's something off."

"If he drives to Malaysia, he will get death penalty."

"Yes. He's got that in his blood. But he's not that dumb. And if he does, then my debt becomes bigger, and my ass is cooked if Mr. Hong..."

"Your debt? Why you talk about your debt?"

Duncan rose ferociously and grabbed Apsara by the hair, his eye twitching.

"Look at me, bitch," he said, placing his face to hers. "We've all got debts to pay. You're just lucky I'm paying yours. But who'll pay mine?

That's the question you would ask yourself if you thought about anybody but yourself. Now get the fuck out of my face."

He spun her around and pushed her forward into a cabinet. She yelled in pain and turned around fiercely, holding her face. She saw Duncan's face was twisted up, and he was trying his best not to cry. Oddly, his eye was no longer twitching.

"What..." she started to say but stopped herself. She stumbled toward the door.

21

"Sveta," Rob said, pushing her as she slept. She was sucking on her thumb like a baby. "Sveta."

She rolled over, away from him, muttering something in Russian. Then he heard the name "Sasha."

"Sveta," he yelled, pushing her hard against her shoulder. She opened her eyes suddenly and turned toward him. Regarding him against the moonlight, which trickled inside through the window. She shuddered and backed against the headboard.

"Oh, Sasha, I didn't mean to leave," she shouted in Russian. "I will do what you say. Please, don't..."

"No worries. Not that wanker." Rob said. "It's me."

"You?" Sveta asked in English, still shaking. "You are here for me?"

"I'll always be here for you, sweetie. When you need me."

"You sent me here alone. You were not in Pattaya for years."

"We needed to go our separate ways, sweetie. Need's a strange thing. It changes sometimes."

"What you need now? Why are you here? You did not tell me."

"I had business. But I figured something out. I think I know how to get you out of here."

"Out of Phuket?"

"Out of Thailand. Into a place you want to be. To give you a different life, a completely different one."

"You say that last time. I end up with same life."

"Better."

"But same."

"I'm hoping it'll be different this time. Trust me again. I've saved you before."

"You act like I have choice, Rob. I cannot go back to Russia, and I cannot stay here."

"You won't stay here. But I can't go with you. That's the deal."

"It is deja vu."

"Ya, sweetie. Life repeats itself, yet again."

PART IV

†

Surat, India

22

At the market in Rander, Niral didn't spot Manu among the crowd, but he felt his presence. He found Val, and they drove back to his house.

The Holi festivities were already underway. Val's wife, Sobha, was back. Two of her cousins were over. Niral relieved himself in the western-style toilet, so uncommon in even middle-class Indian homes, then stuffed the diamond pouch underneath the mattress in the guest room. Following Val's encouragement, Niral climbed to the roof where they had started the bonfire.

Niral could barely tolerate it. The fiery blaze reminded him of memories he would rather forget, and after snacking on vada and khaman and talking with Sobha's cousins about investment opportunities and land purchases with black money, he headed back down to the first floor. Sitting in the living room was a familiar sight. Manu was there, as well as Vikasmama.

"I was speaking with your uncle about the Holi celebration in Dwarka, our first in our new complex," Manu said. "It will be quite extravagant."

"I'm sure," Niral responded. "Is that where Bhai is?"

"Of course. How can the leader of an organization miss its biggest event?"

"Bhai is quite a man, I must admit," Vikasmama said. "I am not a Brotherhood follower, but I admire many of its concepts."

"You should come to a Brotherhood meeting," Manu said. "We have them in schools, markets, libraries, and restaurants. We have built many temples near Surat, too."

"I'd like to see some of them," Niral said. "I've been out of commission for a while."

"Yes," Manu said, rising. "You should see them before your flight, but you will not likely have time. Your flight is tomorrow morning. I've come to drive you back."

"Already? I'll miss the celebration."

"You will see many celebrations on the road."

"I may have to sleep in the car. I guess I'll dream them."

Manu smirked.

"I need to get my things from the room and say goodbye to my family," Niral explained.

"Of course. I will wait for you in the car."

Niral took his duffel bag and placed that inside his suitcase. He was about to climb the stairs when he saw a procession of people descend: Val, Sobha, Amrita, and Viral, one of Sobha's brothers.

"We heard you are leaving. You can't go without eating," Sobha said.

"Where are you going?" Amrita asked.

"Thailand, Amrita. My home," he said.

"Why do you live in Thailand? What do they do in Thailand? How many gods do they worship in Thailand? Who is your favorite god in Thailand?"

Niral answered her questions as well as he could: Bangkok, Sanuk, Buddha. "And as far as my favorite god, I'm not sure."

"Why are you not sure?" she asked. "I like Ambamata." Then she turned away and headed into the kitchen.

"I don't have time to eat," Niral said to Sobha. "I have a flight tomorrow morning. And it takes five hours to get to the Mumbai airport."

"Nonsense," Sobha said. "Eat quickly. You must be hungry."

Niral was hungry. "This is probably the first time someone is requesting a to-go dinner on Holi," he said.

"To-go?" Sobha asked.

"He means like a lunch box," Viral said. "Like the dabbawala."

"Oh, we don't do that here. This is not Mumbai or America. We eat things immediately."

"Come, Niral," Manu said, sticking his face inside. "We will stop at a restaurant on the way."

"Give him a plate," Sobha said. She called Amrita and told her to dump some shak, puri, rice, and dal from a steel thali to a plastic plate and hand it to Niral.

"Thank you," Niral said. "I should be back soon."

"How about the chaas?" Sobha asked.

"Please, Sobha," Val said. "You can make it for him next time."

Niral couldn't give the traditional namaste greeting (bowing with his palms together) while holding the plate, so he said his goodbyes instead. Manu put his bags into the trunk, then went back inside to say something to Vikasmama, while Niral balanced the tray on his lap as he sat in the passenger seat. The entire family came out into the front yard to see him go, something he remembered from his visit to India last time, particularly in Yam Gam.

They drove along the streets, dark in spots but punctuated by bonfires: on rooftops, in pyres in the middle of streets, flaming out of metal cans. Niral ripped a rotli, wrapped the bhinda shak and ate.

"Aren't you forgetting something?" Manu asked.

Niral looked over at him. Manu held up a pouch.

Niral stopped chewing. "You might have lost your entire purpose for coming here."

Niral finished swallowing. He took the pouch with his left hand and massaged it. He felt the diamonds.

"Where'd you find them?" he asked, putting them in his pocket.

"Where you left them, Niralbhai. I followed you to Rander and back to Surat. I am sure you know. I saw you put the diamonds under the mattress. You were not very careful to close your blinds. When you left in such a hurry, I went back inside after I put your bags away and double-checked. You completely forgot your purchase. Your boss would have been very angry."

"I guess you think I owe you?" Niral asked cautiously.

"No more than you owe me for driving you to and from the airport for business with a terrorist and a hater of The Brotherhood."

"Listen, I'm grateful. For all this. And I did plant the bug."

"Our people did not hear anything."

"Maybe it malfunctioned. I don't know. But I planted it under his table in there."

"I see. So you changed your mind."

"It didn't feel right. I remembered what Bhai said. Listening to Talim, seeing his followers, I realized what he said is true."

"I see a bruise forming on your face. Could that be a cause?"

"Yes, they roughed me up when I entered. They thought I could be armed. I am armed in Thailand. It wasn't a stretch."

"No. Have you ever killed anyone?"

Niral didn't answer. "I don't think that's your business."

Manu smiled. "Of course not. You know, we raided that spot shortly after your visit. We did not find a bug, only a piece of one, as if it was crushed."

"Maybe it broke when I was tackled, so it wasn't whole when I planted it. Maybe it fell off. I have no idea. I just know what I did."

"It is possible Talim found the bug. And upon finding it, he crushed it. Meaning you are compromised."

"Maybe. It's possible. But he doesn't know I put it there."

"Who else? He will do his research in that case. If you do have another meeting with him, it may be your last."

Niral ate another piece of rotli. "Look, I just know that after they searched me, he treated me with respect, and the transaction went well. He knows who I am. He knows I was a Brotherhood man who is disillusioned. He kept telling me how I should convert to Islam. That's why I think he will trust me. And we can bring him down."

"We?" Manu asked. "So you are now on board, all the way?"

"I wanted to talk to Bhai about it, but he's away."

"Yes, at the Holi event, which we suspected could be the target. Now, without the bug..."

"I don't think it's the target. I think they're still building a plan. That's the sense I got. He kept probing me, trying to see how much I hated Bhai. Maybe they will try to use me to get inside. If so, that's a long-term plan."

"That would be the best circumstance, I think. An inside man who is actually a turncoat for the other side."

"Yup. If that is what they decide to do, I think it'll be our best chance to bring their plot down."

"Good work, Niral. You might be our secret weapon. While Bhai is ten hours away, we do have another man you can meet with before you leave. He is staying at the same dosa shop. We will pick him up. Instead of Dwarka, he will speak tomorrow at our major temple in Mumbai."

"He is a Big Brother, a Motobhai?" Niral asked, thinking of Narendrakaka's former role.

"No, not technically. He was Bhai's accountant for many years. Now he is an elder, Bhai's second in line."

Niral thought of the audit of The Brotherhood fund. Perhaps it had been done by this person.

"What's his name?" Niral asked.

"Mr. Ghosh. He is Bengali. It is good to have people who are not Gujarati represent The Brotherhood, especially in Mumbai, don't you think?"

"If you say so," Niral said. "I don't know much about the internal politics."

"You will if you stay with us. Of course they are silly, we are all one and equal, but unfortunately our unequal realities, those things that divide us, are not so easily brought down by our ideals. We try, each and every day, and we chip away at them, each and every day."

"You sound like such an educated man. Did you go to college?"

Manu laughed. "Bhen was my teacher. Now Bhai is my teacher. I never went to college. I worked at a Brahmin's farm when I was little, like my father and my brothers. I finished high school; I did well, but I impregnated a girl who became my wife. Then I moved to Surat to work as a rickshaw driver. I tried to do well for my daughter. But I could not make it here, so I moved back home. I kept fighting with my brothers. They were drunks and greedy men, the type of men who ruin many villages today. They sold moonshine. They were promiscuous.

They believed in Hindu superstitions and false idols. That is when I discovered Bhen.

"That became my escape from stupidity. When I began working for the organization, I met Bhai, and he offered to put me in the new village they were building. I happily moved away from my old village, even relinquishing my stake in my family's home and the small plot of land that my brothers and I had purchased together. I had enough. I've never seen them again. But I know what goes on in these villages, among the Dubla. We need to enlighten the people."

"You must read more than what Bhen has written or said. You seem more..."

"Of course I read. I read all the time. But Bhen is my guide. I could tell you I do it simply for a selfish purpose, for self-study, but I must admit, I do it for my daughter, to be her inspiration. I only have one. She is my everything."

"Is she in college?"

"Yes, she is. College in Mumbai. She is a brilliant girl, at the top of class in the sciences. She will be a doctor for sure. But what I am most proud of is that she hasn't taken any Other Backwards Class benefits. She has done everything through merit. We no longer consider ourselves Dubla, Dalits, or anything else. Only Indians. That is what The Brotherhood has taught me, what it has instilled in me, and what I have passed down to her."

"Wow," Niral said, "my parents could never say the same thing about me. I was always a disappointment."

"What I heard you did in New York was heroic. I doubt they are not proud of you."

"Heroic? Is that what you think? I don't feel like a hero."

"Everyone who has mentioned you thinks of you highly. You uncovered the fraud of Narendrabhai and Dilipbhai, you solved the murder of Priya, you discovered the heinous nature of Amrat and Vishal."

"I'd think they'd be angry. I embarrassed The Brotherhood. I showed its true nature to the world."

"Nonsense. I am sure some people feel that way, but they are not our true followers. The organization has become stronger because of the faults uncovered. Now we have no theft from the fund. It is strictly controlled by Mr. Ghosh. You can ask him about it when we come upon the restaurant."

When they pulled inside the lot, Manu asked Niral if he was still hungry. Niral had finished his plate. He shook his head, but said he needed to wash his hands. Manu whistled through the window at a trucker who was drinking tea while on his break. He approached, spoke to Manu, then handed Manu his tea, ran to the diner, and returned with a cup of water.

Niral held out his hands. The trucker poured the water over them. A few morsels remained after, but Niral rubbed his hands and they slipped off.

The trucker smiled. Manu called to him. The trucker hustled over to the other side and took back the tea along with some rupees from Manu.

Meanwhile, someone had slipped inside the backseat and closed the door. Niral, startled, turned around suddenly, afraid it was an assassin ready to strangle him, but instead he saw a short, dark, genial-looking man with a round face. He was dressed in a sherwani and carried a briefcase. Despite his outwardly kind face, he gave a harsh order to Manu to commence driving.

"Yes, sir," Manu said in Hindi, a language Niral didn't understand. As he pulled away, Manu mentioned Niral's name and said something else in Hindi.

"Ah, Niral, yes, very nice to meet you," the man said in English, holding out his hand. Niral turned and shook it. Despite the heat, the man's palm was cold.

"I am Atul Ghosh. Has Manu mentioned me?"

"Yes," Niral said. "He was telling me that you control The Brotherhood fund now."

Mr. Ghosh produced a self-satisfied smile. "Yes, I do. We now have a central fund for the entire organization. Each continent maintains one fund where all donations are initially sent, then they are funneled into the main one here, and we make sure nothing is missing. When expenditures are made at the continental level, they must be carefully documented. North America's Big Brother, Sureshbhai, oversees their fund with Prembhai and Alkeshbhai. Don't worry, no theft like Narendrabhai's can occur again."

"Are the donations still anonymous?"

"We leave that to the Motobhai's discretion. We are not as strict as before. We also allow people to give outside of the official donation nights. We understand people's schedules are hectic these days, and we understand the power of technology, so they can give through wire transfer or donate by credit card on our website. We have done fundraising drives on crowdfunding sites. Our young people are very resourceful. We value and use their ingenuity."

"Don't you think that is a violation of Bhen's dictates?"

Mr. Ghosh looked genuinely surprised. "Not at all. Bhen herself preached against any literal interpretation of texts or commands. We are moving with the times but in a way consistent with her general principles. Believe me, Bhai has been excellent for this organization. He has been strict in the right ways, loose in the right ways."

Niral didn't respond. Mr. Ghosh continued. "We greatly appreciate your actions, Niralkumar. Without your courage we would not have the wonderful organization we have today. We have sought your assistance for years. We tried to track you down in Thailand, but your father believed that perhaps you needed a period of searching after the tragedies you witnessed. Maybe that period has come to an end now?"

"He wants to help us, he says," Manu answered. "He planted the bug, but it was crushed, or it didn't work."

"It does not matter. As long as you want to help," Mr. Ghosh said.

"Yes," Niral responded, his head still turned to Mr. Ghosh. "I can get inside Talim's organization. I feel that he will trust me. He thinks I hate Bhai."

A smile slowly formed on Mr. Ghosh's face. "Very good, Niralkumar. Very good."

PART V

†

Bangkok, Thailand

23

At the airport in Bangkok, Niral stood in the taxi line until his turn came, then he insisted the driver put on the meter ("meter kap") and avoid the highway. He didn't take taxis often, but he remembered Lamai's tips the last time he talked to her, telling him about all the pitfalls of Bangkok.

As they drove up the road, Niral saw someone running toward the cab. He realized it was Apsara. He reached over and opened the door for her. He half-expected her to be carrying a gun. It was almost like he welcomed it.

She was wearing the "I Love Dick" t-shirt again. She caught her breath as she shut the door.

"I brought a taxi for you, Niral. Just for you."

"Duncan told you to pick me up?"

"I am your chauffeur, Niral." She held out her hand. "Give me money."

"God no. Should we switch to the other cab?"

"It is paid by Duncan." The driver was irritated. He began to argue with Apsara, who became theatrical. Niral reminded her not to piss him off.

"What will he do?" Apsara asked.

"He'd take a crow bar and chop off your head, bitch. Read it in a newspaper."

She took out some baht and shoved it in the driver's hand. He stopped the cab. They climbed out. Niral waited by the trunk for the driver to open it, but he didn't emerge from the seat. He seemed to be counting the baht.

"He's gonna drive off with my shit," Niral said.

Apsara sauntered over to him and said something. The driver smiled, then came out and opened the trunk.

Niral wheeled over his bag to the other taxi. They got inside.

"Let me guess, you gave him a free fuck at Scandal?" Niral asked.

"Rob calls it a root."

"I knew it. You don't give a shit about him."

"I give a shit about everybody, Niral. Even you. Especially you."

Niral rolled his eyes. Apsara played with her belly button the rest of the way. They stopped in front of the old gate. Apsara spoke to the driver while Niral wheeled his bag toward the warehouse. He saw Duncan's car parked out front, and the overhead door to the ground entrance was open.

"Where's Rob?" Niral asked Apsara, who was jogging to catch up.

"He should be here," she answered, passing Niral and leading him inside. The ground entrance led into a large, deserted space. The floor was dirt and sand. Duncan and Rob stood in front of a few crates.

"Niral!" Duncan called, waving him forward. "The man of the hour has arrived."

"He's a busy boy. I reckon he looks darker," Rob commented.

"No way. The sun's hotter here," Niral replied as he wheeled up his bag.

"I almost missed him at the airport. But he found me," Apsara said flirtatiously.

Niral didn't respond to her. Instead he said, "So we're all here. Is this a meeting?"

"An important moment in all our lives," Duncan said. "You got the diamonds?"

"Sure," Niral said, sliding in the handle and placing the bag on the ground. He unzipped the bag, found the smaller duffel bag and opened it. He had placed the duffel bag back inside his larger bag once he got to the airport, paranoid about corrupt Indian customs officials. He pulled out the pouch.

"Very nice," Duncan said, taking it from him and holding it up. "I bless this pouch as a symbol of our rejuvenation and renewed future."

"Doesn't seem like you wanted the pouch," Niral noted.

Duncan smiled.

"It's a secondary prize." He placed the pouch upside down and dropped the diamonds into his palm.

"Are those real?" Niral asked.

"You didn't check them?" Duncan replied, looking up.

"Are you kidding? I was surrounded by goons."

Duncan examined him. "I still expected you to do your job, Niral. Part of the payment was for the diamonds."

"That's what I don't understand, Duncan," Niral said. "I bet one diamond is worth a lot more than one of whatever you have in that crate. I didn't check the stones because they took my magnifier away and kicked me out, but I still don't understand the math."

"Yes, you're right," Duncan replied. "One diamond is worth a lot more. But, in the long run, the diamond trade will go south. The drug trade will not. It will continue, as long as there is demand. And Thais want their ya ba."

Duncan pointed to Rob, who took off the cover of one crate and lifted a mint container.

"One of these containers is only worth maybe, I don't know, 300 baht," Duncan explained. "But we'll sell it for 10,000 baht easy. So you can do the math. The diamond is worth a lot more, but doesn't have that level of profit on resale. And we don't need a factory for it. We don't need to sell it in America. We can sell it straight up, right here in Thailand."

"And get hung for it."

"No doubt, we've got to be careful. Rob, check these diamonds against my list."

He rolled them back into the pouch and handed it to Rob, who took out his magnifier and a list.

"So you knew I wouldn't check them?" Niral asked, pointing to the list.

"I wasn't sure, Niral. I know it was a nerve-wracking situation. And I'm sorry I couldn't tell you beforehand."

"Why couldn't you tell me beforehand, Duncan?" Niral asked.

"I just thought it would be better for you to be eased into your surroundings there."

"You knew Bhai would find me first?"

"I didn't know anything for sure. That's why I didn't tell you."

"Where'd you get that shit?" Niral asked, pointing to the crate.

Duncan turned to Rob, who was checking the diamonds against another crate.

"Rob went down to Phuket," Apsara said, rolling her eyes, her arms crossed against her chest. "To Krabi."

"That's right, they ship it from India to southern Thailand, because the Thai police expect it to come in through the Golden Triangle," Duncan explained. "And in India, it's made cheaply, using rupees, so the price is lower."

"Why don't the Muslims sell it themselves?"

"They're making lots of profit already. We also bought some heroin, which they make in Afghanistan for next to nothing. And they don't have distribution here."

"Neither do we. Unless I'm missing something."

"We'll make a system. We have to."

"Why not just take cash for this hit? Easier than selling drugs."

Duncan smirked, his eye twitching. He strolled over to Niral and put his arm around him.

"Again, Niral, it's the long-term idea. Once we build this network, we can keep on making money. It won't be just a one hit wonder. And it'll save us all."

"Mr. Hong won't be happy."

"If he finds out, we're dead men."

"And you'd do this to your poo yai?"

Duncan turned to Niral and grasped his shoulders firmly, so strong that it hurt, putting his face close. "What he doesn't know won't hurt him. This is for us."

"Why do you need the money so badly, Duncan?" Niral asked. "That's what I don't understand."

Duncan glanced at Apsara, then looked away. He turned and walked away from Niral.

"Many reasons that I can't get into now," he said. "But you know how much money we lost to Thanat, which we haven't recovered. That was months ago, but I was counting on it. I have bills, I have obligations."

"We're happy so far," Rob said, continuing to check the diamonds. "I reckon they do want this bloke dead."

"They want to establish a good relationship," Duncan responded. "Still, Niral, you got lucky. I would have taken that amount out of your debt repayment if it wasn't up to snuff."

"I had to run, man," Niral said. "Bhai's people were going to raid the place. You didn't exactly give me a weapon to defend myself if I got ripped off."

"They searched you, didn't they?" Duncan asked. "Just would've meant a lost gun. Anyway, how would you get a gun on a plane?"

"Why me, Duncan?" Niral asked, letting the cat out of the bag. "Rob's the assassin. Have him kill Bhai."

"Rob doesn't know Bhai. He can't fit in like you can. It needs to be an inside job. That's why you're so valuable to them, and why they're going to give us a lot of ya ba and heroin. Plus, I need Rob here to help distribute the shit and continue to run the diamond game."

"When am I going back?"

"We'll give it a decent stretch of time. A couple of months. In the meantime, you'll work with Rob to establish a distribution network in Thailand. And he'll help you to figure out how to kill Bhai. Keep Talim informed while corresponding with Bhai's associates however you want: email, messaging, phone. You did get their information, right?"

"Bhai's associates, yes. But not Bhai."

"Good enough. We can't make it too obvious. You need to flow into his trust. So by the time you go back to make the second exchange, you'll be more familiar to them, a spy who has the confidence of both sides.

It'll be more cost effective than sending you every week. The diamonds are cheaper but not worth the hassle. We can still buy from Shekhat for the majority. I'd rather have you here for that."

"How are we going to distribute the stuff?"

"Rob will fill you in on what we've discussed so far."

"And Apsara?"

Duncan smiled. He approached Apsara, held her by the cheeks, and kissed her. When he released, her makeup was smudged, and Niral noticed what looked like a bruise. Rob noticed it too.

"Apsara's the secret weapon," Duncan said, his eye twitching. "She's got her talons in Nam's gang, her ears open to Mr. Hong's comings and goings, plus her beak in Sumantapat's network too; she can keep track of their drug routes through hearsay. We can steer clear of their territory, and we'll know if they ever get word about us."

"Wouldn't Sumantapat suspect Apsara after Thanat disappeared?" Niral asked.

"His gang knows her real name as Duanphen and her stage name as Tip. Thanat never told them she was going to be at that gem scam. When she runs into their members, she acts like she hasn't seen or heard from Thanat. Sumantapat doesn't know she works at Mr. Hong's club, but the two are at peace, so I'm not sure it would matter if he did. She's just another prostitute who works at a number of places and had a thing with Thanat for a time. But she's got enough of an 'in' that she can keep an ear out for us."

"Sounds randy," Rob said, tossing the bag back to Duncan.

"You think of rooting now," Apsara said, teasing. "I know what randy means."

"We'll lock up here, then I'll drop off the diamonds to Mr. Hong's factory myself," Duncan said, ignoring them and flipping the bag up and down in his palm. "After I drop you guys off on Khao San Road."

24

Upstairs, in their apartment, Rob rushed into the bathroom. When he emerged, he saw Niral holding a gun to him.

"What the fuck, mate?"

"You didn't tell me. Why didn't you tell me about this Bhai shit?"

"Well, Duncan told me not to."

"You've known me for years. You've known Duncan for a year."

"He's my boss. He's paying me. I knew you could take it."

"You called me shaky. Now you think I could kill a holy man?"

"You don't consider that wanker a holy man. You hate that cunt."

"I hate Vishal. I hate Amrat. I don't give a fuck about Bhai."

"But now you do, don't you? However this works out, you'll get out of this vortex you're in. Pretending you're a back-door bandit, dealing diamonds, trying to stay clear of the Dragons. Fuck, man, maybe you need this."

"Don't tell me what I need. I feel betrayed by everyone right now. It never ends. A rock and a hard place."

"I can tell that Duncan means well."

"He means well? How do we know he won't take all the profits and eliminate us? We don't know. He's my poo yai, but he's going behind his own poo yai's back."

"Well, I can run whenever I want."

"Not now."

Niral's arms began to shake as he held the gun.

"Shaky," Rob said, hissing. Suddenly Niral's arms stopped shaking. He aimed clear to Rob's chest. Rob's expression changed to one of abject horror.

Niral put down the gun.

"Fuck, you scared me shitless, mate," Rob said, rubbing sweat from his forehead.

"I didn't shake that time," Niral noted quietly, almost to himself.

"No, you didn't. Not for a second, mate. I reckon you had the eyes of a killer. Which is what you need with this Bhai bloke."

Niral sat on the bed. "All right, let's figure out this kill thing and this drug thing. Two brains are better than one, right?"

25

Sitting in her room at her apartment in Klong Tuey, getting ready to go out and dance at Sumantapat's club Go-Go Rama on Soi Cowboy, Apsara put on her makeup: the light eyeshadow, foundation, and rouge. Her roommate, a ladyboy named Buppha, who worked at a bar in Nana, knocked on her door.

"Apsara, a guy for you!"

Before she could respond, Rob opened the door and stepped inside.

Apsara turned and became animated. But Rob looked dead serious as he shut the door.

"What's the matter, baby?" she asked.

"Why'd he hit you?"

"What? Who?"

"Duncan? Or are you telling me it was a customer?"

"I still..."

Rob charged up, held her chin, and began to lick off the makeup from her cheek.

She tried to push him away. He spit against the mirror.

"I can see it now," he yelled, pointing at her cheek. "Who the fuck did that to you?"

"Nobody," she responded, staring at the spit stain. "I ran into a closet door, okay?"

"You expect me to believe that?"

"It is truth. What do you care?"

Rob took Apsara by the wrists and held her strong. "I care, okay. Don't ask me why, but I do. Now tell me."

"I'm Duncan's mia noi. Not yours."

"You want to be his wife, is that it?"

"I am an Isan cunt. I will never be his wife!"

Rob nodded. "I'm glad you recognize that, you cum dumpster. You're Mr. Hong's property, you're Duncan's mistress, you're every man's whore. So what are you to me?"

"I thought I was your gik. But now I don't want to be."

Rob let go of her wrists. "You're not worth saving, sweetie. You don't have respect for yourself."

"If you think that, go and boom boom your Phuket cunt, slut, or whatever you call her. Your Russian prima donna. I know you go see her. I know you love her."

"You don't understand anything."

"Then tell me. Make me understand, Rob. Because I *don't* understand."

Rob closed his eyes. "It's complicated, sweetie. It's..."

Apsara held his forearms. "You tell me, Rob. Let it out. I will take it."

Rob shook his head. "I've known her a long time. I feel obligated. It's got nothing to do with you. It's got nothing to do with loving her."

"So you don't love her?"

Rob disengaged from Apsara's grasp. He turned and paced around. Then he sat on Apsara's bed.

"I met her in Melbourne when I was an enforcer for a guy named Sasha," Rob explained. "I ran away from Queensland and I fled to Victoria. I needed a job. I didn't realize it was a trafficking operation, that I'd be keeping cum dumpsters in line. Except these girls didn't have any choice. The first thing they made me do was beat up and rape a girl who had tried to run away. Then the other guys took turns ganging her. That was Sveta."

Apsara folded her arms. "So you feel guilty? You?"

"I'd killed at that point, but it wasn't from someone's orders. So that crossed a line for me. I played along, I reckon, but later I visited Sveta and apologized to her. Of course, there were other girls. When they needed to be disciplined, I'd make some excuse and let someone else do it. I'd already proven myself to them, so they respected me. But I made up my mind that I'd save Sveta, someway, somehow. That's when I got that tattoo of her name on my ass to prove I'd feel pain for her.

"I found an agent who'd traffic a girl back to Russia. I looked for the right time to spring her. But then she told me she couldn't go back to Russia. She was in debt there and the local gang that had tricked her and sold her into slavery would kill her if she went back.

"So I looked for another option. I'd met another Russian guy named Boris. He'd worked with Sasha briefly but became sick of his tactics. He wanted to run a more legit place. So he moved to Thailand and with a Thai partner, he'd bought a club in Pattaya. I knew he'd treat her much better than Sasha. At least she'd be free and could keep most of the money she earned. She could send it back to her family if she wanted. So I stole her passport and had Boris get a Thai work visa for her. And one night, I snuck her out. But I couldn't go with her. After what I'd done, I couldn't be around her, and I couldn't stay in that trap. So I went to America instead."

"But then you did come here. And you took her away from Pattaya too. Why?"

"Boris was okay but Sveta wasn't happy. A lot of clients had sick requests. His club promised 100 percent satisfaction, so she had no choice but to comply. Sometimes she would complain and he'd beat her. The money was good, but she was sick of it. When we'd made the deal to free her, we didn't pay Boris. Instead, he'd deduct from her earnings what she owed him. So to get out of the debt, she paid part of it, and I paid part.

"She moved down to Phuket and started working for this half-Thai, half-British guy named Alex. Now she doesn't owe anybody, but she's still not happy. I'd like to get her into a job where she doesn't have to sell her body but can still make good money. It's tough to come by."

"You sleep with her."

"I couldn't for a long time, sweetie. But it happened. She relies on me. But I still can't be with her. It's complicated."

Apsara sat on his lap and put her arms around his neck. "So you will be with me, no?"

"You're still Duncan's mia noi."

"He says he will pay my debt to Mr. Hong, but he does not. He is all talk."

"If he finds out about us, who knows what he'll do," Rob said.

Apsara shook her head and rubbed her nose against his. "I sleep with many men."

"You're more than that to me," Rob said. He kissed her. As she released her lips from his and stared into his eyes, she pulled on his dreads

"Maybe you cut these off," she said. "And one day, when I am debt free, you will visit my family in Isan."

"One day, I reckon," Rob said.

BOOK TWO

PART VI

†

Bangkok, Thailand; Hua Hin, Thailand

26

Planning proceeded well on both fronts. Apsara learned about the drug routes and territories of Sumantapat's dealers. Rob and Niral used that information to steer clear of certain areas and made forays into new territories, meeting potential partners and using word of mouth to ascertain the buyers. Primary users of ya ba included prostitutes, clubbers, and truckers, but the drug was widely used across Thai society. They decided going into the small cities and villages around Bangkok would be a better bet since Sumantapat's gang and others already had Bangkok locked up.

One day, Niral recruited Kan, the vendor near the Muay Thai boxing school who was originally from a village near Kanchanaburi. Kan knew middlemen in adjacent villages who bought their drugs from various sources but weren't dependent on any particular seller, searching instead for the best price for the highest quality product. Rob and Niral visited Kanchanaburi and made deals with the middlemen, armed and ready to use force if they suspected a trap.

Meanwhile, Niral kept in touch with Talim and Mr. Ghosh, convincing both he was duping the other, giving little tidbits of his plans and conversations with the other party, whether true or not, to keep them engaged. Niral knew he would have to be careful, though. Duplicity was possible on their part too. Niral informed Mr. Ghosh that Talim was planning an attack on Shri Diwali, but that the details would be revealed to him on his next trip. He told Talim that a large security presence would be brought in from all over India, possibly the world, for Shri Diwali to guard against his false attack. But a plan to kill Bhai hadn't materialized. Mr. Ghosh was careful not to reveal Bhai's habits or the locations he frequented. Rob and Niral realized that Niral could only gain that "in" with Bhai when he met him again in person and became part of his physical world.

Duncan had kept his word, keeping Niral in Thailand for a couple of months while the drug route was established. But business had been good, and the first batch was wearing thin, so he would be dispatched soon to make another deal. Again, cash would be exchanged for diamonds and more merchandise Rob would pick up in Krabi. Duncan told Niral they would pay less this time and receive more merchandise, essentially an advance on Bhai's assassination. This time Duncan wanted Niral to stay longer so he could meet with Bhai personally and establish a relationship with him. He would look for ways to eliminate Bhai while continuing to feed false information to him about Talim's intentions.

Rob's influence on Niral had increased as they worked together on the drug deals and tried to figure out an assassination plot. Niral's gun skills rose, and Rob no longer teased Niral as "shaky." Sometimes Niral would go to barren spots by the Chao Phraya river to practice. Niral's confidence around women increased, as well; his reluctance around bar girls and prostitutes dissipated. He still didn't trust them, and he still hadn't fucked one. But he no longer minded their company.

One day, Rob suggested trying their luck in Hua Hin. They had gone to the seaside resort town once before, months ago, staying in a cabin by the sea and getting drunk with some British tourists in a Thai club. Rob knew many massage and bar girls on Th Phunsuk and Soi Bintabaht who craved ya ba and especially heroin. He'd avoided selling to them until now.

After they arrived, Rob ventured downtown with the merchandise while Niral lay in a room at a pier guesthouse near Th Naresdamri, staring up at the chipping blue paint on the ceiling and listening to the waves crash against the pillars underneath him.

Bored, he ventured outside. Monsoon season had begun, and while the rain was sporadic, the temperatures had risen. He wiped the sweat from his brow as he strolled down Th Naresdamri, passing an Indian restaurant and curving around an external hotel bar where tourists sat at tables against a stone barrier that guarded them from a massive cliff that dipped into the Gulf of Thailand. When he reached the stairs, he saw the Gulf itself and Hua Hin's uniquely pebbly beach below.

As he climbed down the archaic stone stairs to the beach, he surveyed the scene. Jet skis zipped along the bright blue, wavy water, dragging para gliders, while aircraft carriers hung out against a backdrop of piers and apartment buildings. Where the water made its way onto land, white girls wearing bikinis held hands, afraid to venture in, while Thai boys in their underwear twirled sticks and paced in circles, knee-deep. Thai girls in t-shirts hit each other playfully and fought over designer bags. Families sat on rock formations on the water or, farther back on the beach, lay on blue mats under yellow umbrellas, watching a tourist ride a wild horse while a trainer ran alongside them shouting instructions.

When he reached land, Niral began to walk along the water and saw tiny sand crabs crawling out of the earth. They ran across his feet and ducked into holes, burrowing, hiding, emerging, scattering. The beach was littered with these small holes. A dead jellyfish was caked against the sand.

As the hot wind blew against his face, he peered toward the other side of the beach, where colorful but damaged long-tail boats were docked next to snack spots, hotels, and paths that led back onto Th Naresdamri. He noticed a woman sitting on a lounge chair, wearing a bikini and sunglasses, reading an old novel by Jackie Collins. A chair next to her was empty, but a towel had been placed on it. Niral recognized her. Soon she recognized him too.

They stood there, apart, watching each other. Niral wondered whether he should ignore her. But something compelled him forward. She dropped her book on the chair, took off her sunglasses, and raised her arms. She was shaking.

"I'm going to scream!" she shouted.

"I'm not going to hurt you. You think I'd be this obvious?" Niral asked.

"My husband's coming back. He'll be back before long."

"Calm down. How do I convince you I'm not trying to kill you? It was a long time ago. That plot is over now."

"Is it? I don't think it is ever over for me. Those mobsters, they don't forget. Stan Lorenzo is dead. Have you forgotten?"

Had he forgotten? He hadn't thought of Stan in a long time. He remembered Lauren, Vishal, Amrat. He was sure his father hadn't forgotten. Or Lance. Lance wouldn't forget either.

"I don't work for the Traglianis. I'm not Lucchese."

"You're not?"

"No. Where's Bob at?"

She shuddered, then glanced behind her. "He went to get something to eat. He's been gone a while."

"Don't worry, I'm sure he's still alive."

She stared at him coldly.

"If you don't work for the Traglianis, if you aren't trying to kill us, why do I keep seeing you? And what are you still doing here?"

"Fate, maybe," Niral said after a pause. "I'm amazed too. As for Thailand, it's a nice place, isn't it?"

"I don't know. It's hot like Texas. It has nice beaches. But when I was taking my constitutional, I saw an old man, probably eighty-five, much older than Bob, holding hands with a girl who looked fourteen. I mean, you see it everywhere. And the girls in the massage parlors yelling at every man that passes. It's horrid."

"Yes, that's the reality here. It's not America. Everything's out in the open."

"If you mean Bob's affairs, he's confessed them to me. He's changed now. He's not the man he once was."

"Neither am I."

Niral looked toward the snack shops. He didn't see Bob.

"I'm going to go ahead. Tell Bob I was here. I'm staying at the guesthouse on the pier over there. How about you? That fancy hotel up the steps?"

Linda was silent. Niral turned around and walked back, past the couples and the spider crabs to the steps leading up to the hotel restaurant. He curved around and ended up back on Th Naresdamri, passed some restaurants, and took a left onto Th Dechanuchit. An Indian boy, a tailor's hawk, pointed and shouted at him.

"Where you from, sir? Canada? Pakistan? Please, come in and try. Fine suit, sir. Good price."

Niral ignored him and passed a small massage shop decorated with a laughing Buddha statue that extended into a water fountain. A girl sat on steps leading down to the shop. Weakly, she asked, "Massage?"

Niral knew this would be the tamest of the onslaught he would receive once he turned left onto Th Phunsuk. As soon as he passed a narrow, curving alley, he began to hear the shouts, and then he was grabbed and slapped by multiple hands of skinny Thai girls, shouting, "Massage! Massage, sir! Good time!"

He smiled bitterly and hurried past the onslaught. Two bar girls were playing pool alone at the bar/restaurant down the road. Past that were a few more restaurants. Finally, Niral approached Soi Bintabaht.

It was still daytime. The nighttime crowd and neon lights were not out yet, although even then the scene was nowhere near as chaotic as Patpong or Pattaya. As he turned left onto Soi Bintabaht, he ran straight into Bob Macaday.

"Niral. Why, I..."

"Bob. I thought you were at the beach?"

"What?"

"I just saw Linda. She told me you went to get a snack."

"I must have taken a wrong turn," he said nervously. "Why are you here?"

"On vacation."

Bob smiled awkwardly. Niral could see he was shaking.

"I guess we're in the same boat, then," Bob said.

"I guess so. Did you ever visit that Buddhist temple?"

"Which one?"

"In Kanchanaburi. The one up the hill."

"Oh yes. We did. Of course, we took a tuk-tuk there. Linda wouldn't bike."

"How was it?"

"The monk said some interesting things. They were under construction. Linda didn't think it was relaxing enough, so she insisted we leave. She thought it was a waste of time, but I thought he said some interesting things."

"I was just in Kanchanaburi," Niral recounted. "I wanted to go back to the temple. I motorcycled toward it, but a butterfly hit me in the face, so I skidded out and skinned my knee. A nice couple and their little daughter helped me out. Treated my wound, washed my clothes, fed me at their little restaurant. I was so enamored I forgot about the temple. I'm never less than amazed at the hospitality of some people here. That would never happen in America."

"Some try to cheat you, others try to help you, right?"

Niral smirked.

"Did you want something, Niral?" Bob asked, whispering. "I haven't said a word about what happened."

"No, nothing," Niral responded. "I saw Linda randomly. And I ran into you randomly. Not a big town, or country, after all."

Bob hesitated. "No."

"You're here for a while?"

"We're headed to Pattaya tomorrow. There's a boat that'll take you across. Run by some Norwegian guy."

"Sin city, eh? Linda's cool with that?"

"Sure. She wants to see the country. It's not all sin, is it? There's a beach, I hear."

"True. Where are you staying? Maybe we'll come with."

"Are you serious?"

"Yeah. Maybe. Aren't you going to ask who 'we' is?"

Bob swallowed. "That crazy Australian guy? The butcher?"

"That's what you call him? I'll have to let him know. He should be around here somewhere."

"Look, we're staying at the hotel on the hill. You know it. I haven't said anything."

"What time is the boat? By the way, the beach is the other way."

Bob told him the time. Then he turned around and hurried back down the length of Soi Bintabaht. Niral waited for him to clear it before he followed. Then he saw Rob leaving a massage parlor, being slapped on the arms by some girls. He was carrying the duffel bag with the merchandise, but the bag appeared empty.

"Successful mission?" Niral asked.

Rob expressed some surprise at seeing him. He seemed slightly tipsy and introduced Niral to the girls and the madam, who came out.

They tried to pull Niral inside. The madam said Rob was a friend. They would give Niral a freebie.

"Maybe later," Niral said. "It's not even dark."

"Niral's a careful bloke. He likes to peruse the merchandise before he makes a selection. Ain't long before he loses his virginity."

"I like virgin," one of the girls said, holding Niral's hand. "Better than old man."

They escaped and returned to the pier. Inside the guesthouse, they could hear the sea flowing and receding below the planks.

"Sold it all?" Niral asked.

"What I had. I've still got some reserves in the suitcase."

"Want to try Pattaya?"

"I'm pretty sure I can sell it here. We can hit up Pattaya after I get the next batch."

"I ran into Bob Macaday. Remember the tourist?"

Rob thought. "Oh, yeah. He told me Bob Murphy."

"Regardless, he says he's taking a boat across to Pattaya. We can check it out."

"It's only a short ride from Bangkok. We could go anytime."

"We're here. We don't have to sell anything, just hang."

"Apsara says Sumantapat's got a trade in Pattaya. It's all booked by outfits. Not surprising. Only spot we might make moolah is at Boyztown. If you wanna go poofter again, you're a fit, mate."

"We don't have to go. It's just an idea."

"Nah, we can check it out. I was gonna hit up Pattaya anyway after I got back from Phuket with the next batch. If not for the dope, then for some unfinished business."

"Unfinished business?"

"No worries, mate. I'll mind mine. You hang out with your mate, good ol' Bob."

PART VII

†

Pattaya, Thailand

27

The next morning, Niral noticed Rob's dreads were gone. He looked like an Army private.

He'd gone out the night before. Niral had stayed in and tried to sleep over the sound of waves.

"Didn't realize a haircut was part of the nightlife," he said.

"Reckon a change was in order. Let's go."

They checked out of the guesthouse and reached the pier where the boat was docked that would take them to Pattaya. Niral had looked it up the night before on his smartphone and even bought their tickets with the credit card Duncan had given him.

Bob and Linda were already on the boat. Bob, wearing a sleeveless polo shirt and cargo shorts, was friendly, cheerful even, when Niral and Rob stepped onboard. He didn't act nervous around Rob either, acknowledging him with a head nod. But Linda was still shaking. She stayed inside the cabin with a few other old ladies while Bob and Niral hung out on the deck, the wind in their faces, watching the water and the receding skyline of Hua Hin.

"You still keep in touch with that black man?" Bob asked Niral.

"Lance? No. He doesn't use email or social media."

"Linda's still terrified of him. She won't say what happened upstairs. If he did something and I saw him again, I'm not sure I could control myself."

"Lance was in the Gulf War. Be careful."

Bob smirked. "I've got more connections than you think."

"Really?" Niral asked. "Like who?"

Bob shook his head. "I'm just joking. I'm scared shitless."

"You haven't heard from Vishal, have you?"

"I told you, I haven't. If he's alive, he's living his own life, I hope, because he has every reason to shut me up too."

"Seems like everyone we can think of wants you dead," Niral said.

Bob didn't respond. He went back into the cabin. Rob came over from the other side of the deck, where he had been talking to the captain's friend.

"You sure he'll keep his mouth shut?" Rob asked Niral. "You know him, don't you?"

"Long story," Niral said. "But I think he will."

"That's not very affirmative, mate. We can still finish the job."

"He will," Niral insisted. "He's got too much to lose."

"We'd have to get rid of the wife too, maybe. Who knows what he's gabbed to her? Could get messy."

"Exactly. So let's forget 'finishing the job,' okay?"

"You'll have to explain the connection to me one day, mate. Only fair."

"One day," Niral responded. "Sure."

28

They pulled up to the pier just above Walking Street and docked. During the day, the entrance to the seedy district didn't appear intimidating. In the other direction, bathers lined the beach and tourists stalked the boardwalk. Thais hawked water and fruits. On the water, jet skis paraglided plastic advertisements. Bob stared at the Walking Street sign, nervous now.

"Past that must be the most horrid..." Linda began to say.

"Don't worry, we'll avoid it," Bob answered. "I think our hotel is in Hat Jomtien."

"Yeah, mate, that's your spot," Rob said. "It's family-friendly."

“I guess we can take a tuk-tuk,” Bob suggested.

“Hop a baht bus,” Rob recommended. “Cheaper and more efficient.”

Rob waved at one that was passing, and it stopped. It was painted red, green, and orange. The two benches in the back were full but for one small space. Two men were standing, holding a pole.

“One spot for the lovely lady,” Rob said, holding out his hand for Linda to take, but Mrs. Macaday held her palm up in disgust as she climbed aboard the bus and commandeered the seat. Bob acknowledged Rob’s attempt with a head nod as he climbed aboard and stood next to the men holding the pole.

“Goodbye, Bob. See ya around,” Rob said.

“Goodbye, Niral,” Bob said as the baht bus went off. Rob turned and smirked at Niral.

“He’s been here before. I think he knows Jomtien. And Walking Street.”

“He fought in ‘Nam in the 70s, was stationed in Khorat. Probably came down here.”

“Yeah, I bet he did, mate. Was a busy boy then, I reckon. But then, we never change, do we? Wife or no wife, gik or no gik.”

“Where are we staying?”

“There’s a guesthouse on Soi 12, Th Pattaya 2. It’s next to my favorite massage place.”

“Can’t wait.”

At the massage parlor, Rob was welcomed with the usual fervor by his girls and the madam. But he declined a massage, and the two settled into a simple room in a guesthouse next door run by two women. Like Mr. Hong’s club, it was named “Same Same.”

“Never ones for imagination here, right, Rob?”

“You want imagination, go to sleep.”

“So what’s the plan?”

“You’re the one who came here. You tell me.”

“Did you sell all the merchandise last night?”

“Saved some for my girls downstairs. It’s gonna be a gift, but it’ll get us some valuable info.”

"Cool," Niral said. "So I should just chill while you get serviced again?"

"No, ya dipstick. Go do some investigating on your own. There's Boyztown, I said."

"It's daytime; the establishments probably aren't even open."

Rob smirked. He knelt down near the television and opened a door that hid a safe. He followed the instructions for setting the combination.

"You can check it out at night, when your bugger buddies got their dongers dangling. Meanwhile go up Pattaya 2, where Tiffany's cabaret is. Around are some pool bars. Gab up some bar girls and see if we've got a shot up there. Otherwise, I'm thinking Hat Jomtien. By the way, did good ol' Bob tell you how long he'll be in Pattaya?"

"He said two days. Then they're flying down to Phuket. Might stay down there a while."

"Looks like he's following me around. Rhymes create connections, eh, mate? But seriously, maybe it's better he's out of these parts."

"Exactly. He's finally doing us a favor."

From his duffel bag, Rob removed stacks of rubber-banded baht and stuffed them in the safe. Then he closed and locked it, flipping the combination lock so it spun around endlessly.

"Might as well use what we're given," Rob said. "Now let's have us some fun!"

29

Niral did as instructed. He strolled up Pattaya 2, passing several bars, until he saw Tiffany's in the distance. To its right was a large, outdoor pool hall filled with more than twenty pool tables, a bar, and many girls. He decided to play some rounds with the girls.

He knew the deal. Inevitably, the girl would be named Ka, Ska, Ma, or something similar. She would claim to be studying language in Bangkok but visiting Pattaya on vacation. They would play pool for a while and chat. Then the girl would suggest Niral buy her a lady drink, more expensive than a regular drink, as the girl would obtain some profit from the purchase.

The girl's goal was to induce more lady drink purchases and eventually an appointment in bed. Niral's goal was to sniff potential interest in ya ba by dropping the briefest of hints. He played it extra safe because Sumantapat's men, who controlled most of Pattaya's trade, could be around and listening. Or the girls could rat on him to the police, leading to an arrest or, more likely, a massive bribe of which the girl would obtain a percentage. When he chatted with them, he acted like he enjoyed drinking but wanted something more. He tried to sense whether the girls betrayed interest in stronger substances.

He failed with three girls at different venues of the hall. He couldn't stay in one spot because once he bought a lady drink, the girl would lose face if suddenly he turned around and hit up another. Three at extreme corners of the hall was more than enough. Each balked at his suggestion of higher levels of fun or intoxication, preferring a sexual rendezvous instead.

He left the pool hall and moved onto another bar he had passed earlier. Here, even before buying a lady drink, a girl told him about a spot close to Pattaya Land where he could buy "pills."

When he returned to the room, evening was settling in. Rob was inside, sleeping on the bed. Niral took a shower. When he emerged, clad in his towel, Rob was sitting on the bed, cleaning his gun.

"What'd you find out?" Niral asked.

"That Pattaya's a dead end, mate. Sumantapat's got his claws in this place. Him or some other outfit. Even Hat Jomtien isn't free. It's too risky."

"I heard there's a place on Soi 2, in Pattaya Land, to buy ya ba."

"No worries. The cum dumpsters downstairs were happy to get our shit. They won't gab."

"I mean, do you want me to find out who's selling it?"

"You gammin me, mate? You wanna blow your cover?"

"What cover? They won't remember me. And I'd be buying, not selling."

"They won't remember you, two-face? Forget that. Look, we're here anyway. Let's eat dinner and check out the scene."

They proceeded to a Thai fusion restaurant where they sat on a tatami mat and ate sen yai noodles, tofu, barbecued crab, tom yam soup along with "American fried rice" and a mango wrapped in banana leaf for dessert. They drank Singhas and Johnnie Walker shots to wash it down. They rolled over to the beach and joined the crowds of tourists heading down Th Hat Pattaya toward Walking Street—old, young, and everywhere in between—flanked by endless lines of female and ladyboy prostitutes. As they approached Walking Street, Niral saw an old man speaking to a prostitute next to a tree, holding a bible in his hand.

"Think he'll convince her?" Niral asked.

"Those religious blokes are the perviest wankers. Just getting his kicks before he roots her proper."

The Walking Street sign blazed in neon now. Inside the gate, the crowds became more overwhelming. It was Patpong on hyperdrive—without the cheap merchants selling pirated crap. Neon signs climbed neon signs, clubs towered over other clubs, armies of women were dressed as everything from flight attendants to cowgirls, waitresses and nurses, appealing to any fetish imaginable and holding up signs advertising discounts. Men hustled with plastic sheets, listing threesomes and live sex, more extensive and diverse than the typical pussy shows available at the upstairs bars in Patpong. They shouted "Massage! Sex massage!" and were especially aggressive to those who lingered.

But Rob seemed to know where he was going. They slipped into a side street and entered a club called Delusion. Schoolgirls welcomed them inside. The club featured an upstairs and downstairs, each visible through a glass floor and ceiling. The main stage was a rotating bar—the girls wore nothing but stars on their nipples and skirts covering half their asses, no panties. Seats next to the stage were low, and customers got a full view of a girl's twat when they looked up.

They were led to a booth and given menus. Niral saw two dancers descend the stage and sit on customers' laps—the guys sucked on their tits and fingered their pussies. Next to their booth, drunken Europeans lounged with hostesses.

Upstairs, next to a dance floor with more schoolgirls wearing no panties, bigger girls, sitting on an extended stage, hurled darts at boards from their pussies in a contest for prizes. Through the floor, Niral saw girls having lesbian sex in steaming jacuzzis, while guys watched from adjacent sofas as they were jerked off under their pants by topless schoolgirls.

Niral and Rob each ordered a beer.

"Makes Patpong seem discreet," Niral said.

"Yeah, fucking eh."

"Why doesn't Mr. Hong buy a club here?"

"Duncan told me he used to have a club here until he had a misunderstanding with Sumantapat. He tried the ya ba game, too, but Sumantapat caught on. Some cops on his payroll arrested Mr. Hong when he was in town, just to scare his ass. Mr. Hong gave his club to Sumantapat in return for a free ride and never messed with Sumantapat's territory again. Doesn't even have a club near him. Notice how he's got nothing in Soi Cowboy or Nana?"

"I never got that. Mr. Hong's a Dragon. He's international. Sumantapat's a local guy."

"That's why he's got more influence with the cops."

"Nam doesn't have influence?"

"I don't know the particulars, mate, just work here."

"Yeah. Which club was it?"

Rob shrugged. "Maybe this one, mate."

Two girls approached them, each easing into either side of the booth. Niral's girl put her hand on his thigh.

"Hi, handsome man. Where you from? India?"

Niral didn't feel like explaining, so he nodded.

"I love India. I love my Buddha, but I like Ganesha, too."

"Good for you," he said, wondering if he agreed with her statement. He was about to ship out again to the motherland.

"They make Kama Sutra too," she continued. "We learn lot."

"Yup, lots of learning in India."

Niral looked over at Rob and saw he had his girl's legs open and was examining her pussy. Niral's girl moved her hand up his thigh and caressed his penis. He grabbed her hand and moved it back to the couch.

"Sorry," he said, remembering when a girl had once done that to him, years ago.

She looked offended for a second, then regrouped with a "cool heart" smile and laugh.

"You nervous, baby?" she asked. "We go boom boom whenever you feel good, okay?"

"Yeah, sure." He knew the next step was telling him the rate for the short-time room and the bar fine. But he noticed Rob's girl pouted, slammed the table with her hand, and left.

"Show's over. Let's hit the next dump," Rob said, drinking down the beer in a hurry.

Niral slid over his way and followed him out the door.

"Some nasty muts in there. Gotta peruse the cunts good, else you'll get a disease, mate."

"I've never seen you pass anything up."

"It's been done. Not often, but here's a different ball game. Don't look tight, she could have lesions on the growler or two kids at home and one on the way. That's why they call it 'Delusion,' mate."

30

They returned to Walking Street and went up another side street. They climbed stairs to the second floor of a three-floor complex and entered a club called Barneys. Inside, a white line divided the floor. Girls in lingerie, some in skimpy dresses, were seated on each side of it.

"White lines divide the cunt dumpsters from the coit dumpsters. Left and right."

They sat on a sofa. Rob said, "Got group action here. You can root one in the ass while eating out the other. Or get your Johnson sucked while licking her coit."

"Two of them?"

"Yeah, you're itching for one. Let's start small. I knew you wanted to come to Pattaya for a reason. No worries, I'll pay. Got plenty of baht."

He took out a wad and shoved it into Niral's palm.

"Release that fucking tension, mate. Your shot. I gotta go."

"You're going? Where?"

"I'll check out Boyztown for you. I was just gammin about that. You don't need to go back to that poofter shit."

"Are you sure?"

"You'll figure the way back. Remember Soi 12. You can always call me."

Rob rose and left. Niral put the baht in his pocket. Two girls approached. Both wore dresses. One was big-breasted, the other flat-chested. The latter appeared to be from Isan. "We have two-for-one special," the Isan girl said. "Only 2000 baht compensation fee. No bar fine."

"No short-time room fee?" Niral asked, not sure what else to say.

"2000 baht for compensation. Nothing else."

"How about only one girl?"

"You want pussy or anal?" the Isan girl asked.

Niral shrugged. The Isan girl sat on his lap. The other girl rolled her eyes and went back her side of the line.

"You shy, I know. I give you soapy massage, only 1000 baht. Relaxing, nice. No sex if you no want."

"No sex?"

"You feel good. Come."

She got up and took his hand. He wasn't sure what to do. But he made a sudden decision to release himself and go. They climbed some stairs to the third floor. In the hallway, Niral could hear sounds of fucking from the other rooms. They entered a large room containing a chair, toilet, mat, shower, tub, sink, and duvet, along with bottles of body wash, shampoo, scrubs, and towels.

Niral became nervous as she began filling the tub.

"I don't know about this. Maybe..."

"You relax, sir," she said, standing and closing the door behind him. She put her hands on his shoulders and kissed him on the cheek.

"You sweet boy, I know."

Impulsively, he kissed her on the nose. He remembered how he used to do that to Zaineb, his one and only girlfriend. To his surprise, the girl smiled.

"Very sweet boy. Come."

She led him to the tub, then took off her dress in one movement, pulling it over her head. She was naked underneath.

"Now you be comfortable, sir," she said.

She began to take off his shirt. He resisted, but she persevered. He closed his eyes and imagined her horror when she saw his burned and blotched body.

But she didn't seem phased.

"You don't find this disgusting?" Niral asked.

She touched the blotch. "I see all, sir. You get in accident?"

Niral nodded. "Bad accident."

"It happen, sir. I am not perfect either."

She showed him a small mole near her vagina. He smiled.

"No, you're not." She removed his pants too and found his gun in the holster.

"You dangerous," she said, touching it, but he knocked her hand off and placed the holster on the floor. He helped her remove the pants. She turned off the water. He got into the tub. She climbed on top of him, soaping him up with an exfoliating sponge. He closed his eyes and tried to relax.

She stood and told him to do the same, then turn around. She washed his back, including his asshole. Then she got him out of the tub and dried him.

"You lie down," she commanded, pointing to the mat. He lay on his back and she massaged his body, including his butt. Then she told him to turn around.

"What you want, sir? Sucky, sex, anal, handy?"

"Just use your hand," Niral said.

"You sure, sir? No extra price."

"Yes," he said. She began to rub. He fondled her small breasts and thought of when Lauren had given him his lap dance. He exploded as he recalled fucking her.

Suddenly, he began crying. With a napkin the girl wiped her hand, then the cum on his stomach. And finally the tears from his face.

"What wrong, sir?" she asked.

He shook his head. He pushed her away and got up. He suddenly saw his gun, grabbed it, stood up, removed it from the holster, and pointed it at the Isan girl.

Shaking, she put her palms together in a wai.

"Please, sir, you go. I don't want money."

He put his finger on the trigger and felt himself squeeze it. But he didn't. He regained his senses and put the gun back in the holster.

"Sorry," he said, putting his pants on. "I'll pay you."

"No, sir. Please, if you not happy..."

"I'm happy. I'm happy. Very happy," he kept repeating as he dressed. He put the holster inside his pants in the usual spot, then took out the baht Rob had given him.

"Here's 2,000. For your trouble," he said. He shoved it in her hands. She counted it, looked up, and smiled at him.

"Thank you, sir. If you want, I be your girlfriend for long time tomorrow. I do massage, laundry, sex, or sucky, anything until six p.m. Then I go to job here. That good price, sir."

"I almost killed you. Don't get greedy."

He opened the door and backed out of the room, then hustled down the stairs and went back out to Walking Street.

31

Rob stumbled down Soi 3 and into the heart of Boyztown. He was a bit tipsy from the shots and beers. He approached a Thai boy wearing a thong outside a bar and put his arm around him.

"Listen, mate, wanna get high?"

"What?" the boy asked.

"Ya ba, you fucking wanker. Or we got hezza too."

"No, sir, I take you..." He cupped Rob's balls. Rob grabbed his nose, squeezed it, and pushed him away.

"You fucking fart knocker. I'm trying to help you forget that poofter shit."

He put his hand on his gun but controlled himself. "You fucking wanker. You'll need a toxic blend of shit to get over what you do every night. I know it."

The boy stared at him, trying to form a "cool heart" smile while his coworkers stared at Rob in amazement. He pointed at the tourists passing.

"What the fuck you staring at, you old wankers? Go root your poofs, you sick bastards."

Rob stumbled away quickly, turning back and hurrying up Walking Street. At its conclusion, he ignored the baht bus drivers and rushed to an escalator that transported him upstairs to another complex. The only establishment open was a Russian strip club. He approached it, and two men, one Russian and one Thai, insisted on patting him down.

Rob opened his arms like Jesus.

The Thai man felt his gun. His eyes went wide.

"I know Boris, you cunt," Rob said. "I'm a friend. Tell him I'm here. Rob's the name."

The Russian man nodded. The Thai man slipped inside. Rob smiled slyly at the Russian man, who was big and tall.

"You remember me, don't ya, mate?"

"If Boris lets you in, then I remember you," he responded.

"You know, I'm part Slav, too. That's the good part."

The Russian didn't answer. The Thai man returned, smiled, and let Rob inside.

Rob entered a bright white room filled with several couches and round stages big enough for one girl to pole dance. But no one was dancing, and no customers were in the club. The plastic menu, listing exorbitant prices for drinks, lay on one of the tables.

Rob proceeded toward a neon sign saying "100 Percent Satisfaction Guaranteed," beyond which were the short-time rooms and, Rob knew, a passageway toward Boris's office.

Before he reached it, a skinny Russian girl with sleepy eyes came out, wearing a bikini. She had light bruises on her thighs.

"Mister, you want dance?" she asked, rubbing against him. Rob pushed her away as he entered the passageway, took a left, and approached Boris's office. The door was open.

Boris was sitting behind his desk, smoking a cigar. As he saw Rob enter and close the door behind him, he smiled and stood up, then ventured beyond the desk to shake Rob's hand.

"Rob, my friend. How is Sveta?" Boris asked as Rob took his hand, twisted it, and turned him around. He grabbed his cigar with one hand, put his other hand over Boris's mouth, and bore the cigar into Boris's neck.

Boris screamed, but no sound emerged through Rob's hand.

Rob removed the cigar. "Scream again mate, and the next thing you'll see is a bright red hell."

He spun Boris around and flung him onto the desk. Boris stabbed his back on a trophy. He let out a yelp. Rob threw the cigar at his face, then pulled out his gun and pointed.

"Holler again, mate. I dare ya."

"Look, you fucking fuck. What do you want?"

"I want what Sveta and me paid you. All of it."

"Why?"

"Cuz it's ours. You got no right to own people. Don't you know it's the twenty-first century?"

"You're crazy. You'll never get out of here alive."

"Your bogan cunts were dumb enough to forget my gun. Don't seem like bright bulbs to me."

"I don't have your money..."

"Bollocks! You keep dosh under the desk and in the safe. Empty it, and we'll call it even."

Boris carefully climbed off the desk, his hands in the air. He was breathing hard.

"You really think Sasha ran away?" Rob asked. "You never figured it was a coincidence?"

"People disappear all the time," Boris said. "I didn't care."

Rob followed him around the desk and put him in a chokehold, holding the gun to his head.

"Don't try to press the buzzer, mate. You're just going to cause people to die for no reason. Take the moolah out, and that's it. You get to live. Your lucky day."

Rob released him. Boris, coughing, bent over and lifted a piece of the carpet. He began to turn the combination to the safe.

"How'd you do it?" Boris asked. "They never found anything."

"I lured him into a cellar, chopped off his tongue, his donger, his ears, then the rest of him. I cleaned up well. I always clean up well."

"Sveta was there?"

"No, I freed her after I killed Sasha. She doesn't know he's dead. What she don't know..."

Boris stopped turning the dial. "How do I know you won't kill me after I give you the money, like you did to Sasha?"

"You don't know nothing, mate. But I won't kill you if you follow orders. Sasha was a bad one. I didn't like him. Couldn't stand to see him live."

Boris opened the safe. "Slowly. Take out the money, slowly," Rob ordered, keeping the gun pointed at Boris's head.

Boris began removing stacks of rubber-banded, US hundred-dollar bills. When he was done, Rob pulled him up by the collar and had him open another safe against the wall under a picture.

When Rob had the entire amount in a briefcase, Boris put his hands up again.

"You are mister morality, is that it?" Boris asked. "You killed Sasha because he deserved it?"

"Plenty of people I whacked didn't deserve it. But I know the people who did."

"If you don't kill me, our people will hunt you down."

"You're wrong, mate. If I do kill you, they'll try. If I don't, we consider this shit a business transaction, and that's it. Nothing happened, we both keep our mouths shut. But if I got to kill you, I'll kill you, mate, and everybody in his place. I got no qualms about that."

"How do I explain missing money? I need to pay commission. Patronage."

"Unlike your bogan cunt guards, you're a bright bulb. Figure it out. Charging a few tourists for drinks oughta do it in this dump."

"All right. Just get the fuck out of here."

"Don't you go bothering Sveta now. That ship's sailed, and things won't go well if you try."

"Get out of here, dammit!"

Rob smiled and put his gun in his holster, then let himself out.

The girl was leaning against the white wall, smoking a cigarette. He shoved some dollars into her hand as he walked by. "See, you don't even have to grind me to force a tip, bitch."

Outside, he showed the guards the briefcase. "Business conducted. See ya, mates!"

PART VIII

†

Bangkok, Thailand

32

As Detective Pomrachat Katankug sat at his desk, drinking coffee and combing through the evidence of a murder case in Klong Tuey he had been assigned that morning, he noticed a short man in a gray suit, crouched over and limping slightly, leaving General Toon's office. General Toon Tomechrin was the commander of their division, and his office just happened to be in eye range of Pom's desk. Natthew Sachinkowdon, a junior detective who had become his partner only months before, met his eyes.

"That's Sumantapat," Nat said. "He owns some clubs in Bangkok and Pattaya. I hear he came with a tip."

"Why's a drug dealer coming here with a tip?" Pom asked.

"How do you know he's a drug dealer?"

"Everyone knows but no one knows. Weren't you in vice before you came to homicide?"

"Yes, Khun Pom, but up in Chiang Mai. We don't have the big clubs there, the three a.m. auctions and the women being tied up. The girls are sweet in Chiang Mai."

"Sweet? All Isan hookers there, too; don't know what year they were born. Their mothers sell them to pedophiles when they are two."

"Stop joking, Khun Pom."

"Who's joking? But don't worry, you can go back. Here all vice does is collect bribes from gentlemen like Sumantapat."

"I have never collected a bribe, Khun Pom."

"I hope not. Now let's study the case here. Figure it's a typical lovers quarrel, loss of face, revenge. The internet makes monsters."

"Do we have enough evidence?"

"Prosecutor will need all the evidence he can. Now let's..."

He couldn't finish his sentence because General Toon was standing in his doorway, waving them inside his office. Soon they were sitting across from him, staring at pictures of his children situated next to a pair of incense sticks.

"Three guys disappeared a few months back," General Toon explained after clearing his throat. "A diamond seller named Pornopat Wongsawat and two of his coworkers. Their store was empty. It seems like they packed up and stole their big boss' merchandise. But now we have a lead suggesting it was murder. I want you to investigate."

"Big Boss, we just got assigned a case from Colonel Atitarn. Have Chan and..."

"I've commanded the Colonel to reassign the Klong Tuey case to Chan. You work on this one."

Pom shrugged. "What's the lead, Big Boss?"

"An American tourist in Pattaya blabbed about it. Might be nothing, but we should follow up. Someone overheard him say he was in the store haggling over some diamonds when thugs broke in and killed the three men. They stole the diamonds and maybe money, then cleaned it up to make it seem like the sellers just absconded with it."

"Someone overheard him say it?"

"It's a tip. We don't know if it's reliable. But we know where the space was. It's now a clothing shop, but we can do forensics there. We'll find out if there was a blood bath, no matter how well they cleaned."

"And the witness?"

"You will have to find him. We have a general description. He was overheard saying he was flying to Phuket. So you will have to go down there."

"Is there a reason why this case is important?" Pom asked.

"It's a murder case. You don't think murder is important? Plus, if a farang is involved, we want to make sure it doesn't become a big issue.

You will report to me what you find out from this American. I will have a file for you in two hours. Have noodles outside, come back, and get to work."

33

Niral was busy analyzing a diamond when Shekhat asked him in English, "I have heard a rumor you went to India to buy diamonds. Is it true?" He didn't stop analyzing.

"Would I be here if I did?" he responded finally.

"Maybe you tried it and you failed. You realized this was the best place to buy your merchandise."

"Lots of rumors out there, mate," Rob chimed in. "That's what they are. Rumors."

"I heard you met with Bhai," Shekhat continued in Gujarati. "I have heard you are now a Brotherhood follower."

Niral took the magnifier out of his eye. "I can't concentrate when you ask me questions," Niral said in English. "Where did you hear these rumors? Your brothers in Surat?"

"They are my cousins. My brothers are here. But I have ears everywhere. I hear you bought diamonds from our Muslim enemies," Shekhat answered in Gujarati.

"I'm sure people spin all kinds of gossip. If you want your questions answered, call Duncan and talk to him. We work for him, remember?"

"Remember, there are Hindus in Surat, too. My cousins are there, if you must cut your costs."

"How 'bout you make that discount twenty-five percent, Shekhat?" Rob asked, removing his magnifier. "I'm thinking these diamonds aren't up to the usual snuff."

Shekhat looked at one of his brothers, who stood by watching. "Twenty-five percent," he replied. "Yes. It is yours."

34

"Shonky wanker. Where the fuck does he get off? Don't know why Duncan keeps doing business with him. We should be buying all our shit from that Muslim bloke."

They were inside their Khao San apartment. Rob lay on the bed. Niral leaned against the wall.

"I'd be going to India every other week, man."

"And why not? We'd be making heaps of dosh. And you'd get in with this Bhai bloke if you kept going back. Now all we've got is this Ghosh bloke. You're not within cooee of finding Bhai's weak spot."

"It'll happen. Duncan's being smart. We don't want to make him suspicious. Plus, we needed a distribution network for the ya ba before we get the next shipment."

"What does one have to do with the other, mate? I coulda built that network myself. That's what I'm saying."

"I'm more worried about Shekhat being a spy for Bhai," Niral said, ignoring his last comment. "He mentioned him again. He knows I met him in India."

"If he was a spy, would he be that obvious? That cunt didn't say shit till now. Just another bloke on the grapevine, hearing shit."

Someone knocked on the door. Niral startled.

"Apsara?" he inquired.

"Maybe the landlady," Rob suggested.

"Open the door, you assholes," Nam shouted. "I know you're in there."

Rob sat up. He grabbed his gun, which was inside the holster by the bed. He checked the room, making sure no drug paraphernalia was visible.

Niral waited for him to give the signal, then opened the door. Nam charged inside, holding his own gun.

"Listen, you assholes. Mr. Hong's in town, he wants to see you guys. It's important."

"Right now? They're about to play the national anthem," Rob said.

"You guys stand up in your room and sing it?" Nam asked. "That's admirable. But you can sing it on your cycles too."

35

On this trip to see Mr. Hong, Niral saw a deformed woman on the corner by the Skytrain staircase. She had no nose, only two holes to breathe. Plus, her left leg was shorter than the other.

Niral dropped a couple of baht in her cup. She said "Sawadee Ka" and blessed him with her hand. The same Indians were hanging out with ladyboys outside the club.

Upstairs, Mok was tending bar, as usual. "Mr. Hong is angry," he said simply.

Rob looked at Niral. Nam emerged from behind the blue curtain.

"Give your weapons to Mok," Nam commanded.

Rob's face flamed, but he didn't complain. He gave his holster over, and so did Niral.

"You gonna pat us down too, mate?" Rob asked.

"No, you're good," Nam said dismissively. "Let's go inside."

This time, Nam took them to the club's back office, which was lit up brightly.

Mr. Hong sat behind a desk. Duncan was on one of three chairs. He looked worried.

"Sit," Nam commanded them, and they followed orders. Nam closed the door.

"We have a very distressing situation," Mr. Hong said. Niral felt hot under his collar. He figured it was over. "As you know, we have informants in the police department. Apparently, Sumantapat went to the station in person. There, he reported something very troubling."

"He reported something to the filth?" Rob asked, surprised. "What?"

"It seems this tourist you did not kill said something about Thanat's murder in Pattaya. He described it to somebody. One of Sumantapat's men overheard. You know they are all over Pattaya."

Rob swallowed. "But why report it to the filth?"

"It signals they have more police connections in Bangkok than I thought. Why waste their own men when they can have the police do their work for them?"

"So what do we do?" Rob asked.

"What do *we* do?" Mr. Hong asked sarcastically. "You are the ones who did not kill the tourist like you were supposed to. You think an American, of all people, will stay quiet? It is your mistake. One of you, or all of you, find this American and silence him before the police talk to him. Because if they do, you are all going to end up dead."

"Don't worry, Mr. Hong," Duncan responded. "You're right, it was our mistake. Rob will take care of it. He's our best man."

"He better. I don't want to have to go into hiding or be banned from my own country. I am Thai-Chinese, not Chinese."

"What if we kill the tourist but Sumantapat finds out anyway?" Nam asked. "We can fight him. We've got men and resources."

"I don't want a war, Nam," Mr. Hong responded. "Sumantapat has more numbers and influence. He has the police on his side, too, it seems. We would have to bring in reinforcements from outside. But if you kill this tourist, hopefully he will not find out."

36

Duncan, Rob, and Niral left the bar, walked a few blocks down Sukhumvit Road, and sat at a plastic table, ordering some gooay deeo from the nearby street stall.

"Fuck," Duncan said. "How are we going to find this dickhead?"

"He's in Phuket," Niral told him.

"How do you know that?"

Niral looked at Rob.

"Look bro, we ran into him in Pattaya while we were out scouting," Rob told him. "He told me he was going down to Phuket."

"You fucking idiots. No wonder he was talking about it," Duncan said. "Don't you know that's Sumantapat's territory? What the fuck were you doing in Pattaya anyway?"

"I swear, he didn't say anything about it when we were there," Niral said. “Maybe he said something to his wife, though I don’t know why he would. Probably he got drunk at a bar and just started spouting.”

The vendor brought over their noodle soups on trays.

“Either way, we need to get rid of this fuck,” Duncan said. “It’s a good thing he’s in Phuket. Rob, leave right away and take care of this before you pick up the merchandise.”

Rob nodded. “I’ll take care of it,” he confirmed.

“Who’s idea was it to let him live?” Duncan asked.

Rob looked at Niral. “Look, I just didn’t think it’d be a good idea to have a missing American,” Niral said. “That would have been worse. You agreed with me at the time.”

“Your problem was in the execution,” Duncan said as he stirred his noodles. “You should have waited until after the tourist got ripped off and left the place before you struck.”

“Thanat could have left with him in the tuk-tuk,” Rob interjected. “Then it would have been more difficult to find a good place to take him out. Plus, we thought the moolah was there. We would’ve had to split up. I made the call. It was my fault.”

Duncan shrugged. “Whatever. Just take care of it. My other worry is Apsara.”

“What about her, mate?” Rob asked.

“Before you arrived, Mr. Hong hinted that she was a liability because Sumantapat’s gang knows her. He doesn’t realize she’s our best asset.”

“Sumantapat’s crew knows she was Thanat’s girl, but not that she was at the gem scam, ya?” Rob asked.

“We think so. Niral, go over to her place and make sure her cover’s not blown. I think Nam already went, but from our side...”

“What if they did know?” Rob asked angrily. “You mean you’d take out your own mia noi?”

“Did I say that?” Duncan objected. “I just want to be on top of things. In case you haven’t noticed, that’s what got us into this mess. Not being anal about this shit. Now I want you to leave for Phuket right away. My car’s in my apartment lot. Leave your cycle there. Niral will talk to Apsara. She’s got his materials for his flight to India tonight anyway.”

37

Niral motorcycled over to Klong Tuey. He had never been to Apsara's place before. Rob described the general directions, but since street signs were either sparse or in Thai, Niral had to ask around for the bungalow before he located it.

He parked outside and climbed the stairs toward the apartment that a small boy pointed to. When he reached the door, he knocked. Buppha answered.

She smiled, swaying her hip toward Niral.

"What you want, baby?" she asked.

"Apsara. Is she here?"

"Who is it?" Niral heard Apsara ask in Thai from the back.

"It is my customer," Buppha said in English. "You no want Apsara. You want some lady action."

She put her hands on his shoulders. Niral smiled politely and moved past her. He saw Apsara eyeing him from behind a door, which she then shut and locked.

"Get out!" Apsara screamed through the door. "I don't want more!"

"What are you talking about?" Niral asked. "Duncan wants to make sure you're okay."

"Another customer was here," Buppha said after she had closed the door. "He was loud."

"Who?" Niral asked.

"Thai man. Many tattoos," Buppha added.

Niral knocked on the door hard. "Duncan sent me. Open up."

He waited. She didn't open it.

"Look, if I walk out that door, I don't know who's coming next."

He heard the door unlock. He opened it, entered quickly, and locked the door behind him.

Apsara sat on a mattress on the floor. Her legs were drawn up, and she had her arms wrapped around them. Her expression was blank. Niral didn't see any tears on her face.

"Are you okay?" Niral asked.

Apsara straightened her knees and turned her head. From the light of the ceiling lamp, Niral could see a red line across the bridge of her neck.

"He remind me I can be killed," Apsara said.

"Everyone can be killed, Apsara. None of us are superheroes."

"I don't want to die."

"Neither did I. But now? Sometimes I feel like I'm dead."

"Tell me, Niral, did you dream when you got burned? You told me you slept a long time."

"I don't remember that," Niral said, coming over and sitting by her. "But I dream now. I never talk about it. But they haunt me. I see my old friends."

"They are dead?"

"I guess. But they live on in my head. In the beginning, when I got here, I would dream about them a lot. I'd wake up and hear the Gayatri mantra and think I was in some alternate reality between sleeping and waking. Then I started working for Duncan, and the dreams began to subside. But after Thanat, they started again."

"I dream of my mother and my daughter. I have not gone to see them in a long time. Nam says he will kill them too."

"When was the last time? It's not far."

"I am busy working. I need to pay off my debt and get money for them. But I don't know how much longer I can work."

"You're our best asset, Duncan says. You keep sending us info from Sumantapat's gang. Things are just tense because that fucking tourist Bob blabbed. Rob's going down to kill him. I don't know what to do. I know Bob from the old days."

"You know him?" Apsara asked, surprised.

"Yeah. I'm not saying he's a friend, but I know him. I guess sacrifices have to be made. More sacrifices."

He noticed Apsara's eyes water. She touched his chest.

"Niral, Nam says I will be a sacrifice if Sumantapat finds out about me. I'm scared."

"Don't worry about that fuck. I'll take him out myself if he comes here again."

"You are shaky. I am sorry, but you are."

"Then Rob will. We've got your back."

Apsara swallowed. "I am sorry I said that. I know you will protect me."

She leaned in to kiss him. Niral turned away and stood up.

"I'm sorry. I'm trembling," he said.

"You are nervous. It is okay if you are still awkward."

"It's not that." Niral paused. "You remind me of someone."

"Who?"

"A girl I didn't protect. Someone I let die."

Niral sat down again. Apsara took his face in her hands.

"I'm sure it was not your fault."

"Yes, it was. I fucked her. I used her. I put the value of her life below my need to find out the truth. A lot of people died, but her death is on me. She haunts me the most."

"So you protect me, Niral. You be my hero, and she will go into heaven."

She pressed her lips against Niral's. This time, he didn't avoid it.

PART IX

†

Bangkok, Thailand; Phuket, Thailand

38

Before he took off for India, Niral called Duncan to let him know Apsara's cover wasn't blown and that she would continue to provide information from Sumantapat's gang that would, hopefully, reveal details from the police investigation.

He also told Duncan about Nam's assault on Apsara. He implored Duncan to visit Apsara from time to time to make sure she was safe.

Duncan's reaction was blithe. Niral couldn't believe he had to remind Duncan to look after his mia noi.

The second phone call he made was to his father. They hadn't spoken since his last call, but Niral knew his father was getting regular reports from Mr. Ghosh on the progress of their collaboration. Now, on the eve of his second visit to India, Niral figured he should check in.

"I am so happy, Niral, that you have found The Brotherhood again," his father told him.

"I'll talk to Bhai about some troubling news I've heard from the Muslims."

His father cleared his throat. "Good. I am glad you are working to protect Bhai from these terrorists. But afterwards, I do hope you will settle down and live a simpler life. Even we Kshatriyas should become sanyasis."

"How would I become a sanyasi now, Deddy?"

"You are not too young, if that is what you mean. Meetal has done it."

"Meetal?" Niral asked, surprised to hear her name. "Really? How?"

"She is in Yam Gam too," his father revealed. "She joined her father and mother a year ago. Now she is more devoted than them to meditation and eternal being. If she can do it, so can you."

"Yam Gam?" Niral asked. "I had no idea."

"Visit Narendrabhai. Remember, Niral, your roots are in India. You have a home there too."

39

Nat drove down to Phuket and arrived in the early evening. He checked into the hotel that Pom had booked for him in Phuket Town.

While smoking a cigarette on his balcony, he perused his notes. From Bangkok, he had called several hotels in Phuket and compiled a list of those claiming that a guest matched the American tourist's general description. As usual, the police work would be minute and painstaking, and the search like finding a needle in a haystack. But, as Nat had learned in vice, it had to be done. The devil lay in the details, even when those details were vague.

His first stop would be in Kata, a couple of beaches down from Patong, and he would work his way up. He hoped the tourist wasn't out partying, but if he was, maybe he would catch him as he returned. He would try his luck tonight and continue again in the morning if necessary.

40

Rob's drive down to Phuket was rough. He'd left around noon, about half an hour after talking with Duncan, only stopping twice for fifteen minutes each. By the time he pulled into Patong around midnight, he was exhausted and nervous.

He parked about fifteen minutes from the Boxing Stadium. He took his duffel bag, trekked down to Th Bangla, and stopped in a bar for a quick drink. Then he climbed up to Sveta's flat. He let himself inside with his key and woke her up.

41

Nat arrived in Kata and parked in the hotel lot. He swerved through the half-filled tables of the hotel's restaurant and approached the front desk.

The clerk performed a wai.

"Sawadee kap," Nat said. He took out his badge and showed it to the clerk. "I called this hotel looking for an American tourist. Do you have your log?"

"It is computerized, sir. What is his name?"

"I don't know. The man I spoke to said he recalled someone fitting the description, but he wasn't sure about the name. Maybe you will recognize it."

Nat pulled out the sketch and unfolded it. The clerk scanned it.

"He looks familiar, sir," he replied. "But I cannot say who it is."

"Give me a list of all the Americans staying here and their rooms," Nat requested.

The clerk searched on his computer. "We have three rooms where people signed in with American passports."

"Do you have copies of the passports?"

"No, but we have the passport numbers along with names, countries of origin, and dates of birth."

"I am looking for an older man, mid-fifties or older." He realized he should have asked these questions over the phone. He could have checked the passport numbers from his database in the office. Now he would have to call Pom to check, but he didn't want to lose face by admitting he'd been sloppy.

"I have one couple, both over fifty-five," the clerk informed him.

"Excellent. Give me their information and room numbers."

Nat ran up the stairs and approached the door. He knocked. He took out the sketch and stared at the man who opened it.

42

Rob left Sveta's flat, wearing the duffel bag on his back. He cruised up Th Bangla, peeking inside the bars, one by one, until he spotted Bob Macaday.

Bob was drinking with a bar girl. Linda was nowhere in sight.

Rob strolled up and down the street, a few meters here, a few meters there. After a couple of minutes, Macaday got up, paid the tab, and left the bar, hand in hand, with the girl.

Rob followed him down Th Bangla, then up the beach road. Fifteen minutes later, Bob and the bar girl entered a hotel.

The hotel lobby was filled with drunken tourists. They passed a bar, a restaurant, a swimming pool, and pool table, then entered an elevator. Rob waited behind a few tourists until the doors closed. Then, he tracked the elevator prompts until it stopped. He entered the staircase next to the elevator and began to climb.

At the fourth floor, he ceased, donned a pair of gloves, and opened the door to a curving hallway.

The hallway was empty. Rob proceeded past the rooms.

Then, behind him, he heard a door open and voices echo. He sped up so that the curve would hide him from their line of vision. He stood silent, ready to scurry forward if steps came his way. But the voices receded. He heard a button pressed. The elevator moved. He went on.

He reached a room, put his ear to the door, and listened. Then, he continued down the hallway, looking out for anyone else. Quickly, he returned, took out a card, and swiped at the door's lock.

The red light became a blinking green. Rob opened the door slowly, slipped inside, and closed it just as lightly.

The room was dark. He allowed his eyes to adjust. He felt the wall, then moved his arms within an empty space that he figured was the bathroom. He crept forward until he saw the white moonlight and yellow streetlights peering through the curtains and shining upon a sleeping body.

He took a silent, deep breath. Then he removed his duffel bag, placed it on the floor, gathered himself, and pounced.

He placed his knees on the subject's arms, then grabbed a pillow from underneath the head and pressed it hard on the face. The victim fought, scratching Rob's arms red, but his brute force and strength was no match. After several seconds, the body went limp. After four agonizing minutes, Rob loosened his grip.

Rob closed his eyes and took a few breaths. He climbed off the body, closed the curtains so that no light penetrated, then found the light switch and turned it on. He went to check the body. Staring up at him, eyes wide, was Linda Macaday.

43

Nat thought he had his man, but his questions went nowhere. The man looked the part, but he claimed he didn't know anything about a murder in Bangkok. He hadn't been to Pattaya. The last week, he and his wife had been to Krabi, Ko Lanta, and Phi Phi, and their next destination was San Francisco.

"Have you been to Bangkok?" Nat asked.

"We flew into Phuket. Went in a circle and came back. I've been to Bangkok, but it was several years ago. We didn't buy any jewelry; I can assure you."

"No one tried to gem scam you?" Nat asked, figuring that scenario was likely if Sumantapat was involved.

"Someone talked to me at the Grand Palace. I ignored him. I read about it in the travel guide."

"What did he look like?"

"I don't know. Skinny Thai guy."

Nat felt disheartened. He took the man's contact information in America and went back to his car. He perused his notes. He decided that this late at night he would only try one more spot. It was the farthest away and the one he wouldn't have to go back to: a resort at Rawai on the tip of Phuket Island.

44

Rob was bleaching the last of the blood in the bathtub when he heard a knock on the door. Only the bathroom light was on. He finished the job, took off his gloves, put on another pair, and moved forward. He heard a more forceful knock. He looked through the keyhole, then opened the door.

Bob Macaday snuck inside. As Rob closed the door, Macaday spoke to him in a whisper.

"Is it done?" he asked.

"Yeah, it's done, you bloody wanker," Rob answered, charging past him back into the bathroom. "Your wife's in the bags. Ya happy?"

Bob shrugged, staring at two garbage bags on the floor of the bathroom. His face had gone pale.

"I can't believe it's done," he said.

"What you wanted, mate. Remember that. You got the moolah?"

"It's in a secret spot. I'll get it."

"You better. You try to cut out on the deal, you'll be sorry."

"Why would I do that? Vishal's gonna set me up."

"Maybe you've got something else set up instead. Happens all the time. Double agent."

"I don't. I need out of the spotlight. How is he anyway?" Macaday asked.

"You'll find out. My contact's sporadic."

Rob lifted one of the bags. "Twenty-seven kilos each, I reckon. Sixty pounds, translates to."

"So?"

"So help me take it down to my car, you cunt. I can't do it all myself."

"What if someone sees me?" Bob whined.

"No worries. They'll think you're taking out the trash. Might wonder what you're doing with a tattooed Aussie with red marks on his arms, but it'll be too late. After you check out this morning, no one'll see you again in Thailand. And Bob Murphy won't exist. You won't even be Bob this time."

Macaday seemed nervous. He continued to stare at the bag.

"She was a good wife," he said, "but she was spiteful."

"I reckon they usually are. That's why I don't hitch, and I pick carefully."

"I hope you don't think I'll act that way..."

"Sveta's a sweet gal. She's not spiteful like that. So no worries. Now let's go."

They carried the bags down the stairs. In the lobby, they passed a few drunken tourists, but Rob kept his hand on Macaday's back and led him through.

Only a block away, Rob stopped at his car, opened the trunk, and put the bags inside. Macaday was looking around nervously, shaking.

"Don't lose your nerve on me now, mate," Rob said. "You weren't freaked out when we negotiated this deal, and we'd just chopped up three blokes."

"It wasn't my wife that time."

"You reckon you miss her? Regret it? Too late, mate."

"I'm not saying that. She was a burden, for sure," he said. "Look, I'll get the money."

"And be at Sveta's place after you check out. Six a.m., got it? Be quick, you don't want to be around when the cops come knocking. You've got the address?"

"Above Bangla Boxing Stadium. Got it."

"You lost that bar girl, ya?"

"I told her I changed my mind about the hotel. We went to the next one over. She checked in under her name. I couldn't perform though, kept worrying about this. She went home, I think."

"No worries, we could've used her for an alibi but it won't be necessary if shit goes right. One other thing. Your wife unloaded on the mattress when she passed. Shit, piss, you name it. The sheets are in the bags, and I bleached the mattress. Hope that holds. But you've gotta steal some sheets to replace 'em. Think you can do that, mate?"

"Sure. Whatever you say. I'll find a way."

"Fair enough. See ya in a few."

45

In Rawai, Nat hit another dead end. No Americans were registered at the resort. A few guests did fit the tourist's general description, but they were all Scandinavian—yet another mistake by Nat on his initial call. But Nat didn't want to take any chances, so he woke the Scandinavians and interrogated them anyway, wondering if, due to their fluent English, they were not mistaken for an American by Sumantapat's man.

But he was wrong. They didn't seem to have any clue about Pattaya, gem scams, or anything else, and he believed them. He returned to his car, smoking his cigarette, spitting on the ground, dejected but hoping he would have better luck the next morning in Karon, Patpong, and Kamala.

As he drove up the deserted beaches of this former tourist destination, he noticed the silhouette of a man steering a long-tail boat in the distant Andaman Sea. Normally, Nat wouldn't consider this strange, but it was past four a.m., and no one else was about. He pulled over, got out, and watched the boat as he searched for another cigarette.

Suddenly, far from shore, the boat stopped. One by one, the man dumped two bags into the water. They appeared to be attached by a string to an object, possibly a rock.

Nat swallowed his spit, then coughed and took another drag of his cigarette. It might be a fisherman dumping his extra catch, but he wasn't sure. He decided to head toward the sea to interrogate the individual now that the boat was making its way back.

As the boat pulled up to the beach, Nat was still a distance away, strolling leisurely. As the man docked the boat, he noticed Nat and froze. He was tall, his pants were pulled up above his knees, and he wasn't wearing shoes. His hair was short. In the moonlight, Nat couldn't tell much else, except that a Thai wasn't likely to be that tall.

He held up his hand. "Police!" he yelled in English. "Please wait. I want to talk to you."

The man didn't move. He seemed to get into a stance, then took off running along the beach.

Nat pulled out his gun and fired in the air. "Stop!" he yelled.

Instead of stopping, the man pulled out his own gun and began firing.

Nat yelled. He couldn't believe he was in a shootout.

He felt a sting in his arm. Instinctively, he fell to the floor. When he put his hand on his shoulder, he felt something wet and realized he had been shot.

Part X

†

Surat, India; Phuket, Thailand; Bangkok, Thailand

46

Niral had no problems in customs again. Twice in a row; this was amazing to him. Manu picked him up at the airport.

"How have you been?" Manu asked. "I thought you would come more often."

"I've got business in Thailand too. A lot more business. And every time I leave Thailand, my boss needs to get me a reentry permit."

"But you will help us with Talim?"

"Yes, I've been in touch with Mr. Ghosh."

"He is waiting for you," Manu confirmed.

After a few hours, they reached the same restaurant. Manu asked if he was hungry.

"I'd rather conduct business first," he replied.

Downstairs, Niral was surrounded again by four bodyguards, including the Sikh guard and the two other men who had accosted him months before. Both Bhai and Mr. Ghosh were present. They were sitting butterfly-style and reading volumes of the Gita.

Bhai smiled and stood up slowly, greeting Niral with a namaste. Niral returned the favor.

"I am so happy to hear you are on our side, Niral," he said. "And that you have been conducting a covert campaign. Your father is proud of you."

"Yes, thank you. I just spoke to him and told him I'm glad too. I've been keeping Mr. Ghosh informed of my contact with my boss and Talim."

Mr. Ghosh stood too, using the same namaste greeting.

"And you are meeting them again today?" Bhai asked. "I know that the chip did not work last time. They did not suspect you, even after they discovered it?"

"Apparently not. Talim hasn't said anything to Duncan."

"You are better than a chip," Bhai said. "Now we know that they are planning an attack on Diwali. Have you found out any more particulars?"

"No, but I should at our meeting. I know they want me to coordinate the attack. They believe I hate you because of what happened in New York."

"This is our luck. Will you be in touch once you return to Thailand, or will you report to Mr. Ghosh before you leave?"

"Actually, I convinced my boss to let me stay for two weeks this time. I told him I wanted to spend more time with my family since I had reconnected with them on my last trip. So we have time to work on a way to subvert their plot once we learn what it is."

Bhai nodded silently. "I need to go to Dwarka. I have much to do there. But Mr. Ghosh will be here. You can coordinate our response with him."

"I have enough time to go to Dwarka," Niral said. "We can plan security procedures there."

"Perhaps," Bhai responded. "Speak to Mr. Ghosh about it once you return. I also recommend you visit Yam Gam. You will be even more motivated to help us once Narendrabhai shows you the realities of what is happening in India."

47

Rob appeared bruised and feverish to Sveta as she opened the door to her flat.

"You ready yet?" he asked, charging in past her. He opened a drawer where he kept some clothes and changed into a long sleeve shirt, hiding the red marks on his arms.

"Yes, I am packed," she said, deciding it best not to ask him about his appearance or behavior. "I need to make myself pretty."

"Well, hurry up with it. That bloke come by?"

"No, he is not here yet."

"Fuck! He better come quick."

"What is wrong, baby? I thought you said you will bring him."

"Nah, I talked to him, but he's coming on his own."

Sveta put her arms around his neck.

"Rob, I won't see you again, will I?"

"I'll visit America one day, I reckon."

"I still don't understand why I need to go with this man. Why won't you come with me?"

"It's the best way, sweetie."

"You always leave me behind. Why?"

"You wanna keep working for Alex, be my guest."

"No, I want to go to America. But let's go in the bedroom and fuck one last time."

Sveta put her arms around him and began to kiss him, but Rob heard a knock at the door and pulled away. He approached the door and peeped through the peephole.

"Look, I'll be right back," he said to her.

He opened the door. Before Rob could go out, Bob Macaday rushed inside, rolling a suitcase in one hand and carrying a briefcase in the other.

"Not here," Rob said. "Come outside."

"What is that?" Sveta asked, pointing to the briefcase.

Bob smiled at Sveta and checked out her body.

"Nothing, sweetie," Rob replied. "Just his shit."

"If I will marry him, I want to know what he has."

"She doesn't know?" Macaday asked Rob. Rob closed his eyes.

"Know what?" Sveta asked.

"Let's start with introductions," Bob said, holding out his hand to Sveta. "I'm Bob."

Sveta folded her arms. "You will be my husband?"

"Yes, that's me."

"Why you want to marry Russian girl?"

Bob shrugged and put out his arms. "I love Russia."

"I don't love Russia," she countered. "That's why I want to go to America."

"America's a nice place, I guess."

"Look, Sveta, we need to talk in private," Rob told her, beginning to close the door. "Make yourself pretty in the other room, ya?"

"I want to know what is in suitcase," Sveta insisted.

"Fine," Rob said, grabbing the briefcase. He set it down on the dining table, flipped the locks and opened it. Her eyes widened as she saw stacks of one hundred US dollar bills.

"What is that for?" she asked.

"It's a down payment for you blokes. I'm gonna put it in your accounts so you can use it in the States."

Sveta seemed to be thinking. "If he live in America, he does not have money there?"

"It's a separate account, sweetie. For a rainy day," Rob said. "Trust me, Sveta, it's complicated, and you don't wanna know all the details. Let me handle it."

Sveta shrugged. "Fine. I will make myself pretty."

She turned around, entered her room, and shut the door.

Macaday turned to Rob. "She doesn't know?" he whispered.

"Why the fuck would I tell her that, you dipstick?" Rob whispered angrily in response. "She doesn't know nothing. Only that she's going with you to Carolina."

"How about Vishal?"

"Someone's gonna set her up with a job, that's all."

"Look, I just wanna make sure you're not jerking me around."

Rob grabbed his throat.

"Listen, you fucking wanker, your ass should be grass right now. Isn't that what you say in America? If it hadn't been for Vishal..."

"Vishal would be mad if he knew how you're treating me," he responded, choking through the words.

Rob let go of his neck. "I don't know why, mate. You implicated him in that New York shit."

"He understands," Bob said, breathing heavily and rubbing his neck. "I think."

"Look, you blokes gotta get out of here quick. I had a situation when I dumped the body. I don't know what's going on right now. I should lay low. I can't drive you to the airport, but I've got the tickets and the passports. Plus, a Thai death certificate for a Patricia Murphy, as requested, in both Thai and English."

"What happened? Something happened?"

"Just trust me, Bob. I'll count the money. Once Sveta's ready, I'll call you a cab. Go quick through the security gate. Then dump the cell phone in case they track it. I don't think you'll have a problem boarding the plane. When you get to Carolina, Vishal will have someone waiting for you."

"Indian?"

"Don't know. But he'll know you."

Rob started counting the cash.

"It's all there," Bob said. Rob ignored him and kept counting.

"It was a good idea, planting that story in Pattaya," Bob said. "I was pretty nervous, talking about that in a random bar. Someone could have clipped me then. But it worked. I don't know how..."

"Sometimes shit works, mate. Sometimes it don't. Reckon it depends on if the atoms are in balance."

"I've got a question about the insurance," Bob said. "If you change my name and I'm dead here, how can I collect it? It's under my old name."

"No worries, mate. Only people who think you're dead here are the people I work for. And since you were in witness protection, I imagine your families don't know you're alive or dead, right?"

"Right. I guess I'll ask Vishal."

"Yeah, mate," Rob said, continuing to count, "ask Vishal."

48

Nat was sitting in the sand, his legs outstretched, getting his wound stitched up by a medic. A bullet had grazed his arm and hit the sand. Meanwhile, the Phuket police were searching the ocean, looking for the bags. Gray clouds were gathering in the sky.

"Phone call for you," an officer said, approaching and holding up a cellphone. It was Pom.

"What are you doing down there? Looking for pussy?"

"Better, Khun Pom. Blood."

"Phuket cop called and told us. Why aren't you in the hospital?"

"Just a booboo, Khun Pom. How did your search go?"

"We've canvassed the scene. It was cleaned up well, but nothing can outfox luminol. There's spatter all over the floor, behind the desk, in the bathroom and bathtub. We've recovered multiple DNA samples and are having them tested. Hopefully one or more will get a match in the database."

"Many people could have come through there. I don't know how promising that is. But I might have found something here."

"Getting shot by some random farang is finding something?"

"We're searching for the guy. We're closing the exit points from Phuket."

"Did you see his face?"

"No. We're stopping all tall farangs. I'm hoping there's some connection to this."

"It's unlikely. You know the murder stats. Why were you out that late?"

"Working the case. I spoke to a few farangs at the outer beaches, but I haven't found the witness."

"Once you get stitched up, keep searching. We need to find him to get more information. As you said, even a DNA match isn't conclusive about anything."

"I'll try my best."

He hung up the phone. The medic finished stitching and wrapped a bandage around the wound. A Phuket police detective approached.

"We found the bags, sir. We can't tell if it is one or two bodies, but we believe it is one. It seems to be a woman. Cut up. The autopsy will take a few days. Since we assume it is a farang, we must inform Khun Commissioner. The international press will know soon."

"I want this bastard," Nat responded. "Call me when you have a line-up of suspects. I need to canvas hotels for my other case."

"Sir, the description in your statement is very vague. You want us to stop all tall farangs?"

"Yes. Do your best."

"We must ask our general. Understand, this is our jurisdiction, our case."

"Which is why you want to catch this murderer, right?"

"Of course, sir. With all due respect, detective, we may need to contact you for another statement. Please give us your number and keep your phone on."

49

Manu drove Niral to Val's house. Only Val was awake. He took Niral's bag and put it inside the guest room.

"If you need anything else, let me know," Val said. "I don't work until later."

"Manu will drive me," Niral responded. "Thank you, Val."

All three men ate some nasta. Then Val went upstairs, while Niral and Manu took naps in the guest room, Manu sleeping on the floor. When the two awoke a few hours later, they began talking, Niral lying on the bed, Manu sitting up on the sheet that had been spread out, his arms around his legs.

Niral asked Manu about his family.

"My daughter has passed all her exams successfully," Manu said proudly. "But she will stay in Mumbai to work over the break. Honestly, Niral, I am worried about bad influences there. I think she may hang out with rich people who don't know her origins. If they find out about her..."

"I thought you didn't believe in the caste stuff," Niral pointed out.

"I don't, but others do. It is that imbalance between our ideals and reality, isn't it? And it is not just about caste there; it is more about wealth and influence."

"I know what you mean," Niral said. "Guess that never changes anywhere. But I wouldn't worry. Everyone's got to go through that dance eventually."

"What dance, Niralbhai?"

"Just learning the way things work, you know."

"Yes. Is it like that in America too?"

"Of course. Difference is that in America, everyone thinks they're equal, even though no one is. At least you guys know there's inequality here."

"Hmm. I don't know which is better."

"Neither do I."

Sobha had prepared lunch before she left for work. Niral and Manu ate with Vikasmama and Amrita.

"Did you get me something from Thailand, Niralkaka?" she asked him

Niral hit his forehead. "Oh, I forgot Amrita. I'll get something next time I come."

"Get me something I like, okay?" she asked.

Niral agreed. Then Vikasmama interrupted.

"Niral, your boss in Thailand is an American man? And the merchant here is Muslim?"

"Yes, Vikasmama."

"Think about purchasing from a Hindu. I know a diamond merchant too, and I think he will get you a good price."

Niral smiled at Manu. "I will consider it, Vikasmama. Thank you for the advice."

50

"I just got a call from Rahmat. Are you lost?" Duncan asked Rob. He was calling from the bedroom in his apartment.

"No," Rob said. "There was an incident. I don't think it's wise to move today."

"What about the job? Is it done?"

"It's done. But I had a problem dropping off the garbage."

"What kind of problem?"

"Authority shot at me. I shot back. Near where I dropped off the missus. I had to knock 'em both off."

"Fuck!" Duncan shouted. "Well, at least you got those tourists. But that's the last thing we needed. I hope you iced that cop's ass too."

"Not sure. Looked like the jack fell. I reckon I got him. Been checking the news but haven't seen nothing yet."

"Hold up." Duncan left his bedroom and entered the living room. He picked up the remote and turned on the local news. His wife Lamai was chopping up some vegetables for stir-fry in the adjacent kitchen.

"Tee rak, you want to check the weather?" Lamai asked. "It will be raining soon."

Duncan smiled. "Just want to see what's going on, honey."

He didn't see anything about a murder in Phuket. He switched to a different channel. Then he saw it.

"Oh my God. Another tourist murder? Turn it off, Duncan," Lamai said.

"I know, it's bad," Duncan responded. "But we should know."

"Why, so they can smear Thailand?"

"Farang murders are rare; that's why they get so much press."

"Exactly. So why encourage it?"

"Hold up, honey, let me hear this."

He went back into his room, shut the door.

"You're right," he told Rob. "There's a dragnet in Phuket. They're not releasing a description, but don't move today. We'll figure something out."

"Should I dump my weapon?"

"You didn't already?"

"Ain't got another piece. Can't get another that quick before I meet Rahmat."

"I'd say dump it, but only if it won't be found."

"Not sure 'bout my confidence in that. Think I'll keep it, for now."

Duncan rolled his eyes. "Fine. Just stay put for now. I'll be in touch." He hung up and cursed.

51

Nat drove toward Karon to follow up on his next lead. He stopped at a Norwegian restaurant for breakfast, where he was waylaid by a short burst of torrential rain. When the rain stopped, he resumed his journey, but then he got a phone call from the Phuket police.

"We've already rounded up a number of farang," the detective told him. "You need to come identify them. We can't hold them for long."

Frustrated, he turned around.

At the station, the Phuket police took him into a room to look through a one-way mirror at a number of farang men. All were tall, but they were different heights.

"I don't know," Nat confessed. "It was dark. I saw him in the moonlight. He could look like anything."

An officer entered and introduced himself as General Chaow. "May I speak to you in my office?" he asked.

General Chaow took Nat down a long hallway and into his office decorated with mythological portraits. Nat sat in front of the general's desk and asked if he could smoke, but the general ignored his question.

"Do you know the *Ramakien*, Mr. Nat?" he asked.

"Yes, Khun Chaow. It is our heritage."

"My father was a writer and painter," he explained. "He worked at the Grand Palace for a time, doing touch-ups. He was also a part-time historian and collector. He collected many of these portraits."

"They are very nice," Nat said, looking around. Then he took out his cigarette case and wondered if he should use his injured arm to remove the cigarette or put the case on the table and use his good arm.

"Please, Mr. Nat, no smoking," General Chaow told him. "I would allow you, but I used to smoke myself and I've quit. Quite an accomplishment for a commander of a police division."

Nat smiled, putting away his cigarette case with his good arm.

"Do you know how many versions of the *Ramakien* were written and how many lost?" the general asked.

Nat shook his head.

"Many were written throughout our country's great history, and many were lost during the Burmese Army's destruction of Ayutthaya in 1767. You know that the old kingdom collapsed then. Eventually, the great Rama I regained control, and his family has protected Thailand since. He tried to reconstruct the epic and did a wonderful job of it, including the panels at the Grand Palace. Yet, it is only one version. Rama II had a different version. We don't know how many versions there are."

"Right. I'm sorry, General, but what is your point?"

"My point, Mr. Nat, is that any event has a version, an account, depending on who is telling, and even when one tells his version, sometimes he does not know which version is correct."

"Are you saying I have many versions?"

"I am saying that we cannot indefinitely stop and detain tall farangs in Phuket. We rely on tourism here. Many Scandinavians stay in Kata particularly, and they are all tall."

"This was a murder."

"Do you remember the international reaction when some military men suggested tourists wear wristbands after the murder of a British woman? Yes, we will do the best investigation we can. We will identify this woman. We will talk to the people who knew her. If she was killed by a farang, likely she knew him, and we will build a case. Even if he leaves Thailand, we can extradite him. Don't worry about it. I've spoken with Khun Commissioner, and he confirmed this is the best way to handle things. Go work on your own case."

"That's what I was doing," Nat said, standing up. "How about these guys you picked up? Will you interrogate them?"

"They are random men. It is smarter and more efficient to build a case from knowledge. We preserved some footprints in the sand. We were able to remove one before the rain ruined it, so we will check our suspects against that. We have the bullet from your shoulder in case we recover the weapon. We have also lifted some random items from the scene and will test DNA to see if any suspects were there. Don't worry, we are concerned about any murders here, certainly of a farang. We will conduct a thorough investigation. We will get our man."

52

After lunch, Manu drove Niral to the bank. Once again, he met Val and put the money in his duffel bag. Val asked Niral if he wanted a ride to Rander.

"That would be better, actually," Niral said.

Niral went outside and spoke to Manu. "It's better if you follow behind. I think they'll be less suspicious if Val drives me."

"Okay," Manu agreed.

As Val drove him on his motorcycle to Rander, Niral called Talim. This time, the meeting spot was different.

They drove past the Golden Mosque and stopped at an apartment building. Niral was told to walk into the alley behind it. He turned to Val.

"I don't want you to be late. Go back. I'll get a rickshaw or return with Manu."

"Are you sure? I can wait. I've told my boss..."

"It's okay," Niral said. "Just stop around the corner and tell Manu I might go back with him."

"Be careful," Val told him.

Niral walked through the alleyway. As the last time, it swerved left, but this time a forest was to his right, blocked off by a fence. He continued down the alley but saw no doors to knock on.

The space was deserted.

His cell phone began to ring. He picked up.

"Go all the way to the end of the alley," a voice told him. "Climb the fence and walk into the forest. Remember, you are being watched."

Niral did as he was told. He climbed over the fence, nicking his knee on a jutting wire, then proceeded into the open forest. He wasn't sure which way to go, so he continued forward for about five minutes. Finally, he entered an open field with a tree in the center, where he saw a figure wearing a black uniform and black hood. He continued forward.

As he got closer, he realized the hooded figure held an AK-47 rifle. Niral stopped a meter in front of him. The figure spoke. Niral didn't recognize the voice.

"There are armed men all around, so do not try anything. Do you carry another bug?"

Niral shook his head. "Of course not. Why would I?"

The man felt him up, then told him to take off his shoes. He checked within, turning them upside down, shaking them, using his fingers to trace the lining.

"We don't know who is a double agent or a triple agent," the man said.

"Where's Talim?"

"How do you know I'm not Talim?"

"Your voice."

"Do you think he was Talim?"

"If I don't know who Talim is, how can I believe what he says?"

"Believe us, the stories are true," the man said. "But we are all Talim. We are all followers of Allah and the prophet Muhammed. We have all been wronged by the cursed idol worshippers and especially by Bhai. Tell me, what new news do you bring?"

"I was told I would discuss the false plot with Talim, so I can tell Bhai and get closer to him as they try to mount a defense against the plot. They already know I am working for you. We've discussed possible scenarios via encrypted messaging. Don't you know that?"

"Of course I know that. By the way, we received word from Rahmat. Your partner hasn't arrived yet to pick up the merchandise."

"He has other business beforehand. I'm sure he's just late."

"Well, that is his problem. Whether he picks it up, we have supplied the advance. The plot against Bhai must be successful. Otherwise we will need to foreclose and repossess the difference. Nevertheless, we will need the down payment. Give me the money."

Niral handed over the bag. The man looked inside.

"Very good. Here are your diamonds."

He handed over a small pouch to Niral.

"Can I examine them?" Niral asked.

"You did not examine them last time. I did not hear any complaints. And I have not examined your payment either."

Niral checked inside the pouch to see if the number of diamonds was consistent with Apsara's estimation. She had given him a list, but he decided to forego looking through it.

"I can check them once I get back to my cousin's place. I guess I know where to find you."

"We have decided on the plan to kill Bhai. You will tell him we will strike during the Diwali festival. Four assassins will infiltrate the pilgrims, posing as Hindus. They will not be armed initially, but you will procure them weapons while inside. When you tell him this, we hope he will show you the security procedure and apparatus so we can infiltrate it and hatch the actual plot."

"I thought the plot was for me to poison or kill Bhai myself?"

"That is still being considered. But if we have the ability to achieve a more theatrical assassination, we would prefer that. It will send a clear message, and you will more easily be able to extricate yourself from it. Tell Bhai about this plan. Then we will see what we can do."

PART XI

†

Phang-nga, Thailand; Phuket, Thailand; Krabi, Thailand; Surat, India; Yam Gam, India

---

53

In the late afternoon, Rob received a call from Duncan telling him the dragnet seemed to be called off. Rob checked on his smartphone. The news reported the police were following up on leads, and that tourists and Thais should return to normal life.

Rob went to his car, opened the back passenger door, and placed the briefcase of money inside a secret space under the carpet Duncan had once shown him. Then he drove toward Phang-nga. At the crossing to the mainland, he saw police. He thought of turning back, but the cars in front of him went through, so he took the risk and sighed in relief when he passed without being stopped.

An hour later, he saw the limestone crags perched against the sky, the white sand, and the beaches, but he barely paid attention. He thought about how he had fucked up at the beach in Rawai, how he'd allowed his prey to be found, and what the ramifications would be.

Sveta had texted him hours before that they had boarded the plane, and that Bob was annoying her. He had forgotten to tell her to get rid of her phone, but then the police had no reason to track it. He did hope Bob had followed his orders. He had texted her back, telling her Americans talked a lot and she'd have to get used to it. He received a frowning face in response.

Pasat was standing in front of his restaurant, which was otherwise empty. So were the streets since the tourist excursions from Phuket had been canceled.

"Mr. Rob, did you escape from Phuket, or did you avoid it?"

"They're letting people out now."

"Yes. Very sad. Another tourist murder. It is not good for Thailand."

"Are you concerned for Thailand, Pasat?" Rob asked.

Pasat looked offended. "It is my country, Mr. Rob. I hope it will change, but I love it. We get much business from tourism. I cannot survive without it."

"Of course, mate," Rob responded. He recalled meeting Pasat months before when he had left his tourist entourage to have a meal in a more solitary setting. They started up a conversation about diamonds, ultimately leading Rob to recommend Duncan to check out an alternative route Pasat said he could set up. At the time Thanat hadn't yet ripped them off, and Duncan was trying to explore ways to up his earnings after his marriage to Lamai. Rob hadn't imagined it would lead to a ya ba trade that Mr. Hong had expressly forbid. But then Rob had never been one to follow the rules either.

"I'll grab some gaeng sohm and roti, if it's important to you," Rob said, sitting at one of the tables outside.

"Important to me?"

"All right, I'm heaps hungry for some tucker, I'll admit it."

Pasat smiled. "I will get you some dishes you have not tried, Mr. Rob. Wait."

Rob wiped his brow. The heat had reached its zenith, even as dark clouds covered the sky. But then he felt a drop of rain, and cool air suddenly rolled toward him.

"Reckon I'll eat inside." He entered the restaurant and sat at a table. It began pouring.

"Damn, I hate monsoon season," Rob said. "Noosa's no better."

Pasat brought out some khua kling and khao yam. "Where is Noosa? Is that where you are from?"

"I've hopped around some, but Noosa's a place I stayed a while. Get me some iced coffee, will ya? Still need to cool down."

Pasat returned with the coffee. "My family members have thought of moving to Australia. Would you recommend it?"

"Better off where ya are," Rob said, eating the khao yam ravenously with his fork. "Oz isn't friendly to foreigners. Ain't no better to Aussies either."

"Really? I have heard the opposite."

"Everyone's got their own perspective. Sure, if ya go legally, I'm sure you'll have a grand time. Root a couple of Aussie cunts while you're at it. But go illegal, or hop on a boat, I wish ya luck."

"Yes, I have read about the refugee situation. Our Muslim brothers..."

"Forget about that. Don't mind that shit."

"What, Mr. Rob?"

"You know, that God shit. That religious shit. Don't mind it."

Pasat stopped smiling. "Mr. Rob, if you please, do not speak of our faith that way. You could get in trouble."

"Don't gab to me about it either, then. Look, you're a right bloke, Pasat, but this shit's business. What's the directions?"

"It is the same as last time, sir. No different."

"Don't got the directions for me? I can't remember 'em."

Pasat went back into the kitchen. He came back with a folded piece of paper. He slapped it on the desk.

"Better yet, Pasat," Rob said, looking up while he ate, "visit Noosa. I bet you'll learn something while you're there."

54

In Karon, Nat spoke to a few more tourists who had matched the description. None had been to Pattaya within the last few days.

Next, he drove into Patong and headed to a hotel on the beach.

"Yes, I spoke to you on the phone," the manager told Nat when the desk clerk could not find the name. "But this Bob Murphy and his wife Patricia checked out this morning."

"Where did they go?"

"We do not know, sir. We don't ask. But we wish we did."

"Why?"

"When our maid went to clean the room, the bedsheets were missing and the mattress had a huge stain. Like someone had gone to the bathroom on it. We have the passport number and an address in Texas. But since he paid in cash, we cannot bill him for the mattress. If he stays in Thailand, maybe we can track him down to pay for the mattress, but we will probably forget it."

"Do you still have the mattress?"

"Yes, I believe it is in the storage room."

"Can I see it?"

The manager brought Nat to the storage room. Nat took one look at the mattress and told the manager to keep it.

"What did his wife look like?" Nat asked.

"I don't know. American lady. I take them to the room myself when they come. Not very nice lady."

"Could you draw a picture of her for a sketch artist?"

The manager shrugged. "I can try, Mr. Detective."

"Is someone else checked into the room yet?"

"Yes, I think we filled it an hour ago."

"Can you change them to another room and close it off? I will call the Phuket station. We may need to examine it."

55

By the time Niral reached Manu's car, it had started raining, and Niral was wet.

"Does it rain like this all the time?" Niral asked, climbing inside.

"When it rains it pours, Niralbhai. But this is like nothing. You should see the villages sometimes. There may be some larger storms coming up."

Driving through the streets of Rander, Niral saw Muslim boys running to duck under the tents of day markets. But soon the rain stopped.

"It's like this in Thailand too," Niral said. "Short bursts of torrential rain, followed by sudden stops."

"The heat should dry you," Manu responded. Then he added, "So what did you learn? Did you have trouble?"

"I learned plenty, Manu. They gave me a detailed plan of the assassination plot. It will happen at Diwali, and they want me to get weapons inside. Let's go to Dwarka. I will tell Bhai all about it."

Manu didn't respond at first. Then he said, "We should talk to Mr. Ghosh first."

"Is he at the restaurant?"

"No, he is in Navsari."

"That is next to my mother's village, right?"

"Yes. It is south, the other way from Dwarka. But he may be going up to Bharuch later, which is on the road to Dwarka. In fact, I am supposed to pick him up if he does. We have a big temple there."

"Let's go. I'll get my stuff from Val's house. I don't really want to stay there."

"I thought you would stay. They are your family. I was going to come back tomorrow to pick you up."

"There's no point, Manu. Nothing to do here. I'd rather talk to Bhai about the plot in person and go over it at the temple complex in Dwarka."

Manu nodded. He drove over to Val's house. Niral was still a little wet. He stepped inside the living room. Vikasmama was sitting on the couch. Amrita approached and asked him again if he had brought anything for her from Thailand, but Niral told her he hadn't returned yet. Then she turned and fled up the stairs.

Sobha smiled. She was holding a rolling pin.

"You're wet. Do you want to change?"

"No time. We're leaving for Navsari," Niral said.

"You must be hungry. I am making dinner."

"I can eat on the road."

"You cannot miss another dinner, Niralbhai. I won't allow you to take another plate with you."

"I'm sure there's food in Navsari," he responded.

Sobha held up the rolling pin, stuck her tongue out, and held it up. "My mother used to do this, like she would strike us. You aren't eating any Navsari crap."

"No, you aren't," Val said, coming downstairs. "It won't take long."

Finally, Niral consented to eat. Manu ate with him. Sobha made bhajiya, laddu and shriikhand along with eggplant and potato shak, puri, and khichdi-kadhi. In the meantime, his clothes had dried.

"You should meet this Hindu diamond merchant before you leave," Vikasmama said as they ate, sitting on the floor. "I will set up a meeting."

"We have to go now, Vikasmama," Niral said.

"Stop bothering him, Pappa," Val added. "If he wants a better deal, he will tell us."

"I can't believe a Musulman is giving him the best deal," Vikas said. "I think your mother would say the same."

"If, one day, I need a good deal, I swear I will go to your man," Niral said. "What's his name?"

"Kamalbhai. He has an impressive factory. I'm sure he can give you a tour."

After eating, Niral took his stuff from the room and realized he hadn't checked the diamonds. It would take too long, he thought. He'd check them in the village if he had time.

He waved goodbye to the family, and they drove away into the twilight, past herders whipping their oxen and sadhus in their orange saffron robes and colored faces, smoking as they went home for the night after a day of shaking down homes for funds.

"Are they allowed to smoke?" Niral asked.

"What do you think? Half are frauds. They are conmen, nothing else."

They drove on the highway, then took a detour onto a side road between jungles of trees, the car's beams acting as their only light.

"I wish I had my rickshaw," Manu said. "This car's a bit big for these roads."

"I remember it took us a while to get to Yam Gam from Surat."

"It used to take forever. Even from Mumbai to Surat, it would take fifteen hours. Now with the highway, it takes four or five."

"Progress."

"Yes, with progress comes both ease and complication. I think you will see that."

"Do we have time to stop by Yam Gam? Bhai said I should see Narendrakaka."

"Of course. In fact, I can drop you there while I go check on Mr. Ghosh in Navsari. He said there's a possibility he may have to stay overnight. In that case, you can stay in Yam Gam, and I will pick you up in the morning. I can call you."

"But I didn't tell them I'm staying overnight," Niral noted.

"It's okay. This is India. I'm sure Narendrakaka will not mind. Anyway, that is your home, is it not?"

56

Rob drove through the same route as last time, grumbling as he did. He was still perturbed by how he had allowed Linda Macaday to be found. First time he had ever allowed a body to be found.

The rain had ceased. The sun was setting. Rob drove by beautiful bays and ships filled with tourists clicking their phones and cameras, but even with the crags in the distance, he didn't feel as enamored with the scene as he once had. One sight blurred into another like a series of slides in a view-master moving too fast. What if human perception was wrong? What if time was faster or slower than perception allowed? Were the images of the mind actually straightened out from reality? Was the world superimposed? He remembered telling Boris he would see hell when he died. He hadn't meant it; it had simply come out that way. Maybe his grandma had said it once. Or maybe someone else had.

He turned off the coast and onto the deserted roads. His car's lights were his vision, a spotlight on darkness, illuminating perpetual movement, yet simultaneously still. He thought he made the right number of turns, but then he began to doubt himself. He had no way to contact Rahmat. What if he'd made a wrong turn? He wasn't sure how to go back.

He stopped the car and opened the door. The night air was a bit cooler than the afternoon's serving. He could hear the crickets chirping as he put his foot down on moist soil. Ferns were all around him, trees beyond that, but he could only see in front of him and a little to the sides.

He heard a whistle in the distance. Immediately, he took out his gun and pointed it at the area he suspected. He shouted, "Come out!"

He heard a thunder of gunfire. He ducked and fell on the soil. Then he heard a wild laugh, like a hyena's cry.

"Fucking wankers," he yelled, pulling his head up. He began to crawl toward the door when he heard someone behind him. As he turned his head, he saw a rifle butt flying at him.

57

Nat was inside General Chaow's office again. He perused the Thai mythology murals, including one showing Hanuman jumping over a river and soldiers with animal faces being speared by a large pig. Another slide showed a domestic scene of a princess being offered a chalice by a kneeling prince or servant—Nat couldn't tell which—while her ladies-in-waiting gossiped in the corner.

Nat smoked with his good arm (he had used his other arm to take out the cigarette, moving slowly) and wondered why the general didn't have any family pictures. Suddenly, he was interrupted as two men entered the room. He turned, putting the cigarette out on the general's desk.

The general noticed his move and frowned, but he did not say anything. Nat stood and performed a wai, enduring the pain in his arm, his hands high above his head, and his body bowed. The general nodded slightly. Then he introduced the man next to him.

"Detective Nat, please respectfully bow to Khun Commissioner."

Nat's eyes widened. He had seen Commissioner Prongchat only once in person, at a distance. General Chaow gazed at him angrily, until Nat gave the humblest wai he had ever given.

The commissioner smiled and nodded in return.

"Relax, Detective Nat," Commissioner Prongchat said. "It is good to meet you. Sit; we have much to discuss."

Nat waited until General Chaow had pulled up a seat for the commissioner before he sat himself.

The commissioner tucked his feet slightly under the body of the chair.

"I want to congratulate you on your bravery, Detective Nat," Commissioner Prongchat said. "You came here for one case and almost apprehended a suspect for another crime."

"Thank you, Khun Commissioner. In fact, I have found evidence that could tie both cases."

"Really?" Commissioner Prongchat asked, looking at General Chaow. "I would love to see it."

"The Phuket police are checking DNA in a hotel room in Patong right now, including on a mattress where the victim may have been killed."

Commissioner Prongchat nodded. "Excellent. And how does this relate to your case in Bangkok?"

"Well, I was searching for a witness to a potential murder case, and I believe the woman in the bag may be his wife. Someone might have wanted to scare this man, an American tourist, to cover up the crime in Bangkok, and so killed his wife as a message. Or maybe they killed him too. But the desk clerk did see a man check out who matched both the description of the tourist and the husband who checked in with her. His wife was not with him."

"Hmm. And this man, this witness, is he a tall farang?"

"According to the description, he is not as tall as the man I saw at the beach. Of course, I don't know that this wife is the victim without the DNA."

"Yes, we will try to match the DNA," Commissioner Prongchat interrupted. "But are you eliminating the husband as a suspect in the wife's murder if the two are related?"

"I don't know. I don't think, from the description, that he was the same man from the beach, at least."

Commissioner Prongchat nodded. "I see. They may be unrelated. Maybe this wife is not even dead. We will uncover all evidence and examine it. But I must tell you, we have arrested a man for the murder of the woman at the beach."

"You have?" Nat asked, surprised.

"Yes," General Chaow answered. "You see, you assumed that the man was a farang because he was tall. But there are some tall Thais, are there not? We found one who lives on Phi Phi. He works at a guesthouse there, and occasionally comes to Phuket. He has some prior sex convictions, small stuff, but these types do graduate fast."

"But what evidence do you have?" Nat asked.

"Well, his confession, of course," General Chaow said. "He was picked up this afternoon and questioned."

"What did he say?"

"He says he saw the woman. She was wearing a bathing suit. He followed her, raped her, then killed her by accident. He became frightened and cut her up, put her in the garbage bags, dumped her."

"He said all that? Where did he kill her?"

"He did not say. We assumed it was at the beach, but maybe it was at her hotel."

"You must have asked him."

"He was very confused. Sweating, babbling. Actions stemming from a guilty conscience."

Nat didn't say anything at first. Then he looked at Commissioner Prongchat.

"But you'll follow up on the DNA evidence?" he asked.

"Of course," Commissioner Prongchat responded. "Do not worry, Detective Nat, I will command General Chaow to do a thorough job."

"How about the footprint?" he asked.

"We will check it," General Chaow answered.

"Point is, Detective Nat, we thank you for your service, but this investigation seems to be wrapping up," Commissioner Prongchat said. "Our tourists want to know that a predator has been caught, that they can freely move around Thailand without fear. You can return to Bangkok and continue your other investigation. When they need you to testify at the trial, the prosecutor will let you know."

"I still need to find my witness," Nat reminded him. "And if this Thai man is guilty, maybe he is lying about his motive. Maybe he is working for whoever killed our missing persons."

"Maybe. Maybe. But have you known many Thais able to resist the lures of a farang woman?"

"If the DNA evidence confirms the hotel woman is the murdered woman, and that this suspect was inside the room, I want to come back and interrogate him," Nat said.

"Very well," Commissioner Prongchat stated. "You may return to Phuket at that time. The DNA evidence will take a while to examine. In the meantime, I have spoken to General Toon and told him you will be returning to Bangkok to continue your investigation there. Good day, Detective Nat."

58

Manu sped up a hill and stopped the car abruptly before he hit somebody. It was a woman carrying a pot and ladle. She gave him a dark look, then continued to carry out her duty.

"That was lucky, thank God," Manu said. "Looks like you've come during a festive time."

This strip of the village was lit up by burning torches. Men sat in two rows, facing each other, on a long sheet laid out on the ground, eating from thalis. Women stood, serving them.

Niral remembered the village street from his childhood. The hill seemed to be shorter and closer to the road than during his last visit.

Manu got out and approached the woman holding the pot and ladle.

"Where is Narendrabhai?" he asked, smiling. But Niral didn't listen for the response. He remembered the house. Now it was the only one-story home in a joint row of houses that had all been rebuilt two or three stories higher.

The door was open. He saw Kauntiaunti inside, wearing an old green and red sari, her head covered with her odhni. She was sitting on the floor of the kitchen, one leg out, rolling rotli like in the old days.

He approached her but suddenly doubted himself, recalling the incident at the beach with Vishal. But then he realized she didn't know anything about it.

"Niral?" she asked, looking up and taking the odhni off her head. "My God, it is you."

She began to stand but collapsed on the ground, laughing despite herself. Narendrakaka emerged from the back. He still appeared frail, but he was wearing a crisp white kufni. He helped her up.

"I am glad you have come, Niral," Narendrakaka said. Kauntiaunti began to cry. She stumbled toward Niral, her hand shaking, and put her hand on his head as he bowed.

"Niral!" she hesitated, examining his face. "My God, what happened? What did that monster do to you? I cannot believe my son could orchestrate something like that or that Amrat could murder. But we know now how many things are possible."

"Kaunti, please, calm down," Narendrakaka said. "Roll your rotli for the people. Ketki will be coming soon to collect the next batch. I will talk to Niral and show him around."

"He must be hungry," she told Narendrakaka. "Let him eat. Give him a space and a thali."

"Yes, Kaunti," Narendrakaka responded.

Manu brought in Niral's bags, then tapped Niral's shoulder to signal he was leaving. Niral could see the woman lecturing him from afar, waving the ladle, and Manu smiling as he jogged back to his car. Niral picked up his bags and waved goodbye.

Narendrakaka helped his wife sit, then brought Niral inside the dark interior of the home. It was a space large enough for a small bed followed by a slight passage, also fitting a slim bed, to a backyard and an outhouse.

Niral placed his bags next to the bed.

Narendrakaka hugged Niral. "I am so glad you came. Welcome back to your home. We have been keeping it well for you."

"It's hardly my home. I've only been here once in my life."

"Your mother grew up here. It is your mosal. A man's mosal is his true home. No one will ever love him more than his mother's side of the family."

"What about my father's home? No one ever talks about that."

"Your father was disowned by his family when he married your mother. Just as I've been disowned by my family here for my crime. I can neither be in America nor in my village after I took money from the Brotherhood Fund for Dilip's mortgage. That is why I am doing my penance here."

"I'm sorry to hear that," Niral said.

"Do not worry, Niral. It is not your fault. This happens in India. As for your father, he married your mother for love. But he came from a long line of noble Kshatriyas, and his family had a girl picked out for him. They could not tolerate his betrayal and refused to allow your mother inside their home. So your father sold his property and his land. He no longer has a home there. He considers this village his home in India."

Niral sighed, then changed the subject. "Listen, Narendrakaka, I might have to stay overnight. Is that okay?"

Narendrakaka smiled and grabbed Niral's shoulders. "Of course. You can stay as long as you wish. You should stay longer, but I can show you much even in one night. You should know what is going on."

"What's with the party outside?"

"That is a celebration of Prameshbhai's daughter, Madhuri, obtaining entrance to college in Navsari. Prameshbhai likes to give parties. It helps him reassert his dominance over the village and demonstrate his giving nature. Come, would you like to eat?"

"I just ate. Prameshbhai you said is the Dubla mayor, right? I don't remember a Prameshbhai when I visited last time."

"I heard you were a boy when you visited last time. I'm sure the houses were not this tall either. Nor was there a large house on top of the hill. You will see it when you go out again. That is Prameshbhai's house. He was not mayor years ago. That was Lakshmanbhai, who lives next door. But Prameshbhai, then named Gurio, received an education through OBC benefits, then got a good government post collecting taxes, and soon he was using bribery and deceit to buy land. Now he is the richest man in the village. No Brahmin or Vaishya can compete."

"And he's dividing the village, you say?"

"I don't say, but it is true. The village is helpless. He gives with one hand and takes away with another. The people are frustrated, but they cannot do much. Therein lies danger."

"I guess I should meet him."

"I hear him giving a speech. He likes to give speeches. Come, let us go."

Narendrakaka led Niral outside. As they passed the kitchen, Niral saw that Kauntiaunti was still rolling rotli. The men were still sitting on the strip. Most had finished eating, and their right hands were dirty with the remnants of dal, rice, and shak, but they sat still as they listened to a man who stood at the edge of the long sheet, his voice loud. He was speaking in Gujarati, and Niral could pick up most but not all of his spiel.

"He is saying that hard work can make anyone rise up, just as he has, just as his daughter has," Narendrakaka translated and summarized. "He conveniently does not mention the OBC benefits he had."

"Where is his daughter?"

"Inside the house. She is studying. He wants her to be prepared for when college starts in July."

"Strange. I'd think this would disturb her."

"Who knows what goes on in that house. But even she is a pawn to a man like him."

"These guys are all Dubla?"

"Not at all. No Dubla invited. They are all in their own village. I can take you if you want."

"So he rules over..."

"He does not rule; he mediates. And through mediation, he benefits. Take this dinner. His daughter gets nothing; he gets a stage and gifts."

"But how is that ruining India?"

"This is nothing new. But combined with everything else...you will see."

Prameshbhai had finished his speech. The women came around with jugs of water to pour over the hands of the men, washing the crumbs and sauces into the thalis.

"Are the women being paid for this?" Niral asked.

"Not at all. Free labor. They will eat second, as custom dictates. Come, let us meet Prameshbhai."

The men stared at Niral as he walked past. Prameshbhai, wearing a cream kafni and thick, red odhni, was speaking to a man who had greeted him with namaste.

"Prameshbhai, this is Niral, Heenabhen's son," Narendrakaka said.

Prameshbhai looked at him, surprised, then gave Niral the same namaste greeting and bowing his head.

"Niralbhai. What a surprise. We have heard a lot about you."

"What have you heard?"

"About America, of course. Your heroic actions in the face of unspeakable pain. We are proud."

"In the past, they would have shunned someone who looked like me, right?" Niral asked, remembering some things his mother had told him.

"Do not be ridiculous. That does not happen in Yam Gam, not while I am mayor. You probably do not remember me, but I remember when you first came to this village as a boy with your mother and father. Sure, I was a Dubla then, standing on the edge of the village faliya, but I was watching. You know, many here frown on inter-caste relations, but I knew that with Brahmin and Kshatriya in you, you would amount to greatness."

"I don't feel great."

"If you had told us you were coming, I would have planned a feast," Prameshbhai continued, ignoring Niral's comment. "In the old days, all the villagers would go and greet someone as soon as they came, especially someone from America. Even the Dubla, or at least the ones who worked in the home. But these days everyone is so busy. You must schedule these things. So allow me to introduce you back to the village now, as people are already gathered. This feast will be for my daughter and you, both."

He lifted his hand and yelled. The women had already sat for their meal, but the men who hadn't left stopped walking and paid attention. Niral recalled his father telling him that nothing worked in India because everyone went their own way. That didn't seem to be the case with Prameshbhai and the villagers.

Prameshbhai put his arm around Niral and introduced him as Heenabhen's son. Many people suddenly smiled and nodded at Niral.

"He is an Indian hero in America. He uncovered a murder and

fraudulent plot to defraud a Hindu organization. And he paid the price, as you can see from his scars. Who knows, perhaps he is even an avatar of Vishnu."

Some of the people smiled. Others frowned. Narendrakaka looked embarrassed.

"This feast was for him too. I hope he will stay here long." Then he turned to Niral. "I understand you may be staying in your mother's home," he said, "but my door is open to you too."

His speech ended. Suddenly men rose and began to surround Niral, speaking in Gujarati, asking if he remembered them from his last visit. He did recall some names; the faces were more difficult. But he met everyone, greeted them with namaste, and shook hands. Many older people, as well as women who were now sitting and eating, spoke to each other or Narendrakaka about how big Niral had gotten, how handsome, and how he looked like his mother, as if Niral was not physically present at all.

Younger men either asked how long he was staying or wanted to know more about his actions in America. Narendrakaka had done his penance in the village for years, so everyone knew his crime. They seemed to delight in the fact that the person who had uncovered it was now here, staying under the roof of his victim, the criminal.

But Niral avoided the questions. Narendrakaka sensed his unease and announced that Niral was tired and needed to sleep. Soon, they retired to Niral's family home. They both sat on the bed in the small hallway, staring at a picture of Krishna blowing his flute while gopis hovered around, tiny in the background. Kauntiaunti had become excitable again, but she had been placated by Narendrakaka and was now meditating by counting beads on a rosary in the kitchen.

Niral watched a salamander crawl up the cracked paint of the blue wall.

"So you have decided to help The Brotherhood," Narendrakaka said after a long silence.

"I've decided that the threat is too great for me to ignore it. I guess my father is proud."

"He must be. He should be. Listen, Niral, I have accepted my fate as a fallen man. Now I have given up everything to perform penance. Not exactly a sanyasi but someone who has no material goals. I admit, Vishal was too materialistic. I raised him badly. I was blind to his greed and deceit. He played lip-service to the values I had taught him, and I was too blinded by filial love to see it. I just hope these accusations about him directing Amrat's rage and the mobster's murder are false. Wherever he is, I hope he will come to his senses and seek penance."

"Yes, wherever he is," Niral said quietly. "Hopefully he'll give himself up."

"I don't mean that. There is greater justice than the American courts, Niral."

"You're right; a trial would be a kangaroo court and a show. I don't believe he directed Amrat's rage or set up that mobster's murder. Maybe he had nothing to do with Stan Lorenzo's murder either. Now that I think of it, I can pinpoint a better suspect for that. But Vishal is guilty of one murder."

"Which one?"

"Priya's murder, of course."

"How Niral? Dilipuncle did that."

"Vishal caused it. Trust me. That's all I'll say."

"How? How can you say such a thing?"

Niral stood up. "I heard Meetal was here. But I haven't seen her."

Narendrakaka looked up at him. "Tell me about Priya's murder. Did Dilipuncle not..."

"They are both guilty. Amrat too. Everyone is guilty of Priya's murder, including Priya. Including you. Maybe even including Meetal. Now tell me, if she's here, where is she?"

Narendrakaka hesitated. "She's in a field, meditating. She does not like to be disturbed. She has given up all material things, more than me. At least I work on your parents' mango farm in return for our lodging here, making sure Harshkaka picks all the mangoes and delivers them during the season. But Meetal came here determined to be a spiritual being. And she seems to have reached higher toward Atman than I ever will."

"I want to see her. That's why I came here. So tell me where she is."

"Niral, please do not mention Priya or Vishal. She..."

"I'll mention whatever the fuck I want. Now, if you want my help, tell me where she is."

Narendrakaka stared at the floor. "Okay," he relented. "Go toward Prameshbhai's house and take a left. Walk through the grazing fields and the wheat farm. Behind that is another field. At the end you should see Meetal sitting on a stump under a tree."

59

Rob awoke suddenly as water splashed on his face and body. His eyes blinking furiously, he took in his surroundings. The light was dim, emanating only from a small lamp placed on the floor, but he could see he was inside a room with no windows. The same room where he had picked up the crates of ya ba. He noticed some crates on the floor.

He was naked, immobilized, and standing against a wall, his hands and feet bound to it. Suction cups were attached to his chest, and their wires led down to a small machine.

The man with the scarred face dumped an empty bucket on the ground, smirking as he did. He held a taser in his other hand. The other two men in fatigues stood by holding AK-47s, grinning too.

Rahmat stood respectfully next to the machine, his hands behind his body, wearing a topi and salwar kameez.

"You are awake, at last, Mr. Maric."

Rob coughed. "Can you stop fucking calling me that, mate? And what's your game?"

"Why, it is your real name, isn't it? I like it better than Rob Johnson. The anglicization is fake."

"Look, if you're gonna kill me, just do it. Don't know what you'd gain by it, but..."

"We're not going to kill you, Mr. Maric, unless you deserve it, of course. Tell me, this incident in Phuket, did you have something to do with it?"

"No, you fucking wanker. Why would I?"

"Then why do you have scratches on your arms?"

"My girl likes to scratch. No crime in that, bro."

"And why were you afraid to come here? You didn't know they would stop you. Unless you were spotted during a crime."

"When I'm picking up drugs, I'm careful, mate. I don't want no death penalty if can avoid it."

"Yes. Of course. Please, Mr. Maric, I don't want our collaboration to be fruitless. Obviously, our main partner is Duncan Smith, another fake name I know. But..."

"It's a fake name?" Rob asked. "What's his real one?"

"If you don't know already, maybe you shouldn't be in business with him. Now I'm going to have to insist that you tell me the truth, Mr. Maric. Because if you don't, we will have to zap you with an electric shock. And since you are wet, it will smart more than usual."

"Do whatever you want, you fucking wanker. This is like nothing to me. You don't know what pain feels like."

The scarred man touched him with the taser. Rob screamed. He shook for a few seconds, then breathed heavily and began coughing.

"Fuck you! Fuck you!" he yelled.

"Tell me, Mr. Maric, did you kill the woman on the beach?"

The scarred man moved the taser toward him again.

"Yes! Yes! Okay, mate, what the fuck is the big deal?"

"Why?"

"It's an internal matter, bro. We needed to eliminate a witness."

"What about her husband?"

"How do you know about that?"

"Where is he?"

"He's dead. I killed him. They just never found the body. I ran into that fucking cop so..."

"Mr. Maric, are you working for anyone other than Duncan Smith?"

Rob shook his head. "No, goddamn it."

"I'm sorry, Mr. Maric, the machine tells me that your last two answers are untrue."

"Well maybe your bloody machine's a piece of fucking filth!"

The scarred man zapped him again, this time holding the taser longer. Rob shook forcefully, rhythmically, his eyes bulging from his sockets.

Smoke emerged from Rob's body, his head drooped towards the floor. Saliva dripped from his mouth.

"Believe me, Mr. Maric, this pains me as much as you. Why are you lying to me?"

Rob breathed hard. Then he raised his head. "You think you can break me. But I know my body's finite. It'll break eventually."

"Yes, but do you believe in anything beyond it? We hung you up like Jesus, but you don't strike me as a Christian."

"Nope, this is it, mate. There's no messiah, no revelation. Once I'm dead, it's over."

"Exactly why you should care. But if you accept Allah, you will go to Paradise. You will have seventy-two virgins."

"I'm no virgin."

"No. I imagine you are not."

Rob coughed a bit more, then spit some blood onto the ground.

"Look, why do you care, mate?" he asked, breathing hard. "This has nothing to do with you. Didn't Niral deliver the cash? He's going to do the job on Bhai, bro. No worries."

"Maybe we want more, Mr. Maric. We're giving you quite the spread."

"Still doesn't make sense."

"No, life would not make sense to you." Rahmat sighed. "Bring him down and let him rest," he told his soldiers.

PART XII

†

Bangkok, Thailand; Krabi, Thailand; Yam Gam, India

60

At Sumantapat's club Go-Go Rama, Apsara was dancing naked on stage, smiling on and off at various farang. She stepped off and was about to walk the floor to solicit some "boom boom" time in the rooms when one of Sumantapat's dealers grabbed her arm, a man named Boy. He pulled her to the office as she protested his rough handling.

Inside, she was shocked to see Sumantapat himself, sitting behind the desk normally occupied by the madam, Maem. She bowed deeply to him in the traditional Thai wai. He spoke in a soft voice, punctuating many of his phrases with "ah."

"Please, sit. I know you need to get back to work—money is time—but we have plenty of time here, don't we?"

"Yes, Khun Sumantapat," she answered, sitting as she avoided looking into his eyes.

"Your stage name is Tip, yes? I understand your real name is Duanphen?"

Apsara nodded. Sumantapat smiled. "But when I checked your apartment lease, it says your real name is Apsara. Which is correct?"

Apsara hesitated, running her fingers through her hair. "It is Apsara. Duanphen is the name Thanat used for me."

"Thanat? Who is that?"

"We suspect that is Pornopat's real name," Boy explained. "He used Pornopat under us."

"So you knew him well if you knew his real name," Sumantapat said to Apsara. "Did you work on the gem scam with him?"

"No, Khun Sumantapat. Why would I?"

"Well, I imagine you know he has disappeared, along with a tuk-tuk driver and another gem scam dealer. I questioned some of his associates and they remember him mentioning that a woman would accompany him, pretending to be his wife. They thought it was you, and that you were involved with him romantically."

"I wasn't at the gem scam."

"Which gem scam?" Sumantapat asked, suddenly turning serious.

"Any gem scam," Apsara replied.

Sumantapat nodded. "Ah, I see. Then tell me, why would he give you another nickname?"

Apsara swallowed. She felt herself sweating. He glanced at Boy, who gave her a nasty glare.

"Because we were lovers, as you said. He liked to call me Duanphen. He liked the moon."

"And he never wanted to use you in the gem scam?"

"I didn't say he didn't want to use me. He did mention it as a possibility. But I did not want to be involved. I make my money this way."

Sumantapat glanced at Boy, who took out a knife and began to wipe the blade with his shirt.

"Ah, I understand you have family in Khon Khen province," Sumantapat continued. "A mother and a daughter?"

"Yes. I send them money," Apsara replied.

"You send them money. Your daughter doesn't have a father? Your mother has no husband?"

"No. One is missing, the other is dead. You know Isan men."

"And you are in debt? You work at another club?"

"I work at another club in Patpong. I need to."

"At Scandal, yes? Do you know the owner, Mr. Hong?"

"I work for the madam there, Lek. You know how poor us Isan people are. There are no jobs there. My family needs my Bangkok money."

"I have heard you are in debt to Mr. Hong. That is not true?"

"No, it is not true," Apsara said confidently, looking Sumantapat in the eye. He glanced at Boy.

"What happened to your neck?" Sumantapat asked. "A ring around your neck isn't attractive."

"Jealous lover," she replied. "You know how it happens."

"Yes. Apply more makeup there. You will become less desirable if you have marks on your skin."

"I make plenty of money for the club," she reminded him.

"Yes, you do. The Maem has told me. We appreciate your work. We know you are close to many of our associates too. Which is why I want to pay you more. But there is one catch if you take this deal. You cannot work at Scandal. You cannot associate with anyone close to Mr. Hong, if you already do. We will make you a better part of the organization. We will use you in the gem scam. And maybe other dealings too. I think you already know about them."

"But what if I don't want to? I want to dance. I need the extra money at Scandal."

"You can work more hours here. We will bump other girls for you. This club is much better than any club in Patpong. If you don't have a debt, as you say, I imagine this should not be a problem."

Apsara glanced at Boy, who smiled at her.

"I imagine this should not be a problem?" Sumantapat repeated.

Apsara shook her head. "No, of course not."

"Good. Because if I find out differently, Boy here will take a trip up to Khon Kaen, and you will not like the results."

Apsara stood. "Can I go?"

"Sure. Maem will go over your new pay rate with you later. We will speak again."

Apsara performed a wai.

"I imagine you mourned for Pornopat, Thanat. Whatever you call him?" Sumantapat asked.

"Yes. He was a good man," Apsara replied.

Sumantapat smiled. "I don't think he was. But he was good at the gem scam."

Apsara left. Boy closed the door.

"Why not use her to spy on Mr. Hong?" Boy asked. "If he had anything to do with..."

"We don't know that he did. And anyway, I don't trust her. Make sure you watch her."

61

Niral trekked through the grazing fields and the wheat farm. Only the moonlight illuminated the sky, so he could not see much except darkness, yet he continued on, through tall stalks of grass toward a forest in the distance. His heart began to beat hard. He wasn't sure what to expect.

As he approached the forest, he noticed the outline of the tree Narendrakaka had mentioned since it was centered and distant from the others. He heard a light mum uttering from the tree. From the front he couldn't see anything, but as he moved to the side, he noticed the silhouette of a figure sitting butterfly on a stump. The person's hair was done up and folded in a bun.

"Meetal?" he asked when he was close. "It's Niral."

He didn't get a response. He said her name again.

Still no response.

With his finger, he poked the figure's arm.

Suddenly the head turned. Red eyes glared at him. Hissing emanated from the mouth. He backed away. A noise in the distance spooked him. He considered running. But then he heard Meetal's familiar laugh.

"You think you can disturb a sanyasi's prayer and get away with it?" she asked.

"I'm sorry," Niral said. "I'm leaving tomorrow. There's no other..."

"You will come back. I can see it now," she said.

"You can see the future?"

"Like any other who has penetrated the nature of Brahman, I can see certain things. Whether they are true, or perhaps more accurately, in what temporal way they will manifest themselves, I know not."

"Stop talking like that," Niral said. "You're scaring me."

Meetal laughed again. "You wish there was a light so you could see my face?"

"No. Because I don't want you to see *my* face."

"What happened to your face, Niral?"

"You know what. I was burned."

"Yes, by that vicious Amrat. But I know what he was thinking. He believed he was Parasurama, that the world was going the way of the Kali Yuga. He had to destroy the structures of corruption so that others could bring back purity after his passing. Like all who believe in an apocalypse. His self-immolation was akin to many in political protest."

"Political protest? He killed Lauren. That wasn't protest. That was personal."

"I didn't know her. She was the white girl you were cheating on me with?"

"We were never together per se."

"But I remember asking you about a white girl."

"It was complicated. I feel responsible, in a way."

"How did Amrat know her?"

"I thought you could see all things?"

"I didn't say all things."

"He was her teacher. Her guru. She was in love with him. If there's such a thing as true love, devotional love, she had it for him."

"So why kill her?"

"She was a stripper and a prostitute. He claimed she would never stop. As if that was a reason to kill her. He'd have to murder half of Thailand to be consistent."

"Thailand. Yes, you've found a home in that debased place."

"It's the Land of Smiles."

"Are you smiling?"

Niral shrugged. "I dream of her sometimes. She tells me about her final moments, about finally sleeping with her guru. He told me he did before he burned himself. Sometimes he speaks to me too."

"So why do you blame yourself?"

"I used her to bring down your brother."

"My brother knew her?"

"He employed her, Meetal. He employed a lot of prostitutes."

"I haven't heard that."

"Hardly the most important thing. Land fraud, arson, murder..."

"All lies. I've looked into Atman, my own being, and found nothing to support it. You said yourself Amrat acted for his own reasons."

"True. I know he did."

"So why not go back to America and tell everyone the truth."

"Because the rest are not lies. Vishal is a criminal. And he's a murderer too."

He felt a sharp slap across his face. Shocked, he held his cheek.

"What the—"

He felt a barrage of slaps then, and he bent back to avoid them.

"Niral Solanke, you are the criminal!" she yelled.

"God, what's your problem?" he yelled. "After all that meditation, I'd think you'd have accepted the truth."

"What truth? My brother is still out there. I can see it. He'll return in glory."

"Glory?" he exclaimed, chuckling bitterly. "He's dead, you fucking twat. I killed him."

Meetal breathed heavily. "No, you didn't. I've seen him," she said finally, trembling.

Angry, he pushed her. She fell on the ground. Then he lay on top of her, holding her arms. He couldn't see her, but he could hear her breathing.

"Maybe it's better that you can't see what your brother did to me," he said. "Not Amrat, him. He set this shit in motion. Him and his fucking dick, his bullshit revenge. He made your friend Priya into a whore."

"No," she said, panting, then spitting into his face. He closed his eyes but didn't move.

"Now listen, I don't even care," he continued. "That's the way of the world. What's the big deal, right? It's her body, her money. Kama is a part of life. No one can deny it. But blackmail and using The Brotherhood against itself: that's what your brother did. He wanted to punish Priya because she thought she was superior as a Brahmin. He wanted to show her that he could control her father through money. It's his fault she's dead. And I don't feel bad for killing him after he stabbed me."

Meetal stopped moving. Niral opened his eyes. He could hear her crying.

"But we can still fix things, right? Make sure things work for the greater good?" he asked, laughing. He released her arms and got up. "Why the fuck did you come here anyway? So your brother would find you more easily?"

She wept for a while. Niral breathed in the damp air. He wondered if it would rain soon.

He heard her sit up, imagined her grabbing her knees.

"Without my family, Niral, I had a hard time in New York," she explained. "After the shock in the auditorium, I had a nervous breakdown, and I never went back to Chicago. I quit school without graduating. But everyone I knew had left Queens, so I moved to Williamsburg in Brooklyn. I worked in a cafe, tried to be a hipster or something, but I never felt right.

"I tried to write. At Northwestern, in journalism, I had been trained to write objectively, interviewing people, finding stories, but now I could only write about the conversations I overheard in cafes, and no editor would want content so mundane. I didn't want to write about The Brotherhood either, because it brought back too much pain. So I began looking for experiences and friends that could help my writing. I went to parties and bars. I drank. I tried to find stories, tales of inspiration. I tried to find friends. But in such a large city, I didn't meet many friendly people, and nothing ever stuck.

"I began to read shit about my brother in the paper. The trial of the Tragliani henchmen were front page for a while. I wondered why I had ever considered journalism as a profession, when all they recorded were kangaroo trials and the horrors of the world. I needed peace and understanding.

"I figured a better way was to look inside myself. So instead of writing about the objective world, I began to record my daily thoughts and feelings, like Anais Nin or somebody, thinking it would help fill the emptiness inside me. But it only helped to a point. Writing down my feelings didn't help me escape them, and a lot of times, I couldn't penetrate them completely.

"I decided to take yoga classes. I began meditating consistently. That shit we were raised with, occasionally did but mostly dismissed. And I found it helped. Gradually, I realized I could find myself and deal with my demons through meditation, and India was a much better place for that than Brooklyn. So I rejoined my parents. And it was the right decision. I finally feel I am at home. I always had this nagging feeling in America that I was never whole, even though I'd lived there my entire life."

"But you haven't given up hope about Vishal? That seems counter-intuitive."

"He's my brother. He helped teach me how to read. It's always been us. What do you expect?"

"I expect you to be more enlightened now that you've been meditating on a tree stump for a fucking year."

She was silent for a while. She cleared her throat.

"Did you really kill him?" she asked.

"Yes, because he tried to kill me," Niral responded.

"How about Juan killing that Lucchese guy? And the money?"

"I don't know. Maybe another Lucchese guy pulled the strings. Maybe Bob Macaday. I should have questioned him more. I shouldn't have trusted him."

He wondered if he should have gone down to Phuket instead of Rob. But it was too late. Most likely Macaday was already dead.

"If you killed my brother, I don't want to talk to you, Niral. Just leave."

"I'm staying in my house. Overnight."

"It's not my village. I don't own it. I don't own anything. Not even this stump, not even these clothes, if you could see them."

"I can't see anything. I can't see you. But I can feel you."

"I'm surprised you can feel anything, Niral Solanke. You're a cold man."

"Yes, I am," he agreed. "Completely cold."

62

That night, after her shift ended at two a.m., Apsara texted Duncan and agreed to meet him at the warehouse.

She took a tuk-tuk to the deserted building and climbed the stairs against the moonlight. As she stepped inside the dark office, someone turned her, pulled her close, and grabbed her neck tight from behind.

"Were you followed?" Duncan whispered into her ear.

"I don't think so," she answered.

"I was texting you for hours."

"I was working at Go-Go, baby."

He turned her back around to face him but didn't turn on the light.

"Listen, I just got word from Rahmat that Rob lied. He didn't kill that tourist, and he's working for someone else. Something is going on. When he comes back, I need you to get to the bottom of it. Be more aggressive in your questioning. If he's got another agenda, I need to know it."

"How do you know he lied? This Rahmat is working for you?"

"Just part of the deal. He's got his methods. But I don't think he's going to find out. Rob is tough. Assuming he brings the drugs back here, you need to work on him. He's likely to confide in someone close."

"So now it is good that he is in love with me."

"That's right," Duncan said, pointing at her. "Now it's good."

63

Rob felt water splashing over his face, and he woke up fast, gasping. He was tied to a bed, lying down, still naked, groggy, and weak from the shocks. Rahmat and the scarred man, who held the bucket and an AK-47, glared down at him.

"Are you feeling okay, Mr. Maric?" Rahmat asked. "I apologize for our tactics. I hope you understand."

"Understand? Understand, mate?"

"We must make sure you are not a mole for someone else. The government or anybody else."

Rob glanced toward the foot of the bed, where another soldier stood with his AK-47 pointed at him.

"So what, you believe me now?" Rob asked.

"Maybe you lied, but machines make mistakes," Rahmat answered. "We don't know, but it's not our concern now, as long as you abide by our deal. But I must ask you not to be bitter or to attempt revenge once we release you. We understand why you would want to, but we only wish to conduct business now."

"Understand? Understand?" Rob repeated.

"Yes, understand."

Rob laughed. "Well, I reckon I can't get revenge while you're holding AK's on me."

"I am glad you recognize that fact," Rahmat retorted.

Rahmat gestured to the scarred man, who cut the cords that bound Rob. Immediately, Rob grabbed the scarred man's neck with one hand and twisted his hand with the other, but the scarred man elbowed Rob in the face with his free arm, then, his other arm, free too, lifted the AK-47 to beat him with it.

"Don't!" Rahmat yelled. The scarred man halted. "Don't think you can defeat us, Mr. Maric. We will beat your brains out. We will pummel you with bullets. You will never escape but with the grace of Allah!"

"Fuck your Allah bullshit!" Rob screamed. Rahmat reached over, grabbed him by the hair, and pulled. The scarred man helped him. Rob's arms and legs flailed wildly as they pulled him off the bed and dumped him onto the floor.

"Did you hear what I said before, you stupid kafir?!" Rahmat yelled, backing up with the scarred man. "You are not a whole man like me. Never mind your strength, never mind your skills, never mind your supposed toughness. You do not have fortitude because you have not surrendered yourself to the correct God, Allah, the only God! You have not read the messenger's words, his cries in the desert! No, you merely recite false verses and hold false thoughts, see mirages in your mind. And then you wonder why you are so lost, so constantly dissatisfied, even in this land of so much superficial beauty. Very well! Take away your drugs, Mr Maric, and perhaps you should do them yourself so that you can continue to poison yourself with false pleasures and truths."

Rob gazed up at him, fiercely. But he didn't move. "You can't take me by yourself, you wuss!" he yelled. "Hiding behind your henchmen! Let's get our punch on, mate, you and me!"

"Now, Mr. Maric, I told you the deal if you were released, and you agreed," Rahmat said. "If you do not keep your word, I have no choice to inflict the ultimate punishment. I suppose Mr. Smith can send down another worker in your place."

Rob jumped up to his feet. Breathing hard, he felt his mouth and glanced at his fingers, noticing blood. He flicked his fingers and drops of blood scattered around. The scarred man blinked, AK-47 at the ready.

"Fine, mate," Rob said to Rahmat, gritting his teeth. "I'll be a good boy for you. But you better deliver the good shit. Now come on with it."

64

Niral slept on the floor next to Narendrakaka's bed. Kauntiaunti slept on a bed closer to the back door that led to the outhouse.

Niral was having a dream when a noise awoke him. Lauren had been speaking to him while a smiling Amrat massaged her shoulders. But he couldn't recall her words now. He saw a flashlight and heard whispering voices. One was Narendrakaka's.

Two figures left the home. In the darkness, Niral fumbled for his clothes, dressed quickly, then followed out the door.

The figures were far, but he spotted them on the road, illuminated by a few streetlights. He ran down the hill to the road. They turned left and he followed.

He stepped into a dark passageway with a light at its end. Unable to see otherwise, he ran toward the light and found the passage sloped downhill. At its end, Niral noticed he had entered a village. Two rows of single-story houses stood on either side. A common one-story building was in the middle, helping illuminate both rows with two beams on its roof, and a single streetlight illuminated the entrance. Bonfires raged at different corners, and a few homes had internal lights.

People were out. They had gathered near the far row of houses. Niral could hear shouting, and then he spotted Narendrakaka, along with another man, talking to two young men wearing black shirts. One, clean-shaven, sat on his motorcycle, the other, sporting a goatee, stood by his bike, waving a machete in the air. To his left, a crowd of young men had gathered, holding hammers, sticks, and boards. They were yelling at another young man, who held a board of his own. Niral could see that in a house behind him, two women—one young and one old—peered out of the window fearfully. Other villagers stood around, apparently woken up by the commotion.

Niral hid behind a tree near the entrance.

"Manish, you better give Ravi the dowry you owe!" the man holding the machete said, pointing to the other man on the motorcycle. "How dare you try to get monthly maintenance!"

"You wife-beating scum!" Manish countered. "I'll show you a dowry!"

Manish stepped forward with the board, and the crowd of young men laughed.

"Look at him with his board. Do you think you can hurt a fly with that?" one of them shouted.

"Pranam, stop this!" Narendrakaka begged. "You are drunk. Go back home."

"Why do you defend this thief and liar, Narendrabhai?" Pranam countered. "My brother was duped by his hussy sister. After one day of marriage, she fled, claiming she was beaten. My brother did not lay a hand on her! He did the right thing by marrying her after she became pregnant. Now this Dubla is trying to rob us. He did not even pay us a dowry!"

"We will talk about it with Prameshbhai tomorrow, Pranam," Narendrakaka said. "He will figure it out."

"The hell with Prameshbhai. He is a Dubla too. Manish worked for him, remember? Of course he will favor Manish and Lata. And the courts will favor them too. The Dubla have all the power today."

Suddenly, a mob of men came out to support Manish. They also held boards. Many stood or walked unsteadily, as if they were drunk.

"Look, the Dubla have drank their daru for the day, and now they want to fight!" one of the men yelled. "Come, Dubla, fight!"

"Have you no shame?!" the other old man asked. "These are your brothers. You went to school with them!"

"Shut up, Harshkaka! We know you support your nephew!" Pranam answered. "If he cannot pay the dowry, then you pay the dowry. Someone must pay it. Ravi can't afford the monthly maintenance!"

"Fine, let's have it out," Manish said. "The government tells us we are the same as you. So fine. Let's prove it!"

"Wait!" a woman shouted near Niral. Before he turned, a figure glided past him. When he focused his vision on her, it appeared to be Meetal, clad in a saffron dhoti, her hair in a bun. She was charging toward the Brahmin men.

"Look, it's the Sadhu," the Brahmin man who chided Manish about the board yelled. "What does she want?"

"Stop this nonsense!" she cried. "I can sense you from my stump."

"Oh, too bad, we are interrupting your prayer," he responded. "What an important thing!"

Pranam stared at Meetal, apparently scared. Manish greeted her with namaste. Some of the drunken Dubla laughed, others performed namaste respectfully. The Brahmin lads were similarly divided. Only the one Brahmin man stood up to her.

She approached him, standing steadfast with her hands on her hips.

"What will you do, Sadhu, attack me with your prayers?" he asked. "If you want to stay out of worldly affairs, stay out. Let us live life."

Meetal smiled at him.

"Do you think that I don't see you, Satish, sitting on my stump? I see you laughing at us women, denigrating your own mother. I won't do anything to you. But the women of this village will defend their sister, even if their drunken brothers and husbands will not."

She turned toward the crowd. "Women, grab your knives from your homes. If they want to disgrace our sister, they will have to defeat us first."

She lifted her hand and showed her palm. Inside was a mehndi tattoo of an Om symbol.

A few women in the crowd charged back home. Others emerged from their homes, holding knives.

"This is crazy," the man said. "Women can't fight."

"You can find out if you want," Meetal said.

"Let's go," Pranam told his people. "We'll talk to Prameshbhai tomorrow."

"Are you joking?" Satish asked.

"Come, Satish," Ravi agreed, turning on his motorcycle. "Once they surround us, we might not make it out."

65

Rob was reeling and fuming as he drove away from the village. It was now dawn. Rahmat's men had loaded the crates into the trunk, but Rahmat had confiscated Rob's gun and machete.

He drove several kilometers down a grassy path surrounded by tall ferns. Then he stopped abruptly and shut off the engine. He hit his head several times with his hands, then squeezed it as hard as he could.

He got out of the car and opened the back seat. He checked the secret compartment and saw the money was still there.

He checked the floor and the seat. He closed the door. He opened the driver's seat door again and checked there too. He had lost the directions. How many turns were needed to escape the field?

He tapped his fingers on his jeans. What a crappy turn of events. Almost anything bad that could have happened had happened. He was still alive, but barely.

He heard a sound in the brush. He clenched his fists, realizing he was unarmed. It was possible Rahmat's men had driven out to the field to finish the job. Maybe they hadn't wanted to do it in the village.

But when he saw the figure, he relaxed a bit. It was a boy wearing a topi, carrying a bucket.

Rob raised his hand. "G'day, mate! You know where the main road is?"

The boy stared at him. Then he said something in another language. It didn't sound like Thai.

"What'd ya say? Speak English. Or Thai I reckon."

The boy smiled. He said something in Thai, but Rob didn't recognize it.

"Say it again," Rob commanded.

"Farang," he said. "Farang. Farang."

"I know I'm a bloody farang, you wanker. Where's the main road?"

The boy shrugged, then laughed.

Rob shouted angrily, clenching his fist. "Where's the main road, you bloody Muslim wanker?!"

The boy pointed in the direction of the village and began to run toward a path perpendicular to the road. Rob cursed him again and ran after him.

The boy glanced back with terror as Rob caught him and tackled him to the ground. He heard a brief shriek, then pummeled the boy's head with his fists as he immobilized his arms with his knees. But the immobilization maneuver didn't matter; the boy was dead after several blows.

After the beating was over, Rob covered his face with his bloody hands and cried. Then he began convulsing. He stood up and looked down at the boy: his face was buried deep in the dirt, his head bashed in under his topi, drenched in blood. Rob scanned his torso, his ass, his legs. He was still shaking.

"Bloody fuck, bloody fucking wanker," he muttered, glancing around. He had chased the boy into a section of the path that was shaped like a circle before it narrowed again. Rob investigated the surrounding bush and noticed at one intersection a small stream ran parallel to the road.

Rob paced around again, grabbing and hitting his head. Then he decided to act. He dragged the boy's body into the bush and placed it inside the stream. It was just wide enough to fit his body. Then he dug up wet dirt mounds and piled them onto the body until he was covered.

Rob washed the dirt and blood as best he could from his face, hands, and body. He even took off his shirt and drenched it in the water.

"Stay away from the fucking water, they say. But they ain't me," he said. He went back to the path and used his foot to cover the footprints and the skid marks from the tackle and the beating, along with the blood and brain fragments.

"I can't believe this," Rob kept muttering as he headed back to the car. "I can't fucking believe this."

66

Niral woke up to the sound of roosters crowing. But he wasn't the first one awake. Kauntiaunti was already in the backyard, heating water in a pot on a pyre. Narendrakaka was not in his bed either.

"Niral," Kauntiaunti called through the open door, "Manu is waiting outside. He is talking to Lakshmanbhai. Take a bath with this hot water. I will prepare a nasta."

Kauntiaunti lifted the pot and poured the water into a bucket. Niral noticed it was steaming.

"I'm supposed to bathe with this?" Niral asked as he emerged from the house, stepping on oozing mud.

"You will mix it with the cold water. The kamwali will show you how."

"The who?"

"Kamwali means housekeeper. Our kamwali is Kamkaki. No relation. Do you remember her? She helped raise your mother. She worked for your mother's Motimasi."

"Yes, I do remember," Niral said. He recalled her as a skinny, short, cheery, dark-skinned woman who had given him a stuffed elephant when he had come to India as a boy. And he realized now that Kamkaki was probably the old woman he had seen peeking out of the house the night before.

"But today, Kamkaki needed to work at a farm," Kauntiaunti continued. "So Lata, her niece, is filling in for her."

Another woman, much younger and darker-skinned, dropped the laundry in the backyard of the next house and skipped over the border, a small irrigation canal made of cement. She looked like the woman who had been in the home with Kamkaki. "Lata works for Lakshmanbhai but fills in for us. She can show you how to work the faucet."

Lata smiled at Niral and picked up the bucket, resisting Niral's attempt to do so. "Please, Niralbhai, allow me," she said in Gujarati. She carried it toward the outhouse. Niral followed.

The outhouse was small but big enough for a faucet, large bucket, small bucket, and squat toilet. It was covered with spider webs in every corner, and it smelled like a dunghill.

Lata placed the bucket of steaming water on the ground next to the empty large bucket positioned under the faucet. Turning on the faucet, she filled the large bucket halfway with cold water. Then she demonstrated how he could use the small bucket, equipped with a handle, to fill the cold-water bucket with hot water. After a few pours, she threw the small bucket into the steaming bucket and stood up straight, smiling.

"If you need anything, let me know," she said, brushing against him as she left. Niral wondered if the brush was on purpose. He undressed and placed his clothes on the windowsill, away from a spider web. He wet himself with the cold water and used a small slither of soap he found on the windowsill to lather himself. Then he filled up the cold-water bucket with the hot water and bathed.

When he was done, he turned on the faucet, filled the cold-water bucket halfway, and repeated the procedure. As he was rinsing himself, he noticed a tiny slab of brown on the wall. He recalled wiping his shit on it many years before, when he had come as a boy, and it was still there.

Lata came in again. She saw him naked and smiled.

"Do you need anything else, Niralbhai?" she asked.

He noticed she had a fit, smooth body with a lump on her stomach. He could feel himself getting aroused, his penis engorging. Immediately, he tried to stop his impure thoughts, but he didn't consider covering his genitals.

"No thank you," he said reflexively.

But then he thought.

"How about shampoo?" he asked.

"What?" she replied in Gujarati.

He touched his hair and began rubbing his head.

Her eyes went wide, and she smiled in recognition. She performed namaste and left. A minute later, she returned with the shampoo and handed it to Niral.

"Let me know if you need anything else, Niralbhai," she stated. She hung around for a few seconds, then left. Niral washed his hair. Then he locked the door with a small latch and jerked off, releasing the sexual tension and hopefully finishing his arousal for Lata. He washed his hands and penis with the soap and water. Then, he used the toilet and cleaned himself with the same small bucket.

He heard someone trying to open the door. He unlocked it and stuck his head out. Lata was right outside. He asked for a towel. Lata nodded, left and, a minute later, returned with the towel.

He thanked her, took it, and dried himself with the door open as Lata stood by, but this time, already depleted of desire, he ignored her gaze. Then he took his clothes and marched back to the house, clad in the towel.

As he dressed in new underwear and another shirt, Narendrakaka entered.

"Niral, Kauntiaunti has made a good nasta of khaman, batata poha, and sev for you in the kitchen. Manu is waiting for you outside."

"Yes, Narendrakaka. I will dress and come out."

Narendrakaka watched him as he dressed.

"I see you do not wear your janoi," he noted.

"I don't know what happened to it. I don't care either."

"You don't care? Even now that you are helping The Brotherhood?"

Niral thought, then turned to Narendrakaka. "It is a sign of the old ways, Narendrakaka. The caste ways. We are beyond caste, aren't we?"

"We should be. But unfortunately, India is not, nor is this village. Anyway, Bhai's conception is equality without taking away duty. The janoi represents the duty of a Brahmin or a Kshatriya. Since you are both, you are doubly duty-bound."

"Am I? Maybe that's why shit weighs on me so much."

"Listen, Niral, I know you followed us last night. I know you saw what happened."

"Meetal's a crazy bitch. I didn't think she had it in her. Especially after sitting on a stump for a year and all."

"I was surprised too. But she commands much respect from the women in the Dubla village. Much more so than from the Brahmin women here, who take her for granted."

"How do the Dubla women know her?"

"Word travels fast when a Sadhu comes. Sometimes they bring her lotuses they have picked. They leave them at her feet while she prays."

"So they knew how to act last night? How'd she even sense it was happening from over there?"

"I don't know the answers to your questions, Niral. Maybe, like Arjuna's questions to Krishna, they are futile. But I do know one thing: that Manish will go to Prameshbhai this morning before Pranam does. He believes it will give him the upper hand. I told him this is a mistake, but he insists. I suspect, as usual, that the entire incident was set up by Prameshbhai himself. Pranam Rokhad goes around with his daughter, Madhuri, and Prameshbhai secretly approves of the union, but only in return for loyalty from Pranam.

"Prameshbhai instigated this incident because he wants land back that Manish bought from him. Manish has worked on this land for years and saved money to buy a patch to farm on his own. With real estate prices rising crazily, he couldn't get much with the amount he had, but Harshkaka helped him out. After holding out for months, Prameshbhai sold the land to him for a discount because he wanted to seem like the benevolent, wealthy Dubla, giving back to his own people. But now he will insist Manish pay the dowry to Pranam to settle their disagreement. He will loan Manish the money, with the land as collateral in case of non-payment, knowing that Manish will probably struggle in the future. Most likely he will get back the land, worth much more than the loan."

"Why do all this?" Niral asked.

"To win all ways, Niral. This is savvy politics. Divide and conquer. It has worked well for our adopted country, no?"

"So Lata, she was impregnated and beaten by Ravi?"

"No one is innocent in these affairs. Harshkaka is a good man, but Manish is greedy. I wouldn't be surprised if he and Lata fabricated the beating so they could file a domestic violence case against Ravi, knowing the judge would institute monthly maintenance fees from him. Who knows, maybe Manish ordered Lata to seduce Ravi when they attended school together with the intention of becoming pregnant. But in that case, Manish miscalculated. He didn't think Ravi would demand a dowry from a Dubla girl. Sure, the courts might not require it, but this is India all the same."

"If it's not legally required, why do they need to give a dowry?"

"This is India. A family will be shamed if they don't give something. They may not look guilty in the eyes of the law, but they do in the eyes of Hindu society. So both sides are miserable. Only Prameshbhai prospers. Yet again."

"So this misery will drive Islam into the village? The Dubla seem pretty set on Hinduism."

"That is because Meetal gives them hope. Without her...believe me, a few Dubla on the outskirts have already converted. And the converts are the worst. They have been preaching. They've beaten up hijra during their wedding or janoi visits. They are not afraid of hijra curses."

"And the Hindus do nothing?"

"They are spineless. They need true leadership, but greedy men like Prameshbhai won't deal with that headache. It is easier for him to continue exploiting his own people than to protect them."

"How about the Brahmins? They seem rich to me. With their big homes..."

"They are. Which is why they do not care about what is happening. They have become spoiled, like our fellow Americans."

When Niral finished dressing, he followed Narendrakaka into the kitchen and sat on the floor. Lata served his nasta on a small silver plate, along with a cup of spicy hot tea that was rich in masala and ginger, with only a slight batch of brown fat on top.

As Niral ate, Manu and Lakshmanbhai entered from outside.

"Niral, I will get your bags," Manu said. "Are they packed?"

"Yes," Niral answered. "Are we in a hurry?"

"Mr. Ghosh is waiting in the car," Manu responded, going to get the bags. "He has spent the time talking to Lakshmanbhai."

Lakshmanbhai greeted Niral with namaste. He was a rotund man who wore a mustache. "I am so happy to see you again, Niral. You probably do not remember me from your last visit."

"Actually, I do. In my memory, your house was huge. I remember coming down a large, spirally staircase."

Lakshmanbhai laughed. "Back then, I had an upper floor, which was basically an attic, but yes, there was a steep, rickety staircase leading up to it. Your boy's imagination must have furnished the rest. Now, however, I have four floors."

"Did you sell your land?"

"Yes, Niral. The prices kept going up, so we have all sold land to finance better lives. Also, jobs are plentiful now, especially in Navsari and Gandevi. Only the elderly hang around in the daytime now. Before, when the Dubla did all the work, many Brahmins would sit around all day, only tending to the farms when necessary. If you go back farther, before Indira Gandhi, the Dubla did not have their own villages even, and many lived in the wadi itself. And still some do live there today. You can visit your mother's cousins, who still live deep in the wadi, along with their own Dubla."

"Maybe another day," Niral replied.

"Yes, Niral, another day. Please do return. Before you leave, I want to thank you for what you are doing for The Brotherhood. I have been a loyal follower for many decades. I introduced your Motimasi and your mother to Bhen's philosophy."

"Have you tried to spread it among the Dubla too?"

"Niral, I used to be mayor of this village but no more. I don't have the influence I once had. I wish I did."

Manu re-entered the kitchen, carrying the luggage. Niral finished his tea quickly. As he was about to rise, Lata rushed over with a jug and washed Niral's hands by pouring water over them, into the dish. Then she gave him a napkin.

He wiped his hands, then stood and thanked her, touching her shoulder.

"Thank you, Lata," he said. "I hope things work out for you. I really do."

Lata did namaste. "Come again, Niralbhai," she said in Gujarati. "I hope to see you again."

After saying goodbye to Narendrakaka and Kauntiaunti, he waved to the few villagers who had come to see him off. In the past, he recalled the entire village would see someone off, certainly if they had come from America.

He gazed across the faliya. Prameshbhai was standing on his porch in front of a doorway, a towel over his shoulder, watching. Niral waved goodbye; Prameshbhai addressed him with namaste, then bobbled his head out of respect. Behind Prameshbhai, he saw a figure emerge from another doorway. He thought he would finally see Prameshbhai's daughter, Madhuri, but instead he recognized Manish, who waved at him.

"I guess I'll never see Prameshbhai's daughter," he muttered, returning the wave, then getting into the car. "She must be studying."

In the back, Mr. Ghosh was perusing some papers that were spread across the seat.

"Niralbhai," Mr. Ghosh announced without looking up. "We have much to discuss."

"Yes, we do," Niral responded.

"Prepare yourself for a long ride. We will stop briefly in Bharuch, but then we will head to Dwarka. So you will see Bhai, as per your request. I am planning to leave tomorrow morning because I need to be in Ahmedabad, and they say a major storm may hit in the afternoon, so I need to arrive before that."

"I'll prepare myself for whatever comes," Niral responded.

"Good, Niralbhai. Now let us talk."

67

As Rob pulled up near the warehouse in Bangkok, late at night, a torrential downpour began. He had driven a long time. The police had stopped him at checkpoints twice. Worried, weaponless, and shirtless, with scrapes on his face and blood stains on his pants, he had been prepared to drive off the road if the police had asked to check the trunk, knowing full well he might be shot down. But between that and sitting in a Thai prison awaiting death, he preferred the quicker option.

Yet the police didn't care. They were looking for illegal Burmese or Malaysian immigrants, not farang, and since his papers were in order (thankfully, Rahmat had given him back his passport and his work permit), he had been allowed through, not once, but twice.

Finally, things were bending his way again. Balance was the way of the universe, and if there was a God, certainly he owned a tipping scale.

Rob had retained his phone. Sveta hadn't texted him again, but her phone likely didn't work overseas. She should have reached North Carolina already. Oddly, Duncan hadn't texted him again for an update until that morning. Rob had texted back, telling him he had the merchandise and would inform Duncan upon his arrival at the warehouse.

He tried to wait out the storm, but he lost patience. He stepped out, ran to the warehouse, then unlocked and pulled up the overhead door. He ran back, drenched completely, and drove the car inside.

He got out, closed the overhead door, and locked it from the outside. Then he used another key to enter the regular door and locked that from the inside. He took the suitcase from the secret hiding place in the trunk. He checked that his own motorcycle was still parked in the garage, then he climbed the staircase to the fifth floor. He stepped through a door that led to an external staircase and waited in the dark.

The rain ceased. Rob continued to wait. Finally, a motorcycle pulled up and parked outside. It was Niral's motorcycle, but Niral wasn't driving it.

The driver ran up the stairs and hugged Rob fiercely. Rob held her tight, then they kissed for a minute.

"I'm so happy, Rob," Apsara said, holding his face, then noticing the scrapes. "But what happened to you?"

"Nothing. No worries."

"Sveta is gone?"

"Yeah, she's gone. For good."

"I am yours. And you are mine."

"That's right, sweetie."

"Is that it?" she asked, pointing to the briefcase on the floor.

"The rest of the moolah. You put the other one I gave you in a safe deposit, right?"

"Away. It is away."

"Better keep it safe. Pay off Mr. Hong in batches, so he doesn't get suspicious."

"I want to pay him now. I worry."

"Yeah. I worry too, sweetie, and I'm Aussie, I'm not supposed to worry. Anything change that makes you worry more?"

Apsara shrugged. "Duncan knows."

"What does he know?"

"That you lied about killing the tourist. And he says you are working for someone else."

"Fucking wanker. How'd he know?"

"Rahmat."

"Motherfucker. I knew that wanker set that up."

"I see the cuts on your face," Apsara said, touching them. "What did those Muslims do to you?"

Rob shook his head. "No worries, sweetie. Nothing I ain't been through before."

"Let's run away with this money, Rob. Go to another country."

"Not so easy. We gotta get you a visa. That'll take time. If Duncan knows, I might not have time."

"Then come with me to Isan. We live there."

Rob felt her cheek. "I never felt this way before about any girl. Bloody hell, I'm fucked, sweetie."

"We live in Isan."

"They'll track us there and kill us. Pay off Mr. Hong first."

"Then they will think something."

"Let 'em think. Long as you and your momma and your baby..."

"I don't think you'll be paying off Mr. Hong," a voice said from the staircase. Apsara turned around. Boy stood on the third step down, holding a gun.

"Khun Sumantapat will love to know about your debt to Mr. Hong,"

Boy said to Apsara. "And your affair with this farang. I'm sure it will make his day."

"So you work for Sumantapat?" Rob asked.

"I sure do. And I thought this lovely lady did too. Tip, Apsara, Duanphen, whatever your name is. Yes, he will be glad to know you work for Mr. Hong."

"What do you want?" Rob asked.

"That briefcase, to start," Boy answered. "It is money, yes?"

Apsara cursed at him in Thai.

"One more curse, and I will shoot you, princess," he said in Thai. "Give me the briefcase."

Rob picked it up. "Fine, if you'll go away and don't say nothing."

Boy smiled. "First the briefcase," he said.

Boy climbed the staircase. As he stepped onto the landing, Rob swung the briefcase with a backhand and hit Boy in the head. It didn't dislodge the gun from his grasp, but Boy was discombobulated enough for Rob to drop the briefcase and grab Boy's neck in an armlock from behind. A shot rang out. Rob choked him hard, but the gun remained in Boy's hand.

Apsara grabbed the briefcase and ran down the stairs. Boy poked Rob in his eyes with his fingers, but this motion also dislodged the gun from Boy's hand, and it fell on the floor.

Rob shouted in pain and covered his eyes, allowing Boy to wiggle out of the chokehold. Through watery eyes, Rob saw Boy lunge for the gun. Suddenly, it began raining again. Rob kicked Boy in the stomach as he reached the gun, and it slipped from his grasp.

Boy breathed hard, the wind knocked out of him. Rob took this opportunity to lift Boy up by the shoulders, his biceps under Boy's armpits. Boy kicked backwards, hitting Rob partially in the balls. Rob yelled, but didn't let go.

"You fucking farang," Boy screamed. "Get out of Thailand, you fucking farang."

"You like to fly, you Thai fuck?" Rob countered. "Come on, fly!"

He dragged Boy to the edge of the landing, twisted and threw him into the rain. He heard a long, vague scream before a dull thud.

"Wanker!" Rob exclaimed. "You wanna be Thai, die in Thailand, you sick fuck."

The rain suddenly stopped. Rob wiped the tears from his eyes. He saw Boy on the ground, his arms and legs stretched out, shaped like a swastika. But he didn't see Niral's motorcycle. It was gone.

Book Three

Part XIII

†

Bharuch, India; The Road, Gujarat, India; Near Lamba, India; Near Apex, North Carolina

---

68

The ride up to Dwarka was long. They stopped briefly in Bharuch, where, from the outside, Niral admired a marble temple dedicated to Bhen. A staircase with serpent arms representing Shiva led up to a majestic rendering of Bhen, her palm out with one hand and the Bhagavad Gita in the other. On the arch above the doorway a statue of Vishnu sitting on a lotus was perched. Niral's favorite god, Brahma, the creator, was absent.

"Bhai has built many temples since Bhen's death," Manu explained. "This was built recently."

"How is he getting the money?" Niral asked.

"Donations, of course," Manu answered. "He has eliminated corruption in the donation scheme and increased donors, expanding the organization."

"Well, it is a nice temple," Niral said, remembering Amrat's words about the potential deification of Bhen. "But Bhen is treated like a god."

"More like an avatar."

"Yes, an avatar, maybe."

"She is an avatar, Niralbhai. She has changed the world for the better, as many avatars have done: Rama, Krishna, Jesus, Gandhi."

"If you say so, Manu," Niral responded, noting to himself that they were all men. "Where is Brahma?"

"I believe he is depicted inside. I would show you, but it looks like Mr. Ghosh is returning, and we have a long trip ahead."

They drove up via a few highways and stopped twice to eat. At the first stop near Kheda, Niral and Mr. Ghosh ate inside a roadside restaurant. Manu declined to eat with them and left. Niral was offended.

"He's acting like he's low caste," Niral complained to Mr. Ghosh. "He's supposed to be equal."

"Equality is not a perfect algorithm, Niralbhai," Mr. Ghosh said. "He prefers either to eat alone, or gossip and chew paan with the truckers. That is his way, as a driver. You must understand, even if you eliminate caste, you will not eliminate social roles and their differentiations. And why would you want to? That would be totalitarianism."

"I do recall Bhen defended the caste system to some extent."

"It was a system meant to order society and create a ladder of responsibility. Certainly, it was corrupted, but there is something to be said for the vision. The German philosopher Nietzsche also admired this concept, I believe."

"I guess. But Manu is proud of his non-caste status. Why would he choose this?"

"Ask him, Niralbhai."

As they waited by the car while Mr. Ghosh used the toilet, Niral broached the subject. Manu laughed.

"Mr. Ghosh is my boss. We are not equals in that sense. Do you like to eat with your boss?"

Niral thought back to his days in the office with Stan and eating his meals with Lance.

"No, I never did. That's true."

At their next stop near Rajkot, Niral decided to eat with Manu. They went to the back of the non-vegetarian restaurant, while Mr. Ghosh ate a vegetarian thali inside, alone.

They sat on overturned buckets, conversing with a couple of truckers who were driving through. They rolled tobacco-filled paan and offered one to Niral.

"I've never had one with tobacco," Niral said. "Can you make one without it?"

Manu smiled. "Yes, we can make one without it."

Niral changed his mind and stuffed it in his mouth. He chewed it on one side of his mouth like the other men, tasting the sweet areca nut and the dry tobacco, spitting on the ground regularly.

"They've tried to stamp out paan here," Manu said. "The spit causes pollution, and the tobacco causes mouth cancer. But we still do it."

The other men smiled. Niral saw their teeth were brown and decayed. He swallowed the paan, keeping as much of the tobacco inside his cheek pocket as possible, then spitting that out onto the ground.

A dark woman wearing a purple sari laced with gold trimming came out twice, carrying a thali for each man. Each thali contained two shaks, two rotli, dal-bhat along with a mango pickle, and a steel glass of chaas. Afterwards, they also drank a cup of masala tea.

Manu told the two truckers that Niral was visiting The Brotherhood complex in Dwarka, but he didn't reveal Niral was from America. After they left the men, Manu told Niral the reason.

"You never know people's motivations or thoughts, Niralbhai, especially in India. You must be street smart here. If they knew your true origins, they might want to rob you."

A few hours later, as the sun began to set, they approached the sea. Niral asked if they had reached Dwarka.

"We are not stopping at Dwarka yet, Niralbhai," Mr. Ghosh told him from the backseat. "I want to show you another temple we have built. No one knows about it yet, but we are planning to unveil it on Diwali. This temple is up on a mountain and by the sea, about an hour from Dwarka."

69

Rob waited nervously for Duncan to arrive. The rain had started and stopped again. Rob was drenched, having dragged Boy's body into the garage. He had called Apsara, but she had not picked up her phone.

He heard a motorcycle approach. Rob had locked the overhead door. Duncan opened it and rode his motorcycle inside. Rob closed the door after him.

"So you got everything?" Duncan asked, seeing the car. "Went off without a hitch?"

He turned off the motorcycle. As he turned, he noticed Rob's red eyes. A gun was pointed at Duncan's back. "Not without a hitch, mate," Rob said. "You know about the hitch."

"What's this about?" Duncan asked incredulously, his eye twitching. "You seriously double-crossing me?"

"I want to talk, Duncan. About why you got me electrocuted by a goddamn Muslim."

"Electrocuted? What do you mean?"

"I'm not beating around the bush, mate. I know you've been spying on me. I could have forgiven that, but this shit is less forgivable."

Duncan raised his arms. He grinned in an embarrassed, conciliatory way.

"Look, Rob, I didn't know they would electrocute you, man. I just told them to get information, to make sure you weren't double-crossing me."

"I don't believe you, mate. But let's say I do. What do you know?"

Slowly, Duncan disembarked from the motorcycle and used the kickstand to stabilize it. "That tourist isn't dead. You're working for someone else. Pretty concerning shit."

"Yeah. Concerning shit. Reasons, Duncan. But nothing to do with you, mate."

"You're splitting your drug proceeds?"

"No. The other connection's got nothing to do with the drugs. That's our game, but it's gonna be an even game from now on."

"If you didn't kill the tourist, why his wife? Or was that someone else?"

"No worries, mate. Trust me, Bob is far away. He ain't going to rat."

"Maybe not, but the police are investigating Thanat's murder based on something he said. Looks like we've avoided trouble on this lady's murder though. They arrested a Thai man."

"Told you it wasn't me."

"Actually, you told me it was you."

"Forget that. Let's talk business."

"You want it even, is that right? This is Thailand, there's a structure."

"I'm not a Dragon, mate. And neither of us are Thai. I found Pasat for you; I got you this lead. And I'm not giving you a choice. I'll do the distribution. Half and half is workable, ya?"

Duncan shrugged. "Okay, I guess that's workable. How about Niral, Apsara? We cut them out?"

"Employees, not partners."

"Fine," Duncan said, lowering his arms. "What now?"

"Now we get rid of this Sumantapat soldier I just whacked."

"What Sumantapat soldier?"

Rob smiled. He led Duncan around the car. Duncan saw Boy laying on the floor, his arms outstretched.

"Fuck. What happened?"

"Seems he had a lead."

"Here? Shit!" Duncan shook his head, his eye twitching rapidly again. "I wonder what else Sumantapat knows. We'll get buried from both sides if there's a war. We need Apsara to get info."

Rob swallowed. "Don't do nothing, mate. I'll talk to her."

Duncan looked up at him. "Why?"

"Trust me, mate. I know what to say."

70

At Raleigh-Durham International Airport, Bob and Sveta dragged their bags through the "Nothing to Declare" customs lane and into the terminal opening. While Sveta was still complaining about Bob's snoring on the plane, Bob tried to concentrate on the people waiting for new arrivals. He saw a sign saying "Franklin and Yuliya," corresponding to their new identities. The man holding it was a tall Indian with a goatee, who wore a black suit and a tie.

Bob raised his hand. The Indian man held up his hand sternly, his chin high.

"Did Vishal send you?" Bob asked as he approached.

"No, my cousin Ashok. You know him, right?"

Bob swallowed. "Do you know Vishal?"

The man smirked. "You mean the archcriminal cousin? Don't know him, but I wish I did!"

"What's your name, young man?"

"Hemraj. Pleased to meet you," he said, shaking Bob's hand. "And very pleased to meet you," Hemraj said to Sveta, staring into her eyes as he kissed her hand.

Sveta smiled, staring at him directly.

"That's my new wife, Hemraj," Bob told him.

"You sure know how to pick 'em, bro," he replied, slapping Bob on the back, then abruptly turning. "Let's ride."

Hemraj didn't help with the bags, just led the way to the pickup lane. He called someone on his cell. A Mercedes appeared in a few minutes, chauffeured by a short Indian man who got out and helped put the bags in the trunk.

Bob and Sveta rode in the back, Hemraj in front.

"So how do you know my cousin?" Hemraj asked, turning.

"He didn't tell you?" Bob responded.

"Nope. Just told me you needed a lift up to the house."

"So you live with him?"

"Yeah, it's a big house. My mom tells me to get married and move out, but I don't wanna leave my family. See, my mom's sick. And I've got a special relationship with my girl."

"What's your special relationship?"

"We're tight, but we do our own thing. Some Desi girl would be ordering my ass around, but my girl's white. She's chill. And she's got class."

"Plenty of white women ordered me around," Bob said. Sveta rolled her eyes.

"You gotta pick 'em, I guess," Hemraj replied. "Desi girls in these parts, they're real stuck up. Their dads own motels, and they think they're in the *Social Register* or something. But my girl actually is! Her dad's a pharmaceutical giant. She's never worked a day in her life. Sits on boards, does philanthropy, shit like that. Knows how to give back."

"I know a thing or two about that," Bob said, nodding. "But why not marry her? You'll get an inheritance. Your kids..."

"Her dad can tell I'm not in it for her money. And I'm not. I love Ashley to death, but I'm down here, and she's up in New York mostly. She comes back sometimes. You say you've been on boards?"

"I know your cousin from way back. Let's just say that."

Bob put his hand on Sveta's, but she took it away.

"I love Indian culture," she said to Hemraj. "I see all the Indian movies back in Russia. Akshay Kumar, Shah Rukh Khan..."

"I'm American, baby. I don't watch that Bollywood shit. Maybe you can talk to my dad."

Sveta frowned and gazed out the window.

71

From the highway, Niral, Manu, and Mr. Ghosh took a right into a vine-strewn path that ended at a gate and was not visible from the road. Niral didn't see any signage, but he noticed a path curving up the mountain past the gate. Next to the gate was a metal detector and detection machine with conveyor belt manned by a seated guard who was drinking tea. Two other guards stood by the gate, holding rifles.

"The foot of the mountain, Niral," Mr. Ghosh explained. "Any visitor must be thoroughly screened before entering. All vehicles will be screened as well, and the only ones allowed up are cleared vehicles like ours."

They exited the car. Each held their arms up and were patted by the armed guards. Then the guards searched the car, including the trunk.

"So the festival will take place here?" Niral asked Mr. Ghosh while waiting by the metal detector.

"Yes, the main part," Mr. Ghosh replied. "But tell your friends it will be at the Dwarka complex so we can easily apprehend them."

"Sounds good," Niral said carefully. "Is there one temple here or many?"

"One temple with four levels. It is magnificent. The pilgrims will stay at the complex overnight, but in the morning, they will be transported here. They will not be told beforehand. They will be screened thoroughly for any weapons, contraband, etc., at both locations. Then they will have to climb the mountain up the path. It is meant to approximate the climb toward moksha and enlightenment. You will see."

Bags from the trunk were placed on the conveyor belt and screened. Then the three men were required to pass through the metal detector. Beforehand, Niral emptied his pockets into a tray. He took out the pouch of diamonds, which he recalled he had never examined. He placed them in the tray too, and it entered the detection machine.

"Later," he said to himself, smiling. He passed through the metal detector. The tray was on the other side, and he placed the items in his pocket again. But he didn't see the pouch of diamonds. He began to panic.

"Where are my diamonds?" he asked.

The guard sitting behind the machine held up the pouch.

"Not allowed," he said in Gujarati.

Niral turned to Mr. Ghosh. "Why? I need them with me. I can't lose them."

"I'll call Bhavesh, the head of security," Mr. Ghosh replied.

While Mr. Ghosh called, Niral sat in the car with Manu.

"Looks like you saved the diamonds yourself this time," Manu said.

"Who knows what I saved. I haven't even examined them. They could be glass for all I know."

"You never know with Muslims."

"Right," Niral said quickly. "Look, is this place the only surprise I'm getting today?"

"Only Mr. Ghosh knows what surprises he will spring."

"Is Bhai up there?"

"I believe Bhai is at the Dwarka complex. But we will head there later."

"We'll catch the Muslims this way," Niral said, swallowing. "I'll tell them it's the other complex."

"Yes," Manu confirmed. "It will be easy to eliminate the threat that way."

Mr. Ghosh slipped inside the back seat and closed the door. He held out the pouch to Niral.

"Exceptions are made only for you, Niralbhai," Mr. Ghosh said as the gate slid open. "Let us proceed."

72

The Mercedes pulled inside a gated complex, up a path, and around an active fountain mounted with a statue of Bhen holding out her palm. The house was as large as Hemraj had mentioned, three floors and ten windows spread across the length of it, the windows barred with silver columns centered by Om signs. The edifice was white marble.

"You have large family?" Sveta asked. "Who lives here? Hookers?"

Hemraj laughed. "Guess we're all hookers, right? No, I've got my dad, mom, two uncles, my sister, my brother, me, and Ashok. My older cousins are married and live separate."

"You have big family," she said.

"Yup, but not always a happy one. Trust Ashok will tell you about that at some point."

"Well, why are you telling us?" Bob asked he stepped out of the car. "I mean, are you proud of your problems?"

Hemraj stepped out and faced Bob. "Ashok didn't tell me much about you, but said you'd be a trusted asset. Don't know what that means exactly, but I imagine you'll have to know this shit anyway, eventually."

Hemraj said his uncle would get the bags. When Hemraj pointed toward the chauffeur, Bob was temporarily confused, then realized the uncle and chauffeur were one and the same.

They approached the big doors of the house. It reminded Bob of his old house in Forest Hills with its protective lions and marble colonnade. The Witness Protection Program had given him a run-down, one-story home in El Paso. Now he felt, in some way, like he was returning home.

Hemraj rang the bell. A minute later, a maid answered. She was Hispanic, in her twenties, and was dressed in an apron.

Bob could see Sveta was relaxing more, blown away by this extravagance.

The maid smiled at Hemraj and waved them inside. Immediately, they heard moans coming from a side room through a closed door.

"Don't mind that," Hemraj said. "It's my mom. She ails sometimes."

An older man, dressed in a sweater, descended a twirling staircase. The staircase reminded Macaday again of his former home. The chandelier was higher in this house, however, and the staircase wider and taller.

The man hobbled a bit, but he made it down and reached out his hand to Bob.

"Mr. Stewart," he said. "Ashok has told me much about you."

"And what is your name?" Bob asked.

"I am Sunil, Ashok's uncle. Hemraj's father."

"Very nice to meet you too," Bob said, shaking his hand. Then Sunil greeted Sveta with namaste. She mimicked him back and nodded.

"I love Indian culture," she said.

Sunil smiled. "I am so glad. Come. Ashok is waiting for you upstairs."

A young woman glided down the stairs, dressed in a tight black dress that accentuated a bony butt. She was carrying a martini glass.

"Ashok says only Franklin should come up," she told Sunil. "I'll get his wife a cocktail."

"I'm Dharini," she told Sveta, taking her by the elbow. "What do you like to drink?"

"I don't know," Sveta replied, giggling in excitement and nervousness. "Maybe martini."

"Come along to the bar, sweet pea," Dharini said. "There's tons of excitement in there."

Hemraj took Bob upstairs, but stopped at the top of the staircase and pointed to a door at the far end of the corridor.

"He's inside. I'll leave you alone."

Bob passed six other rooms and two bathrooms. When he knocked on the last door, it slid open a bit, and he let himself inside.

The room was large and spacious. A bed was on the right, the headboard perpendicular to Bob, while to the left, a large mirror with a gold frame and lightbulbs glistened on a dresser. The entire room was white—the blankets, bedsheets, carpet, even the curtains that hid the sunlight and reflected back the bright white lights of various chandeliers.

At the foot of the bed, a man sat, wearing a black tuxedo and holding a cane. His right hand twitched furiously and made the cane vibrate.

He looked up at Bob. Bob didn't recognize his face. It was an odd face, where the eyes were set unevenly and the mouth drooped, yet the bone structure held. As the man stood, Bob realized he was tall enough, and his body frame skinny enough (though he now sported a belly) to be Vishal Patel.

"I can't believe it," Bob said, not moving. "It's like seeing a ghost."

"Same to you, Bob," Vishal said, in a voice deeper than before and holding out his left hand. "Nice to see you again."

73

They drove up to a parking lot below a large rectangular base of sandstone carved with swastikas and Om signs.

"The pilgrims will have to walk this length," Mr. Ghosh said. "It is not far, but it is a bit steep. Guards will need to line the path to make sure no one deviates. They will arrive from many of our temples across India to help. There will be hundreds of them. They have been screened for total loyalty."

"Won't you need guards inside the temple too?" Niral asked.

"Yes, but the bigger challenge is outside, particularly on each landing. You see, the pilgrims will be stopped on the landing and perhaps, for some unlucky ones, on this level below. A screen will show these pilgrims what is going on inside the temple. Only a select few will be let inside. Some will be top Big Brothers, heads of various parts of the organization. The rest will enter by lottery, and a different batch will go inside each floor."

"How will the lottery work?"

"They will pick numbers at the Dwarka complex before they leave. Based on this, they will gather in groups to be taken by bus to this venue. They will climb up by group, and the first group will be allowed inside the temple. Then, as they are leaving, the other three groups will proceed before the first group, leaving them in the back. I'm afraid there will be too many pilgrims to accommodate everybody into a group, but I hope the rest of the pilgrims will consider the climb worth it."

"So Bhai will officiate at each temple?"

"No. He wanted to, but Mr. Shah and Bhavesh, our security officers, changed his mind. Now the other ceremonies will be officiated by Big Brothers from around the world. The plan is Sureshbhai from the US in North America, Mukeshbhai from Singapore in Asia, and me, but that could change. Bhai will only be officiating the ceremony at the top temple, unless he changes his mind again."

They climbed a slope up to the landing. The landing, shaped like a square, was covered with sand. A fountain in the middle of it was made from sandstone. Past the fountain was a simple square construction where, arched on top of the doorway, was a statue of Brahma. He was four-headed and seated on a lotus, holding the Vedas, rosary beads, ladle, and water utensil. A large screen stood to the right of the building.

"This is the level of Kama, and to an extent, Brahmacharya, which, while it emphasizes chastity along with learning in the first stage of life, is less relevant today than before," Mr. Ghosh explained. "Brahma is depicted less often in our scriptures than any other god but is more associated with Kama."

"I used to worship him," Niral explained. "After I returned home from Brooklyn. He was the creator. I thought I was a creator."

"Yes, Brahma is the creator of the universe," Mr. Ghosh affirmed. "The birth of all things, including desire."

Within the temple, on its walls, Niral saw a portrait of Saraswati playing her veena. He also passed engraved scenes of Krishna flirting with gopis, of Shiva dancing, and of his sons, Ganesh and Kartikeya, playing in front of their mother, Parvati.

"I thought this temple was dedicated to Brahma," Niral said. "Krishna is an avatar of Vishnu."

"Yes, but its focus on Kama lead us to include scenes of revelry, including the playful Krishna."

"What about Shiva? He is the god of destruction."

"Yes. But here Shiva's role as god of dance and sexuality is given prominence. Too much Kama, especially addiction to it, leads to the individual's destruction, doesn't it? Sometimes even society's."

Niral nodded but didn't respond.

"Only part of Shiva's identity is depicted on this floor. Shiva is shown as a householder and a yogi at times. His householder status is emphasized on the next level, which is dedicated to Artha and Grihastha."

Niral proceeded along a brown rug to an elevated stage. A large picture of Bhen was mounted on the back wall. Below that, on the stage itself, were smaller statues of Brahma and Saraswati, anointed with garlands and chandlos. A box meant for yagna, a microphone, and a stand with a copy of the Bhagavad Gita rounded out the highlights.

Next to the stage was a small passageway leading to a back area. A few rooms were on the side, the doors closed. Closer to the main entrance, a staircase led down to a basement.

"Will those be closed off?" Niral asked.

"Guards will cordon off those areas, and ropes will block them just in case." Mr. Ghosh confirmed. "The speaker will wait to come on through the back way, so while guards will be stationed, we probably won't have a rope there. Temple maintainers, about three to four per floor, are present, plus ample security. Bhavesh, on the top floor, will explain the security set up. Come."

74

This time, they reversed their positions: Bob sat on the bed while Vishal stood in front of him, holding the cane in his left hand now, his right hand shaking inside a besom pocket.

"I was in the Caribbean this whole time, Bob, in different places. First, I went to the Caymans, where I'd stashed the money, but I thought I'd be too conspicuous there, so I fled to Grenada. I befriended some med school students, but a bunch were Indian-Americans, so I got nervous and decided to leave again. I moved to Trinidad, where it was easier to fade into the Indian population because they are ignorant and clannish and don't mix with the other races. I grew a beard, colored my hair white, gained some weight. But I always felt my face could betray me. I heard of successful facial transplant surgeries in the Caymans, so I went back and had the procedure."

"You look hideous, Vishal. But in a good way. If I hadn't expected you, I wouldn't have known it was you. The face is awkwardly set, but I wouldn't necessarily question its authenticity."

"I would. But that's the deal. I needed to make sure I wasn't caught, so I took the chance. There are some side effects. I take this medication to keep down inflammation from the surgery, and that's why my hand shakes. I'm not sure I still need to take it—it's been a while—but I don't want the face to blow up."

"Why come back to America?"

"To settle business, Bob. I got sick of the Caribbean, but more importantly, I got sick of not being in the game."

"What game are you in now, Vishal?"

"Every game, Bob. More than before."

"Do your relatives know you're you?"

"No. They think I'm Ashok. He was a distant cousin of ours who lived in Trinidad. No one had heard from him in a while, and no one had ever met him outside of Facebook. We knew he had mental problems, and his parents had died a while back. I made inquiries about him when I got there. He was a hermit who lived on the edge of a swamp.

"I was hesitant to search for someone who could identify me, but I was a little sick of being so detached from my former life. It's possible Ashok wouldn't have noticed me at all, and that I could have made small talk with him without acknowledging my identity, but somehow I wanted him to know me and ask me back as a cousin and family member, to have that real blood connection I didn't have with any of the other Indians in Trinidad. And that's why, despite the risk of him telling someone, anyone, about my existence, I decided to seek him out.

"I rented a boat and rowed over alligator-filled slush, making my way to the small, isolated hut. I disembarked and called out his name. As I entered the hut, I found his body decomposing. He had been dead many days, but I guess no one interacted with him enough to check up. Looked like there had been a storm and a portion of the hut had collapsed and hit him in the head.

"So I buried him. I cleaned and rebuilt the hut. I started living there. I liked the isolation it offered, plus I was able to go to the Indian village when I wanted. Sitting there, I would stare at this picture of him with his mom and dad. Our facial structures were similar, and I remember he was about my height.

"That's when I got the idea of a facial transplant. I contacted a doctor in the Caymans, and we made a pact. An Indian guy had died in a car accident in Guyana. His face was intact and preserved, and he looked similar to Ashok. The body had been signed away for organ donation, but the doctor was able to get it from corrupt government officials, and the surgery planted that man's face onto mine. I had to be looked after for complications for many months, but the drugs have worked since. When I got here, I told my cousins I had been in a fire and my face was scarred, so I had replacement surgery.

"I learned enough about family history to make small talk with Sunil and his brothers, Rujul and Ronak, who have recollections of Ashok and his parents. I guess I was convincing, because they forgot the rumors about Ashok's mental problems and isolationist nature. I explained it away by saying I'd been busy. See, Ashok had been well-respected once, on his way to becoming a medical doctor, but his parents' deaths had collapsed his will. And believe me, my 'coming back' has had a major impact for the better on this family, which is why they revere me. I've brought harmony, prestige, money, and The Brotherhood into their lives, among other things."

"How'd you get back in the country, Vishal? By using Ashok's passport?"

"I could have done that, but I didn't want trouble at immigration, with my face and all, especially given worries about terrorism. So I hopped on a boat with a bunch of Chinese and Cuban illegals. We got off in Mexico and, with the help of some very professional agents, crossed the border into Texas. The Cubans were going to Florida, and the Chinese were going up to New York. Funny since I bought a house in Florida for my dad way back that the government seized, and I wanted to revisit it. But that wasn't the way I should have gone, so I hopped a ride with the Chinese, and I got off in North Carolina. Ended up making good contacts that way."

"But now you can't get out, unless you go by boat again."

"Oh contraire...just like my man Rob gave you fake passports, I was able to fix a fake passport here. I know a guy who stole a government printing machine and has this high-level service in Virginia. Plus, someone at the social security office had to be bribed. Cost me a lot of money and time, but now Ashok Patel is a US citizen, on paper, with a social and everything."

"So we're both missing men who are still alive."

"Yup, buddy, we are."

"But with my new identity, how do I collect insurance from Linda's death?"

"You're still alive on paper. We haven't killed you. We'll submit the death certificate to your insurance company and reroute the payment to a P.O. Box here. Then you can cash the check with your old ID. You do have that?"

"Yeah, stuffed it in my suitcase before I went through security."

"Good. Then that won't be a problem. You lost the Feds, right?"

"The Marshals. Yes. I told them we were heading to Thailand, and we didn't need any more protection. That should be that."

"They might get suspicious about the insurance if they find out. Let's hope they don't. I'm sorry about Linda."

"Yeah, well, she had to go eventually. I just helped her along. She was miserable anyway."

"Sure. You got some sweeter pussy instead."

Bob's hands were shaking. He got up and began to pace. Vishal limped over to the bed and sat.

"What happened to you?" Bob asked, deflecting the topic away from Linda. "With the limping and the cane. It's like you really were in an accident. Was it on the boat?"

Vishal shrugged. "Well I was. Courtesy of our mutual friend Niral Solanke. But not on the boat. Before I fled New York."

"What did he do?"

"He took something precious from me. But actually, it was the best thing that happened. Now I don't lust after women. I don't have to. That takes pressure away."

"Damn. He cut it off?"

"One shot in the Manhasset Bay. I thought I was a goner. I think I lost consciousness. I was underneath the water, then suddenly God must have given me consciousness again because I found myself drowning. I shot out of the water. I remember coughing and spitting. I didn't see anyone around. I collapsed on the beach, holding my crotch, praying the blood would stop squirting. It seemed like I lay there forever. Next person I saw was Juan's mother. She was my live-in maid, if you remember. She must have woken up when she heard the shot. She took off my clothes, wrapped me up in a blanket and tied my shirt around my wound. Then Juan came back with his cousin, who was a surgeon. Saved my life."

"I'm sorry Juan died. Why Tragliani?"

"Unfinished business. But it's still unfinished. That's why I need you."

"Listen, Vishal, I'm sorry about testifying against you. I had no choice. They wouldn't let me walk without it, and I figured you were far away or dead..."

"You still owe me for that. Plus this."

"Going near the Traglianis again isn't what I had in mind."

"Well, you better get used to doing what I tell you. Because you owe me for a lot. Now it could go another way, Bob..."

Bob put up his hands. "I didn't mean I wouldn't, Vishal. But why do you need me?"

"Alicia Tragliani's network is bothering my interests there, and she doesn't even know it. But don't worry, you won't need to go against the Traglianis. For now, I need you to talk to Hemraj's girlfriend, Ashley Simmons."

"Talk to her about what?"

"She's on a board that's looking to give construction rights for my property in LIC to our old friend Brendan Carty. Remember him? Back from disgrace in Montana, now rejuvenated as stellar businessman and patron saint of foundations. Took back Ledacorp, too."

"Wow. I didn't know Brendan was back in the game. But if he knew I..."

"We'll do it smoothly, Bob. It's a plan."

"Back up to New York?"

"After you get settled in. Your new wife is going with you."

"She doesn't even like me."

"She will. She'll have to."

"Let me ask you something, Vishal," Bob said after a pause. "If Niral shot you, why not have Rob take him out? And how do you even know Rob? Did I just get lucky running into him after he killed those gem scammers, telling him how ironic it would be to die after being in witness protection?"

"Everything works out, Bob. Somehow, in this universe, it does. Rob did me a favor a while back. He knew Niral too. So now he does the favor of watching Niral for me."

"Why?"

"Because I need Niral alive. He's family. He's important to me. And so are you."

75

Niral, Manu, and Mr. Ghosh left the first building through the front doors and, leaving the car behind, climbed a steep gravel path up toward the second level.

"We are going the way of the pilgrims," Mr. Ghosh explained, "but for your information, there is an internal road we can travel up by car and an elevator in the back one can take up to the different levels. During the event, those routes will be available only to maintenance and security personnel."

As they climbed, Niral noticed the second level's base was made of black granite. Again, Om signs and swastikas were carved into the stone. On the landing, the ground was covered with loose gravel that might have sparkled, but with the sun going down, the shine was less pronounced, providing a soothing effect. In the middle was a large lingam. Water sprung from its tip and cascaded down into a bowl underneath. The lingam was flanked by statues of Parvati and Kartikeya, holding out their palms. Parvati's breasts were large and pronounced, her waist tight. Kartikeya was muscular and held a spear.

To the right of the temple, Niral saw a large screen.

The temple itself was rectangular and constructed with black granite. Shrubs and greenery decorated its top. A short staircase led up to large doors covered with decorations of serpents, more Om signs, and swastikas. The staircase railings were also serpents, punctuated by serpents' heads, their tongues sticking out as devotees approached. Between the staircase and doors were statues of Shiva and Ganesh holding up their palms, made from Ashford black marble.

Within the temple, on its black granite walls, were engraved pictures of Shiva, Parvati, Ganesh, and Kartikeya in their household. A black rug led up to a stage similar to the first temple, with its large picture of Bhen, a yagna box, microphone, and Gita, but in place of statues of gods, there were garlanded and chandloed lingams. The side rooms and basement were also identical, but the interior of the temple was wider.

"The outside looks like it's set up more for Kama than Artha," Niral said. "But the inside appears true to the intention."

"The lingam is mistakenly considered to be a phallic symbol, Niral-bhai," Mr. Ghosh said. "But the presentation outside is deliberately ambiguous. It is meant to show the interplay of Kama and Artha, particularly the first leading into the other. As well, in the ancient tradition, sexual desire only appears in the householder stage of life, so that is represented here. Remember that Parvati is the goddess of fertility, love, and devotion."

"I see," Niral said, nodding.

"Come," Mr. Ghosh said, taking Niral's arm. "Let us go to the next temple."

76

Bob descended the stairs to the first floor of the home. He had showered and changed into a peach shirt and white pants after Rosa, the maid, had shown him his new room. He was tired from the flight but knew he should talk to Sveta before he went to bed. Vishal had told him they were flying out with Hemraj the next morning.

Sveta was inside a large lounge, draped thoroughly in red velvet, drinking a martini with Dharini. They sat on a couch next to a fancy bar that included beers on tap and liquors laid out on the counter. Both women were drunk.

Bob could see the fluff under Sveta's eyes as he walked in. He knew she was tired too. On the plane, they had both slept on and off, distracted by little things.

"Sveta, my darling, should I show you our room?" Bob asked. "We should go to sleep. We have work to do tomorrow."

Sveta looked at him like she was seeing him for the first time. "Don't worry about me, baby," she said, waving her hand, "I drink with my girlfriend here."

"Your wife says she hasn't had a girlfriend in a while," Dharini added, laughing. "All the girls in Thailand were bitches."

"I'm surprised by that," Bob responded, towering over her, his hands on his hips. "I always thought they were friendly."

"Not when you compete with them, baby," Sveta said. "The ones with the braces were the worst."

"I liked the ones with the braces, darling," Bob said.

Sveta sneered at him. "Go away, old man," she said, pushing him in the stomach. "Why don't you go rape some teenagers?"

She started to laugh. Bob grabbed her arm and lifted her up. Her glass fell onto the carpet. The drink spilled out, but the glass didn't break.

"What is your problem?" Sveta asked.

Bob grabbed her shoulders and pulled her body in front of him.

"Look, my darling, you better get your act together," he stated in a measured tone. "We need to sleep now. We have work tomorrow."

Dharini stopped smiling, placed her palm over her drink, and paid attention to the proceedings.

"What work?" Sveta asked. "Rob promised I will be free. Free like a bird!"

"No one's free in this world, darling. We've all got duties, even when we think we don't."

"Yes? Yes? They beat me bad, old man. They beat me so bad..."

"Tell me about it in our room." Bob said, taking her firmly by the arm and dragging her toward the door.

As he did, he turned to Dharini. "I'm sorry, she'll have to catch up with you later."

Dharini shrugged. "Whatever," she said, watching them intently.

Bob pulled Sveta up the staircase as she repeated "They beat me bad! They beat me bad!" with Sunil watching critically from the door of Hemraj's mother's room. Bob could hear Hemraj's mother wailing as he pulled Sveta into their room, threw her on the bed, and closed the door.

"Listen, Sveta, you don't have to like me," he roared. "But if you want to stay here, you'll have to do what we say."

"I want to call Rob," Sveta said, sinking to the floor, her back to the bed. "I don't like it here. It's like the other places."

"What other places? What are you talking about?"

"In Australia. In Pattaya. I was slave. Men will come and rape me now."

She climbed back onto the bed. She lay back and opened her legs. "I will get ready so they don't bruise my thighs."

"Damn," Bob said under his breath. "No, you..."

He pulled her up by her shoulders as she began to remove her panties from under her skirt.

"No rape, Sveta," he said, shaking her. "Unless you consider me a rapist."

She swallowed and looked at him straight on now. She smiled.

"You have a wife before, sir?" she asked. She released her panties and began to unbutton his pants. He looked uncomfortable.

"Of course," he answered. "I'm not young."

"Divorced?"

"She had an unfortunate accident."

"Did you love her?"

Bob shrugged. "Once."

Sveta pulled down his pants and boxers, exposing his penis, which steadily rose.

"Mmm," Sveta said, tapping the tip. "A banana cock. I like."

77

They climbed up a pathway of blue limestone tiles to the next landing, which had a square base also made of blue limestone. The landing was, again, entirely laid by blue limestone tiles. A huge statue of Vishnu stood in the middle of the square, holding a lotus flower, conch, sudarshana chakra, and, unlike in many depictions, a large spear.

The building, flanked by a large screen, was blue too, one floor, and shaped like a trapezoid. Before the entrance was a large statue of Rama, holding a bow and arrow in one hand, palm out in another.

"Dharma!" Mr. Ghosh shouted suddenly. "Vishnu is the greatest symbol of this, as he is the preserver of earth and the source of avatars who descend when the world is in trouble."

The walls within the temple were engraved with scenes from the Ramayana featuring Rama, Lakshmana, Sita and Hanuman. A blue rug led to the typical stage, except statues of Hanuman, Sita, and Lakshmi blessed the visitors. Their skin was beige, not blue, contrasting the color scheme. The rest of the layout was similar too, except that the roof, through the trapezoidal arch, allowed sunlight into the temple through blue glass, although Niral had arrived too late in the day to see the full effect.

"When the building is fully lit, it inspires worshippers like no other except for the final floor," Mr. Ghosh said.

"These seem like different temples to me," Niral said. "Why do you call them floors?"

"Niralbhai, we like to think of it as one experience. A worshipper who comes to this temple should climb and see all levels to get the full effect. That is why we call it one temple."

Niral turned to Manu, who had been silent this entire time.

"Manu, have you been here before?" he asked.

"My first time, Niralbhai," Manu replied.

"What do you think of it?"

"It is sublime. Like climbing to Atman."

"Yes," Niral said, nodding. "Like climbing to God. Mr. Ghosh, who will conduct the ceremonies at each temple and how?"

"I will let Bhavesh explain that to you, Niralbhai. Let us ascend to the final level. I think you will be impressed."

78

Sveta had her head on Bob's chest as they lay in bed together after they had made love. Sveta had downed a few glasses of water to help sober herself up. She was crying a bit, though she had not explained why.

"Rape? Really?" Bob asked, remembering what she had said earlier. "I didn't know."

"Why would you know, baby? But you can assume for me, no?"

"Who raped you?"

"A bad man named Sasha. I will tell you story from beginning, baby, if you like it. I lived in small town in Siberia. At university, to take my mind off my studies, I shoot heroin, and I become addicted. It is common in Russia.

"I borrow money from a gang for drugs because I did not want to burden my family. I was supposed to take care of them, baby. My brother, Kolya, he had rare condition, and he depend on me. I paid for hospital and drugs from a part-time job I have. But then he died. I think the doctors were very bad, and they did not treat him right. I become sad, and I want to get out of Russia.

"I meet my ex-boyfriend one day. He worked for gang. He tried to sell me heroin again, but I say no. We talk and I tell him I want to leave Russia. He say I can pay off debt by working in another country. I make more that way and send it back to them, and later to my mother. He says he has contacts that can take me to Australia.

"One day I run away. I do not tell my mother. She did not know about my debt. She was still sad about Kolya, but she had job, and without hospital bills, I think she can support herself until I send money. My father is gone, living in St. Petersburg. So I take the plane to Australia. My ex-boyfriend, he gets me visitor visa and says his friend Sasha will get me job and lawyer for permanent status. I think he care about me. I am very naive.

"I meet Sasha at the airport in Melbourne and he drive me to building at edge of town. He is very nice, so I do not suspect anything. But when I get to building and see it is in deserted area, I become nervous. He ask me to come to building, but I say no. He smile and take me by the arm. When I get to the building, I turn around and try to run, but a group of men come out and grab me. I scream and scream but they drag me inside. I remember Sasha is laughing. Inside, they throw me onto bed. They beat me and they laugh. One by one, they rape me.

"Baby, I never knew such evil people before that. Of course, I was not with best people in Russia, but even they do not enjoy cruelty and suffering. And it only become worse."

"Wow," Bob said. "What happened after that?"

"They took my passport and my money. Every day I have to service many men. Sometimes fifty. Some were nice, but most were bad. They were from all over the world, not just Australia."

"You were a sex slave."

"Yes. I was in prison with other girls. They were from Russia, Eastern Europe, and Central Asia. We were given soup, porridge, things like that to eat. We had to go to the bathroom in front of each other. If a girl refused to do something, they beat her up and raped her. One day, a girl tried to run away through high window. They caught her and slit her throat in front of us. We watched her die.

"Strange, but this did not scare me. It make me think of escape more. I was thinking of suicide and how to do it, but if I try to escape and they catch me, I will die anyway. Every day I dream of escaping. I think of Kolya in heaven, my mother behind her kitchen, cooking borsht. And yet, I could not go home. I will be too ashamed to face my mother. So I really had no idea where to escape if I make it. Maybe America. That became my dream, but even there, I know I can end up same way.

"One day I put plan into action. Why not. I run away through high window. I get to highway but before I get driver, they catch me. I think they will kill me, but maybe they think I am too valuable. And that is when I meet Rob. He is not like the others."

"How was he not like the others?"

"He was not cruel. He apologized."

"Apologized for what?"

She paused and wiped away a tear. "For raping me."

"Rob raped you?" Bob asked, looking at her neutrally. "I guess it's not surprising."

Sveta looked up at him. "Why is it not surprising?"

Bob realized he had said too much. He shrugged. "I don't know."

"He had no choice. Rob was new, so Sasha told him to beat and rape me. He did what he was told, and then they all had their turn. I hated him until he came and apologized. No one else did."

"So you became lovers?"

"We did not have sex like lovers until much later, when he come to Thailand. But yes, he loves me. He told me he will free me, and he did, with help of another pimp named Boris. Boris was Sasha's partner before, but they fought over how he treated us girls. He moved to Thailand and started real club in Pattaya. He sponsor me for work in Thailand. Rob stole my passport from Sasha, and we left in the night. He saved only me, not the other girls.

"Rob sent me to Thailand, but said he cannot come with me. So he went to America, where I wanted to go. When I get to Thailand, I become afraid same thing will happen to me, that I trust the wrong person and I am sold to another man. I think about running away from the airport in Bangkok. But Boris is not bad at first. He gives me an advance and an apartment in Pattaya. He is not slavedriver. But later he becomes bad too. Thank goodness Rob came to Thailand then. He help me pay off my debt to Boris and send me to Phuket. I have better time everywhere I go, but nowhere is good."

"Well, it sounds like this job will be much higher on the scale," Bob said. "I know you've had a wild ride, darling. I knew another girl who had a wild ride too, but not as wild as you."

"What girl?"

"Her name was Lauren. She was an artist in New York. Also a hooker. I guess I can't stay away from girls like you."

"You will see her when you are up in New York?" Sveta asked jealously.

"I wish I could. But she's dead."

"Oh."

"Yes. Seems like a lot of women die around me."

"Like who?"

Bob cleared his throat. "My wife, of course."

"Did a pimp kill this Lauren? I will kill him then."

"Not a pimp exactly. A guru."

"Like a Hindu guru? They are in America too? I watched many Bollywood movies in Russia so I was ready for mantra in Thailand. Chana Chana!"

"Yup. That's the guy. But word is the pimp was involved too."

"A pimp and a guru."

"Yes. What a world."

"Do you want revenge on this pimp and this guru?"

"The guru already's met his maker, darling. The pimp still has to receive his due."

79

The final path was tough to climb. It was steeper than the other paths, plus the ground was smooth marble, making it difficult to grip.

"Getting to moksha is the most difficult journey of all, and this makes the point," Mr. Ghosh explained. "Almost everyone who lives long enough and makes an effort can climb the ladder of pleasure, wealth, and duty. But moksha is another story."

"Yes," Niral pointed out, "but those who are mentally prepared for moksha but not physically fit cannot get up to the temple this way,"

"This is why we have the elevator," Mr. Ghosh replied, laughing. "But you are right. On Diwali, we will only allow the physically prepared to climb up. We cannot accommodate everyone anyway. So it works out."

As Niral neared the top, the path became even steeper, but he was able to hold onto a marble railing and pull himself up. At the pinnacle of the climb, Niral was able to observe a domed temple made of white marble similar to the Taj Mahal. The top of the dome, however, was etched with stained glass of many colors. The building was much taller than the other temples, being at least three stories. Against the setting sun, with a flicker of rays budding through the horizon, the temple appeared almost mythic.

The screen was present again. The large square, laid in white marble, was centered by a statue of Bhen, holding the Bhagavad Gita in one hand and pointing a finger up with the other. In front of her was a fountain shaped like a swan.

"That is Brahma's chariot," Mr. Ghosh explained. "Here we approximate the journey to Brahman and the flight from samsara to moksha."

A huge marble staircase, its railing shaped like the wings of a swan, led up to the front doors, decorated by pictures of Laxmi and Parvati, holding out their palms. Over them, suspended from wires, was a statue of Saraswati, seated on a white lotus and playing a veena. Niral could hear music emanating from the walls of the temple, a soothing drone of soulful shlokas.

Inside the cylindrical marble walls were carved bas reliefs of scenes from both the Ramayana and the Mahabharata. A glass floor emitted white light from underneath. Above him, limited to the right side, Niral could see three levels of balconies. The top floor seemed to be under construction. The second floor appeared empty. The bottom floor included statues of figures such as Ganesh, Durga, Indra and other gods, this time robed as well as garlanded. Etched into the stained-glass dome were scenes from the avatar myths, including the story of Prahlad and Holika.

A large statue of Arjuna kneeling and praying to a standing Krishna stood to the left of a tall, round stage equipped with a microphone and stand. Farther ahead was another shorter stage, this one rectangular in shape. A statue of Bhen was at the back, one hand holding the Rigveda and the other palm toward the viewer. White curtains hung down the walls on either side of the stage.

"Impressed?" Mr. Ghosh asked Niral as the latter looked around.

"Where will Bhai be? On this stage or the other?" Niral inquired as he noticed where the rooms were located. The layout was similar to the other temples, but with additional doors. Niral didn't see a basement this time, or at least no staircase leading down to one.

Mr. Ghosh appeared taken aback by Niral's practical response to his question. But he went along with it.

"We can speak to Bhavesh about the actual plans," he replied. "Come with me."

Mr. Ghosh used a card to unlock a door, and they entered a staircase. They climbed to a second floor. Mr. Ghosh unlocked another door so they could enter the landing.

Niral was confronted by sages in yellow robes. Some were dressing statues of gods that were not visible from below. Others were anointing their heads with kum kum powder or rotating thalis and praying.

"These rishis are at every level," Mr. Ghosh said. "We did not see the previous batch as they were inside. Because we have so many gods here, we must employ them. They are dedicated to Bhen."

"Do they live here?"

"Yes, they do. It is better that way. Unlike other temples, we don't have a problem with homeless sadhus hanging around here. We intend to keep it that way when we open."

They approached a guard at the edge of the landing. Equipped with a rifle, he stood by a door.

"Here is Paul, Niral," Mr. Ghosh said, introducing him. "He is Christian, as his name attests. But he is Hindustani. He is dedicated to The Brotherhood."

"You are the famous Niral," he said, his eyes wide. He put his palms together and bent over.

"Whoa, I'm not that great," Niral complained.

"I have heard how you defended The Brotherhood in New York," Paul said. "We are all grateful."

Niral cleared his throat and touched Paul's head when it was clear he would not rise until he was blessed.

"Yes, well, I did what I could," he responded.

Paul rose, smiled, and opened the door. The three men entered a curving hallway and passed a control room filled with guards seated at computers, apparently monitoring different parts of the temple complex, followed by an empty room, a gym, and bathrooms. Finally, they reached a kitchen where two men were drinking tea.

Mr. Ghosh did namaste. "Mr. Bhavesh, this is the famous Niral I have told you about," he said.

Bhavesh stood, greeted Niral with namaste, and shook his hand. "A pleasure to meet you, Niralbhai. I have heard many great things."

"Yes, I'm sure you have."

The other man smiled shyly. He was younger. Bhavesh told him to stand.

"This is Bilal, my assistant."

"Bilal," Niral said. "That is a Muslim name?"

"Yes," Bilal said. "I am Muslim. But Hindustani."

"He will defend Bhai with his life," Bhavesh said. "So I am told you will assist us with the security operation during Diwali."

"Yes, I hope to," Niral responded. "I've been wondering how it will be set up. Mr. Ghosh just told me to ask you."

Bhavesh laughed. "Yes, he wanted to keep you in suspense. Well, I imagine he has told you the general plan of how the event will proceed, how certain groups will be allowed entry into a certain building and then will fall back?"

"Yes, he told me that."

"For that to work, we need a large number of guards who are well-trained and understand the procedures. That means guards up and down the paths, at least ten on each landing plus six inside each temple. So for the first three buildings, I plan to have at least fifty guards. All the pilgrims will go through the metal detector and will be searched bodily. They cannot have any material positions on them but their clothes. They will be given pre-screened bottles of water so they do not dehydrate. So I will need at least twenty guards down at the first landing too. If you add guards on the paths, I'd say about 100-120 guards will be necessary below this building.

"This building is the most work. I say about fifteen guards on the landing, ten inside on the main floor, another five on the first balcony, which will not be open to the public, but we will need security there too. On the second balcony, we will have five other men to act as snipers. About twenty men will be manning the security cameras. Then Bhai will have his entourage of six bodyguards. The head of his personal security, Mr. Shah, may also come, but we are not sure yet."

"He will meet Mr. Shah at the Dwarka complex," Mr. Ghosh noted.

"Yes," Bhavesh said, sounding annoyed. "So we will have plenty of security."

"Is it really necessary to have that many guards here?" Niral asked. "How about at the Dwarka complex?"

"Mr. Shah is in charge of the personnel at Dwarka," Bhavesh said. "But the main event is here. We are on high alert, as you know. After the situation in Ayodhya, the Muslims have sworn revenge."

"What situation?" Niral asked.

"It is not important," Mr. Ghosh said, staring at Bhavesh. "Since you will be steering the terrorists to the Dwarka complex, we will have enough guards there to meet and detain them. Then we can question them thoroughly and gain the upper hand, finally destroying this threat forever."

"Exactly," Niral countered. "So why have so many guards here? Why not move more to the complex?"

"You never know what can arise," Bhavesh said. "We will have thousands of pilgrims, and there could be other threats."

"I want to speak to Bhai about this," Niral said. "I have concerns about the way it's going to work."

"What concerns?" Mr. Ghosh asked angrily. "You have not said anything this entire time about any concerns. Did Talim tell you something you have not shared with me?"

"No," Niral replied. "But I've thought of a potential problem."

"Let me think. That you will be vulnerable after these men are caught?" Mr. Ghosh surmised.

"Yes, that's part of it," Niral admitted.

"Hmm. You are right," Mr. Ghosh said. "We must plan an exit strategy for you. Come, let us head back to the car and drive to the Dwarka complex."

He grabbed Niral's arm, but Niral resisted.

"First, Bhavesh, can you explain how Bhai will reach the podium and where he will be beforehand?" Niral asked.

"We don't know yet which podium he will use," Bhavesh explained. "The middle podium is higher, but he will be surrounded by worshippers, which might be a security challenge. The back stage is more secure, but he will have less access to the people. We are working on that.

"In regards to where he will be beforehand, a staircase at the end of this hallway leads down to a chamber, where three rooms are located. One is Bhai's room. He can enter the ground floor from there or descend to other levels via an elevator. A cellar is accessible too. Would you like a tour?"

"We should get to the complex, Niralbhai," Mr. Ghosh insisted. "Bhai may sleep early."

"A quick tour won't hurt," Niral said. "Please, Bhavesh, show me."

PART XIV

†

Bangkok, Thailand; Dwarka, India; Kings Point, New York

80

Early the next morning, Rob headed to Klong Tuey and knocked on Apsara's door. Buppha answered, wearing a cut-off t-shirt with an American flag on it.

"Buppha, where's Apsara?" Rob asked.

"I don't know. You tell me what you want."

"No time, Buppha."

"She not here. She come back late last night. Then she leave."

"You know where she went?"

"No know."

"Let me look around," Rob said, barging inside. Buppha sighed and put her hand on her hip.

Soon, Rob charged back out of Apsara's room. "She took her suitcase with her? Looks like clothes are missing."

"I look like her mother to you?"

"Look, I'm not in the mood to play games, Buppha. You tell me..."

"I know nothing, Rob. I not awake when she leave. I hear her shut door. That is it."

Rob cursed to himself. He hadn't received replies to his texts or calls either.

"If she comes back, tell her to call me right away, Buppha. Got it?"

"Got it, sir," Buppha said, saluting him.

81

The three troopers: Bob, Sveta, and Hemraj, look a flight from Raleigh to LaGuardia Airport in New York City, where a limo hired by Hemraj's girlfriend, Ashley Simmons, picked them up. It drove them to Great Neck, Long Island, where the driver stopped and bought a hero sandwich from a local deli for himself. He proceeded to drive them up to the neighborhood of King's Point, where they were dropped off in front of a colonial-style mansion made of brick that overlooked Manhasset Bay. After emerging from the limo, Ashley Simmons, a beach blond, curvy babe wearing a tight sundress and sunglasses, ran up to Hemraj and kissed him passionately.

Sveta poked Bob. "I don't think we will have this relationship," she said.

"You never know, darling," Bob replied, winking.

Bob approached the bay and peered at a larger mansion in the distance.

"Vishal's house," he said to himself.

"What, baby?" Sveta asked, touching his arm. She had followed him.

"Nothing," he said, turning to her. "Listen, you should really stop saying 'baby.' Sounds so cheap, like you're still hustling for tricks. You're married to a proper lord now. You should act, you know, genteel."

Sveta blushed. Then she smiled. "Okay, darling," she said.

"That's better," Bob responded, kissing her forehead. Then he put his arm around her and walked her back to the mansion. He held out his hand to Ashley, who had finally stopped kissing Hemraj. "Nice to meet you," he said. "Franklin Stewart."

"Sorry, sir," Ashley said, speaking with a light southern accent. "I haven't seem Hem in a while." She smiled and shook Bob's hand.

Initially, Ashley scowled at Sveta, but soon hid her disdain with southern charm and a warm smile. She took Sveta by the arm and kissed her cheek.

"Your name?" she asked.

"Julie," Sveta responded, trying to hide her Russian accent unsuccessfully.

"Julie is originally from Russia," Bob explained. "It's Yuliya, but for Americans, it's Julie."

"Very nice to meet you," Ashley said. She released Sveta's arm and took Hemraj's arm instead.

"Let's go inside. I'll have my maid bring you some lunch."

They entered a short corridor, then a spacious living room. Ashley fled briefly while Bob and Sveta were seated on a velvet couch, facing a large television. Hemraj hunkered down on an adjacent couch. Both were covered with a red and black pattern that seemed middle eastern. A table made of pink ivory unified the space.

Ashley re-entered the living room, marching like a storm trooper, her head held high. The maid, a Bangladeshi woman in her forties, followed her, carrying a tray of tea cups and a pitcher. She placed the cups on a table, then began pouring. Hemraj smiled at her with what Bob thought was a knowing look.

"Well," Ashley said, taking her tea cup as she slid down next to Hemraj. "I hope you like chamomile. I love this particular blend. I bought it at the Union Square market the other day."

She gestured for the maid to leave the tea pitcher on the table and go.

"Why were you in Union Square?" Bob asked.

"Lunch with an old friend. You remember Carly, don't you?" she asked Hemraj.

"Yeah," Hemraj responded. "Beer pong bitch."

Ashley slapped his thigh with her free hand. "Only the mean boys called her that," she said to Bob, as if in a secret conference.

"Girls too," Hemraj muttered.

"Now she's an analyst at Goldman Sachs," Ashley explained. "She's doing pretty well."

"You two met at college?" Bob asked. "I mean you and Hemraj."

"Chapel Hill," Ashley said proudly. "Over there it's like Harvard. No one up here knows it's a top school."

"Ashley's dad gave a big donation to Duke, and they still wouldn't take her," Hemraj teased. "So Chapel Hill was the next bet."

"Believe me, Chapel Hill's like, I don't know, what's a top public school in New York?"

"Gay-ass CUNY," Hemraj said.

"Binghamton," Bob said. "SUNY. That's where I went."

"Really?" Hemraj asked. "A said you went to Columbia."

"Oh, I went there for a year," Bob responded, trying to save himself. "Well, less than a year. My grades in high school weren't so great." The truth was that he hadn't gone to Columbia or Binghamton either. He'd attended Bronx Community College and took classes at Hunter College for two years before he had dropped out. He'd worked as a janitor before the Reagan Revolution had inspired him to become an investment banker and make his fortune.

"Yes, us 'children of privilege' need to live up to so much," Ashley said.

"You haven't worked a day in your life," Hemraj reminded her.

"Foundations are work, honey. And you weren't Duke bright either. Not like your sister."

"Well she got lucky. And look at her now. Annoying, good-for-nothing lush. Still better than the fucking Air Force, though."

"His brother's a patriot," Ashley said, laughing. "We all admire him."

"I work for a living," Hemraj countered. "I build things. A real job."

Ashley rolled her eyes. Sveta thought Ashley was ignoring her on purpose. She was about to say something, anything, but then the Bangladeshi maid brought in a large tray of small sandwiches, salad, silverware, and plates. She placed the plates and silverware next to the tea cups. She poured Ashley some more tea, then asked Bob and Sveta if they needed anything else. Bob smiled at her and said he didn't. He took a sandwich of ham and brie cheese.

Ashley dismissed the maid. During the silence that followed, Sveta thought she should speak, but then forgot what she was planning to say.

Instead, Ashley spoke to her.

"Julie, what school...oh, yeah, Russia," she said dismissively, waving her hand. Sveta wished for Dharini's company again.

"She's from a very prestigious university in Siberia," Bob said.

"But you met her at a runway, right?" Ashley asked.

"Look, enough of the histories," Hemraj butted in. "Why don't we get down to business? I'm sure Frank would appreciate that."

"Franklin," Bob said. He figured he should be addressed formally now. "Ashok wants me to be on your board, Ashley."

"I'm on many boards. The one A mentioned is the Council on the Future of the Long Island City Project: CFLIC."

"Yes. That one. It's not the community board, right?"

"We advise the local community board, which makes the final decisions on what gets built and what doesn't, where it happens, and how and who does it. They've been locked for quite some time on this property. There've been protests too."

"That's where the Great Fire took place, right?"

"Yes, where the mad priest destroyed that crappy Spray Mecca known by some as the Graffiti Building in the so-called Arts Center of Queens. Directed by Hemraj's other cousin, as it turns out."

"There's no evidence of that, though that'd be pretty bad-ass," Hemraj said, shrugging. "Either way, Ashok says he wants to make things right. It's only fair after what happened, whether Vishal did it or not. And since we've got our shit together as a family now, he wants to help out. Says you'd help too," he said to Bob.

Before Bob could respond, Ashley cut in. "Honestly," she said, "I've heard the Spray Mecca was an eyesore and there were plans to shut it down anyway. These artist-wannabes make it seem like Shangri-La now, but the place was filled with hookers, porn stars, and drug addicts. That strip club won't be missed either. Only The Dock, a restaurant on the East River, had substantial value by itself. But now the entire area is wealthy and gentrified and everyone wants a piece of the pie.

"Some buildings are still standing but everything's been on lockdown for years. The land was bought through an organized crime front and ownership was frozen during a trial that sent away some mafia men. Then the federal government seized it. But bureaucracy went nowhere. They never put it up for auction. Later they sold it back to the city. Now they're letting the community board decide whether to sell it or keep it as city property, and either way, what should be built there, who will get the contract, and what general terms the buyer/builder will agree on, such as using a percentage of union labor, having a space for artists, etc. And we advise for that."

"And there's a spot open on the board?"

"Yes. I've been tasked with filling it. I understand you're a veteran of boards in the city. So if you want it, it's yours."

"I do, but it's not for me," Bob said, turning to Sveta. "Meet your new board partner: Julie Stewart."

82

Amrat was burning. He floated in the air, palm up, blessing Niral. While he had fallen temporarily, Amrat said, Niral was rising again and reaching his potential. Amrat had been wrong: Niral had strength and quality of vision. He might be an avatar after all. But Niral shouted back that Amrat was a murderer. Couldn't he be reborn as a mouse and stay out of his dreams?

Lauren was laughing. Vishal was laughing. Then Stan and Lance approached, arm in arm, pointing at Niral, calling him a murderer too. How dare he judge someone else?

Niral awoke. Manu was breathing deeply on a bed above him. Niral sat up suddenly, trying to remember where he was.

He recalled the previous night. They had descended the temple and driven to the Dwarka complex, struggling through hoards of sadhus congesting the thoroughfare. They had approached the gate, been searched by security guards, and let through.

The complex was spacious and shaped like a hexagon. Mr. Ghosh noted that Shri Holi had been held on a large stage in the middle of the complex that featured a statue of Bhen. Beyond it were three temples dedicated to each major God. They were spaced out equally, but compared to the Lamba complex they were small and could only fit a maximum of twenty people each. On each side were small temples devoted to lesser gods and goddesses like Ganesh and Amba. Beyond that, on the actual structure of the complex, were offices and residences.

After touring the temples, Mr. Ghosh led Niral and Manu to their rooms. Manu's room was first. Niral noticed it was small but did not say anything until he saw his own room, which was larger and had a more comfortable bed. Yet he decided not to say anything to Mr. Ghosh.

Instead, once Mr. Ghosh left, he walked back to Manu's room and offered to switch. But Manu declined, saying he was okay with the arrangement.

Back in his room, Niral got the chance to check the diamonds. He sighed in relief that they were real. He began to think about the plan ahead. He wondered if he should call Talim or Duncan, who had been strangely uncommunicative. But he was interrupted by a knock on the door. He put the sack of diamonds back in his pocket and opened the door to find Mr. Ghosh.

"Mr. Shah, the head of Bhai's personal security service, would like to speak to you," he said.

"I prefer to speak to Bhai directly," Niral responded.

"You will have time tomorrow. He is asleep right now."

"I thought we had to leave early tomorrow."

"Bhai wakes up early."

Niral proceeded down a hallway, outside to the open space, and across to a different side of the hexagon. Inside a dining room, he saw a large man with a mustache wearing a green, military-style uniform. He had an insignia on his arm shaped like an Om sign with additional curves on its sides, but Niral wasn't sure what rank it designated. He was flanked by two men he had met before: the guard with the slight beard and the Sikh guard who had handed him the chip.

"The hero is here," Mr. Shah said, clapping and smiling sinisterly. He held out his hand. "Good to meet you, Niral Solanke."

"Seems like everyone has heard great things about me," Niral responded, shaking his hand.

"Some great, some not so great," Mr. Shah said, holding out his arms. "You did embarrass The Brotherhood. Perhaps others will not say it..."

"You're the only one who has said it," Niral responded stoically.

Mr. Shah laughed. "It is good you recognize your flaws. Honestly, I told Bhai I was not convinced by your transformation. How can a man change so quickly to defend an organization he does not believe in and join a cause he would not fight for?"

"I'll fight for it."

"Yes, but why now? Because your father tells you that you should?"

"I've been in a spiritual place a long time, Mr. Shah. Thailand has gods everywhere. I hear the Gayatri mantra every morning when I wake up. But I haven't been moved by it. When I came here and I met the terrorists who want to harm our people and the world, I felt it."

Mr. Shah smiled. "You were moved to a higher purpose. You truly are a Kshatriya. And once you gain a deeper understanding of why you fight, perhaps you will be a Brahmin as well."

"I thought we did not believe in castes anymore."

"Old habits die hard, Mr. Solanke. Without our social roles, we are nothing. Simply sadhus praying for moksha and salvation. Leave that to the Buddhists, those who live life as though it is merely a gateway to ahimsa. But we Hindus know that life is more than meditation. It is action. It is dharma. We are all on different planes of understanding and behavior. Haven't you read the Gita, the Vedas? All are different; all have different purposes. Yes, God is in everything, He is omnipresent and omniscient, but we have different paths to Him. And if some group wants to bring down our world, like the Rakshasas of the past, we have an obligation to fight them."

"Obviously, I agree with that part. But I see Manu being treated differently, as if he's still a Dubla. He is more intelligent than many of you, and he is dedicated to The Brotherhood. Why should he be relegated to that?"

"Relegated? Hmm, have you asked him what he thinks? I believe he prefers what he has. Why should we change that, force him into uncomfortable behaviors?"

"That's what I told Niral earlier," Mr. Ghosh added.

"Yeah, that's what you all say," Niral said, "but I don't think it's right."

"Mr. Solanke, talk to Manu after you leave us," Mr. Shah said. "His preference is our desire. Now let us discuss Shri Diwali. You will lure Talim's men to us. Will they arrive after the pilgrims have been transported?"

"That would make them conspicuous, wouldn't it? Their plan is to meld into the crowd of Hindus. It would be better if they believed that until the end."

"But how will we know who they are, and how will we capture them?"

"I can identify them. Your men can keep an eye on them. We could apprehend them before the transportation arrives, either at night or in the morning."

"If they plan to strike at night while the pilgrims sleep, which would make sense, we can apprehend them then. But I would prefer to make the capture after the pilgrims leave, so innocent people are not hurt."

"The plan isn't set yet, but I can recommend they sneak into a section of the complex before or even while the pilgrims are being transported. They don't know about Lamba, so that would make sense if they believe the ceremony will be held here. By the way, how will the pilgrims be transported?"

"Buses."

"And how will pilgrims be let into this complex originally? Will they need an ID?"

"They will be checked for weapons. There is no other criteria. This is India; we must be welcoming."

"So it would be easy for them to sneak in as Hindus and not be noticed. They will have a false sense of security and won't see what's coming."

"Good. We will surprise them and capture them alive, then question them about their activities. But if we know Talim's location, we can nab him simultaneously."

"I can try to find out," Niral said.

"Yes, please do. That would be very valuable information."

"What will happen to me after they are caught? I can't go back to Thailand. If my boss finds out about my double-cross, he might kill me or feed me to the Muslims."

"We will work something out for you," Mr. Ghosh said. "But you must speak to Bhai."

"How? Isn't he asleep?"

"Yes, but you can speak to him tomorrow morning, after he awakes," Mr. Ghosh said. "Before we leave."

While sitting around the dining room table, the group of men consulted a map of the complex and went over the exact plans of the

Shri Diwali event. After discussing it for a while and working out some kinks, they ate a Gujarati thali dinner on the same table.

"Mr. Ghosh still isn't comfortable with the Gujarati emphasis we have here," Mr. Shah teased.

"I have learned to appreciate Gujarati cuisine," Mr. Ghosh responded.

As Niral was leaving to head back to his room, Mr. Ghosh approached him.

"Niral, I can speak to Bhai for you about the aftermath of Shri Diwali. You can stay, and we will protect you. It is the least we can do."

"The situation is more complicated than you think. So I want to talk to Bhai directly."

"Fine. Wake up early, at dawn."

Back in his room, Niral called Duncan, but the call went to voicemail. Then he called Talim's number.

"Just in case the call is traced, we will not speak long," the voice stated. It was a different voice. "Where are you, what is the progress?"

"I'm in Dwarka. I'm laying the trap."

"When you return to Thailand, we will discuss the exact plan."

"Do you want to meet in Surat again?"

"It is too risky. Better if you stay with Bhai and learn his ways."

"I thought you wanted a theatrical assassination."

"Once you learn his ways, we can discuss the best plan."

"Okay, what if I get a chance to kill him?"

"If it is a clean chance, take it. Otherwise, be conservative. We have time to strike."

The man hung up. Niral wondered how he could direct Mr. Shah's men to Talim when he wasn't even sure who Talim was.

Niral thought about calling his father, but he decided not to.

As he stared at his bed, he began to think about his future and about the decisions he had to make. But this didn't last long. He didn't want to think too much. He decided to leave the room and take a walk. He ended up at Manu's room. He knocked on the door.

Surprisingly, Manu was awake and opened the door. Apparently, he had been praying, as he held a rosary in his hand.

"Have you eaten?" Niral asked.

"Yes, Niralbhai. Do not worry."

"I want to feel like a layman," Niral said. "I don't deserve extravagance."

"Aren't you a layman in Thailand?" he asked.

"Yes," Niral said. "But I'm not low enough."

83

Rob took the elevator to the seventy-seventh floor of Duncan's apartment building. As he marched through the curving hallway to Duncan's door, it brought to mind his journey to Linda Macaday's room not long before.

The door opened, and Lamai stood there. Under a short dress, a bump appeared, and Rob finally realized why Duncan had wanted to deal drugs despite the risks.

"G'day Lamai. How ya going?"

"I'm well, Rob."

"How's this little lad?" he asked, reaching over and rubbing her stomach.

"He's more than halfway grown now. Sorry we never told you. We didn't go around telling people in case there was some miscarriage. But it's obvious now. Only a few months now until he delivers. I hope."

"No worries. It'll be fine. You still working?"

"Yes, but I will be going on leave soon. I would like to go up to my parent's home in Chiang Rai to have the baby. It is an old tradition in our family."

"Duncan's going too?"

"We will see. If he does not have to work. He is not supposed to come, but times change."

Rob didn't see Duncan, but he could hear him speaking on the phone behind a closed bedroom door.

"Why don't you sit and I will make you a drink?" Lamai asked.

"No worries. I don't want you to stress yourself out."

"Nonsense, Rob. I enjoy it. You should have dinner with us too."

She walked over to a blender and a cutting board where she had already gathered papaya, lychee, and a mango.

Duncan's door opened. "Rob, get in here," he commanded.

"Guess I'll take a raincheck," Rob said, getting up.

Duncan's room was dark. The curtains were closed, and only a desk lamp illuminated it. The only place to sit, other than the desk, was Duncan's bed, so Rob stood and listened.

"I spoke to Niral. The Bhai assassination is still on track. But this Sumantapat thing is worrying me. If he finds out about his soldier..."

"He's cut up and buried. I didn't take a chance this time with the river. There's a shore where Niral practices shooting sometimes. It's deserted."

"Good. Now we need Apsara to track what Sumantapat suspects."

"Might be a problem with that, mate. I can't find her."

"Where'd you look? She might be at work tonight."

"She called Scandal to say she's going home and not coming back for a bit."

"Home? Like to Isan?"

"That's where home is, ain't it?"

"It's the start of the week. Why would she..."

"Listen, mate, there's something I didn't tell you. Apsara's the one I met at the warehouse. That's how I know you're spying on me. And she's the one Sumantapat's bloke followed."

"Shit!" Duncan hissed. "So she's run away."

"I reckon so. She's not picking up her phone. Guess this shit scared her. Plus, Nam worked her over. She's getting it from all sides. And I don't know what you've been doing to her."

"What does that mean?"

"Using your mia noi to spy on me. That's not cool, mate."

"If you think she loves you, you're wrong. She got close to you because I told her to. I had to protect what's mine. I don't know you as well as Niral. You're a better worker, but that doesn't mean I can trust you."

Rob swallowed. "Look mate, whether she loves me or not is none of your business. Not anymore. So leave her alone. I'll deal with her."

"That's not fair. She owes me."

"She owes Mr. Hong."

"I put her on a pedestal. She would have gotten a lot more shit from Nam otherwise."

"I know you beat on her. If you were anyone else, I'd crack your skull for that."

Duncan laughed. "You're a pussy-whipped fool, man."

Rob pointed to the door. "You've got a pregnant wife. Tend to that, mate."

"I am tending to that. Why do you think I got involved with these Muslims, and Thanat before that? I need the money for our future."

"Too bad your fancy plans keep messing shit up for us."

"We've got a network now. We need to build on that and make sure loose ends are tied up. Niral has to deliver on Bhai's assassination. Otherwise we're in major debt—and danger."

"Only Niral can deliver on that. But something's gotta be in it for him. Or are you planning to get rid of him afterwards?"

Duncan hesitated. "I'm not," he said carefully. "Are you?"

"No. He's my friend, mate."

"Yet you're not willing to make him a partner."

"Apsara's an employee too. Doesn't mean we don't pay them."

"Niral knows I'll relieve his debt from Mr. Hong."

"Good. How about Apsara?"

"I've been paying it down for her services."

"I'll take care of it now. Like I said."

"She knows about Thanat. She might be a liability in Mr. Hong's eyes."

"I'll worry about that."

"You might have to worry sooner than later. That was Mr. Hong on the phone. He's coming back to Bangkok in a week. If the Sumantapat situation is still hot and he finds out, we'll have a problem. And now no one's on the inside to tell us what's what."

"Maybe I should take a trip to Isan. Get her back here."

"Do what you have to do. I can start distribution on spots you have locked down. And I'll make the purchases from Shekhat until you're back. Do you know where her village is?"

"No idea. She never told me the name. You?"

"No. Just said it was near Khon Kaen."

"I'll ride up there."

"Take some merchandise in case you can find another market up there."

"All right. Take care of business here. And don't turn Mr. Hong against me. Or I'll know."

"You've got to trust me. We are partners now."

Rob smirked. "All right, partner."

84

Niral heard the Gayatri mantra in the distance. He felt like he was in Bangkok, except instead of sleeping in a bed with Rob, he was on the floor, by choice, in Manu's tight, inferior room.

The sun was coming up. Following the dream he had featuring individuals from his past, Niral had sat up for nearly half an hour, thinking. Now he heard Manu rise too.

"Niralbhai, the sun prayer follows the mantra," Manu muttered groggily.

"Do you want to do it?"

"I do it every morning. Just not this early."

"I want to meet with Bhai. You can do the sun prayer."

"Bhai directs the sun prayer himself. Come."

They rose and took quick baths with cold water instead of waiting until the water heated up in the tanks. Yet, by the time they entered the open complex, the sun prayer session was almost over. Niral saw a massive group of devotees, most men dressed in nothing but a wife beater and pajama pants, the women in panjabis and simple saris, beginning with a namaste, then continuing to stretch their hands over their heads, bending down to their feet, getting on their knees, stretching their butts in the air, swooping down and up, then back to their knees, and rising back up with a namaste. This action was repeated with numerous prayers, with everyone, including Bhai and Mr. Ghosh, facing the rising sun as they accomplished the technique. Speakers blasted the prayers, and Mr. Shah and the other security guards, armed with rifles, watched the crowd for any malfeasance.

Niral and Manu got in two stretches before the session ended. Then Bhai, holding a microphone, spoke:

"Brothers and sisters, pray for peace and sustenance, pray for our father the sun to keep our world going. And pray for Indra in heaven and Vishnu the operator too."

They recited another short prayer.

"We will have the daily nasta now," he announced. "The next prayer is at noon, before lunch."

He handed the microphone over to Mr. Ghosh, who gave it to an assistant. As they made their way to a washing station set up nearby, Niral approached Bhai. The Sikh security guard blocked his path, but Mr. Ghosh told him it was okay.

"I'm glad you take security so seriously," Niral said to the guard, who scowled.

"How was your trip, Niral?" Bhai asked as he washed his hands and feet in a brass bowl. He was dressed in a wife beater and white pajama pant, blending him in with the other men. Niral could see his janoi sticking out from the wife beater strap on his shoulder.

"Tiring," Niral replied. "The trip took all day. Had some good paan though."

"Be careful. That will rot your teeth. And it is a pollutant. They have banned it in certain parts of Gujarat. You know Gujaratis are more forward thinking than anyone else."

"So you say."

"We've banned it in this complex."

"I'm not chewing any now."

"I am glad to hear it," Bhai said, wiping his hands with a cloth as a servant wiped his feet.

"I was wondering," Niral asked, "how did all these people get into the temple complex?"

"They line up before dawn to share in the prayer. They are thoroughly screened. If they have any objects that are not allowed inside, they will be kept for the owners at the entrance, but only if we determine it is not some kind of weapon. After nasta, they leave for their day's work. Often they will return for the lunch prayer. They are true devotees."

"No sadhus?"

"The sadhus are frauds. I don't allow hypocrites in my complex," Bhai said.

"Shouldn't we welcome everyone?"

"A man who pretends to be holy while living a life of vice is no man. He is lower than an animal. Even a carnivore has more dignity. Also, they harass the devotees and the visitors. We cannot allow them. There are enough temples in Dwarka for them to stalk."

"Do you charge the visitors?"

"A small fee," Mr. Ghosh said. "They can buy a monthly or yearly pass. The true devotees buy it."

Bhai closed his eyes and recited a prayer to himself. A rishi, dressed in saffron robes and carrying a brass dish, came forward and anointed Bhai's forehead with kum kum powder and dry rice.

"We have a Sadhu," Niral announced.

"He is our priest. This is different," Mr. Ghosh said, laughing. "You should talk to Bhai now. We can take you into his prayer room where you can converse. Then we should get going."

"Actually, I wanted to talk to you about that, Bhai," Niral said. "I would rather stay here."

Bhai turned to him. "Stay here? For how long?"

"I have more than ten days until I go back to Thailand. I want to learn from you."

"Didn't they already inform you about the security situation?"

"I can learn more about that, but that's not what I meant." Niral bent down on his knee and performed namaste to Bhai. "Teach me like Krishna taught Arjuna about the eternal way. I have been a sinner in Thailand. I have been empty spiritually and dead to life. Teach me the way of life, Bhai."

Bhai smirked. "Now you wish to learn?" He glanced at Mr. Ghosh. "What a transformation," he continued. "You've agreed to protect us. Now you seek to be us. In only a matter of..."

"Say no, and I will leave and still keep my obligation to trap Talim," Niral replied. "But if you say yes, I will be transformed as a person too."

"Don't you need to tell Talim..."

"I did. I spoke to him last night. He does not expect another meeting. We will keep in contact while I am in Thailand, and I will keep him abreast, as he expects."

Bhai nodded. "How will you return? Manu must drive Mr. Ghosh to Ahmedabad today."

"I'm sure there must be a way. A train, a bus..."

"Bhai," Manu said, greeting Bhai with a namaste, "I will return to pick up Niralbhai when he requests, if Mr. Ghosh confirms this is acceptable."

Mr. Ghosh shrugged. "Of course. If Niral is sincere in his thirst for knowledge, then we are obligated to give it to him. Your father will be very happy, Niral."

Niral bowed deeply. Bhai smiled at Mr. Ghosh.

PART XV

†

Bangkok, Thailand; Khon Kaen, Thailand; Long Island City, New York; Kings Point, New York

---

85

Nat stumbled into the office. One arm was limp; in the other, he carried a briefcase.

"Working hard?" Pom asked, smiling. "You look tired. I thought you were on vacation."

"I didn't leave Phuket right away," Nat responded, placing the briefcase on his desk. "I poked around more hotels. But no match on the witness. I'm convinced it was this Bob Murphy. And I think this dead woman was his wife. But it will take a few more days for the DNA match to confirm that."

"Meanwhile, they have charged this Thai man Panit," Pom said. "Now they say he followed her to her hotel room on Patong beach and killed her there. If you are right about the connection, where is our witness? He may be dead too."

Nat smirked from the pain in his arm.

"I thought the bullet went through?" Pom asked.

"It grazed me, Khun Pom, but it still hurts. And the more I use it, the more it hurts."

"You are able to take out your cigarettes?"

"I use one arm when possible."

"Good. At least you can still smoke."

"Listen, I want to go back to Phuket when this DNA match comes back. I want to question this Panit. But I need you to fight for me if General Toon says no."

"Why would he say no?"

Nat shrugged. "Same reason that General Chaow found this Panit and put the blame on him."

"You think it is a setup?"

"I think they are more interested in appearances than truth. What about your side?"

"DNA will take time, as you say. But speaking of General Toon, he got another visit from Sumantapat today. He asked to see us both when you came in."

"Let's go," Nat said.

Toon was reading a memo when the two detectives inquired at his door. He put down his memo, cleared his throat, and gruffly received them. They both greeted their superior with a wai, then sat.

"Nat," Toon started, "Khun Commissioner told you to return right away. Next time, you must follow orders."

"Yes, Big Boss," Nat responded. "I wanted to find the witness if I could. I know how much this case means to you."

General Toon grunted. "Yes, well there is a complication. Another man is missing here."

"Another gem dealer?" Pom asked.

"A man who worked with the gem dealers." He paused. "I want to be frank, gentlemen. You know I am honest, not like other police commanders. But sometimes, we must skirt the edge of the law for the greater good. We know drugs are a major scourge in Thailand. Especially ya ba."

Pom and Nat nodded.

"You've seen a gentleman named Sumantapat come to my office. He owns some clubs in Bangkok and Pattaya, and gem businesses too. Not exactly a man of great reputation. I don't claim he is nearing nirvana anytime soon. But I do trust him. The men who disappeared worked for him. He believes they were killed because they discovered a large drug enterprise operating in Bangkok and the surrounding area. Of course, drug enterprises are not news, but the Narcotics Suppression Bureau has confirmed there is a new seller on the street with purer ya ba at higher prices. So we are concentrating on this new dealer. We don't know anything about him or them. Sumantapat has only one lead, and we should follow it up."

"Were these men buying ya ba from this dealer?" Nat asked.

"He does not know."

"So how did he get this clue?"

"I would rather not reveal that information. The lead is a go-go dancer who disappeared recently. She was this Pornopat's girlfriend. We believe her real name is Apsara, although we can't find a record to substantiate her identity. She also goes by Duanphen, and her stage name is Tip. She is from the Khon Kaen province of Isan. The exact location of her village is uncertain, but it is likely she went home to care for her mother and daughter. One of you should go up there. Find her and make her talk. I hope this drug angle does not exist, but if it does and we can link these crimes, we will all be winners."

Nat turned to Pom. "We are both waiting on DNA results. I guess we don't have much groundwork right now."

"You go, Nat," Pom said. "You're young and fond of travel. I will follow up on both DNA trails. Either way, your trip to Phuket can wait until the results come."

"What trip to Phuket?" General Toon asked.

"If the DNA match confirms it is the woman," Nat replied, "and that she was killed in the hotel room, I would like to interview this Panit and see if he knows the whereabouts of the husband."

General Toon frowned. "You can always call him. Or I will speak to General Chaow and they can ask him. The girl is more important. I have a hunch."

"How can I find her if I don't know where her village is?"

"Start in Khon Kaen city. Ask around at the university, clubs. Maybe someone knows her. I doubt she started dancing in Bangkok."

"Many do, Big Boss. Many do," Nat said under his breath.

"Should I follow up on this new man's disappearance?" Pom asked. "Do you suspect where he was killed, like with the gem dealers?"

"Unfortunately, we have less leads on the murder scene. But I can give you the file."

"Can I speak to Sumantapat?" Pom asked.

General Toon cleared his throat. "If you must. But be respectful, please."

"Always, Big Boss," Pom replied. "Always."

86

"Why did you involve the police?" Maem scolded Sumantapat, sitting across from him in their office at Go-Go Rama.

Sumantapat leaned forward on his chair, a self-satisfied yet calm look on his face.

"You don't see the wider picture, Maem. The police are our most powerful weapon."

"What if Tip tells a detective about the drugs? We will get the needle."

"Ah, Toon won't let that happen."

"Toon is not the only one there. You should send a few men up, kill her family, and burn her village to the ground. Then torture her until you learn the truth about Porn."

"I already lost my best man. I don't want to keep losing men, not while others can do the work for me. Toon will tell us what the detective learns. Once he finds where she is, we can finish the job."

Maem ran her hand through her hair as she rocked back and forth. "Do you really think this is related to the new ya ba on the street?"

"Why, are you interested in trying it? Ah, we just got you off the heroin."

"Very funny. That seems like another dangerous angle."

"I will never back down from another dealer, Maem. We have the biggest operation around. We will crush our competition, but first we need to find out who they are. Mr. Hong and the Dragons are at the top of my list, but my spies haven't seen any unusual activity. Don't worry, Maem. Work the girls. Enjoy life. Sanuk."

"Yes. Land of Smiles. I am always smiling."

She got up, faked a smile, then opened the door.

"That's my girl," Sumantapat said, slapping the desk. "Keep smiling!"

87

Rob had been in Khon Kaen for nearly a week. He had spoken to students at Khon Kaen University and visited every go-go club, massage parlor, and girly bar in town, showing Apsara's picture on his phone and using all her nicknames. Many people didn't speak English, but Rob utilized the little Thai he knew. No one recognized her, or at least they claimed they didn't.

Her phone was always off when he called. She didn't answer her texts. Buppha hadn't heard from her, and Rob realized that he had never inquired into her life outside of their immediate circle. He didn't know if she had any girlfriends or acquaintances in Bangkok or beyond. Their conversations, when not punctuated by Apsara's frustrations about money, had usually been superficial and flippant.

He knew the major facts that she had revealed: her family's poverty, her father's death at an early age, selling her virginity for her boyfriend's benefit, his abandonment of their only child, being kidnapped from the Bangkok bus station and chained for days as a sex slave, then escaping and, out of desperation, selling herself to a madam, who then put her up at a Bangkok auction, leading to her debt to Mr. Hong.

She could have suffered a far worse fate. Mr. Hong had helped her, at least, by loaning her money to send to her family and giving her a decent percentage of earnings at the club. But no matter what, she kept falling farther into his debt. And her story, that serious side Rob believed she only showed to him, inspired him to steal from Sveta, his last project, to save his latest honey dove.

Had she paid off Mr. Hong or just took off? Or had she fallen into Sumantapat's clutches? The latter appeared more likely. The murder of Linda Macaday and his strong-arming of Boris had been for nothing if Apsara was dead and the money had disappeared. He decided to drown out that possibility. He held onto the assumption that she got scared and ran to her village to hide. Reunited with her family, she was waiting for Rob to find her.

From his hotel room on Th Glang Meuang, Rob called Duncan. Through Duncan he could find out whether Mr. Hong's debt had been paid, but then Rob might have to explain Bob Macaday, and he didn't want to fall into that trap. Apsara had left in a hurry. It was unlikely she had paid off Mr. Hong before she left.

"I'm on my way to meet Mr. Hong," Duncan said. "Any word on Apsara?"

"No, mate. Haven't found anything."

"Fuck. Well, I'll let him know the tourist is dead, and I'll mention Apsara only if he asks."

"Wise, mate. Only if he asks. How's business?"

"Kan's been a boon in Kanchanaburi and the villages. I've hit up a couple of Bangkok spots, the ones you recommended. Demand's high for Rahmat's shit. We should consider raising prices."

"Be careful, mate. Don't wanna get too loud."

"How about on your side? New markets?"

"I've been subtle about it, but I've pushed. Sold a couple of saucers, but I think the villages are a better bet."

"Are you coming back?"

"I'm gonna make one last push. Take another trip through the villages. Maybe a crack at Khorat when I'm passing through. It's a big area."

"Okay, but it's better if you come back sooner. If she's gone, she's gone. Can't do anything about that."

Rob paused for a second. "You happy about that, mate?"

"Why would I be happy about that?"

"No worries. We'll gab later."

Rob hung up. But before he could think, he received another call.

He didn't recognize the number. It started with a zero and it was long. Rob decided to pick up.

"Ya?"

"Rob?" He heard Sveta's accent even in his name.

"Sweetie...how ya going? You wait till now to call me?"

"You haven't called me. You care if I am dead?"

"Course I care, sweetie. I checked up on you in my own way. Wanted you to settle in. If you like your life, you can forget about me."

"You know what I am doing? Where I am?"

"You're in New York? That right?"

Sveta paused. "Yes. How did you know?"

"Told you. I keep in touch."

"And what am I doing?"

"Reckon I don't know that."

"I am going into a board meeting. I am Julie Stewart now."

"Got you Americanized already... Board meeting? What kind?"

"We are going in right now. Save my number. I will call you later."

He heard her hang up. He looked at the phone. The screen went back to its default.

"Board meeting?" he asked himself.

88

The board meeting was conducted inside a large conference room on the fifth floor of the newly renovated church building. As Tim McNally had never sold the building to Vishal Patel, he was able to capitalize on the fire's fame and rent out the property for vast sums of money to different groups, including city boards and their ancillaries, using the funds to help the church. The building that once held Tony's Diner stood too, but now was a Latin fusion tapas bar.

Bob Macaday, now publicly named Franklin Stewart, waited across the street in Ashley's limo, next to the location of the former Spray Mecca. It was now a fenced off, arid area of shoveled dirt and weeds.

A large crowd had gathered in front of the church building, holding signs protesting sale to any private entity. A ragtag group of artist-types, anarchists, union activists, construction workers, housewives from the nearby projects, and former members of Occupy Wall Street were led by a city councilman named Vince Stevens, who railed against private development in the area and demanded that the site be preserved for the public. He cited the high costs of living that were displacing working people and the success of nearby P. S. 1 and other similar venues. He demanded that the city keep the property and use union labor to build a museum where the Spray Mecca had once stood, along with an artists' studio overlooking the East River where The Dock had been and a housing project on the Gigglies site where local citizens could live affordably in rent-controlled housing and be shielded from gentrification. He pounded his fists and posed for the cameras as he announced his entrance to the church building with a group of concerned citizens.

Ashok had purposely installed Sveta on the board so Bob wouldn't be recognized by any board members or reporters. But Bob was curious, so against Ashok's advice he had tagged along.

Once Vince Stevens had entered the building with his entourage, some people kept yelling slogans, but many protesters began to break up and chat among themselves. Bob saw one subsection was mostly young and white, mixed with assorted people of color. He figured these were the artists and hipsters. There were working-class mothers, mainly Black and Hispanic women, and men wearing construction hats. Then, a group he had previously missed: older white men with long hair and dirty jeans. Old school hippies, Bob thought, who had hated the Reagan Revolution and everything it had stood for. Would he have become like them if he hadn't proceeded on his path?

He began to consider his past when he saw a familiar figure on the steps, walking up separately from the rest of the crowd. The man entered the building and disappeared. Bob's window was shaded, so he couldn't see the man clearly. He figured most black guys looked the same, so he might be mistaken in his identification.

A few minutes later, the man emerged from the building and watched the crowd while pretending, Bob believed, to be loitering. Bob rolled down his window to take a clearer, closer look, and he realized he had been right. What a strange coincidence. Running into the man who had terrorized his old wife as he was sitting in a limousine waiting for his new one. Just as running into Rob, a man who happened to work for Vishal, had been a coincidence that had led to the death of his old wife.

What had motivated Bob to leave an easy life in Texas, armed with a fake identity but stuck with an annoying, spiteful woman he wanted to love but didn't trust, back to his old life in New York City, but this time in disguise? Perhaps the same impulse that had motivated him to change his situation from a poor mick janitor in the Bronx to a successful investment banker in Manhattan, making so much money so quickly that he was able to retire early and live on his investments. But that money was gone now, and to remake his life again, he would have to guide others and be guided by others.

Lance moved past the crowd now and scanned the wider scene. Bob tried to roll up the window to reshield himself, but Lance spotted him before he was successful. Lance appeared as shocked as Bob when Bob had made his identification of Lance. But Bob made sure there was no reunion. He immediately told the driver to pull out and speed away. Lance ran behind the vehicle, but the limo beat a light and lost him.

89

In the late afternoon, Pom received the DNA results from the gem store. He called Nat, who was driving up to Khon Kaen.

"We matched blood samples to each of the three victims," Pom said. "So we are reasonably certain they died there."

"Or maybe they all had nosebleeds."

"With the blood spatter evidence from the luminol, it is reasonable to assume..."

"Yes, Khun Pom, with due respect, I am joking with you, as you do with me."

"Mr. Nat, you are a funny one."

"Anything else?"

"Yes, hair samples from two different people, but not the victims. One is male, Caucasian, the other female, Mongoloid."

"They could have been customers from before."

"Yes, but they are leads. Unfortunately, neither are in our criminal database."

"We can send the Caucasian sample to different countries."

"Yes, but which ones? And that will take time. I think it is better to work the street. If this new ya ba is related to this gem store murder, then our Klong Tuey ladyboys might know about it."

"You're going back into groundwork, Pom? That is my job, no?"

"I've been in homicide longer than you. Believe me, I have contacts by now."

"Any word on my DNA?"

"Not yet. But if I hear about it, I will give you a call."

90

Bob returned to Ashley's mansion in Kings Point. There, he convinced Hemraj he had a panic attack, which were sometimes caused by long waits in cars, and had sped home to rest. Hemraj took the limo back to LIC to pick up the women.

When the threesome returned, Bob met them in the living room and told Hemraj he felt better now. But when he asked the women what had transpired at the meeting, Ashley didn't respond, giving him a steely southern glare.

"Thank you for leaving us, husband," Sveta said. "We waited long time outside with crazy people yelling."

"I couldn't help it, darling. I had a panic attack. I couldn't go outside, so I had to return."

"You couldn't go to a park nearby?" Ashley asked. "There are plenty of them."

"He almost died, Ash," Hemraj said. "Isn't there any compassion around here?"

Sveta frowned playfully, then hugged Bob.

"Are you okay, baby?" she asked. "I am sorry."

"Yes, I'm fine now," he said, hugging her back. "I'm sorry about those animals. Tell me, are we winning?"

Sveta shrugged. "Nothing is decided."

Ashley rolled her eyes and, while playing with the hem of her dress, sat down.

"This was the community board's public hearing on the issue," she explained. "I announced CFLIC's recommendations for the properties—commercial buildings, including a shopping center and entertainment complex. That's the best plan to develop Long Island City and make money for the owner. People will come from Manhattan for that. They'll come from Eastern Queens and Long Island for that.

"Next month, the Arts and Cultural Affairs Committee will report their recommendations. The board plans to vote the month after, but politics can cause delays. We anticipate the votes are tied between the board members nominated by city council member Vince Stevens and those appointed by the Queens borough president. Stevens, influenced by the City Council's progressive agenda, wants an artist studio or working museum dedicated to avant garde art, from which they can make money and fame for the city, while the borough president wants affordable housing for the local people of Queens. Vince Stevens is a city council member, but he is local too. He is fighting hard for a combination, but we think we can work him."

"And then he can turn his members?" Bob asked, sitting on the adjacent sofa, Sveta by his side.

"Yes, that's the plan. Stevens and his supporters booed us when we announced our recommendations. One by one, they made speeches denouncing the plan. Now he and the Queens borough president will go to the media and rile people up. It's similar to the mob's original plan. Gentrification will displace people and kill art. Blah blah blah. So we will compromise by including some rent-controlled condos, which will keep the Queens borough president happy, and a small artistic restoration and studio space, which, along with whatever he wants—campaign contribution, endorsement by a friendly entity, whatever—we hope will help bring Vince Stevens to our side.

"While his followers don't want any sale to a private entity, they might compromise on a contractor who uses union labor and provides an artistic restoration. CFLIC still needs to vote on which contractor it recommends for the bid once the board, in turn, tells us what terms they expect the contractor to live up to. And I'm fairly certain Julie's vote will give it to Hemraj's company. The board still needs to approve the sale, and then there's bureaucracy—we've got to negotiate on the zoning laws and variables, the Department of Buildings needs to approve permits, etc. But we don't see a problem as long as the board agrees with the vision and all parties are reasonably neutralized."

"It pays not to be married," Hemraj said, kissing Ashley on her cheek after sliding beside her.

"Won't they figure out your relationship to Vishal, if not to you, Ashley?" Bob asked. "I'm surprised they haven't already."

"Vishal is missing, maybe dead," Hemraj answered. "I'm family, but I don't have any direct connection to him. How can they punish me for that? I'm a businessman from North Carolina, expanding my business here."

"You're not local," Bob noted. "I imagine the others are. Why would they give it to you?"

"We increasingly dominate the motel game in eastern North Carolina. I've built convention centers there too. My overall success in real estate development kills the competition. Unfortunately, these days, merit isn't enough."

"Who are the other contenders?"

"A large number," Ashley responded. "But only two have a realistic shot because they have influence. One is Brendan Carty, a hedge fund guy who finances real estate developers but seems, for whatever reason, to be interested in becoming a developer himself in this case, and a construction firm we believe is a front for the Tragliani family."

"The Traglianis?" Bob asked, shuddering. "I can't believe you would consider anybody..."

"That's a rumor. No one can prove it. But that also means, influence or not, that firm isn't likely to get the contract because it might cause a media storm that could expose everyone involved."

"Good thing," Bob said. "So then it's Brendan or Hemraj."

Ashley looked suspicious. "Do you know Brendan Carty?" she asked.

"I'm a veteran of boards," Bob explained. "I hear names."

Ashley rolled her eyes. "I was hoping if you knew Brendan Carty, you could help us one-up him. But I guess we'll have to rely on your knowledge of board procedures. Look, I'm sorry about your panic attack. Maybe you shouldn't come along next time."

"Yes, it's these cars. Sometimes I get..."

"Husband," Sveta said, rubbing Bob's thigh. "Do not worry. I have cure. Let us go to the bedroom."

91

Duncan climbed the steep stairs and, as usual, saw Mok behind the bar. Mok noticed Duncan's eye twitching. He winked at Duncan, then made him a Mai Tai.

"Don't worry, Mr. Duncan, I know what you like," Mok said, handing it to him.

"Thanks, Mok. You're a real keeper."

"How long have we known each other? We are like brothers."

"Yeah, when I first came up these steps, you were here. I was nervous about meeting Mr. Hong, but you were joking the entire time. Put me at ease."

"You don't seem at ease now, Mr. Duncan. Drink your Mai Tai, and you will feel better."

"What mood's the old man in?"

"He is not bad. I think he get pussy last night."

"He gets pussy every night, when he wants it anyway."

"So do you, Mr. Duncan. So do you."

Duncan raised the glass to him and drank. "To us. Brothers."

Mok raised his shirt sleeve and showed Duncan his tattoo. "Why you never join the gang? You three are stubborn."

"We're not Asian. Except Niral, but he's the wrong kind."

Nam emerged from behind the blue curtain. He was wearing a gray suit with white stripes. It was rare for him to be dressed up. Apparently, he had been listening to the conversation.

"You don't need to be Asian, Duncan, just have balls of steel," Nam commented.

"Remember, I'm the honest guy," Duncan replied. "How would it look if I had a Dragon tattoo on me?"

"I still say you're a pussy, Duncan. That wife pussy-whipped you."

"She did. I admit it. How about you, Nam?"

"No time. Too busy fucking girls."

"Hope they're girls."

"I'm not like pretty boy, Mr. Boyztown. Where is he? I haven't seen him in a while."

"Around. On business."

"What's he call business?" Nam waved his hands in an effeminate manner.

"Is Mr. Hong here?"

Nam stopped and straightened up. "Straight to business. Did you take care of the tourist?"

"I'll tell Mr. Hong."

"He wants me to tell him before he sees you."

"Then you can tell him yes."

Nam nodded and went back through the curtain. Duncan waited nervously. He finished his Mai Tai, then handed the glass to Mok, who shrugged.

"Boss is acting like he's Big Boss," Mok whispered.

"He's not," Duncan said. "Don't forget that."

Nam returned. He bowed and showed the way with his arm. "Boss will see you now," he said.

Duncan proceeded to the back table where Mr. Hong sat, dressed in his beige suit, a bottle of Johnnie Walker in front of him. He did not stand up. Duncan greeted him with a deep wai.

"Sit, my son," he said. Nam moved to pour the Johnnie Walker into shot glasses, but Mr. Hong's hand stopped him.

"Let the poo noy pour. Sit, Nam."

Duncan sat on the vacant seat at the table while Nam pulled up a chair. Duncan poured the shots for all three men.

Mr. Hong raised his glass. "To dead American tourists," he said.

Duncan smiled. Each downed their drink. Duncan coughed—the shot went down too soon after the Mai Tai.

"If you cannot take Johnnie Walker, Duncan, how can you take Bangkok?" Mr. Hong asked.

"I've taken it well, Mr. Hong. I think."

Mr. Hong nodded. "Duncan, I did not want you involved in the violent side of our business. I wanted you to be my pure arm, passing on my wisdom and legacy without the trash. I was happy when you married Lamai. Though you did not need me as a sponsor anymore, I knew you would never abandon me. And you have not. But your new family's needs led you to trust this Thanat, and even after death he haunts us. The tourist's death is good, but loose ends still remain. We can't forget that."

Duncan's eyebrow twitched. "What do you mean, Mr. Hong?"

"Nam's contacts say another Sumantapat soldier is missing. Probably some unrelated hit, but the police are working harder now. They checked Thanat's murder scene and found DNA samples. They may find a link to us."

"I hope you're not saying what I think you are saying, Mr. Hong."

"Duncan, you are like my son. But the others are not. It may be better to cleanse them from the palette. You can find other help. I can give you one of Nam's men."

"I trust Rob and Niral," Duncan said. "They've helped me a lot. Especially Niral."

"Niral killed Thanat. Rob made the mistake of not killing the tourist."

"And now he has."

"Which means he is more of a risk. And what about Aspara?"

"My mia noi," Duncan said under his breath.

"Your mia noi is missing. Have you noticed?"

"Yes, Mr. Hong."

"She called Scandal and said she is going home. Without asking me, she went home. I will send Nam to Isan, and he will send her to her eternal home."

"No, Mr. Hong," Duncan said.

"Don't tell me you are in love with this girl? What happened to your wife?"

"That's not why I said that," Duncan said, trying to regroup. "I sent Rob to find her."

"I see. He knows where she is?"

Duncan shook his head. "No."

"Let him bring her back," Nam said. "Then we can finish them all at once."

"Sumantapat might have told the police about Apsara, since she is missing from their club too," Mr. Hong said. "Let's hope they don't find her first. She is the biggest problem right now. Tell Rob to finish her. We can deal with him when he comes back."

"Rob's tough," Duncan noted. "He won't be easy to kill."

"We will trick him," Mr. Hong said.

"I'll take him," Nam said. "Then killing that Boyztown toot will be like nothing."

"Niral is my poo noy," Duncan reminded Mr. Hong.

"Yes, but what can we do? Think of me. I will lose so much money. Apsara owes me a debt, and so does Niral."

"Didn't Niral originally owe his debt to Mr. Chang's men in New York?" Duncan asked. "They might be angry if we kill him."

Mr. Hong thought, then nodded. "True, Duncan. I will ask Mr. Chang's permission for Niral. But the others must go."

92

Rob drove his motorcycle to the villages outside Khon Kaen, showing pictures of Apsara at random corner stores and homes. Most people didn't speak English, but they were willing to cooperate, using hand gestures when they realized Rob's Thai was limited. But he didn't find anyone who recognized her. He drove from village to village, not knowing where he was going. Until he got a hit—kind of.

A young man standing on his porch came down the steps—it was a house built on stilts. He smiled as he took Rob's phone, viewing Apsara vertically, then horizontally.

"Nice phone," he said. "How much?"

"I'm not selling the phone, mate. And if you swipe it, you're gonna get it."

Rob grabbed the phone and put it in his pocket.

"Wait, sir," the young man said as Rob began to pull away. "I know this girl."

"Rubbish," Rob replied, stopping. "What's her name?"

"She had stage name."

"There's a club around here?"

"In Udon Thani."

"You sure? Which one?"

"Near Nutty Park, sir. I don't remember name."

"Any bloke in this village go with you? Can he tell me the same shit?"

"No one, sir."

"I don't believe you. Scrawny village kid just rode up to Udon? How'd you afford a club?"

"You believe me, sir. Give me reward."

He held out his hand. Rob put up his arm as if to strike him. The boy fled down the road. Rob rode away in frustration, but he began to think. Should he go up to Udon Thani? The rural areas were vast, and searching this way was like trying to locate a needle in a haystack. If Apsara had danced in an urban area, it would be easier to locate her, and Udon Thani was a better bet than Khon Kaen for making money from foreigners. The drive was only an hour and a half. He could give it a shot, and on the way back visit Khorat. Meanwhile, he would continue to try calling her phone.

93

When Nat arrived in Khon Kaen, evening had fallen. He avoided an elephant on Th Si Chan and headed to the megaclub Kam on Th Prachasumran. It was the biggest in town, featuring several different types of clubs within its large complex.

As Nat rushed past flames, flashing lights, and water fountains, he was greeted by a young lady dressed in a classy, zip-front, white dress. She greeted him with a wai.

"Sawadee kap," he said in Thai, nodding. "Is Piti here?"

"Who?"

"She works here. She's a dancer."

"I'm sorry," the hostess said, smiling. "I don't know all the girls' names. Why don't you sit down? I will get you a drink menu and ask for the girls."

"Sure," Nat said. He followed her into the dark club. It was empty. She motioned him toward a leather cushion behind a small table, where he sat. He took out a cigarette with his one good arm and his match pad with the hurt arm. He was trying to use his injured arm more despite the lingering pain.

But when the hostess returned with the drink menu, she told him he couldn't smoke. He rolled his eyes and put his cigarette and matches back. Then, he glanced at the menu and ordered a Singha.

The stage was shaped like a miniature Tower of Babel, with one circular pillar on top of the other and a pole above that. Music was playing, yet no one was dancing. But a moment later, two girls wearing identical bikinis decorated with flowers took the stage. Their panties appeared oversized from the back, and Nat was surprised they weren't wearing thongs. The hostess returned with the beer.

"She will be out in a minute, sir."

Nat drank, his finger twitching, wishing he could smoke as he watched the girls dance. One twirled around the pole while the other sat on the bottom pillar, her legs apart and dangling, smiling at Nat.

A short, skinny girl wearing the same bikini slid next to Nat, taking his hand under the table.

"Look who it is," she said. "Why are you back?"

"Case. Work," Nat said simply. "I'm looking for a bar girl."

"Why come here? This is a club."

"I meant go-go dancer. She might work both. Do you know an Apsara or Duanphen?"

"Long names."

"Stage name is Tip."

Piti's eyebrows raised. "I know a Tip."

"She works here?"

"Yes, for the last six months."

"It's not her. Unless she started working recently or long before."

Piti shrugged her shoulders.

"How often does she work?" he asked.

"Maybe two or three times a week."

"Can't be her. Listen, this girl has a boyfriend named Pornopat. Heard of him?"

"No. Sorry. Why don't you move back, Nat? It's not fun without you."

"Isan is long gone from my memory, Piti. I feel more Lanna now."

"You will always be Isan. You can't change that. Your Lao roots are in your blood. Are you still impregnating young girls?"

Nat gave her a nasty look. "No. That was a mistake. I've changed."

"That's why you went to Chiang Mai?"

"Exactly. I needed to change my life. I didn't want to be like every other Isan kid, living their entire lives for their selfish parents. Think about your father. You dance to feed his appetite for women. You might as well sleep with him yourself."

Piti slapped him on his injured arm. "Have you no shame, Nat? Have you seen your parents?"

Nat grimaced as he rubbed his arm. "No, and I don't plan to. I need to find this girl."

"Any picture? I can show it around."

With his good arm, Nat took out his phone. He showed Piti a picture of Apsara. General Toon had emailed it to him, having received it from Sumantapat.

Piti took the phone and analyzed the picture.

"This is the girl," she said.

"What girl? You know her?"

"No, but a few days ago some farang asked about her."

"Did he mention her name?"

"He did to the girl on stage now."

Piti waved at the girl, who strolled over as the next shift arrived. Piti showed her the picture and asked for her name.

"He say Ploy, or Apsara. Yes, that her," she said in broken Thai. Nat guessed she was from Laos.

"This farang, what did he look like?" Nat asked.

"He was tall. Very tall. He had bald hair. Short hair."

"He said 'mate,'" Piti added. "Like in the movies."

"Australian?" Nat asked.

"Or British."

"If he said 'mate,' I think he is Australian," Nat said. "Did he say where he was staying?"

"I think he say Coco," the other girl said.

"That's on Th Glang Meuang, right?"

"Yes, Nat," Piti said. "Will you go now?"

"This is the best lead I've had, Piti. This is coming together better than I expected."

Nat rose joyfully, then grimaced and grabbed his arm. Piti rose with him.

"Tell me you will visit your parents, Nat," she said. "Do not deny your heritage."

"My heritage is dead, Piti," Nat replied, rushing out. "Thank you for your help. Sawadee kap!"

94

Though Duncan had insisted on ordering in, Lamai had made a large dinner beginning with nam prik num, an appetizer consisting of garlic, green chilies, rice, and pork, followed by Lamai's favorite dish, Kanom jeen nam ngeeo, consisting of noodles in a pork and tomato broth, and finishing off with a desert of lychee ice cream.

When they were done eating, Duncan felt bloated, but his eyes must have been twitching because Lamai asked him if everything at work was okay.

"Tell me, Lamai, do you think I'm a good person?" Duncan asked.

Lamai smiled. "Tee rak, why would I marry a bad person?"

"True. Why would you?"

"Is something troubling you?"

Duncan shrugged. "Things are tight. I might have to let someone go."

"You mean Niral or Rob?"

"Yes. I'm not sure I can afford them."

"You can pay them less."

"They might not stick around then."

"But they would have a choice."

"I'm sure the tourist agency has let people go they couldn't afford to keep."

"We are good about retaining people. It is our Buddhist duty."

"They hire people based on their looks. Is that a Buddhist duty too?"

Lamai slapped Duncan's arm.

"It's true. You had to include a picture with your application. Even the bowling alley has only pretty girls."

"Well, Buddha must like pretty girls."

Duncan smiled. "Like you?" he asked. They kissed.

"Listen, Duncan, if you are troubled, you should go to the temple," Lamai said, touching his arms. "We can go together. Talk to the monk. He helps me."

"I don't know."

"Better yet, when we go up to Chiang Rai, I can take you to my local monastery. They will teach you more about Buddhism."

"Then I can reach nirvana. But enlightenment won't help me provide for this family."

Lamai took his head in her hands.

"Tee rak, you are a great provider. I would not have married you..."

"How can I be a good person and a good provider?"

"All good men are. My father is. He provided, and he's a good person."

"Wasn't he in the Thai military?"

"He helped defend his country. That makes him bad? He was a monk for a few months like every Thai boy. After the military, he got a job and provided. But he never lost his faith or his morals."

"After we go up to Chiang Rai, I might have to return to Bangkok more than I thought."

Lamai let go of his head and leaned back in her chair.

"You can stay in Bangkok. If it is so important..."

"If I don't have Rob and Niral, I'll have to do everything myself."

"We will go to the temple here in Bangkok. And you can make peace with yourself. And whatever happens happens. I intended to be alone with my family in Chiang Rai anyway."

"Fine. We will go to the temple."

"Yes. And once I start maternity leave, I will go to Chiang Rai. By then maybe you will have decided that Rob and Niral are worth saving, and you will come with me. Or you will decide to terminate them and work alone in Bangkok, without your wife or your friends. It will be your choice."

PART XVI

†

Dwarka, India; The Road, Gujarat, India; Near Surat, India; Bangkok, Thailand; Khon Kaen, Thailand; Kings Point, New York

---

95

In the morning, Niral was dressed in a saffron dhoti and wore a janoi. Kum kum powder was anointed on his forehead in the shape of a lingam. Palms together, he knelt to Bhai, who blessed him. Then he rose, feeling the warm embers from the yagna.

"I am proud of you, Niral. In only a week, you have learned much. I believe you will fulfill your duties as both a Kshatriya and Brahmin. The abolishment of the caste system increases individualism and equality but also chaos and selfishness. A man like you, forged with two duties at once, will carry on the torch of social consciousness combined with our overall goals of justice, equality, and spreading to all mankind The Brotherhood enlightenment."

Niral performed namaste again. "Bhai, I have learned more about Hinduism than I ever knew. Your teachings have opened my eyes to the endless breadth of our faith and reinforced the importance of our victory in India. Thank you for that."

"Remember what we have discussed. Even as you wear other uniforms, you must not forget who you are. Your core must remain strong."

"Yes, Bhai."

"Now go. Another storm is coming. Hopefully you will reach Yam Gam before it strikes."

"Should I meet with Talim again?"

"First, go to Yam Gam and see Narendrabhai. Bring him my message, and inform him of your activities."

"Yes, Bhai. But I have only so much time..."

"Then go to Yam Gam and don't return to Surat. You may correspond with Talim electronically and allow us to see your plans without censorship."

"Yes, Bhai."

"Now go. Manu awaits outside the gates."

"May I call my father first?"

"I have spoken to your father about your progress. He is proud of you."

"He will be here at Shri Diwali?"

"Yes. You will be united at the moment of your greatest honor."

Niral repeated the namaste and returned to his room. He undressed, bathed, and dressed again in his street clothes, making sure that the diamonds were in his pocket. He packed his bags, including the copy of the Bhagavad Gita that Bhai had given him.

Outside the gates, Manu waited against the car, his hands behind his back. He was chewing, but Niral didn't see any spit on the ground. After they had driven five minutes, Niral asked him about it.

"A man at a shop gave me a tiny paan," Manu explained. "It contains no tobacco, and it won't fill up my mouth enough that I will have to spit. So I can chew, enjoy, and swallow."

"You could still get mouth cancer, though."

"That is if you overdo it, Niralbhai." They continued to drive.

Then Niral said, "You know, I can drive too, Manu."

"I know you want to be equal, but I would not trust you on these roads, Niralbhai."

"Equal but different. This is what Bhai taught me."

"I am glad you chose to stay."

"Yes. I was with Bhai a lot. He has some strange habits."

Manu laughed. "You focused on Bhai's habits?"

"No. But I did notice them."

Manu shook his head. "I don't want to know the habits of my teacher."

"Maybe he is an avatar."

"Bhen was an avatar. Bhai is a great man. It is too soon to know if he is an avatar."

"Let's ask Mr. Ghosh," Niral suggested.

"Mr. Ghosh would say yes."

"Yet you don't?"

"The Brotherhood has changed my life, Niralbhai. But we should follow Bhen's teachings not to judge too quickly. Still, if I see a clear sign, I will believe."

They drove on. Niral went to sleep. When they arrived at a restaurant in Rajkot, Manu awoke Niral and informed him that four hours had passed.

"I see clouds," Manu said as he ate inside the restaurant with Niral. "We shouldn't stay too long."

"How was the storm a week ago? Dwarka didn't get hit."

"Yes, the storm was mainly near Navsari and Surat. There was minor flooding in my village, but nothing too bad."

"This time people seem more concerned."

"Modi has built the dam. They shouldn't worry. But people think like in the old days. Always worrying."

They finished their thalis and left the restaurant, acknowledging the truck drivers on the side of the road.

"Were you more comfortable inside or outside?" Niral asked.

"I feel comfortable with you, Niralbhai," Manu said, smiling.

Another four hours later, they reached Ahmedabad. Once again, they sat in a restaurant, this time eating idli sambar, a southern dish of rice cakes and lentil stew.

"Is Mr. Ghosh still here?" Niral asked.

"He is back in Navsari. He may be headed to Ayodhya soon."

"Do you know why Bhai left Ayodhya for Dwarka?"

"After the court decision to separate the Babri Mosque area, many Hindu organizations, including The Brotherhood, worried there would be more attacks by Muslims. Dwarka is safer, more beautiful, and has the heritage of a democratic India back when Krishna's influence was present."

"But Mr. Ghosh said something about a situation in Ayodhya. That the Muslims swore revenge. Did he mean 1992?"

"I have heard a rumor. When Bhen was ailing, Bhai decided to build a large temple dedicated to her in Ayodhya. During a rally to announce it, a Muslim terrorist tried to strike with a bomb. Thankfully, Bhai's bodyguards shot the terrorist as he got out of his car. The bomb exploded, but it just killed the terrorists."

"Not anyone else?"

"I have not heard that."

"How did they know he had a bomb?"

"I heard Mr. Ghosh acted as an intermediary. He pretended to be sympathetic to the Muslim cause in exchange for money. Since he was an accountant, perhaps the Muslims believed him. Either way, they told him about the plot, and he tipped off the guards."

"And kept the money, I assume."

Manu laughed. "I don't know. He probably put it in The Brotherhood fund."

"Yet Mr. Ghosh doesn't travel with bodyguards."

"No, but he does employ chauffeurs like me. This is what I heard, Niralbhai. I am not, uh, privy to all information."

Niral laughed at Manu's use of the word "privy." They paid and left the restaurant. During the drive, they listened to Brotherhood shlokas recited on the radio. Then, Niral said, "So Talim has had an inside man before and been betrayed."

"If it was Talim, then yes. But Mr. Ghosh was a high-ranking member of The Brotherhood. In their eyes, you are a former believer who has left the organization but can still infiltrate it."

"Still, it's concerning."

"What you are doing is very brave, Niralbhai. I salute you." He took his hands off the wheel and performed namaste to Niral.

As they passed Bharuch, the clouds became grayer. "I hope we reach Yam Gam before it rains. Otherwise, we can divert to Surat and stay at your cousin's house until the rain stops."

"It might not be torrential," Niral said.

"Torrential? What does it mean?"

"It might not be that bad. We can drive through rain."

"I hear it will be bad. We will see."

About half an hour later, it began to rain. The drops pounded on the windowpane, and they could barely see in front of them.

"I see what you mean," Niral said. "We have monsoons in Thailand, too, but this looks worse."

"We're too far from Surat. But we are close to my village. I will try to navigate us there. Otherwise, we will have to pull over and wait in the car."

"Your house sounds better."

"Yes, we don't know how long this will last."

Manu drove slowly, his head arched forward. He was focusing on the road he could see. He took a right down a narrow road and then a left.

"We should avoid side roads, but since the situation is not bad yet, we will try to reach my village through them," Manu said. "It is a calculation because if we get stuck, it will be much worse."

"I trust your judgment," Niral said.

They continued driving slowly and making turns. Niral could hear pounding thunder.

"Damn," he said. "It's like God's angry."

"He should be angry, Niralbhai."

The car stopped. Manu pressed the pedal. Niral could hear the wheels turning.

"Try going back," Niral said, but Manu was already one step ahead. He reversed quickly, then propelled forward. The rain seemed to pound harder. Now, nothing at all was visible, but Manu kept driving, his head arched forward even more. Particles of rain were seeping through slight cracks in the car and squirting on Niral's face.

Suddenly, the car stopped again. The wheels kept turning. Manu reversed, but the car would not move. He drove forward again.

"We are close enough, Niralbhai. We should run to my home."

"How far is it? Maybe we should wait inside."

"It shouldn't be far. I am fairly certain we are inside the village. I believe we are only several meters away."

"Fairly certain? You believe?"

"I cannot see, Niralbhai!" Manu yelled. "I can only sense. Trust my sense."

Niral swallowed. "Okay, if you say so. Should I open the door?"

"No, wait until I run around to your door. But unlock it."

Niral unlocked his door. Manu took a deep breath. Then he struggled to open his own door. The strength of the rain pushed him back once, but Niral bent over, and they used all their collective strength to open it enough for Manu to slip outside. Then the door slammed shut.

Niral straightened up and waited. He couldn't see anything or anyone. He didn't know whether Manu would survive the onslaught. And he couldn't remember being in such natural danger since his fights with Martin on the East River and with Vishal in Manhasset Bay.

The rain continued to pound. He didn't hear anything else. For all he knew, Manu had been swept away or drowned. He should have insisted they wait inside.

Then something slammed into his door. He could see Manu pressed against the glass. Apparently, the rain had pinned him. Niral pulled the latch and pushed against the door, battling the weight of the rain and Manu. On the first thrust, he didn't have the power to open it. He backed up and cursed. Then he looked up and didn't see Manu anymore.

He pushed again. This time he was able to open the door a bit. As he placed one leg out, he stepped onto an uneven surface. He slipped his body out of the door as it slammed shut, and a barrage of rain engulfed him. He tripped over the uneven surface and fell into a puddle of water, struggling to rise up against the rain and wind. He spit out water that had engulfed his mouth and poured through his nostrils. Looking down and around, he realized the uneven surface was Manu's body. He bent over and picked him up by his shoulders. He considered opening the car door but decided instead to drag him, moving backwards, toward what he hoped was Manu's home.

He backpedaled until he tripped over something hard and landed on something harder. He hit his head, yelling out as Manu's body fell on top of him. But he didn't see rain. A green awning was above him. And when he turned his head up, he saw, upside down, a row of homes.

He pushed Manu's body to the side and sat up. Manu's eyes were closed. Water was bubbling from his mouth. Niral turned him around and pounded on his back, trying to get the water out of him while, in English, he screamed for help.

One door opened. A skinny woman wearing a wet, dark blue sari rushed out, holding a broom. She seemed ready to strike Niral, but when she saw Manu, she screamed, dropping the broom.

"Are you his wife?" Niral asked in English.

She didn't understand, so he asked again in Gujarati. To this, she assented.

"Let's get him inside," Niral said in Gujarati. He put Manu's arm over his shoulder and helped him up. Manu's wife took the other side. An old man peeked out another door, then closed it again.

They dragged Manu inside the home and placed him on the floor, face up. His wife left briefly to grab the broom, then locked the door from the inside.

Niral jumped on top of Manu and started pushing his chest with his palms, with no result. Thinking quickly, he changed positions. He lifted Manu up by the shoulders, got behind him, created a fist with both hands and pushed up on Manu's sternum, simulating the Heimlich maneuver.

On the third thrust, Manu's mouth ejected a stream of water. His eyes opened, and he coughed loudly.

His wife bent over him, asking him if he was okay as he breathed hard and tried to get his bearings. Niral plopped down on the floor, tired and relieved. Then he noticed an old woman, hunched over, standing in the archway to the kitchen. She put her palm up at him and smiled. He put his palms together and greeted her with namaste.

96

As Bob put on his jogging suit, he watched Sveta sleeping, curled up with her thumb in her mouth like a baby. He often watched her in the early morning before he ran to exercise and clear his mind, remembering how he would watch Linda too, but with far different thoughts.

Avoiding Kings Point Road and Gatsby Lane, he ran along the beach overlooking the Manhasset Bay. As he passed the view of Vishal's old house, a black man holding a gun ran out of the bushes. Bob stopped running and stumbled a bit, but didn't fall. He felt his heart pound faster. He thought he was having a real panic attack. But then he recognized Lance, wearing a jogging suit of his own.

"Bob, my brother," Lance said, pointing a pistol at him. Bob backed up toward the water and began to recompose himself.

"What's the meaning of this?" Bob stuttered. "My name is Franklin."

"That's what you call yourself these days? They make you WASP in witless protection?"

"I don't know what you mean," Bob said. "I'll scream, and the police will come."

"Jews always call the cops, I know that. But they didn't last time in Forest Hills, Bob. Because you didn't scream last time neither."

A wave of water hit Bob's ankle, and he shuddered.

"Before Niral left, he told me this is how Vishal passed," Lance said. "Drowning in this bay right here. Maybe you'll go the same way, Bob."

"Just tell me what you want."

"Wherever they put you, in Wyoming or wherever, must've been a sweet spot. So why you back? And why you with these council people working on that contract? Can't be a coincidence."

"I'm here with my wife."

"Gave that twat a sweet ride last time. Don't see her rich ass now."

"Linda's dead, you bastard. I remarried."

"One of the blondes? Which one, Heidi or Lauren Conrad?"

"Her name is Julie."

"I'm thinking the tall, awkward one with less class. I'd pin that on you, Bob, in the tradition of Cherry: you got that eye and good looking out. That definitely what we looking for."

"Look..."

"Let me lay it out for you, brother. I'm wondering if this Indian guy is Vishal's cousin who wants the contract. And if he's shacking up with the other blonde, that's a conflict of interest right there."

"Why do you care?"

"Cuz I live on the other side of this bay. I play volleyball on that sweet spot where Vishal passed. You dig?"

Bob froze. He felt larger waves engulf his shins, and his feet were now buried in sand underneath the water.

"You own Vishal's old house?"

Lance took out a piece of gum, unwrapped it with one hand, and put it in his mouth. "Black man owning a house like that? This country ain't that progressive yet. But I work for the man's ass."

"Who?"

"Who you think, brother? Your old comrade, Brendan."

Bob swallowed. "Brendan owns it?"

"Sure, the Feds sold it to some developer, and when Brendan come back from his long vacation, he thought, I need some peace and quiet. I need the shit Vishal stole from me. Cuz, you know, he used to own the house before Vishal. That's what he told me, anyhow."

"But how the hell do you know Brendan?"

Lance laughed, throwing the wrapper the on the ground. "Every once in a while, that facade of the genteel noble breaks, and out comes the mick in you, brother. You don't fool me. I see you. Just another pedophile. Another hard dick."

"How the fuck do you know Carty?"

"Who're you to be making demands on me? Look what I got, look what you got."

"All right, calm down."

"It's a good story, brother. But not one you need to know. Yet."

"Fine. So what..."

"I want the dirt, brother. Why you staying with this board bitch Lauren Conrad, and how'd you get Heidi on it? You looking to buy the contract?"

Bob cleared his throat. He looked back. Vishal's house was still visible but hindered by a light fog. The waves had receded and the water was gone, but his feet were still stuck in the sand.

"I'm not looking to buy, but I'm helping Hemraj."

"Vishal's cousin? I knew it. Why?"

Bob shrugged. "Feel I owe it to Vishal, I guess."

"You come out of witless protection for that? Hard to believe. He's giving you a cut, ain't he?"

"Yeah, sure, I guess."

"You guess? Well, you're gonna work for me now. I'm gonna take pics of Hemraj and this Conrad together. We'll get her ass off the board, and your wife'll vote for Carty's piece."

"And what if I don't help you?"

"It ain't difficult to guess, brother. You'll take a long swim in the bay. You'll meet Vishal all right, but it ain't gonna be light when you do."

97

When Rob woke up, his mind had cleared and he felt a sense of purpose. He was confident this foray into Udon Thani would lead to Apsara. She would explain why she had left, and they would escape and live happily in some place where he could be a normal human being for once in his life.

He took the elevator down to the reception desk, wearing his duffel bag that contained his machete, his gun, and a few saucers of ya ba along with baht earned from sales. He also held two smaller duffel bags in each hand, which he planned to attach to his motorcycle. One contained changes of underwear, the other toiletries. Duncan had kept the car since he was selling the majority of product, while Rob was subjected to living a scant and frugal life, which he was used to anyway.

As he approached the desk to check out, a voice called out "Sir!" in English. Rob turned to see a short Thai man who wore a tan suit holding up a badge.

"Police, sir," the man said. "May I ask you some questions?"

Rob didn't like the gleam in the cop's eye. He figured it couldn't be the same cop who shot at him in Phuket, but he doubted his purposes were good.

"Sure, mate. What's it about?"

"You are Australian?" Nat asked as he scanned Rob's features. This man seemed as tall as the one who had shot him in Phuket. But Nat couldn't be sure.

"Ya, mate. Been in Thailand a while, though."

"You speak Thai?"

"Only a little, mate. Sawadee kap. Sorry for not saying it. Know I should have done the wai thing too."

"No worries. This is what you say?"

"Sure." Rob laughed, winking at the hotel desk clerk. "Mind telling me what this is about? I'm about to ride out."

"Yes, yes," Nat said, chuckling, reaching into his pocket with his right arm. He took out the phone, then put up his left arm slowly to turn it on and put in his passcode.

"Funny, I need to move this arm very slowly. I got shot here."

"Shot? Wow, you really are a cop," Rob said, but didn't laugh.

"Yes, yes. You know, I never had to draw my weapon before that."

"You get shot around here? I know Isan's poor. Crime rate must be high, too."

"Yes, we do have desperate people here. Poverty does that. But no, I got shot in Phuket."

He turned the phone toward Rob and showed him the picture of Apsara.

"Do you know this girl?"

Rob moved his head forward and pretended to peruse it.

"Nah, never seen her."

"Well, look again. These Thai girls all look alike to you farang, no?"

Rob shook his head. "I'd know her if I'd seen her. I've known plenty of Thai girls, and that don't look like one I know."

"You have many giks, yes? You are a tall, handsome farang."

Rob shrugged his shoulders. "I reckon I do all right."

"Yes," Nat said, putting the phone away. "I imagine you do."

Rob handed over his room key and passport to the desk clerk. "What this girl do, anyway?"

"I can't talk about the case, Mr..."

Rob hesitated. He stuttered. "Johnson...Maric."

"Johnson Maric. What a name!"

"Yeah, I like it." The desk clerk, a young girl, matched his passport to the name in the book and crossed him off. She looked at Nat but didn't say anything.

"Right," Rob said, straightening up. "Love to gab more, officer, but I've got to jet off, mate."

"Yes, yes. One more question, Mr. Johnson Maric. Have you ever been to Phuket?"

The color went out of Rob's face, and Nat noticed it.

"Phuket?" Rob stuttered. "Sure, I guess. I don't remember."

"You don't remember? I'm sorry, sir, but it is a memorable place."

Rob opened his arms. "Been all over, mate. Seen so many fucking islands. Ko Samet, Ko Samui, that full moon place."

"Ko Pha-ngan."

"Yeah. How can I remember?"

"You don't forget Phuket, sir. Have you seen the crags?"

Rob didn't respond. His mouth went dry, and a drop of sweat dripped down his forehead.

"Your trip can wait, Mr. Maric. Why don't we go over to the police station? I'd like to ask you more questions."

Rob swallowed. "You came all the way up here from Phuket?"

"I'm a Bangkok detective, sir. Natthew. Nat for short. You don't want to know my last name."

"Bet it's long," Rob said, looking outside.

"Sure, it is Sachinkowdon. Now..."

As Nat turned to guide Rob outside, Rob struck him across the face with his elbow, sending Nat crashing to the floor. Then Rob, dropping one his bags, ran out to his motorcycle.

Nat covered his injured left eye with his right hand, while his free eye tracked his suspect. He tried to rise with his damaged arm, but it was too painful as the clerk's screams engulfed his own. But he freed his right arm and rose with both. Then, standing, he took out his pistol with his right hand and pointed it toward the motorcycle, but it had pulled away.

He gave chase. At the end of Th Glang Meuang, the motorcycle took a left toward the bus station and Khon Kaen University. Getting his car would take too long. He put his pistol back in his holster and removed his cell phone, using his damaged arm again to put in his passcode. Then he dialed the number for the tourist police since he didn't know the number for the main police station.

98

Early that morning, Duncan and Lamai took a tuk-tuk to a temple near King Rama V monument.

"Tee rak, this is the temple I go to every morning," Lamai told him.

Duncan stared at her as if he was regarding her for the first time. "You go to a temple every morning?"

"Of course. I was raised a good Buddhist girl. It gives me peace. I learn more about myself, and it helps me understand the world."

"I don't know you," Duncan said.

"Well, now you will, silly boy," she replied, slapping Duncan's cheek playfully. "It is at the edge of this park. A zoo is close by. Sometimes I go there when I want to think."

"I never knew you were this serious. Usually we just joke around."

"We Thais are taught that, you know. Don't take anything seriously; always make a joke of everything. But some girls do think."

"Mmm..."

As they got out of the tuk-tuk and Duncan paid the driver, Lamai turned to him.

"I am not like other girls, Duncan. I am not like the Isan trash in Patpong."

Duncan swallowed, his eye twitching. "I wouldn't have married you if..."

"No, you wouldn't have," Lamai said firmly, leading him toward the temple. They removed their shoes and placed them at the foot of a short staircase that led up to a small temple with a golden stupa. A few women stood on the steps, praying, while upstairs two other women lay prostrate, their arms outstretched and their palms firmly waiing.

A young monk was lighting an incense stick next to a miniature reclining Buddha. A larger, more earnest Buddha towered above him.

Lamai performed wai, closed her eyes, and prayed quickly, then, smiling, made small talk with the young monk, who was an apprentice to the monk she had come to see. He nodded and left, then returned with the older monk, then left again. Lamai gave the older monk a deep wai.

The older monk, laughing, told her to sit on the other side of the Buddha, where the three of them could be alone, though worshippers lay only a meter away. He introduced himself to Duncan as they followed Lamai into the corner, telling him in English that he was handsome. Duncan acknowledged him with a nod, but didn't answer. He sat on the floor next to his wife, their legs tucked under them, feet away from the Buddha.

"I am so glad to meet your husband at last, Lamai," the monk said in Thai, sitting as well.

"Yes, and he is glad to be here," Lamai responded.

The monk smiled. "He does not look glad," he said. Then in English he stated, "My son, I am sorry we are in a temple, not a brothel."

Lamai pretended to slap the monk. Duncan's eye began twitching again.

"I am sorry," the monk said to Duncan. "For a monk, I can sometimes have, uh, inappropriate humor. What do you call it? Toilet humor?"

Duncan shrugged. "I don't know. I'm sorry, my Thai is only average," he said in Thai.

"This is okay. I want to practice my English. Please, let us speak English!"

"Okay," Duncan assented.

"Tell me, son, are you troubled? In Thailand, we don't worry; we smile. But please, tell me if you have problems. I will advise you."

Duncan seemed hesitant to speak. So Lamai said, "His finances are not good, and he may have to lay off one or both of his workers. He wants to know what he should do."

"I see," the monk said. "This is a common problem. Son, I am afraid I cannot give you the answer, but I can tell you how to see the problem you face in a different light. Do you know the difference between altering perception and solving a problem?"

Duncan nodded. "Yes."

"In the West, you always want to solve problems. Spread democracy, kill this dictator, clean this country. We, on the other hand, look with a gleeful eye and ponder how we can view a glass differently—half empty or half full."

"Sure," Duncan said, a bit removed.

"In addition, we don't simply see the problem as an either/or. Do this or do that. Let me give you an example. Do you know how Buddha became enlightened? It was not, as some think, simply through prayer or asceticism, but rather through a Middle Way, which was between these. After leaving his kingdom where he was raised a prince, Buddha tried to live a life as an ascetic. He decided to eat only a leaf or nut a day, so he became frail and emaciated, and he almost starved to death. But then a village girl named Sujata gave him payasam, a rice pudding, saving his life. They say he also floated the expensive rice bowl on the water, willing it to float in the middle, but who knows if this is true. There are many variations of the story, but the real lesson is: this is why we value women. To feed us!"

Lamai pretended to slap him again. Duncan became uncomfortable with how close she seemed to the monk. His eye twitched furiously.

"Now look," the monk continued, "what I really mean is, extreme solutions are not necessary simply to implement them or to prove a point. You believe this decision has been laid upon you because society tells you it must be one or the other. But can you truly say you cannot find a Third Way—splitting the difference and satisfying everyone?"

"I've told him he can pay them less, rather than firing them," Lamai said.

"Of course, that is one way. But we cannot presume to understand Duncan's business. He must make the decision. I merely suggest that he be more creative and look at the situation not in terms of solving a business problem but rather like he is soothing over a personal matter."

"A personal matter," Duncan repeated. "Yes, that's what it is."

"It is?" Lamai asked.

"Maybe he sees that it is now," the monk said. "Is that so?"

Duncan nodded. He rose. "Thanks for the tip, man. Lamai, I've gotta go." He turned abruptly and left the temple. As he was putting on his shoes at the foot of the stairs, Lamai caught up to him.

"That was very rude, Duncan. You did not wai or anything?"

"Seems like a chill guy. I don't think he minds."

"Duncan, are you jealous?" She grabbed his chin and turned his face to her. "He's a monk."

Duncan slapped her hand away.

"Going to the brothel, baby," he said as he turned. "That's where I belong, right?"

99

The rain continued to pound outside. Some had seeped under the door, but it flowed inside a ditch on the floor that acted like a moat. It was near capacity, but so far, it had been a buffer against flooding.

Manu lay against the wall, still resting from the incident. His wife Sita was cooking in the kitchen, while Sita's mother sat on a mat, awaiting the meal.

Niral's headache had subsided after Sita had administered a cold, wet cloth to the lower back portion of his head. Recently, he had been speaking to Sita's mother in Gujarati. It was not traditional for a mother to live with her daughter after marriage, but Sita's mother had nowhere else to go, and Manu had kept her, citing Bhai's dictums of liberalism and compassion.

"My greedy brothers would have regarded her as another mouth to feed and kept her out. But due to Bhai's teachings, I am different," Manu said.

"Your parents?" Niral asked.

"They are dead," Manu said. "Many people die early here. It is normal."

"So Sita's mother didn't mind..." Niral stopped speaking, realizing the subject might be sensitive. But Manu smirked.

"If you mean Sita's unwed pregnancy, of course, it was not seen well.

We initially planned to run away. But the Dubla are more forgiving than other castes. Her mother embraced our union, and we were married in due course. I understand because our daughter is our only future too."

Sita charged inside with a pot which she placed on the mat. She glared at Manu harshly, then marched back into the kitchen.

Niral looked at Manu.

"She is not angry at you, Niralbhai. She is angry at me. Because of our daughter."

"Why?"

"Manu spoils her," Sita said, bringing in another pot and a bowl of rice.

"I let her be herself. Is that not The Brotherhood way?"

"The Brotherhood Way is being modest and pure. Not a hussy," Sita responded.

Manu became angry. "Don't make assumptions, Sita. Mumbai is not all about..."

"It is today. You see all the vulgarity in the movies, on the billboards. Look Niralbhai," she said, turning to him, "in the old days, my mother would work all day for the Brahmins in our village. They would give her food for her trouble. Only when Indira Gandhi raised the minimum wage did she get money, and then they stopped giving food, the cheap people. Now when we work, we earn money and make our own food. We are dignified and do not seek favors or cheap rewards. My daughter did not take OBC benefits, even though that was the easy way, because we insisted. But now she is selling her body to pay her tuition, instead of working an honest job."

"She has an honest job," Manu said angrily. "Do not believe vicious rumors."

"Her friend called and told me."

"That girl is not friends with Gayatri anymore. They had a falling out. She is trying to ruin Gayatri's reputation."

"But you did say she has rich friends," Niral recalled.

"Yes, and to impress them, she must sell her body," Sita went on.

"Her friends are a separate issue," Manu responded. "She works hard as a tutor for high school and college students. I know my daughter."

"Well, prostitution is work," Niral said, though he immediately regretted it. Sita gave him a shocked, nasty glare and looked like she might hit him with the pot she was holding.

Manu swallowed. "It is work for girls without honor. It is work she is not doing."

Sita huffed and returned to the kitchen. She called out angrily that the food was ready, that they could sit down. Niral stood and walked over to Manu.

"Do you need help?" he asked

Manu shook his head. He tried to stand but struggled. Niral helped pull him up by his armpits.

"I'm sorry for making your wife mad," Niral said.

"Sita is always mad. Right Sita?"

Sita didn't respond. It sounded like she was rolling rotli.

"Don't worry, you saved my life, Niralbhai," Manu said. "I am indebted to you forever."

"Don't say that. I did what anyone would do."

They sat by the food and recited The Brotherhood food prayer. Then they began to eat and tried to watch television, but the connection was not good, so they gave up and ate in silence. Afterwards, they lay down in the back room to sleep. Unlike his mother's home, the apartment had a bedroom beyond the kitchen and hallway that contained three beds.

Manu offered Sita's bed to Niral, saying husband and wife would sleep together in the same bed.

"Are you sure? Won't you kill each other?" Niral asked.

Manu laughed. "We fight all the time. We are married!"

Niral offered to sleep on the floor.

"It may get wet. We may have rats. Who knows. Trust me, take her bed."

They could hear the rain pounding on the back door beyond the room. Niral sat on Sita's bed.

"Do you think we'll be able to make Yam Gam tomorrow?" Niral asked. "Or Surat?"

"The rain isn't supposed to last all night. This is what I heard. We will see how flooded the land is in the morning. Due to the irrigation and dams the government has laid, we may be able to travel, but we will have to avoid side roads. Getting out of this village will be the hardest task. Still, I know a long way around that might be easier. Thankfully Yam Gam is now on a major road."

"Good. No offense, but I don't want to stay here for another day."

Manu smiled. "I would not either if I was you, Niralbhai."

"Do you think we can make it to Mumbai? Or to Surat?"

"We will see, Niralbhai. Let us see tomorrow."

PART XVII

†

Sands Point, New York; Bangkok, Thailand; Near Khon Kaen, Thailand; Near Surat, India; The Road, Gujarat, India; Yam Gam, India

---

100

A long time had passed since Bob had stood inside Carty's home. Carty's home, then Vishal's home, then the government's home, and now Carty's home again. Strange how events twisted and turned, how individuals were overthrown and replaced and yet able to rejuvenate themselves and return to their origins.

The ceiling of the interior hallway of the mansion, a construction of brick and limestone that tried to imitate the style of The Gilded Age, displayed a scene from the Judgment of Paris. Nude Greek Goddesses Hera, Aphrodite, and Athena were posing for Paris on Mount Ida, holding their various bribes to influence his decision on their beauty contest. Hera held out her palm, offering Europe and Asia; Athena held a spear, offering skill in war; and Aphrodite gave him a fruit, with Cupid hovering below with arrow pointed. Paris took the fruit, a decision which ultimately lead to the Trojan War and the foundation of Rome. In this version, Hermes looked over Paris's shoulder, while Apollo, sitting on a cloud and playing the lyre, watched in amusement from afar.

The mansion was much different than Bob's old home in Forest Hills or Sunil Patel's in North Carolina. The wide hallway that looked like a museum gallery separated into rooms at every turn. A marble staircase at the far end, out of view, led up to a second floor, which was similar in layout. The rooms were majestic; the ceilings were covered with paintings from Greek and Roman mythology imitating the style of either Nicolas Poussin or Peter Paul Rubens, and the floors filled with lesser known marble sculptures by Auguste Rodin and Alexander Milne Calder as well as bronze sculptures by Giuseppe Moretti. The paintings of John Singer Sargent and his American contemporaries mixed with the occasional Renoir, Monet, and Cezanne that decorated the walls. Carty had inherited the works from the previous owner, who had added their hefty prices to the bill after deciding to live the rest of his cancer-shortened life among the beaches of the French Riviera and the Greek Islands. Carty wasn't a great collector, but he was cognizant of the appeal of art. He preferred the image of the culturalist to the actuality of taste, yet he had developed a few rooms with contemporary works by newer artists, shopping in the same Chelsea galleries Bob Macaday had perused to fill his Forest Hills home.

Bob had always been jealous of this building, wondering how the men who invested his money could seem so much wealthier than him. Yet he had believed, wrongly, that his focus on philanthropy and the arts had made him a superior individual, above reproach. He thought that even if the sleazy hedge-fund managers were found out, he would live to be one of those childless men of wealth who would, Carnegie-style, leave a lasting legacy of social and artistic merit.

Vishal, on the other hand, had showed little interest in art or in leaving such a conventional legacy. He had left the paintings and sculptures where they were, true, because like Carty, he understood their impressionable power, but he rarely built upon them except as a tool to engage young women. He did visit galleries in Chelsea and Soho to meet young female artists and models. He did bring them back to this mansion and showed himself off as a wealthy patron of the arts, but this was merely a strategy to woo them into his prostitution ring.

Vishal wanted to be a ringleader of a secret, erotic society like in the film *Eyes Wide Shut*, and he tried to imitate its famous sequence in many of his own orgies. Most orgies would take place at this mansion. Only his workers' orgies were held at his apartment in Murray Hill.

Priya would set up the rooms and place masks, g-strings, and stripper lotion for the girls in the dressing room, then Juan would drive her back to NYU before the orgy began. Vishal wasn't a fan of the grotesque, so he frowned upon costumes that were too ornate, but he did encourage his investors to wear blander robes and masks when they pulled up to his mansion in their chauffeured cars, though many investors did cheat and wear more extravagant costumes.

Bob remembered one orgy that had changed the trajectory of his life. While taking a break, Bob had slipped into an empty room and discovered a painting that depicted Hindu Gods and Goddesses sitting in Indra's court, done in a slick, modern style that showed little understanding of Hinduism. It had no message, ambiguity, or complexity whatsoever, no icons, symbols, or movements that signified something deeper, yet it did betray a natural talent for painting. It struck Bob that Vishal must have acquired the painting himself since Bob didn't recall Carty owning any Asian works.

Vishal, maskless, had entered the room holding a glass of Sazerac and asked Bob if he was having a good time. Bob, his white, plain smile mask resting on his head, asked Vishal who had painted the work. Waving his hand, Vishal told him an amateur prostitute in the audience had donated it; he certainly wouldn't have spent money on it. Bob asked to be introduced to the young lady, and Vishal had called Cherry. She had entered completely naked, wearing a white sad mask. Vishal had encouraged Bob to take her to a private room upstairs, and their affair had begun, since Bob had insisted on taking off her mask as he made love to her. Afterwards, they had talked. She had told him her real name, narrated her ambitions and pitfalls. He had praised her talent and pledged to help her career if she would keep seeing him.

The orgies initially excited Bob, but they always led him to be depressed afterwards, and after a while, he began to prefer the individual company of ladies who made him feel special, unlike his shrewish, annoying wife, Linda. Lauren became his favorite. While he loved the sex and often reimagined it when working or masturbating, he could have lived with being apart from Lauren. But her death had hurt him to his core. Even as they had formally reconciled and moved into witness protection together, he had blamed Linda for Lauren's death and for Stan Lorenzo's murder as well. For Bob had been the one, not Vishal, who had told Roberto Tragliani about Stan's blackmail attempt from his investigation into Bob's infidelity, how his wife's greed might lead to the downfall of their enterprise. Bob had also invested in Coleman, thinking the investment would lead to a creation of a greater Long Island City, a cultural hub superior to the strip clubs and run-down buildings that stood there. Yes, he had believed he was doing something greater. He didn't realize Tragliani would resort to murder. But now he had resorted to murder too, and he didn't feel too badly about it.

The Traglianis wanted him dead because of his betrayal. Whether Alicia Tragliani knew about his role in Stan Lorenzo's death was unclear, but it didn't matter. He didn't feel bad about pinning Stan's death on Vishal, since Vishal had stolen his money when he'd absconded with Ledacorp and Coleman's funds. And now Vishal thought Bob owed him for setting Bob up with a new identity, a new life, a new wife, and for facilitating Linda's murder. But Bob knew Vishal owed him, so working with Carty didn't seem like a bad idea. Except Carty might still be angry that Bob, like many other investors, had betrayed him by withdrawing his money and reinvesting with the younger, smarter Vishal when the housing collapse had hit, benefiting handsomely from the gamble and sending Carty packing to Montana. Bob would have hit rock bottom if he had stuck with Carty. The move was common sense, but Carty had trusted him not to pull out. At that point, he had owed Vishal and screwed Carty. Now, it seemed, it could be the other way around.

Bob finally heard commotion on the back steps, which he could not see. Lance was speaking loudly, explaining his surveillance operations, and he could hear Carty's faint voice, resoundingly effeminate despite its command. Vishal had been a fast talker, an aggressive businessman who always saw an opportunity. But his ex-boss didn't come across the same way. He was a much better schmoozer, someone more like Bob Macaday himself, a polished individual who didn't need to try to influence people.

He flitted down the hall, dressed in a light blue bathrobe made of microfiber with a white silk lining. Macaday often wondered if Carty was gay, but he knew Carty had two sons, strong lions named Seamus and Lachlan, so he never broached the subject or investigated further. He thought of Carty as an aristocratic dandy from the nineteenth century who had become too complacent and self-involved when the financial crisis had hit. Now Bob wasn't sure what to expect. Brendan Carty was back. He had taken back what Vishal had taken from him, and now he wanted what Vishal wanted.

When he saw Bob, Carty ran down the hallway, his arms outstretched like an eagle, enveloping Bob in his arms but touching lightly, then moving back before Bob could return his hug, his arms still outstretched, his smile wide and far-fetched like a jester.

"Bobby, how've you been? I thought I'd never see you again. New York can't keep anyone away for long, certainly not when you're stuck in hick country. I got tired of white people, Bobby, honestly, too many damn white people in Montana. Cowboys riding horses in KKK hoods, holding towns hostage. Women saying 'Fer sure' like some Cali circus. Country saloons in Billings, lame comedy sketches in Bozeman. How many hikes can you do? How many mochas can you drink? How many games of polo can you play? That's why the first thing I got upon returning was a capable black man on my side. Isn't that right, Lance?"

"Whatever you say, brother," Lance said, chuckling.

"Well, enough about myself, my old friend. Where have you been hiding out? Oregon? Florida? Please tell me it was some place exciting."

"More exciting than you can guess, Brendan. But I'm back now. That doesn't matter."

"How can it not matter? You were out there for years...or did you come back long ago?"

"Perhaps we can talk business."

Carty laughed and turned to Lance. "Business, he wants to talk business. He just got here. Why don't you bring out the cookies, Lance?"

"Chocolate chip? Or the dark chocolate?"

"The ones imported from Belgium. Lance likes them with low-fat milk, but I know you're too sophisticated for that, Bobby. If you want milk, I can make you a white Russian."

"No thank you."

“Then I’ll have a white Russian, Lance. And a cigar.” He put his arm around Bob and guided him down the hall.

“Let’s go into the lounge. You remember it. It held that huge painting by John Singer Sargent that looks like Madame X except the lady is wearing a red dress. Who knows who it is. Probably someone famous from that time, but I’ve never figured it out.”

They entered the room. Bob remembered the bar. It was well-stocked. Lance came inside carrying a box and went behind the bar. Carty made sure Bob sat on a green, velvet-cushioned seat made of mahogany. Then he flit his arms, raising his left hand while fluttering over to the bar, holding the cigar in his mouth and waiting until Lance lit it with a match. And he blew out smoke several times before he spit out a small portion of the cigar, which he had apparently held under his tongue, into a brass saucer.

He held up his left hand again as he spoke. “Bobby, let me give you the gist. I don’t know what brought you back. For whatever reason you’re still with Vishal’s interests. I’m sure the Traglianis would love to chop you into pieces, yet you returned to help that little weasel’s cousin. But Bobby, you should be helping me. Someone stole your money. If Vishal’s dead, as Lance tells me, then it might be his family members. Maybe they promised to give back your cut if the Long Island City property went to them. I know it’s your dream. I read your testimony, that you wanted this cultural fairyland in that spot. So maybe your intentions are good. But let me tell you, once everyone knows this Patel is Vishal’s cousin and shacking up with some blonde bimbo on the board, he’s done. Then I can create your cultural fairyland. I can get your money back from the people who stole it.”

“That’s what I don’t understand, Brendan. Why are you back? Why are you interested in the Long Island City development?”

Carty laughed out loud. “You don’t see me as a beacon of progress? Am I a voice of the people or a voice of the divine?” He laughed again.

Bob remembered Carty being pretentious and arrogant, but nothing like this.

“Bobby, I know your origins are working class, three generations back of Irish immigrants. And I’m proud of my Irish background too;

hell, I've got an Irish name; I gave my kids Irish names. But one thing I'm not is Irish. My ancestors are Scotch-Irish actually, Scots who lived in Ireland, the ones who came over early and built this country. Do you think I would sit around in Montana forever, riding horses across ranches and buttfucking heifers in boots?

"My people go way back. I'm part of a legacy. I had two trust funds and a whole lot of cash. Sure, I liked running a hedge fund, but I didn't need it. So I became lazy. I liked the parties; I liked showing off the art, but unlike Vishal, I had some stake in culture. Too much so that I began to trust the economy and the instincts of my workers, instead of thinking outside the box like Vishal. Give him credit; he learned what I taught him, and he applied what I hadn't. He saw my weakness. I didn't. He's a son of immigrants; he had nothing to fall back on.

"I felt bad for the investors who lost their money. I was ashamed, so I moved away. But I never lost anything. I had nothing to lose. It was like a circus to me. But my territory had been taken over, and by who, some uncultured, new money cretin? I let time pass, figuring he would fall on his own.

"You know, I believe in fate. I'm a big believer in it. The moment I brought him here, and he looked around, amazed at the possibilities of this place, I knew he would one day own it. I even told him that. Isn't it strange how we purposely stab ourselves in the foot, bringing in people we know could cause our downfall, hell, who must by nature cause it? Read history; witness your own life. That older wife who brings in the babysitter or secretary for her husband, even though she knows, she can sense, that she will be replaced. She does it anyway because this is the natural order of things, and she must fulfill her role. She must facilitate the metamorphosis of her situation, the progression to destruction.

"Now look. A new money guy like Vishal, a hungry man, must by nature fall because he becomes too greedy; he makes the wrong friends; he bets on the wrong horses. And he knows he will. He might go to jail for securities fraud, he might die, but he must go. And men like me, even when we fall, we never die. We aren't in the papers; we don't live on lists, but we keep living, and we keep coming back, don't we?"

Lance handed Carty his white Russian, then placed a tray of dark chocolate cookies on a table next to Macaday, along with a glass of milk.

"Good idea. Great lecture," Bob said, taking and sipping the milk. "But Vishal's not dead."

Carty glanced at Lance, who shrugged. "Ain't too surprising, I guess," Lance said. "Niral told me he shot him, but he didn't see him die."

"You met him?" Carty asked Bob.

"He's the one who sent me, Brendan."

"So he's behind his cousin," Carty said. "Even better. But how do I know you're not lying?"

"I guess you don't. I can call him, but that would be too convenient."

"One call, and he's in a federal cell. Is this too easy?" Carty asked Lance.

"Forget about him," Bob advised. "He's too slick. He'll evade it somehow. Let's focus on frustrating his ambition."

Carty nodded. "So you will help us, willingly?"

"If you get me what you promise. The property developed the way I want it and my money back from that fucking thief."

"The money will be more difficult," Carty said. "But the property shouldn't be hard. I'll get the pictures and information in the right hands. But should we wait to reveal Vishal's status and location?"

"Yes, for now," Bob said, dipping the dark chocolate cookie in the milk. "We'll make him suffer. We won't give him the easy way out."

101

Finally, Nat had the DNA results from Phuket: the DNA on the mattress matched the corpse they found. In addition, the Royal Thai police had acquired Patricia Murphy's picture from the El Paso police department and matched it to the corpse's head, as waterlogged and slightly decomposed as it was, using a computer program comparing facial structures. They still awaited DNA results from the toothbrush in her El Paso apartment to confirm her identity.

While the El Paso police initially seemed reluctant to cooperate, citing jurisdictional concerns, they now seemed eager to help. They searched for Patricia Murphy's family members but didn't find any in El Paso or elsewhere besides her husband. However, they were on the verge of acquiring a warrant to search her phone records and other information.

The El Paso police also sent a picture of Robert Murphy, Patricia's husband, who the Thai police considered a missing witness. The commissioner considered releasing it to the press, but first they pressed Panit, the man in custody, to reveal if he had taken Robert's life too.

The suspect's DNA had not been found on the mattress, which was a blow, but General Chaow assumed this was only because he had taken proper precautions or merely got lucky. Many other strands of DNA had been found there, but so many people had stayed in the room, and so many maids had cleaned the beds that most were likely irrelevant. Still, they were kept for possible future matches. The Thai police awaited the arrival of Bob's toothbrush to check his DNA, but his DNA's presence on the mattress, at least, would not be surprising or revelatory since he had certainly slept there.

"They should check this Borisslava Maric's DNA on the mattress," Nat told Pom over the phone. "I've got swabs from his toothbrush, which he dropped. I think he's the guy, not this Thai Panit."

"You know our resources are limited. They are not going to check every DNA sample. Plus, they have their man. They just want to confirm he is guilty."

"I would go interview the suspect again, but I don't have time. I need to follow up on this Maric. Maybe you can go instead."

"I'm still investigating this go-go dancer Apsara here. I've talked to ladyboys in Klong Tuey, and now I'm standing inside her apartment. Turns out her roommate is a ladyboy. She says this Apsara had some boyfriends, especially two farang named Rob and Duncan."

"Ask her if she knew a Borisslava Maric. He's Australian. I've got his passport right here. I'm going to mail you the DNA swabs, Khun Pom. Promise me you will try to match them up."

Pom sounded upset. "Remember your place, Junior Detective! Do not ask me to promise you anything!"

"I'm sorry, Khun Pom. I don't mean disrespect. I just want the truth."

"We are in the wrong profession for truth, Natthew," Pom said softly. "But I will try."

"I will also fax you a copy of his passport. See what you can find out about him. I'm working with Khon Kaen police here to track him. Oh, and remember this: I think his nickname is Johnson."

"Okay, I will ask. You've had to draw your gun twice now, Natthew. Please, be careful."

"I know. Since we have to pay for it out of our own pockets, we should conserve bullets," he said, reciting an old Thai police joke.

When Pom hung up, he turned to Buppha.

"Do you know a Maric? Australian?"

"Maric? I don't know. Duncan and Rob. Rob might be Australian. Or British."

"How about a Johnson?"

Buppha shrugged. "Before, a Thai man would come by."

"Pornopat?"

"Yes, that was his name. He made me uncomfortable. Very slick, a bad Thai man. But Apsara, she called him something else."

"What?"

"I don't remember. But she called him something else."

102

Now on the run, Rob decided to avoid Udon Thani. The police dragnet would be higher in a city. So he headed back to the village where the boy had given him information.

He found the boy standing next to the stilts of his house. Seeing no one else was around, he took out his gun and forced the boy up the ladder. Inside, his grandmother seemed to be convalescing.

"What do you want, sir? I am sorry about before. If you did not find this girl..."

"Shut up. Tell me, how long have you lived in this village?"

"My whole life, sir."

"That's good, mate. Let me stay here. Don't tell anyone else I'm here.

Bring me food and drink when I want. If you tell anyone, I'll shoot your grandmother."

"Okay, sir," the boy said, swallowing. "What do you want to drink?"

"I'll tell you when I want to drink," he said, sitting in the corner. "Listen, do you have a phone?"

"Not one like you..."

"But you have a cell phone. Like a shitty cell phone, ya mate?"

The boy took out a small flip phone and gave it to Rob, who called Duncan with it, but the call went to voicemail. He tried again. On the third try, Duncan picked up.

"Hello?" he asked.

"Third time's a cinch, mate."

"Rob? You got another phone?"

"I've got to cover my tracks, mate. Bit of a situation."

"Situation?"

"Sure, nothing I can't handle, but I might have to stay out of sight for a bit."

Duncan didn't respond. He seemed to be thinking.

"Mate?"

"Whatever it is, deal with it. You can't come back here."

"What you mean? We're partners. Or did you forget?"

"Not anymore. Mr. Hong wants you eliminated. You and Apsara."

"Why me? I'm..."

"A liability, in his eyes. Look, I'm doing you a courtesy. I could have just done what he wanted, lured you and Apsara back and had him kill you both. Find her and get the fuck out of Thailand."

"Mate, if this is some trick meant to keep me out of the game..."

"If you step foot in Bangkok again, you're a dead man. I might want to get out too. That's all I can say now. Trust me."

Duncan hung up. Rob looked at the phone, then smashed it against the floor in frustration.

The boy stared at his phone, now in pieces, astonished.

"Now you can get me that drink, mate," Rob mumbled.

103

Niral and Manu woke up early. They no longer heard rain pouring outside. When they ventured to the front door, they noticed the moat had overflowed and water had seeped over the living room floor. However, the level was shallow, and the flow hadn't extended into the kitchen.

Gently, Manu opened the door. A light tide of water poured inside, and Niral could see the road was flooded by a stream of water three inches deep.

"This is okay," Manu explained. "The road is slightly dipped in the middle to keep water away from the homes and steer it out of the village. It will be worse outside, but if this is how bad it is here, I don't think we will have a problem driving to Yam Gam."

So they said goodbye to Sita and her mother, then slowly drove out to the road in the early morning light, their shoes, socks, and feet soaked. They swerved around to an alternative road, where the water was twice as high and trees were overturned and uprooted. After fifteen minutes of driving, Niral saw a naked boy stroking the head of a woman who wore a drenched sari. She was sitting in the water and leaning against a tree, her eyes closed.

"Should we check if she is okay?" Niral asked.

"It is up to you, Niralbhai. I don't advise it."

They stopped. Niral got out and approached the couple.

"It rained a lot, and we were trapped in our hut," the boy muttered in Gujarati, pointing toward a structure several meters away, a collapsed shack of corrugated metal that Niral had not noticed.

"It fell on us," he continued. "My father is dead. My mother is breathing badly."

Manu waded toward the metal shack and peeked inside.

"A body is in here," he confirmed. "It seems to be crushed. I don't think we can do anything."

"Have you called the police?" Niral asked the boy.

The woman opened her eyes. Tears emerged, and she began muttering what Niral assumed was her husband's name.

"Satu, oh Satu, you stupid man..."

Niral took out his phone and asked Manu for the police's phone number. Once they had called, Manu recommended they move on.

"We can do nothing, Niralbhai," Manu said. "He is dead."

"The police should be here already."

"They have many places to go. They cannot save everyone. Neither can we."

"These people shouldn't be living in a shack."

"It is common, Niralbhai. On my way back, I can try to resettle them in the village. I did not know they lived here. Or who they are. It has been a long time since I have been down this road."

Niral rubbed the boy's head and turned to go. The boy shouted for him to stop.

"Sir, please, help us. Give us money and food."

Niral turned back, but Manu held his arm.

"I will take care of them when I return," he said. "Don't worry."

They proceeded to the car and drove away. Niral looked back and saw the boy standing, staring.

They continued to see devastation. Dead bodies, crying children, and families sitting on the side of the road. This included the main road.

"Does this happen often?" Niral asked.

"I haven't seen this level of catastrophe in some time. We have monsoons often. Only a few people die. But there are so many people in Gujarat. Of course, there will be some casualties."

"What is Bhai's solution? Has he addressed it?"

"Bhai is a spiritual leader, not the chief minister. He wants more shelters built for those in harm's way, but even the Dubla have their villages, so ultimately God will choose who lives and dies, who suffers and does not."

"Bhai keeps talking about saving people, but he means only spiritually?"

"We've gone beyond Bhen's focus on spiritual transformations. We do social work now. But we must plan strategically. One day, we may have the huge following we envision, but today, we must work project by project, like building my village. It was laid on a relatively high surface and with a dipped road to minimize damage during floods."

"How about the farm lands?"

"Farmers are happy about the water, of course, but we are already at the end of mango season, so it could be a boon or a curse. It depends on the crop. But I am not a farmer, Niralbhai."

They continued to drive slowly down the main road. The water level was less here, maybe an inch up. An hour and a half later, the water level became higher, and Niral saw ahead the faliya of Yam Gam.

Manu turned the car and drove up the slope. The faliya, being on raised land, was not flooded, as the water had simply drained down into the road. Yet Kauntiaunti was sitting on the porch, weeping. Lakshmanbhai was comforting her.

As soon as the car stopped, Niral opened the door and rushed to her, slogging through the muddy road.

"What happened?" Niral asked.

Kauntiaunti was shocked to see him. "Niral. God, how happy I am to see you!"

She rose and hugged Niral. Then Niral began to feel tight in his stomach.

"Meetal," he said. "Is she okay?"

Kauntiaunti didn't answer.

"She is missing, Niral," Lakshmanbhai responded.

"Missing? For how long?"

"She usually comes home when it rains," Kauntiaunti said. "Or she stays in the Dubla village. But..."

"You've checked the field?"

"The Dubla women have searched it far and wide," Lakshmanbhai said. "They suspect foul play. They are angry."

"Narendrakaka is with him?"

"No, he is in the Dubla village, overlooking another tragedy."

"What tragedy?"

"Manish is dead."

"How?"

"The village was flooded. It is on a lower elevation, so this happens often, and the people know to head to their roofs. But some children were watching television in the communal building and were trapped when the flood came. So when Manish and Harshkaka found out, they waded out in the rain to rescue them. Harshkaka said the water flooded into the building when they opened the door, but he was able to take two children on his shoulders and two by their hands. He closed the door as he left so the water couldn't flood the place completely, but while Manu was trying to rescue the other two children, the television, which was plugged in, crashed into the water and broke. It electrocuted Manish and the two children, or at least this is what we believe."

"My God," Niral said. "Where were these children's parents?"

"Huddled on their own roofs. They assumed their children were at friends' houses when the rain began, and that they had climbed to their friends' roofs."

"Wow," Niral said, looking at Manu. "More people dying. But I think Meetal is alive. I can't believe she could..."

Kauntiaunti began crying. Niral looked at the flooded road curving toward the Dubla village.

"I'm afraid the situation is even worse than I have portrayed, Niral," Lakshmanbhai continued. "One of the children described a young man of Satish's description encouraging the children to stay inside the building as it began to rain. Then someone who sounded like Pranam, according to Lata, called her cell phone and told her about the children trapped inside. Some Dubla say it was a setup, that the brothers expected both Manish and Harshkaka to die so they could settle the dispute. Manish had just paid a portion of the dowry, but he could not afford the entire thing. Now with his death, Prameshbhai will get his land back. Perhaps he will give some money to Pranam. This is what they say. Personally, I believe it."

"That's terrible," Niral said. "But it sounds far-fetched. How could they push the TV? By remote control?"

"Far-fetched or not, it is believed. A gang of Dubla marched to the Brahmin village at dawn. They could not find Satish, but they took the brothers by force, tying them up and parading them into the Dubla village. They are holding them hostage, threatening to burn them alive unless Satish gives himself up. The Brahmins are gearing up for a counter-offensive."

"And the police?"

"No one has called them. It will only make things worse."

"And Prameshbhai?"

"He is holed up in his home with his daughter, Madhuri, armed with a rifle. The Dubla women, suspecting he had something to do with Meetal's disappearance, have warned him not to leave the house. You can see one of them guarding the house there."

Niral looked toward Prameshbhai's house and saw her. She wore a purple sari and held a stick.

"A stick is no match for a rifle," Niral observed.

"Yes, but if he fires, he will be overwhelmed. Women are in the back and side of the house too."

"He hasn't called the police? I thought they were in his pocket?"

"I suspect he assumes that calling them will only inflame the situation and lessen his grip on power, possibly destroying it. He believes he can talk and deal his way out of it, as he always has."

Niral shook his head. "A piece of work," he said.

"I will call Mr. Ghosh," Manu told Niral, taking out his phone. "He is close by."

Niral didn't say anything. He turned to Lakshmanbhai. "I'd love to help search for Meetal, but it sounds like this situation in the village is more important. Take me there."

Lakshmanbhai smiled. "I am glad you will help the Dubla."

Niral turned to Manu, who seemed to be speaking to Mr. Ghosh.

"Manu," he said. "Look after Kauntiaunti."

Manu finished his sentence, then said, "Niralbhai, I have to pick up Mr. Ghosh. He is close by and can come."

Niral rolled his eyes, but he suppressed his natural impulse to dissuade assistance and said, "If he wants to help, I guess he can come."

Niral consoled Kauntiaunti again, assuring her that Meetal would be found. Kauntiaunti said she was praying to God, that she couldn't live with losing another child. Niral was moved by her comment. Sure, he and Meetal had fought when reconnecting, but after seeing how she had changed, and after losing so many others in the past, he couldn't accept her potential death. But now he had a greater duty to fulfill, and he couldn't get caught up in personal matters from long ago. So he controlled his emotions and told Kauntiaunti he would be back shortly.

He followed Lakshmanbhai down the road toward the village. The water level was several inches high on the road, but when they entered the Dubla village and descended the slope, the level became much higher. By the time he saw the communal building, standing around where he hid last time, they were waist deep in water. Lakshmanbhai told him to keep moving. Niral worried about infection from the water, which was filled with dirt and debris, but he kept on.

"Thankfully the building is made of wood," Lakshmanbhai said. "Harshkaka closed the door, and that stopped the current from spreading. Otherwise, it might have killed him and the other children too."

Niral could see men standing on Kamkaki's roof holding shovels, pipes, and flaming wood sticks. One man held a rifle. Inside Kamkaki's home, Manish's dead body, along with two children, lay on tables, side by side, just above water level. Someone had anointed their foreheads with kum kum powder and dry rice.

Niral followed Lakshmanbhai up a staircase to the roof. There he saw Kamkaki, Lata, and two other women in a corner weeping, being comforted by Narendrakaka. In another corner, Harshkaka, holding a rifle, stood over two men who lay on the floor, faces down, hands, feet, and mouths bound.

Several young Dubla men stood next to Harshkaka. A few wobbled a bit like they were drunk. One of them, whose eyes were red, held a flame and pretended to kick the bound men as he taunted: "Let's drown them in the water."

"We will get Satish first, Pankaj," Harshkaka replied coldly. Narendrakaka saw Niral, got up and rushed to him.

"Niral, I am glad you are here," he said.

"How do they have guns?" Niral asked.

Narendrakaka was startled by the question, but he answered quickly. "An old Dubla found them in a shed. They were stored long ago for emergency purposes. The idea was to scare people, but we discovered they are loaded with real bullets."

"Prameshbhai?" Niral asked.

"Yes," Harshkaka said, turning around. "We will go to Prameshbhai's home armed with the rifles. We will force him to surrender and face justice."

"Harshbhai, I know you are angry, but this is crazy!" Narendrakaka exclaimed.

"Don't lecture me, Narendrabhai! I may be your employee in the wadi, but I have dignity, too. Here, we are the masters. For too long we have allowed the Brahmins, and hypocrites like Prameshbhai, to treat us like dogs. We put up with their tricks and their threats, watching them grow richer and richer while we did the labor and received nothing. Now that they have murdered my nephew and these poor children, we will finally take what is rightfully ours."

"Prameshbhai will call the police if you approach him with a rifle," Narendrakaka insisted. "They will hunt you down and kill you. Do you think that will be good for Kambhen or Lata?"

"We will have justice in this village. One way or another."

"Remember, you are brothers," Lakshmanbhai said. "Allow me to negotiate as an in-between."

"With all due respect, Lakshmanbhai, you are a Brahmin too," Harshkaka reminded him.

"I was a fair mayor of this village, if you remember."

"No mayor was ever fair," Harkshkaka said. "I agree, it was our fault for electing Prameshbhai, but he has gone too far. When Narendrabhai explained his methods to me, I did not believe him, but I have seen the light now. Come, these boys' parents require justice. Cut the bindings off their feet. We will march these rogues to Prameshbhai's porch."

The two Dubla smiled and, taking out knives, cut the bindings off the brothers' feet, making sure to nick them in the legs so they would squirm. Then, the brothers were picked up by their arms, which were tied behind their backs, and pushed toward the staircase, the Dubla men yelling, "Come on, sisterfuckers, come on!"

Harshkaka led two middle-aged men, who seemed visibly sad, to the staircase. Niral assumed these were the children's fathers. Narendrakaka turned to Niral. "We must stop Harshkaka. He will seal his own doom."

"What should we do?"

"I don't know. Call Bhai."

"Manu has gone to pick up Mr. Ghosh from Navsari," Niral said.

"Good. Hopefully he will arrive in time."

"But what can he do?"

"Talk sense, maybe. Look, in case the Brahmins come with their own mob, the other man with the rifle will stay here to guard the women. This village could become Rwanda fast. We need someone with sense in both places. You can stay behind to comfort the women or go reason with Harshkaka and Prameshbhai. It is your choice."

"I've never been able to comfort anyone," Niral said, remembering Lauren. He watched the women and saw Lata's once lustful gaze had turned to unalterable sorrow.

"Okay, then I will stay here," Narendrakaka said. "You go with Lakshmanbhai and try to talk sense into Harshkaka and the other men."

"What do I say?"

"Say what I've said. Preach the principles of our faith."

"I don't think he wants to hear that. Our faith created the caste system."

"I meant The Brotherhood. Harshkaka is better than the others. He has listened in the past, although he has not converted from his ritualistic ways."

Niral nodded. Harshkaka and his men were well ahead but just past the village, Niral and Lakshmanbhai caught up to the group's tail end. Niral scanned the road to see if a Brahmin mob was marching from the other villages. He didn't see anyone, so he continued to follow the Dubla mob. As they approached the slope, Niral caught up to Harshkaka.

"Harshkaka, what do you hope to gain from this?" he asked.

"Niral," Harshkaka said, smiling briefly. "I am sorry we did not meet last time. I was busy in your mother's wadi, and we were not invited to Prameshbhai's dinner. Do you remember visiting as a boy, how I would throw mangoes down to you that I caught in my net?"

"Vaguely. I mean a little."

"I still remember. You have grown so big. I'm sorry you had to discover the realities of the world."

"Maybe there is a better solution," Niral said. "What if Prameshbhai steps down as mayor and pays restitution to the families?"

"Why would Prameshbhai admit to the murders? He will never do that. He must learn he cannot get away with such maneuvers. I am not a violent man, but I will fight for right."

As they approached, Niral saw that a crowd of Dubla women had surrounded Prameshbhai's home, all carrying sticks. The Brahmins of the faliya watched from their porches, speechless. Prameshbhai was standing in one of his two doorways, holding his rifle slackly in his left hand as a Dubla woman yelled at him.

When he saw Harshkaka's mob approach with Pranam and Ravi, he rushed inside the house and closed the door.

"Prameshbhai!" Harshkaka roared. "Do not be a coward and hide from justice. Do you see these men, your lackeys?"

He pointed to Pranam and Ravi. The women stepped aside for the men. Pankaj kicked Pranam in the back, and he fell forward onto Prameshbhai's stairs. Ravi met the same fate.

"What do you want?" Prameshbhai yelled from inside. "I have not done anything. Let me mediate your dispute. I am the mayor!"

"We've had enough of your mediations, Prameshbhai!" Harshkaka yelled. "Come out and face justice, too."

"Justice for what?"

"What, he asks? You ordered these men to lure me and Manish into the communal building so you could murder us. We know your ways. You claim to be innocent of all things. You will do this: give Lata the farm, release her dowry debt from Ravi, absolve the marriage, and order the Brahmins to give us Satish. Then we can talk about monetary restitution. Otherwise, you and your daughter will suffer the same fate as these young men. And it will not be pretty."

"Leave Madhuri alone! She is innocent."

"But you are not. So come out."

"I will call the police. They will have you all arrested."

"You will die before they arrive," Pankaj shouted. "Your house will burn. Call the police, if you dare." He took out a bottle of kerosene, opened it, and began pouring it on Pranam and Ravi. Both men were shaking.

"We will burn them like the Muslims did to the Hindus in Godhra," he said, laughing.

Suddenly, another door on the porch opened, and a girl rushed out. She was light-skinned, had long hair, and wore a white slip. She blocked Pranam from the kerosene and was doused too.

"Just what we wanted," Pankaj said, grabbing her hair. "This is your daughter? No wonder we never see her. So pretty..."

He fondled her breasts and laughed. Some Dubla women looked disgusted but didn't say anything. Niral could see Harshkaka was uncomfortable, but didn't intervene in the molestation.

"Put your rifle on the ground and come out," Harshkaka ordered Prameshbhai. "And I promise you, we will not hurt your daughter."

Behind him, Niral heard a car driving up to the faliya. Meanwhile, on the road below, he heard voices, like a crowd of people marching.

The car stopped abruptly, and Mr. Ghosh got out. But Niral decided to do something. He ran up the stairs toward Prameshbhai's house and stopped halfway. He faced the Dubla crowd.

"This is wrong!" Niral shouted. "Prameshbhai will surrender, he will make right his wrongs, but do not hurt anybody!"

"Who are you, an American?" Pankaj asked, still holding Madhuri by her hair. "You talk about justice. Where is the justice in America?"

"Calm down, brother. This is not the way," Niral said.

"I will not calm down. I will show you justice!"

Pankaj took the flame and lit Madhuri on fire. She shouted and fell into Pranam, who also became enflamed. Ravi managed to run a meter away, but another Dubla grabbed him and shoved him onto the stairs. Meanwhile, his brother and Madhuri continued to burn, and the crowd heard their blood-curdling screams. Pankaj moved to torch Ravi, too, but a shot rang out, and Pankaj fell onto the stairs. Niral turned to see that Harshkaka had shot him, his arms trembling as he held the rifle.

A Dubla woman shouted that Prameshbhai was escaping out the back. A number of men ran to track him down. Meanwhile, Niral turned to see Mr. Ghosh marching forward, followed by a crowd of Brahmins, led by Meetal. She wore a saffron robe, and her skin was darker than he remembered. They had Satish, and his hands were bound.

The couple continued to shout and scream as they burned, the Dubla women staring at them, horrified and helpless. The couple fell to the mud and rolled, but they kept burning. A few Dubla women stepped forward to try to stamp the flames with their feet, but they were unsuccessful. Finally, one ran to Prameshbhai's backyard to get a bucket of water.

Meetal held up her hand. "The Brahmins have decided to do the right thing and hand over Satish. He has confessed."

The Dubla woman finally came out of the house and doused Pranam and Madhuri with water. But it was too late. The charred bodies were deceased.

Satish cried as he fell to his knees before the fathers of the dead children and related the story of Prameshbhai's plot. Niral witnessed the charred bodies and the dead Pankaj on the steps and listened to Satish's sick story of murder and greed. His blood began to boil, and he began to feel angry.

Meanwhile, Prameshbhai had been captured and was brought forward. He appeared simultaneously resigned and terrified. As they approached the crowd, a Dubla tapped Niral and gave him his rifle to hold as he picked up the flame Pankaj had dropped.

Satish continued to confess the plot, the fathers sobbing as they heard the reason why their children had died. "We wanted to kill Manish and Harshkaka and the children. We hoped they would all drown. We wanted revenge for Lata. We wanted the farm so we could sell it for more money. Vishnu, Prabhu, I am sorry. Please, don't spare me. I deserve death. I deserve..."

Niral snapped. Before he knew it, he was beating Satish with the rifle butt. No one stopped him. They all watched while Niral beat in his skull.

As Niral caught his breath, astonished at his own sudden, violent action, the Dubla with the flame gestured that he should finish Prameshbhai too.

Prameshbhai was shaking, his head down. "You killed my daughter. Please kill me, too."

Niral shook his head. "I'm done with that," he said, handing the rifle to a father, then turning and walking away, as if in a trance. "Let him kill you if he wants to."

The father reared back with the rifle but hesitated.

"Enough, Ramonbhai," Harshkaka said, his hands up. "Enough."

PART XVIII

†

Yam Gam, India; In and Near Khon Kaen, Thailand; Kings Point, New York; Bangkok, Thailand

---

104

Once evening had struck and the sun was setting, the bodies were ready for their ritual cleansing by fire: three bodies, dead of electrocution, including one man and two children; two charred bodies, one man and one woman; a man shot through the chest; and a last man whose skull had been beaten in like a pumpkin. The seven lay side by side near the stump where Meetal worshipped, washed, dressed modestly in white, and covered with chandlos and ghee, atop bamboo constructions on separate pyres of wood which men and women, Brahmin, Vaishya, and Dubla alike, had spent the day gathering.

Meanwhile, another gathering was taking place inside Prameshbhai's home. Narendrakaka, Lakshmanbhai, Meetal, Niral, Manu, and Harshkaka were in attendance. Mr. Ghosh led the meeting and was waving his arms around as he spoke. "We need a Marshall Plan for this village! Do not worry; Bhai will provide. This will be The Brotherhood's greatest triumph. The people have had a shock, but this was needed to bring a truly communal village to order, one where men will be equal under God, not masters and slaves!"

Lakshmanbhai said, "We still need someone to lead. Who will handle the funds? I imagine you will not stay in the village."

"I respect you greatly, Lakshmanbhai, but I think many can rule here simultaneously," Mr. Ghosh replied. "Of course, Bhai will be the leader, the spiritual guide. But it is better to have a council, with one person representing a caste. From conversation, I have gathered Meetal is close to the Dubla, or the Halpati as they prefer to be called. Narendrabhai is respected by the Brahmins. And perhaps your wealth, Lakshmanbhai, has inspired the Vaishyas. Each of you will represent the various needs of each caste until these councils are not needed anymore. Right now, they are needed, until the revolution progresses."

"You forget that Meetal has sworn to live as a sanyasi," Narendrakaka said. "As have I, with less limits. How can we..."

"Don't you wish to serve The Brotherhood again, Narendrabhai? Bhai is willing to overlook your past transgressions. And it is Meetal's choice, but I feel she desires deeply to help the Halpati. It will not be a tremendous amount of labor. I have already seen you act for the common good."

"I, too, have the support of the Dubla," Harshkaka noted. "I am not saying I want to be on any council, for I wish to avoid politics as much as possible. Perhaps it is better for Dubla to stay out, so as not to be corrupted as Prameshbhai was."

"If you wish to represent the Dubla, I don't mind," Mr. Ghosh said. "But if you do not, I think Meetal has the support of the Dubla women especially, and she is well-respected in this village."

Meetal stood up. She had been sitting on the floor, her legs crossed. "If this is to be a great revolution, why are we talking about a divided government? We should have none, shouldn't we?"

"Did Iraq work without a government after the dictator's fall?" Mr. Ghosh asked. "There may be chaos. This structure will lead the way toward brotherhood and peace."

"How about the money?" Lakshmanbhai asked. "How will we receive it, and how will it be allocated? Will there be one account..."

"Always you who asks about money first, Lakshmanbhai," Mr. Ghosh joked. "We can make Manu in charge of communication and transactions. He often moves between Dwarka, Bharuch, and here. He's been a driver for a long time, but he's always wanted a greater role in our organization. He was born a Halpati, so this will be our lower caste component. He is very intelligent and will..."

Niral stepped outside to take a breath. He descended the stairs and decided to keep walking. In the distance, he heard Dubla women reciting communal prayers near the pyres. Niral had spent much of the day taking long walks as the villagers worked collectively and discussed the fates of bodies and men. He was shaken by his actions and hadn't changed clothes yet or washed; Satish's blood was still on him, and the burning bodies were still on his mind. Only when Manu had discovered him was he summoned to the meeting, where he had learned how the community had proceeded in the aftermath of the drama.

As an initial step in healing caste wounds, Narendrakaka, Lakshmanbhai, and Harshkaka, with Mr. Ghosh's guidance, had decided to burn the dead together. Villagers from every caste had trekked into the woods to gather bamboo, timber, and kindle, while others had helped moved the bodies from the Dubla village and Prameshbhai's house, and still others had cleansed the bodies as possible, then dressed and ornamented them. Then villagers had gathered in back of Prameshbhai's house where Prameshbhai and Ravi were tied up so they wouldn't be spotted from the road. They had discussed whether they should be imprisoned indefinitely, allowed to reintegrate with the village, or burned along with their peers. Some feared freeing them would ruin any attempt to salvage the disastrous event and refashion it as a liberating and revolutionary moment, since they would likely run to the police. Finally, Harshkaka had decided to move the pair to the Dubla village and place them under house arrest until their fates could be decided, with Dubla, Vaishya, and Brahmins assisting in the transport.

Now these men of the village were making decisions about its future while Niral continued to pace and ponder, walking down the faliya path toward the slope, then back again. He remembered Amrat's burning like it was yesterday, his own leap and tumble into the drainage pipe. The slitting of Lauren's throat, the destruction of sinful establishments. He hadn't waited to see if that led to revolution. He doubted it had. The cycles of corruption, greed, power, and violence had likely continued. Why would an orgy of murder here—part deliberate and part passionate—lead to anything better?

One thing he did accept was his identity as a murderer. He couldn't discount Vishal's and Thanat's deaths as accidents. Whether cold-blooded or hot-blooded, violence was part of his nature, he realized. Years ago, while sitting in his small apartment in Brooklyn, staring at dilapidated buildings filled with welfare recipients, wondering if his book could be published or if it would sell, did he ever imagine his world would crumble as it had?

His worries had been a luxury. Now, his worries did not matter. His actions led to death, one way or another. He had promised murders still. He knew from the myths that the avatars killed, in some cases massacred, yet were deified as incarnations of God. Had his actions been right, or were they wrong, or were they somewhere in the middle? Was he a man born to lead and save, to vanquish evil and rescue good, or was he just a normal man muddling along who passively murdered when convenient because he did not have the backbone to stand up to the powers that pulled his strings? Did he even care?

Niral sat on the cliff of the slope leading to the still-flooded road and began to ponder these things, but when he found them pointless, he began to block them out of his mind again, until he couldn't any longer, and he began pondering again, not knowing which way to go.

He heard someone approach. When he turned, he saw Meetal. Her saffron robes were torn and her hair, bunned up, was slightly disheveled, so that a strand of long, slightly curly, black hair hung down and stuck out an angle. She sat by him.

"I believe you now, Niral Solanke," she said. "You killed my brother. You're a killer."

Niral nodded. "I am."

They sat in silence. Niral listened to the mating song of crickets, males for females.

"They'll cremate them in the same space that I pray," Meetal said. "I should object."

"Too late. I assumed it was your idea."

"You assume too much, Niral Solanke."

"So you'll be a politician now? From journalist to hipster to sanyasi to council member?"

"The Dubla need me. Especially the women. I'll continue to pray."

"Will you? I'm not so sure."

"What do you think about me, Niral? Truly?"

"Your mother thought you were dead. I didn't believe her. No way you could die this early, with so much to prove. I don't think you were born to pray to a deity forever."

"I needed to disappear to ingratiate myself toward the Brahmins. To protect my Dubla. And the women behaved like I thought they would, rallying for me."

"See, a politician already. You didn't even need Mr. Ghosh."

"Maybe I am my brother's sister."

"And your father's daughter. He didn't become Big Brother simply through devotion," Niral said.

"He's back in a position of governance. I just wish Vishal was alive to see it."

"Maybe he's a cricket now, singing for a woman. Like he never could in his past life."

"Very funny. I really didn't know about Priya. That my brother would do that to her."

"He did. And he scarred my face, my body, my soul. It was him, not just Amrat. He put everything in motion."

"If you say so. Either way, you vanquished him, just like you killed Satish. If people do bad things, you destroy them. Like some avatar."

"Plenty of people who die are innocent."

"Not when you kill them," she said.

He looked at her sharply. "You ask me what I think of you? Truly? I think you're a bitch. And a fraud."

Meetal smiled. "I'm sorry you think that. But will your thoughts patch those scars on your face? Come, Niral. Let's go obliterate the dead."

105

Lamai was at work when Duncan heard the doorbell rang. He was sitting in his room, wearing pajamas. Ya ba containers and baht bills were spread over his bed as he worked on a spreadsheet on his laptop. He was calculating his sales and deciding where to sell his merchandise without attracting suspicion. He had lost two people, Rob and Apsara. Niral was essential to bring in needed merchandise, yet he was still out of the country, and Mr. Hong's verdict on him was undecided. With Sumantapat and the police on the prowl, and with Mr. Hong bearing down, Duncan figured he was safer staying out of the immediate Bangkok area and dealing with a credible source Rob and Niral had worked with before: Kan near Kanchanaburi.

He heard another ring. Hurriedly, he placed the ya ba containers and money under his mattress, then saved the spreadsheet and shut his laptop. He felt mocked by a laughing Buddha that Lamai kept on the desk, so he turned it around, then thought better of it and turned it back.

When he peered through the keyhole, the last person he expected to see was a small man wearing a suit and holding up a police badge. He felt a pang in his chest as he opened the door.

"Sawadee kap!" the man said.

"Sawadee kap. Can I help you?"

"Are you Duncan Smith?" the man asked, reading from a pad in his other hand.

"Yes."

"Sponsor of Borisslava Maric?"

Duncan's eye began twitching as he scanned the badge. The man placed it back in his pocket.

"What is this about?" Duncan asked.

"My name is Detective Pomrachat Katankug. May I come inside? I have some important questions to ask you. If you do not mind."

"Sure, I guess," Duncan said. He let Pom inside, then closed and locked the door.

"A nice place you have here," Pom said, looking around the apartment. "Very far up. We police officers don't live so well. We only get paid once a month. We have to purchase our own firearms, bullets, uniforms, cars, bikes. Even our own badges."

"I'm sorry. I know you guys work hard."

Pom smiled. "Yes, we do what we do out of love for Thailand."

Duncan offered Pom a seat on the couch, but Pom continued to stroll around the apartment, peering at odds and ends.

"You know," Pom continued, "they mainly keep me in Klong Tuey, dealing with the scum: drug dealers, ladyboys, prostitutes. Not often does a case take me to an apartment like this."

"It isn't so great," Duncan said. "Only one bedroom."

"Yes, but you have a pool upstairs. A gym too. Mr. Duncan, what do you do for a living?"

"I'm a jewelry merchant."

"How does that work?"

"I buy polished diamonds from an Indian merchant. I have them made into jewelry at a factory here, then I sell the pieces abroad."

"Where abroad?"

"Mainly the US."

"And you are American?"

"Yes. But I am a Thai Permanent Resident. After the ten-year period passes, I hope to become a Thai citizen."

"So you know our language. May I speak to you in Thai?"

"You can speak to me however you want."

Pom smiled. "Yes. Let's stick to English. I need to practice. What does Mr. Maric do for you?"

"He examines and purchases diamonds from the merchant. He delivers them to the factory."

"You cannot do this yourself?"

"I am on the research end. Looking for new opportunities."

"It must feel good to be a boss. Any other employees?"

Duncan's mouth was moving as he thought of what to say, and realizing this, he stopped.

"Yes," he replied finally, stuttering. "One other."

"What does he do?"

"He sends the merchandise to America. Customer service for the clients."

"According to my records, you sponsored one person," Pom said, taking some papers from his pocket and unfolding them. "Unless he is Thai."

"Well..." Duncan began saying, realizing he was sweating. "He was sponsored by Mr. Hong, the owner of the jewelry-making factory."

"I see. But he works for you?"

"No...well, he works for both of us. For Mr. Hong, mainly. He gets the jewelry from Mr. Hong's factory and sends it to our clients in America."

"Do you pay him?"

Duncan swallowed. "What does this have to do with..."

"Maybe nothing. But if this employee is doing work not allowed on the work permit, he can be fined and deported. Where is he now?"

"In India. On vacation."

"On vacation? I see. I assume he has a multiple-entry visa?"

"Of course. Everything by the book."

Pom smiled. "Yes. Well, I can have my colleagues at the immigration office look into this later. I am more interested in Mr. Maric. Where is he now?"

"On vacation."

"You gave him vacation, too?"

"Every day is a vacation in Thailand, right, detective?"

Pom smiled. "Sanuk mai krap. This is our culture. Where is he on vacation?"

"I believe in Isan somewhere. With his girlfriend, maybe. I don't know."

"What is his girlfriend's name?"

"I'm not sure."

"Apsara? Duanphen? Ring a bell?"

"Yes. Apsara. That's it."

"You don't know her?"

Duncan shook his head.

"What if I told you, Mr. Duncan, that her roommate has seen you in her apartment. And also a tall Australian named Rob. Is this Mr. Maric?"

"Yes, that's him."

"So he goes by Rob?"

"Yes. Rob Johnson."

"Nickname?"

"Yes."

"And you know Apsara? You know she is a go-go dancer and a prostitute?"

"Yes. I didn't admit it because I am a married man."

"Married to a Thai woman?"

"Yes. My wife, Lamai." He pointed to a picture of them dressed in traditional northern Thai clothes with her parents and sister. Pom considered it with passing interest.

"Do you own this apartment?"

"She owns it."

"You can own a condominium in Bangkok in your own name. It is not like land."

"Yes, but we don't know what the future holds, when laws could change. We decided it would be safer for her name to be on the mortgage."

"And what does she do?"

"She works at a travel agency."

"I see," Pom said, writing this down on his pad. "Where in Isan does Apsara live?"

"I wish I could tell you. I've never been to Isan."

"Most people never go."

"Do you mind telling me what this is about? Are Rob or Apsara in some kind of trouble?"

"Well," Pom said, shrugging. "I suppose it does not hurt to say. Your worker is suspected of assaulting my junior detective. And he's wanted for a murder in Phuket. Has he ever been to Phuket?"

A sharp pain hit Duncan in the chest, but he masked it as best he could. He was afraid he might be blushing, though.

"For vacation, I think," Duncan responded.

"Another vacation. Does this man ever work?" Pom laughed. Duncan tried to laugh along, but he wasn't very successful.

"I think he has a girlfriend down there, too," Duncan said. "You know, a mia noi."

Pom smiled. "Yes. We know how it is. What is her name?"

"She's Russian, I think. Sveta. Something like that."

"And where does she work?"

"I don't know. Probably at a club."

"We will follow up. Do you have business interests in Phuket?"

Duncan shook his head.

"In Isan?"

Duncan shook his head again.

"And this Mr. Hong, where can I find him?"

"I'm not sure if he's in town right now. He's Thai-Chinese. He's often in Shanghai or Hong Kong."

"Where is his office?"

"He owns a club called Same Same in Sukhumvit. That's where he conducts business."

"Okay, Mr. Duncan," Pom said, writing down the information. "I need phone numbers for Mr. Maric, Apsara, Mr. Hong. Can you write them down for me as I use the bathroom? Is it in here?" Pom asked, opening Duncan's bedroom. Duncan leaped to stop Pom.

"No, this is my bedroom," he said. "Please, it's this door."

Pom smiled, peering into the room quickly before closing the door. "Of course. I will leave my pad here. Write the numbers down."

He dropped the pad on the sofa and entered the bathroom. Once the door closed, Duncan checked the entrees earlier in the pad, but didn't find anything he didn't already know. Except for one reference to a "Coco" in Khon Kaen, as well as a phone number to the police department there.

He heard the toilet flush, so he turned the pages back and began to write the numbers from his smartphone. Rob had called him from a different phone so he hoped Rob had destroyed his old one.

Pom emerged from the bathroom as Duncan was writing Mr. Hong's number. Then he turned and handed over the pad.

"Thank you, Khun Duncan," Pom said, taking it. "I will be in touch if necessary."

Duncan nodded. At the door, Pom turned to him. "Be careful who you hire and who you spend time with. This is difficult in Thailand, I know. We aim for sanuk at all costs, but sometimes the costs of freedom and fun are great."

Duncan performed a wai to Pom and closed the door. Then he bent over and cursed, holding his head tightly.

106

Rob sipped coconut water through a straw, then burped and placed it on the floor. He stared ahead at the boy, who was sitting in the corner, his arms around his knees.

"Ever done ya ba, mate?" he asked.

The boy shook his head.

"But you know what it is, ya?"

"My friends have done it."

"So why not you?"

"Messes up your mind, sir. It is not good."

"Not good. This shit is my livelihood. Let me show you."

He took a container from his duffel bag, opened it, and took out a pill, holding it between his thumb and forefinger.

"Don't seem so harmful. Looks like a damn Tums. Though I prefer Rennie. Yummy, yummy."

The boy shrugged.

"Never had one myself," Rob continued. "Can ya believe it? I sell it all around, but I've never tried." He examined it. "How does it make you crazy, mate? Why don't ya explain it?"

"Like you take twenty Red Bull, sir. That crazy."

Rob smiled. "Crazy like that, mate?"

He put the tablet in his mouth and began chewing. "This is sweet stuff," he said. "Chocalee. I heard they call it that in Chiang Mai. Bloody hell."

The boy looked over at his grandmother, who was sleeping.

"No worries, mate, I won't hurt your grannie, long as you keep doing what I say. Now tell me, what's your name, mate?"

"Som."

"That your full name?"

"Somchai."

"What's that mean?"

"Something like dignified man."

"Really?" Rob took out his machete. "You ain't gonna be dignified when you lie to me."

"I don't lie to you, sir."

"You saw that girl in Udon Thani?"

"I did, sir."

"If you lied to me that time, it won't count. But you tell me the truth now."

"I did not lie. I see that girl."

"How'd you get up to Udon?"

"I go with my friend. His name Wat. Wattana."

"He's got a bike?"

"Yes, sir."

"She give short time to Wat?"

"No, sir. Her friend did. But I see her."

"I've heard young Lao girls give short time up there. Nutty Park, right? Can you take a ride up with Wat and ask around for me?"

"I will do so."

"If you don't come back in twenty-four hours, your grandmother's gonna get it."

"I will come back. Do not hurt my grandmother."

"Any girls giving short time here in the village?"

Som appeared uncomfortable.

"Out with it, mate. Must be heaps of cum dumpsters here. How do they fill up the clubs in Bangkok and Pattaya?"

"Sure, sir. A girl who goes to school with me gives short time to village men at home when her father goes gambling. She tells her father she gets money by selling newspapers. But she is too lazy to sell newspapers."

"How old is she?"

"Thirteen."

"Can you get her here without her yabbering?"

"Sure. I tell her there is a client, and he does not want to go to her home."

"Good. You think she'll take ya ba as payment?"

"I don't know, sir. She does not do ya ba."

"Well get her here. Long as she's willing. I don't want no sex slave. I'll cut off your head and feed it to the pigs if you're bringing me some strung-up slut."

"No, she is willing. She needs money."

"All right. Get me this Wat and this girl, and bring 'em here. Don't want no one else knowing, got it? No one else."

107

Night had fallen in Khon Kaen, and Nat was back in his room at Coco. He had spent much of the day strategizing with the Khon Kaen police to find Maric and Apsara, and tagged along on a few raids of villages on the outskirts of Khon Kaen, leading to minor drug possession charges and nothing else.

Nat smoked on his small balcony and considered how the pieces fit: how was Pornopat's murder related to Patricia Murphy's in Phuket? Why was Robert Murphy missing and Panit suspected? Why was Maric looking for Pornopat's girlfriend up in Isan, and why had she run away?

He called Pom, who informed him of his conversation with Duncan, and that Maric was known as Rob Johnson.

"This Duncan is strange too," Pom said. "He works directly with Fan Hong, an international businessman who owns clubs in Sukhumvit and Patpong. I've heard rumors Hong is a member of the international Chinese gang the Dragons. They have Korean, Thai, and farang members too. Maybe Rob works for Fan Hong."

"So talk to Fan Hong. Could he be peddling the strong ya ba the general told us about?"

"Possibly. Maybe that's the connection. More interesting than a murder in Klong Tuey, huh?"

"Or a vice bust in Chiang Mai. I swear, I never took a bribe there. Many cops did."

"Why bring this up? I have seen your honesty and dedication. But it also worries me. We don't know what others are doing. I have a wife and children at home. Don't be too interested in truth. You must consider survival too."

Nat was silent for a minute. Then he said, "Is that a threat?"

"No, Natthew. I would not threaten you. But I have been around longer. My honest partners were transferred. Those who dug too deep."

"Khun Pom, my partners have shook down tourists for bribes and beat out confessions from prostitutes. They've thrown cocaine into cars and harassed men who unknowingly slept with underage prostitutes they pimped themselves. I refused to play that way. I know some people on top are corrupt, too. But I entered this profession knowing there is no money in it. I focus on my honor. That is what drives me. I would have had a lousy life in Isan. Every day is better than that."

"Natthew, I wish you luck. I truly do. I will talk to this Sumantapat first, get his take on Fan Hong before I make that leap."

"Good luck. Keep me informed, and tell me when you get the additional DNA."

"Good luck to you too, Natthew."

108

Bob and Sveta were lying in the guest bedroom upstairs, holding each other, when they heard a shout from downstairs. Sveta thought Ashley and Hemraj were having another fight. Bob and Sveta, on the other hand, had grown affectionate. Sveta treated Bob like a real husband, knowing their futures were intertwined. He treated her better than any man had, yet she still thought about Rob, despite his constant betrayals.

"Let's see what that is," Bob said, getting off the bed.

"Another fight, baby. But they make up. They have strong relationship."

"Even the strongest can crumble, darling. If they're so strong, why won't they marry?"

"Their plan will fall apart, baby."

"Oh, is that all?" Bob asked, opening the door and descending the stairs. Sveta followed.

In the living room, Hemraj stood, watching TV, and Ashley was a few feet behind him, her hands clasped awkwardly.

On TV, Vince Stevens, speaking at a press conference, held a picture of them kissing outside their home. He railed against corruption on the council on the future of the Long Island City Project.

"This is Vishal Patel's cousin with a council member. My sources tell me they are living together. He's bidding on this property through his front company. We don't need Vishal Patel's family anywhere near this project or any corruption on this council. I've asked the mayor and governor to use their influence. Remove Ashley Simmons from the CFLIC, and deny Hemraj Patel's bid on the property due to conflict of interest. The victims of Vishal Patel's arson deserve better."

One of the reporters asked how the council was appointed.

"I'll look into that," Stevens said, raising his finger. "Believe me, we will investigate that thoroughly."

"Shit!" Hemraj shouted when he saw Bob. "How the fuck did they find out?"

"I'm sure they have spies everywhere," Bob said.

Hemraj turned to Ashley. "So much for turning Vince Stevens."

"Someone must have got to him first," she said. "Alicia Tragliani?"

"I don't know, but what do we do?"

"We deny the charges," she said. "You all move out."

"Deny? They have a picture of us smooching. They'll find out about Chapel Hill, that we're together."

"So call A. Talk to him."

Hemraj took out his cell phone, cursing as he did. Sveta turned to Bob.

"Not good, husband," she said, taking on the formal tone she used as Julie Stewart.

"We will see, darling," he answered, listening to the phone conversation. "We will see."

109

Brahmins, Dubla, and Vaishya, along with a few Kshatriya and Sudra, surrounded the funeral pyres of the dead, the group divided only by gender. The men, standing on the left, wore white kafnis, and the women, standing on the right, wore white saris and covered their heads with their odhnis. Mr. Ghosh joined Narendrakaka, Lakshmanbhai, and Harshkaka in reciting prayers for the men. Kauntiaunti and the other women echoed them. Niral, finally bathed and dressed in new clothes, stood with Manu. Meetal sat on the ground, between the men and women, eyes closed, praying to herself.

When the recital was finished, Harshkaka, in tears, ran over to Lata and Kamkaki to comfort them. A Dubla holding a thick piece of flaming wood stood by the pyre, ready to light it when the word was given. But first, Mr. Ghosh raised his hand and spoke.

"People of Yam Gam, I know I have met many of you already, but allow me to introduce myself formally. I am Atul Ghosh, a senior Brother of the Brotherhood organization. Many of your fellow villagers are also devotees of our organization: Narendrabhai, Lakshmanbhai, Niral, Meetal, and Niral's mother, Heenabhen. All over Gujarat, all over India, and all over the world, we have spread a message of tolerance and equality. We have smashed the inequities caused by the caste system, dictatorship, religious fundamentalism, capitalism, and communism. We have used our founder Bhen's reinterpretation of the ancient Hindu texts, the Vedas and the Bhagavad Gita, to lead the way. We have emphasized not one god or two but the Trinity of Gods as a unifying foundation for the enlightenment of the soul, the ultimate reality available to all people after a certain number of lives.

"Atman is the goal of all human endeavor. But sometimes we have forsaken our social duties on this path toward individual transcendence. While we do not condemn—to a reasonable extent—pleasure or money-making, we also cannot tolerate corruption among people with power, and we have increasingly moved in when we have been needed, or when terrible tragedies like yours have occurred.

"We have built villages for Halpati throughout Gujarat where there were unacceptable living conditions or gross inequities. Bhai, our leader, has agreed to rebuild your Halpati village on a higher level so you will never be flooded again. We will also reconstruct your homes to rival the lavish Brahmin homes built from new wealth through land sales. We don't believe in redistributing wealth or punishing those who have money, but we will infuse capital to those who have been subject to historical and real injustice. We encourage wealthy Brahmins and Vaishyas to donate to our fund to make this easier for us. We only have one fund. We use it to do good.

"As for the political situation: this Prameshbhai has done you great wrong. I hear he has cheated people for his own benefit for many years. He will never be your mayor again. I have kept him and Ravi in the Halpati village for their own protection. Some have called for their execution, but we will be humane, as is our tradition. Slowly, we will allow them back into the fold of the village. We will see how and if they change. Also, we need Prameshbhai's signature to right his contractual and financial wrongs. And Ravi can still be a good father to Lata's child, God willing.

"Though I understand what I am saying is illegal and may hurt my organization, please do not contact the police; they are in Prameshbhai's pocket and will not help us. We will form our own police force to handle internal disputes. Many have broken the law and committed murder here. I know they were acts of passion. They must be pardoned for us to move forward with our society.

"Furthermore, we will need to construct a new democratic system to change the exploitative system of the past, as Krishna did in Dwarka, which happens to be The Brotherhood's headquarters for symbolic reasons. We will have an election. But for the transition period, I will appoint three people you all trust and to which different groups can go to for assistance: Narendrabhai for the Brahmins, Meetal for the Halpati, Lakshmanbhai for the Vaishya and other castes. If you have a problem, contact them. Meanwhile, we will begin drawing up a democratic election process in the village that features a council like this rather than one mayor."

One Brahmin raised his hand. He was shaking. Mr. Ghosh called on him, but then he seemed reluctant to speak.

"Yes? Ask your question, brother. Do not be afraid."

"Narendrabhai was corrupt in the past," he finally stated. "Plus, he is close to the Dubla. How can we trust him as our representative?"

Narendrakaka closed his eyes.

"This is a good question," Mr. Ghosh said. "What Narendrabhai did was a long time ago. It was not corruption but a mistake, an act of love that had bad effects. This is why he exiled himself here: to do penance. But he has learned his lesson, and Bhai has forgiven him. He was one of Bhen's original followers and does not have caste prejudice in his heart. He will be an impartial and effective representative for the Brahmins."

A Dubla raised his hand. "Many of us worship Gods other than the trinity," he said. "Will we be forced to worship the trinity and not our Gods?"

"Of course not," Mr. Ghosh responded. "Hinduism and The Brotherhood are all encompassing. God is everywhere and in everything. All Gods make up Atman, and the ultimate reality can be attained through worship of any and all Gods. But I urge you to beware of Islam. We will not tolerate a religion that seeks to blot out all others."

A few Dubla glanced at each other. Niral wondered if they had converted in secret, but then Mr. Ghosh concluded the questioning, Lakshmanbhai gave the word to begin the cremation, and Niral lost focus on the Dubla glances. Fathers and mothers cried as the children burned, then Manish, the murderous Dubla Pankaj, then his victims, Pranam and Madhuri. And finally, Satish. Niral closed his eyes. Vishal and Thanat entered his mind. Why should he regret any of them?

Narendrakaka approached him and touched his shoulders.

"Do not worry, Niral," he said. "He did not deserve life for what he did."

"He probably did," Niral responded. "But life is life. We can't take things back."

"He has reached his next life. Hopefully, it will be a better one. Niral, will you continue your involvement in the village? We need you."

"I have to return to Thailand and prepare for the Diwali operation. I considered visiting Talim in Surat today, but I don't have time. I fly out tomorrow morning. I need to leave in a few minutes."

"I'm sorry you are stuck with that mission, but I am glad you are dedicated to The Brotherhood again. Your father would be proud."

"My father, proud of this? I don't think so."

"Believe me, we will do wonderful things here."

"You're so quick to believe in this mission. Like you believed in Dilipuncle."

"Yes, but that was done in secret, Niral. That was my mistake. Here, an entire society, once divided, is coming together to rebuild a disaster zone."

"You're using their lowest moment as an opportunity to build your following. Now I agree it's good for them, and I'm all for it. I'm just saying, maybe you saw the way before anyone else."

Narendrakaka smiled. "Thank you for the kind words, Niral. But I know what I did with Dilipuncle was wrong. This will be my redemption."

"By the way, Bhai gave me a message for you. Seems rather redundant now."

"What is it?"

"He said, 'Keep the village sound. We need sound villages,'" Niral said.

Narendrakaka laughed. "He meant keep the Muslims out. Despite this horrible tragedy, which words cannot begin to describe, I believe this restructuring will accomplish that. Not a moment too late."

"Are you sure Islam hasn't seeped into the village already? I saw a few Dubla give each other strange looks when Mr. Ghosh announced that Islam would not be tolerated. You may have potential terrorists on your hands."

"Maybe. It could have seeped in from the outskirts. Consider what Pankaj said, comparing his action to the massacre of Hindus in Godhra. He didn't compare it to Hindus torching Muslims in revenge. What did it mean for him to put himself in the shoes of a terrorist Muslim?"

"He's dead now. Does it mean anything?"

"People live on after death, if not on the ground, then in the memories of other people."

"I know. Look, I should grab Manu and get going."

"Okay. No need to say goodbye to everyone if you don't have time. Their minds are on other things. And you know how Indians like to say goodbyes. Entire villages follow cars."

"Not anymore, it seems," Niral said, then he performed namaste. Narendrakaka touched his head to bless him.

Niral gestured to Manu. They walked up the dark field back to the village.

"You haven't said much since the incident, Manu," Niral said as they trudged through the dark. "Do you want to?"

Silence continued.

"Are you afraid of me, Manu?" Niral asked. "After what you saw me do? I think I am afraid of myself."

"Niralbhai," Manu said slowly, "Quite the contrary. I have been silenced by awe. I know now that you are an avatar."

"What?" Niral asked. "How?"

"You can save lives, and you can take them. You saved my life. You tried to convince the village not to turn to violence, and then, when they did not listen, you took revenge on a bad man so the village would not explode further. Believe me, Niralbhai, it would have been worse if you had not killed Satish. You have changed this village with your will and skill. You will protect The Brotherhood and this nation in a few months. I will do my part, Niralbhai, for you. Whatever you ask. I am at your beck and call. I am yours, Niralbhai."

110

Pom considered discussing his new evidence with General Toon but decided to visit Sumantapat first, knowing his conversation would lead back to the General anyway.

He drove to Soi Cowboy and walked down the strip, peering at the clubs. He had been here on cases often but for entertainment only once, when he had gotten drunk with American pilots stationed at U-Tapao soon after the start of the War on Terror. That was many years ago, shortly after his stint as a monk and before he had met and married his wife.

He found Go-Go Rama and entered. Immediately, he was met by girls in sailor outfits. Bored girls in bikinis stood on the stage. He showed his badge and asked for Sumantapat. The girls were shocked and ran away. But Maem came over and, after attempting to placate him with smiles, apologies, wais, and bows, ultimately led him to her back office where the short, rotund Sumantapat sat, counting some baht, piling one on top of the other very carefully.

"Ah, please sit, detective," he said. "You are lucky I am in today. I do not come to the club often. I stay home with my wife and children."

"Believe me, Khun Sumantapat, I also like to be home with my wife and children when I can."

"How old are your children, sir, if I may ask?"

"Not old enough. Or maybe too old. They are on the brink of manhood. Two boys, twelve and eleven."

"Ah, at that burdensome age. Yes, I have two boys myself, and they are the same age."

"Wow. That is a coincidence."

"You know, ah, my wife pushed them out fast after my marriage. Yours too?"

"Yes, Khun Sumantapat. We were too eager."

"Now we know what a condom is. Ha ha! I don't like to work too much. I own my clubs, and I let my people do my work. But now I keep losing my workers, so I must do more. For us family men, it is not good to work too much. We shouldn't spend too much time in places like this."

"Yes. I cannot avoid them due to the nature of my work, yet, I do not enter places like this for pleasure."

"Exactly. Men like us have intelligence. Isn't that what Buddha valued above all? We do not judge the behavior or actions of others, but we do not taint Thailand by involving ourselves in such filth. I trained to be a monk, you know. I thought that would be my path until this route intersected and forced me to another. Now I am just a businessman. An ordinary man who will never reach nirvana. Strange how we think we will become one thing in life, and poof, something turns us wayward?"

"Yes. Very true. May I talk to you about the case of your missing workers? General Toon..."

"Ah, General Toon is a man I respect. That is why I went to his office. And I saw you as I passed. I told General Toon, that is a man I want investigating this case. Perhaps I saw myself in you."

"Thank you for the compliment, Khun Sumantapat. I wonder, this go-go dancer, Apsara, you reported her missing on your second visit with General Toon. You thought she had information on the first case and the disappearance of your second man."

"Yes. Have you found her?"

"No. We are still trying. I wonder why you thought she could help."

Sumantapat smiled. "I have been rude. Do you want a drink? I will have Maem..."

"No thank you. I don't drink alcohol."

"Very well. To answer your question, we found out she was the gem dealer Pornopat's girlfriend. I told General Toon."

"Yes. But her disappearance...why did you think..."

"She didn't show up to work. Then we realized we couldn't verify her identity. We called her Duanphen, and her stage name was Tip. But her apartment lease named her Apsara. General Toon told me she has no identity card. Apsara also called Pornopat a different name, Thanat, and we suspect that was his real name. Strange, isn't it, how no one seems to be straight?"

Pom nodded, then paused. He said, "Do you know a man named Fan Hong?"

"Fan Hong?" Sumantapat laughed. "What a question. How do you know him?"

"It's just a question."

"Honestly, I am not surprised you asked. I found out Duanphen worked at Fan Hong's club too, a club at Patpong called Scandal. So I have a feeling he may be involved."

"Would he want to hurt your workers? Ruin your business?"

Sumantapat nodded. "He might. He thinks I pushed him out of Pattaya. You see, I wanted his club, and he would not sell it to me. He was doing illegal things, not worth mentioning. The police raided him, and he had to pay a large bribe. He said I had stuck the police on him. Nonsense. If such things were possible, he could have done the same thing to me. Anyway, he became sick of police raids, and he needed money, so he sold me the club. I kept expanding in Pattaya, and now I own many clubs there, while he only owns two clubs in Bangkok. So he may be jealous."

"And for this reason, he killed your gem dealers and your right-hand man?"

"It is your investigation, detective. But I am not surprised you mentioned him."

"How about a Duncan Smith, Rob Johnson, Borisslava Maric?"

"Farang names. Never heard of them, and they bore me. I doubt a farang could commit these crimes. Look at the case in Phuket; they thought a farang had killed that tourist, and it turned out to be a Thai."

Pom swallowed. "Yes, true."

"I love our people, but we must be realistic about the nature of some of our countrymen. Not all the problems are caused by Burmese immigrants, sir."

"You told General Toon there is a new, more potent ya ba on the market."

Sumantapat stared at him coldly.

"I don't follow the ya ba trade, sir. My men heard about it through gossip."

"I wonder if, in your opinion, Fan Hong could be selling it."

"I don't know him to be a drug dealer, but I would not be surprised. I have heard he has many international connections. But again, this is gossip. I don't follow the ya ba trade."

"Of course," Pom said, standing up. "I will have some officers follow up with family members of the victims, including your right-hand man. Perhaps we can find out the source of this gossip."

"Boy was my best man. He is especially missed. That is why I am more and more alarmed. The killings are getting closer and closer to me."

"Do you need police protection?"

Sumantapat laughed. "No, sir. Thank you for offering. I am protected, believe me. But Boy thought he was, too."

Sumantapat continued to count his baht. As Pom turned to leave, Sumantapat said, "I can provide you one piece of information. Before he disappeared, Boy mentioned following Duanphen to some warehouse near the Chao Phraya river. I don't know the location, otherwise I would tell you. He suspected Duanphen of doing something underhanded and thought maybe she would head there again. I didn't recommend following anyone around, but he thought it might lead to the killer, so I gave him my blessing. And then they both disappeared. I did not mention it to General Toon, but I thought you should know. Look, I am merely a businessman. I don't get involved in such things. But I'm sure you will keep me up to date on the investigation, yes? And thank you, detective. You do a service to Thailand."

111

Rob began feeling the effects of the ya ba. His mind wandered at a more rapid pace, and he knew he couldn't control himself much longer. He wasn't sure why he had taken the pill. In Noosa, he had taken ecstasy, introduced to him by an older man who had taken him in after his escape from his foster home. That had been many years ago, before he had gone to Melbourne and worked for Sasha. But it had started him on his path. And he thought, perhaps, since his path seemed to be ending, why not go back to where it began?

He got up and began pacing the room, cursing Apsara one second for being a heartless bitch who had used him for money, and another second hoping she had used her wiles to escape slavery and penury. He had helped Sveta many times but had grown tired of her. Maybe he was suffering for this betrayal. But then someone had to be up there, a titanic god, to exert such justice. No, most likely it was a tipping of the scales, a full rounding of the situation back to its origins. Not merely a condition of natural selection, for he did acknowledge he was still alive because of his facility to murder, but also a recharging of the atoms that had propelled him originally, then returned to their dormant state and now were ready to go berserk again. What goes up, must go down. It was gravity, simple science, chaos to order back to chaos. And now that he had seen the crags of Phuket, eaten passion fruit, papaya, mangoes, and lychee and all the rest, now that he had experienced Candyland and the promise of God's lila, as the Hindus would say, it was time for his world to crumble.

He heard the door open. Som peeked in, then entered, followed by a boy and girl. The boy, Wat, was taller and gruffer looking than Som. The girl was short and compact. She had a childish face and wore a low-cut dress that partially revealed her developed chest. The grandmother had awoken, but she lay still, watching the proceedings with care and suspicion. This grandmother has been around, Rob thought. She's seen shit go down. She's a survivor, just like me.

Wat grabbed the girl's shoulders and pushed her toward Rob, who noticed Wat held a stick in his left hand. A skinny stick, a wonky stick, but a stick.

Rob sat down, crossed his legs, and waved the girl forward.

"G'day! What's your name, sweetie?"

He took her by the waist and forced her onto his lap with a tender precision that made her smile.

"Boonsri," she said.

"What's it mean, babe?"

"Beautiful, sir," Wat said. Then he scolded the girl in Thai.

She put her arms around Rob's neck.

"She's a good girl," Wat said. "Do what you want to her. It will cost only 300 baht. Like nothing for a farang."

Rob smiled. "You reckon what I can afford, mate? I haven't got a brass razoo."

Wat glanced at Som. "What?" he asked Rob.

"Means I'm broke, mate. I only got some ya ba. One pill. That's the same price."

"Ya ba?" Wat laughed. "Are you joking, sir? I don't do that crazy drug."

"Come on, mate. I can see it in your eyes. You've got that hunger. I can see you lighting up and sniffin' that jack."

Wat looked at Som again. "You are not with the police?" he asked Rob.

"Nah, mate. Hell, I told Som here not to dob in cuz I'm avoiding the boys in blue. Or brown, that is."

Wat swallowed. "Okay, ya ba pill is okay. But two pills."

"Going price for one is 300 baht, bro."

"Not in Isan. No one has that much money."

"Which makes it a good spot to do business. One pill. I root girl."

Wat smiled. He came forward and held his right hand out.

"What are you, pimp?" Rob asked nastily, grabbing his wrist. "Doesn't she get a percentage?"

Wat was taken aback. He dropped the stick he held in his other hand.

"Yes, sir," he said. "I will give her the money later."

"Don't believe you. Give it to her now."

"But I don't have it now."

"Som never said nothing about a pimp."

Wat swallowed. He turned to Som, then back to Rob. "Som told me about the girl you want," he said. "I will take you to the Nutty Park club where we saw her."

"Except you've never seen her. Now you expect me to fuck a child. Very classy."

"I have seen her. I will take you to..."

"You fucking pimp cunt!" Rob yelled, pushing Boonsri to the floor. "I'll show you how it feels!" He grabbed his machete from his bag and sliced Wat's right arm off. A second later, the blood began gushing out. But Wat didn't scream. He was too shocked. He just watched, eyes wide.

Rob took Wat by the neck, turned him around, and forced him to his knees. Then he speared the machete through Wat's pants into his asshole.

Now Wat began to scream.

"See, this is what it feels like, you fucking wanker!"

Rob pierced him all the way through till the blade came out through his prostate, then sliced down, ripping his penis and nut sack in half.

"You like that, you rapist fuck?!" Rob shouted. Wat, still alive, shook violently in an expanding pool of blood. Rob heard the grandmother hyperventilating. Boonsri screamed once, but Rob showed her his blade, which quieted her. She crawled into the corner and crouched there.

Rob's eyes met Som's. He quickly dashed for the door, opened it, and ran out, but Rob was right behind him, He grabbed him by the neck and perched him on the railing of the porch.

"Say sayonara," he said.

"Please sir, please sir!" Som repeated.

"You wanna feel what it's like before you die?" Rob asked, putting the blade to Som's asshole.

"No sir, no sir!"

Rob laughed like a hyena and pulled him back onto the porch.

"Didn't think so, mate," he said.

112

After consuming a quick meal of noodles and eggs at a food cart on Th Glang Meuang, Nat returned to the megaclub on Th Prachasumran. He parked his car in front. A different hostess performed a wai and led him inside to the same couch. He wore an eyepatch now because of Rob's elbow assault. This time, through his good eye, he saw a number of well-dressed young men sitting at a table near the stage, cheering on two dancers.

Once again, he ordered a Singha and asked for Piti. Once again, she came over and sat next to him.

"What happened to your eye?" she asked. "Did you go back home?"

Nat laughed. "I would have more than an injured eye if I went back home."

"So what happened?"

"Battle with a suspect. Pulled my gun."

"Oh my God," Piti said, putting her hand over her mouth, but smiling.

"That's why I chose this job, Piti," he said, accepting the Singha from the waitress and paying for it. "Action and adventure."

"It is better than this life," Piti said. "This club..."

"Looks good to me. You've got multiple rooms."

"As if we have time for that. This town sucks."

"I see the frat boys are out."

"Khon Kaen University Freshmen. They think they're so great. Probably went to Wittayayon."

"It's downtown, so they think they're superior. Except they hate..."

"Yes, that other school with a similar name. I've seen fights in here."

"Their lives won't amount to anything. I don't care how slick their blazers are."

"Yes, they will never be you," Piti said, laughing.

"Look, I came back to ask you about afterhours underground clubs, massage spots, auctions for women who want to sell themselves to brothel fronts from Bangkok and Pattaya."

"There are more in Udon Thani, but I have heard rumors of spots here too."

"So tell me about them. I need to find this Apsara girl."

"That other Tip mentioned it to me."

"So ask her. And that Lao dancer I questioned last time."

"Do you want me to ask all the girls working now?"

"Why not, Piti? Why not?"

"And these frat boys too?" she asked, pointing to them. "They might have seen her on campus."

"A go-go dancer taking classes?" Nat laughed. "Sure, why not, Piti? Why not?"

PART XIX

†

Khon Kaen, Thailand; Bangkok, Thailand; Kings Point, New York; Near Mumbai, India

---

113

Nat's interviews led him to befriend the frat boys, who thought it was cool that he was a Bangkok cop originally from Isan. Once he assured them that he only wanted to find the girl and didn't care about their activities, they agreed to lead him to an underground auction near Nakhon Lake. Nat gave them a ride in his car and parked across the street, turning down the VIP option offered by an attendant outside the door.

Inside, several Thai men sat at round tables, drinking shots and smoking cigarettes. On stage, a few old women, their faces expressionless, were stationed on chairs with numbers hanging from their necks. A madam was speaking Thai into a microphone, describing the qualities of #3. The boys found a table.

"A bunch of elephants today," one of the boys said.

"How much does one go for?" Nat asked.

"Depends. It's an auction. Low as sixty baht for these heifers."

Nat asked him for a cigarette and got it lit. Then he waved at the madam. One of the young men got up and raced up the stairs.

"Where's he going?" Nat asked.

"The madam's daughter went to Wittayayon with us. Sometimes she's up there playing pool. Rune's been trying to get lucky."

The madam stopped describing #3 and rushed over to Nat. Smiling, she asked if they wanted a drink. Nat took a drag and asked her how much #3 was.

The madam thought and smiled.

"She is cheap, only 300 baht, sir," she said. "Special offer."

"Tell me," Nat asked. "How long have you been doing this?"

The madam seemed taken aback. "Long time, sir. We've had girls a long time."

"I saw a girl way back. She's from Khon Kaen. Maybe she's been here?"

He placed the cigarette on an ashtray, then showed the woman Apsara's picture on his phone. The woman's face dropped.

"You know her?" Nat asked.

"She here many years ago," she said. "I tell her, you are very pretty girl, you can make more money as dancer. She said, okay, but I want money now for night. So she sit on auction. All men want her, so we start bidding. Finally, one man buys her. I give her part of price, and she goes with him. Later that night, when we are closing, man comes back and says young man attacked him as he entered his home. He beat him up, she took his money, and they drive away together. I never see her again. This is very bad girl."

"Are you sure it's her?"

"Yes," she said, taking the phone and staring at the picture. "She is older here, but it is same girl."

"How long ago was this?"

"Many, many years ago. She looked like teenager then."

"Do you remember her name?"

"She gave some name: Ka, Ska, you know the normal, same same. But I don't forget the face. I've had many bad girls, but none ever beat up or robbed a client in his home. Our girls don't do that. You hear that in Bangkok, but not here in Khon Kaen."

"Do you know where that client is now? The one who got robbed."

The madam stared at Nat, and her expression changed.

"No, he is random man. Why do you care? Where did you get that picture?"

"She's a friend," Nat said, putting the phone away and picking up the cigarette. "She's missing."

"You're a cop, aren't you?" she asked, horrified.

Nat shook his head and took another drag. But the madam wasn't convinced.

"We will pay the bribe," she said. "Whatever it is. Just don't shut us down."

Nat looked at the men, then at the ladies on stage.

"Doesn't look like you do much business anyway," he said.

"We don't make much, just liquor sales and commission. These ladies have no other income, so they are grateful to these men. Please, this is how I feed my daughter."

"She goes to Wittayayon, doesn't she?"

"A public school, sir. We don't have much. Our rice fields did not grow, so we moved to the city. This is my livelihood," she said, putting her palms together.

"You haven't seen this girl recently, right? You would tell me if you had?"

"Of course, sir. Please don't take us to the station. We will pay the fine here."

Nat put out the cigarette in the ashtray and stood up. On the staircase, he saw Rune, hand in hand with a curvy Thai girl wearing a t-shirt and ripped jeans.

"These after-hours establishments are a menace. What do you contribute to Thailand? Nothing."

He took out a card and handed it to the madam.

"If you see that girl again, hear anything about her, remember her name, or have any other information, call me. Don't worry, there's no fine today. But whatever you do, don't lose that card. I paid for it myself."

114

Duncan motorcycled to Patpong and parked. He had left the car in the garage at the warehouse. He used it only sporadically, when he knew he was about to make a sale.

He hurried through the crowd and entered Scandal. He passed Lek and skipped up the steps to the second floor. Behind the curtain in the back space, Mr. Hong sat with Nam, drinking Johnnie Walker and counting baht. Duncan wondered if all Asian bosses drank and counted money all day.

"Duncan," Mr. Hong said, trying to stand, then falling because he was drunk. He laughed. He wasn't wearing his jacket, but Nam was. "Nice to see you, son. Please, sit."

Nam nodded at Duncan sternly.

"I know you're leaving tomorrow, Mr. Hong, but I wanted to check in with you about the situation," Duncan said as he sat across from them.

Mr. Hong smiled. "Must we talk business on my last night? I expected you earlier."

"I got caught up. I found out something about Rob."

"Has he found Apsara? Gotten rid of her?"

"No, he's suspected of assaulting a police officer in Isan. Now they are searching for him and Apsara."

Mr. Hong's face turned cold. "So our worst fears are realized. We need to get him first."

"Problem is, he destroyed his phone. So I can't lure him back to Bangkok."

Mr. Hong looked at Nam. "Nam, your men must get him. But first, find out where Apsara went. Use the methods you deem fit."

"Do you think that will help find Rob?" Duncan asked.

"Finding one might find the other. Do you know where Rob is?"

"Before destroying his phone, he called and told me the cop was chasing him. He mentioned a 'Coco' in Khon Kaen. I looked it up. It's a resort there."

"Then Nam will head up to Khon Kaen. Or we will send someone else."

"Who?" Duncan asked.

"Not you, my dear poo noy," Mr. Hong said, laughing. "I have requested back up from headquarters. We cannot be short-handed at a time like this. Who knows what could boil up, especially if Sumantapat finds out. We are even getting men from New York."

"New York?"

"Yes, New York. Which reminds me of our friend Niral."

Duncan swallowed. "Yes, Niral. Listen, I need him. I need to go up to Chiang Mai, and he knows the business..."

"Don't worry, Duncan. Mr. Chang has informed us that Niral is not to be harmed. In fact, we intend to make him a greater part of the organization."

"Oh, that's great, I guess..."

"This is a strange time to go to Chiang Mai, Duncan," Mr. Hong continued.

"Lamai needs to visit her family before the birth, and they want me to be involved in planning for the baby."

"You are a family man, and if you must go, you must go. Niral can run your side of the business. He will be a 'busy boy' as poor Rob used to say. Where is Niral, anyway? I have not seen him in a while. You should have brought him with you. Instead of killing him, we could have congratulated him."

"I was afraid you would kill him," Duncan said.

"Nonsense. Kill Niral?" Mr. Hong laughed. "Bring him by tomorrow. We'll be picking up the men from the airport tomorrow morning. Maybe he will have friends among them."

"The airport? What time?"

"In the afternoon. Around two. Nam will drop me off in the morning. So, the poor boy, he will be waiting around for a while."

Duncan swallowed. "Yes, I'll bring Niral by in the late afternoon. Before you open to the public for the night."

"Excellent. Sorry I will miss him, but Nam will be here. Now pour us some more whiskey, poo noy."

Duncan poured the whiskey, his eye twitching, his hand shaking.

"Is there anything else, Duncan?" Mr. Hong asked.

"No one else came to see you, did they?"

"Like who? Sumantapat?" Mr. Hong asked, slapping Nam on the back.

"No, Mr. Hong," Duncan said, putting the bottle down. "I meant the girls. Sanuk mai krap."

115

Bob held Sveta in the dark, staring up at the ceiling where glow-in-the-dark stickers were oriented like the solar system.

"Whatever happens, Sveta, we must be willing to adapt," Bob said.

"You are telling me?" she asked, looking at her thumb. "You don't see how I have adapted?"

"You are not the only one. I have been on this earth longer than you."

"I don't think you have adapted like me. Growing up in Russia, then Sasha in Australia..."

"You have no idea, my darling."

"Why don't you tell me, then?"

"There will be time to tell you, Sveta. It is an epic."

"I don't want to be Sveta anymore. I like being Julie Stewart."

"I'm working to make sure you stay Julie Stewart and I stay Franklin Stewart and we live happily ever after. Which is why we must get up right now and say we've decided, after thinking it over, that we should move out. I found a place in Queens to stay. If we wait until morning, the media will surround us, and we'll be associated with Ashley and Hemraj in the press. That's the last thing we want. Hell, I'm surprised they haven't come already."

"Do you think they will let me stay on the council?"

"As long as we're not spotted, Ashok has reason to keep you on. Now let's pack our stuff quickly."

He turned on the light. She rose groggily, running her fingers through her hair.

"I'm sure you've had more daring escapes than this," Bob said.

"This is why I do not unpack my things anymore, husband. I keep them in my bag because I know I will move soon."

"Yes, me too, my darling. There's no point when you were born to run."

"But I am getting tired, husband," she replied. "I am getting very tired."

116

After leaving Sumantapat's office at Go-Go Rama, Pom had called Buppha, who had given him her phone number for information in return for a get-out-of-jail-free card if she got busted on solicitation. He asked her only one question: if Apsara had called Pornopat Thanat. Was that the name she remembered?

"No, it was a different name," she answered in Thai.

"Thank you," Pom said.

"Is this considered information?"

"I'll call back," Pom said and hung up.

Pom wasn't sure what this meant. Did Apsara have a nickname for Thanat? Why did she call him Thanat to Sumantapat but not to his face? How many names could one person have?

He realized he needed to look more into Thanat's past the next day when he returned to the police station. But first, following up on Sumantapat's tip, Pom had driven up to the river to check out a few warehouses. Now, in the middle of the night, he approached a deserted warehouse near a Muay Thai boxing school.

He entered the unmanned gate and parked in the empty lot, then walked up the smooth dirt path to the entrance of what seemed like a garage. The doors were bolted with a lock. He peered through a crack but couldn't see anything. He turned on his flashlight, aimed it within the crack, and thought he saw a car in the distance.

He climbed up the adjacent steps, checking each floor carefully, but he didn't find much but old furniture, ashes, waste, and litter. It seemed like the warehouse had once been an office building, but a fire had consumed it. He made a note to check the property's ownership once he got back. He decided not to make a call to the station as he didn't want to scare anybody hiding around.

He wasn't finding much of consequence, but he had seen ya ba and heroin stashed within anything under the sun, so he decided to check each floor. And on the fifth floor, he finally found evidence of life.

He turned his flashlight into a room that appeared to be a functioning office. He felt around for a switch, found one, and turned on the light.

The room had a green carpet and red walls. A large desk decorated with Buddhas was its only piece of furniture. No pictures were on the walls, no papers on the desk. The side drawers were locked, but the middle tray opened. Inside, Pom found a picture of a pretty Thai woman. She looked familiar, but it was not Apsara. She didn't look Isan. She looked Lanna.

He continued to dig in the tray, taking out papers and examining them. Among them was an invoice of a diamond sale between Anil Shekhat of the Shekhat Brothers and Duncan Smith of Emblem Jewelry. And then the picture made sense. It was Duncan's wife from the picture in his apartment.

If Boy had followed Apsara to a warehouse, this was likely the one. She had been coming to see Duncan, who worked with Mr. Hong. Both employed Rob Johnson, Borisslava Maric, or whatever his name was. Rob had been up in Khon Kaen, perhaps looking for Apsara. He had killed someone in Phuket and assaulted Nat twice. But what was the motive? Perhaps they were in the drug game and in competition with Sumantapat, which could explain the murders of Thanat and Boy. But where was evidence of a drug connection? That's what he needed to find.

He scoured through the papers again but could not find anything of importance. He thought of shooting or breaking the locks to Duncan's drawers, but decided it was better to get a warrant.

As he was about to leave the office, he noticed a door on the left. He opened it and saw a staircase. He decided to take it down to where it led.

Down five flights of stairs, he was confronted by a large, heavy door. He twisted the knob and opened it.

He seemed to be inside the garage. The light was on, and the front door was open. Several meters away was the car he had spotted through the crack. It was a black sedan. He drew his gun and looked out the front door but did not see anyone there.

He approached the car and looked inside the vehicle. He didn't see anything suspicious. But the trunk would have to be checked. He could call the police station now so officers could secure the property while he got a warrant the next day. But as he took out his cell phone, he heard a loud blast.

He felt pain in his back and dropped the phone. A split second later, the pain turned immense, and then he saw blood on the car. He looked down and noticed his chest was bleeding.

He turned around. He still held his gun, but it was limp in his hand. From behind two barrels, he saw Duncan, aiming the rifle at him.

He began to lift his gun, but Duncan fired again, this time at his left shoulder. Blood spurt out as the force of the shot smashed him against the car, cracking the window. The gun dropped, and he began to slide down.

117

As they neared Mumbai, Niral realized he still had an hour to spare before the checkout counter opened at 5:30 a.m. for his 8:20 a.m. flight. Manu suggested a dosa place he had visited when dropping off Mr. Ghosh.

"Is it a trap like the last place?" Niral asked.

"Bhai is not there, Niralbhai. We can eat in peace."

It was a small, dingy place. Most tables were free. The waiter was gruff and unshaven. He waved them toward a table against the window. But Manu asked if they could have a table next to the wall instead. The waiter waved again, speaking violently in Marathi.

"They do not have the manners of a five-star restaurant, but the dosas are the best I've had," Manu explained. "You will see."

"Why always dosas?" Niral asked. "Can't we eat...?"

"We could have pizza, Chinese food, McDonalds, whatever you want, Niralbhai, especially in Mumbai," Manu said. "But don't you want an authentic Indian dish before you leave for months?"

"I remember having bad pizza in Navsari when I was a boy, so Indian is the better bet. A dosa is better than a Gujarati thali, but maybe they have uttapam here? Or idli sambar?"

"Believe me, only the dosas are good here. Now look, Niralbhai.

While you are in Thailand planning the Diwali defense, I will continue your work here."

"My work? You mean The Brotherhood's work?"

"Isn't it one and the same?"

Niral chuckled. "Manu, do you believe, truly, that I'm an avatar?"

Manu nodded. "Certainly, Niralbhai."

"Then you wouldn't mind following my orders, even if, at times, they might seem contrary to the interests of The Brotherhood?"

Manu swallowed. "What do you mean, Niralbhai?"

"Sometimes things aren't as they seem, Manu, and only an avatar can truly discern truth. Otherwise Krishna wouldn't have had to lecture to Arjuna the Gita."

Manu nodded. "Yes, Niralbhai. He had to make Arjuna understand."

"And what did he make him understand? That killing his own family members was right because they were on adharma's side. Sometimes violence is necessary to preserve dharma, no?"

"Of course."

"And, sometimes a course that seems wrong may ultimately lead to right. Think about all the times Krishna tricked people in his life but for the right reasons. Remember how he fooled Duryodhana into wearing underpants when he went to see Gandhari, thus weakening his thighs for Bhima's mace? How he urged Bhima to break the rules of combat to see justice done? There are too many examples to mention."

"Yes."

"How God sanctioned a bloody war, despite the death of great noblemen like Bhishma, to see, ultimately, the just Yudhishthira rise to the throne?"

"What are you saying, Niralbhai?"

"I am asking if I have your complete loyalty, Manu. There will be a treacherous road in front of us. You might not understand why I am asking you to do some things, but your absolute loyalty is necessary to the right cause. Are you willing to be completely loyal to me?"

Manu put his palms together. "Yes, Niralbhai, of course I am. You saved my life; you saved a village. May I kneel before you?"

Niral put his hands over Manu's palms. "Not here, Manu. We need to maintain our social facade."

Niral ordered the rava masala dosa, Manu the mysore masala dosa. And then, while they ate and drank tea, Niral noticed something and asked Manu a question as he sat there, shaking.

"Is this why you wanted to stop here?" Niral asked, pointing to something written on the wall. "Because these dosas are good, but not that good."

Manu averted his eyes. "I was too nervous to say anything, Niralbhai. I didn't want it to be true. I hoped it was gone. I had seen it on my last trip here. I do not want to admit that Sita may be right. It is too shameful."

"This could be another Gayatri."

"That is her number. I wanted to cross it out when I saw it last time. But I could not touch it. What a shameful father I am."

"You came here because you wanted to believe you had dreamed it. And in case you hadn't, that I would do something about it. Is that right?"

Manu nodded. "I was hoping that you could advise me, Niralbhai."

"How about this: I will call the number now. And if she speaks in a sexy way to me, I will tell you, and at least you will know."

Manu swallowed. "Whatever you think is best, Niralbhai."

Niral took out his cell phone. He dialed the number written on the wall.

"Whether she is doing it or not, she would be asleep now." He winked at Manu while the phone rang.

After several rings, a groggy woman answered. Niral tried to don an Indian accent, but he spoke English since he didn't know Hindi.

"Hey, is this Gayatri? For a good time?" She didn't respond at first, so he repeated it in Gujarati.

"Yes, baby, but it's late," she said, putting on a sexy voice to the extent she could. "Do you want to come over now?"

Niral rolled his eyes and hung up. Manu looked intent.

"She cursed at me and hung up. She must get a lot of these calls."

Manu smiled and laughed.

"See, I told you to relax," Niral said. "There's nothing to it!"

Niral asked the waiter to borrow a pen. The waiter grumbled but complied. Niral began crossing out the message.

"Why are you defacing my wall, sisterfucker?" the waiter screamed. Manu stood up.

"We are defending the honor of a great woman, you imbecile. How dare you allow people to write scandalous things on your wall?" After crossing out the message, Niral was able to stop a fight. They didn't finish their dosas or their tea. They left the restaurant laughing.

"You have relieved my mind so much, Niralbhai," Manu said. "Or should I say Lord?"

"Never call me that," Niral said angrily. "Did they call Krishna Lord in his time? They simply respected him as a wise equal."

Manu put his palms together. "You have done more for me than I deserve. Even more than The Brotherhood. Thank you, Niralbhai."

"Here's more," Niral said. He took the bag of diamonds from his pocket and held it out to Manu.

"What is this?" Manu asked, taking it.

"A gift. A girl who turns down OBC benefits must need money. Sell them in Surat. And consider this a down payment. I will get you more when I can."

Manu shook his head. "This is too much, Niralbhai. I don't deserve this."

"You saved them once before, remember? And you deserve more than you think. Believe me, Manu, the righteous will prevail if we follow the right path."

Glossary of Terms: Thai

Arahant (also known as Arhat)—Someone who has achieved Buddhist enlightenment and/or nirvana, the ultimate goal of the Buddhist path.

Auction—In Thailand, often done in the late hours at illicit bars or warehouses to "auction" women. During the event, women are seated on a stage and wear numbers. Men can bid on them to either take them home for sex or "own" them in other ways, depending on the type of auction. Often the women do this voluntarily to pay bills or debts, but sometimes force may be applied.

Baht—Monetary currency of Thailand.

Baht bus (also known as a songthaew)—A pickup truck with an open back and two long seats that picks up passengers for a fee. They usually take set routes and sometimes don't leave until a certain number of passengers are aboard.

Bar fine (also known as compensation fee)—A fee paid to take away a bar girl, go-go dancer, or masseuse from her establishment to have sex with her. This is in addition to the fee paid for sex and sometimes may be added even if going to a short time room (see below) within the establishment. The room might have its own fee, too.

Boom boom—Slang for sex at Thai bars, usually in exchange for money.

Buddha (originally named Siddhartha Gautama)—An Indian prince from the 5th or 6th century BC, who gave up his royal lifestyle and escaped society to become a monk and reach enlightenment. Through his life and teachings, his followers created Buddhism, one of the major religions of the world and the primary religion of Thailand.

Buddhism—The major religion of Thailand, derived from the teaching of Buddha. There are two major strains of Buddhism: Theravada, which is the one prominent in Thailand, and Mahayana, which is prominent in countries like Japan.

Burma—Now known as Myanmar, a nation to the west of Thailand, where many illegal immigrants in Thailand come from. These immigrants are still colloquially known as Burmese.

Chocalee—Slang for ya ba (see below) in northern Thailand due to the strong chocolate smell and taste it often leaves in the mouth.

Compensation fee—See "Bar fine."

Cool heart (also known as Jai yen)—In Thai, it means keeping a cool and composed manner in a tense situation, often dissolving the situation through laughter, diplomacy or compromise.

Faen—A boyfriend or girlfriend.

Farang—A foreigner. It literally refers to those of Caucasian race, although it can be used colloquially to refer to any foreigners.

Gaeng sohm—A sour orange curry from southern Thailand made with fish, turmeric, and pineapple. It is often eaten with roti, a flat bread.

Gik—A casual mistress or "fuck friend." A gik is less formal than a mia noi (see definition). Often, a male or female has multiple giks they can call to hang out with.

Golden Triangle—An area near the borders of Thailand, Laos, and Myanmar where opium and ya ba is made and trafficked.

Gooay deeo—Wide rice noodles, usually fried with chicken, egg, squid, and/or garlic oil. Typically, you can get this dish or some variation of it at street stalls in Bangkok.

Grand Palace—A complex of buildings in Bangkok where the Kings of Thailand have had official residence since the 18th century. It includes panels of mythological drawings from the *Ramakien*, the ancient Thai epic.

Hanuman—A central figure in India's epic *Ramayana* and Thailand's similar *Ramakien*. Hanuman is an ape-man who is a strong devotee of Rama. He is the God of celibacy, a yogi who can control his senses, and a Brahmachari (devotee of Brahma) who can perform selfless actions (bhakti).

Isan—A large area of northern Thailand often regarded as the poorest section of Thailand. Many prostitutes, bar girls, go-go dancers, and masseuses in Bangkok and other larger Thai cities originate from Isan.

Johnny Walker—An American whiskey often drank in Thailand.

Kanom jeen nam ngeeo—Northern Thai dish consisting of noodles in a pork and tomato broth.

Karaoke boat—Essentially a river cruise, either for a few hours or an entire day or night, where you can listen to music and participate in karaoke.

Kathoey (also known as a ladyboy)—A transgender Thai.

Khao yum—A traditional spicy, southern Thai rice salad dish.

Khon Kaen University—A public research university in Khon Kaen, Thailand.

Khua kling—A southern Thai dish of roasted meat and curry paste. It is usually spicy and dry.

Korp khun krap—Thank you; said by a male.

Krap/ka—Krap is often used after a phrase to connote that a male is saying the phrase. Ka is used for females.

Ladyboy (also known as kathoey)—A transgender Thai.

Lady drink—A special drink a patron buys for a bar girl that usually costs twice as much, or more, than a normal drink. This usually suggests that the patron is interested in buying the girl's time, possibly leading to short time or long time (see below) later in the night.

Lanna—A Thai ethnic group from northern Thailand, named after the ancient Lan Na kingdom.

Lao—Of ethnic or national origin from the nation of Laos, north of Thailand. Many northern Thais and Thais from Isan have Lao cultural attributes, and some prostitutes in northern Thailand originate from Laos.

Long time—Paying a prostitute for her time where the patron will keep her overnight or through the next day, depending on negotiation.

Long time fee—Fee paid for sex with a prostitute for a "long time." The patron may also have to pay a bar fine to take her from the establishment where he met her (bar, go-go club, massage parlor, etc.).

Lose face (also known as sia naa)—Loss of honor for a Thai. In a public situation, causing a Thai to lose face could result in them behaving in an unexpectedly violent manner.

Lychee—Small round fruit with rough skin and a soft white interior.

Meter kap—"Meter, please." Said when in a taxi, especially from the Bangkok airport. Taxi drivers often deliberately don't put on the meter and charge exorbitant amounts of money when they get their (usually foreign) passenger to their destination, so it helps to insist on the meter.

Another common scam is taking the highway and charging a fee, so a passenger can also insist on not taking a highway.

Mia noi—A minor wife, or mistress, common among men in Thailand of various backgrounds.

Middle Way (also known as the Middle Path)—Major doctrine of Buddhist philosophy that emphasizes a middle way of moderation between sensual indulgence and asceticism. It is the concept that leads to the Noble Eightfold Path to nirvana, which is right understanding, right thought, right action, right speech, right effort, right livelihood, right concentration, and right mindfulness.

Monk—A priest in Buddhism. Every Thai male is expected to be a monk for a short period of time in youth. Monks are highly respected in Thailand.

Nam prik num—An appetizer consisting of garlic, green chilies, rice, and pork.

Nirvana—The ultimate goal of the Buddhist path. Enlightenment or liberation.

Noble Eightfold Path—See definition within "Middle Way."

Payasam—A rice pudding known in India as kheer.

Pha nung—A cloth worn along the lower body that resembles a long skirt.

Poo noy—Within a hierarchical social position in Thailand, it is considered the junior position (literally "little person"). Poo noys are supposed to show obedience to elders, known as poo yai (literally "big person") and not question them. Poo yai, in turn, sponsor poo noy, buy things for them, etc.

Poo yai—The elder in a hierarchical relationship in Thailand, the Poo yai sponsor the Poo noy and give them favors when possible.

Pussy pong—A demonstration in Thai bars where a woman shoots a ping pong ball, and other objects, including bananas, out of her vagina. This could be shot at other performers or at the audience.

Ramakien—Thailand's national epic, similar to and derived from India's *Ramayana*.

Red Shirts—Slang for a Thai political movement called the United Front for Democracy Against Dictatorship, initially favoring the policies and government of former Prime Minister Thaksin Shinawatra.

Roti—A flat bread, usually eaten with a curry in southern Thailand. It could also be filled with fruits and other things and eaten as a dessert or snack.

Same same—A common phrase in Thailand, used to suggest that something is similar, whether a hotel, meal, etc.

Sanuk—Fun. It is a major aspect of Thai culture where even work is meant to be a pleasant activity. The opposite is mai sanuk, meaning one is not having fun. Often, this will be rectified by Thais with an activity that is sanuk.

Sanuk mai krap—A question asking "Are you having fun?"

Sawat dee krap—Hello; said by male.

Sen yai noodles—Wide rice noodles used in a variety of Thai dishes.

Short time—Paid sex with a prostitute that lasts one to three hours.

Short time fee—Fee for "short time" sex with a prostitute (bar girl, go-go dancer or masseuse).

Short time room—A private room where a prostitute from a bar or go-go club will take a patron for sex. Short time connotes that there will be a brief sexual exchange. There may be an additional fee for using the room, in addition to a bar fine and short time fee.

Sia naa—Losing face in Thai society or a Thai social situation. Also see "losing face."

Singha—A Thai beer. Other Thai beers are Tiger and Chang.

Songthaew—See "baht bus."

Stupa—A structure, usually with dome and a pointed top, that is a Buddhist shrine. However, it can have a variety of designs.

Sucky—Slang for blowjob.

Sujata—In Buddhist history, a milkmaid who gave Buddha payasam, ending his seven years of fasting and leading to him to develop The Middle Way as a philosophy.

Tatami mat—Flooring material used in Japanese-style rooms.

Tee rak—Thai slang for sweetheart.

Thai-Chinese—Thai people who are ethnically Chinese. They are the largest minority group in Thailand, have been integrated into the country for over 200 years, and play a role in the Thai economy, military, and political class.

Theravada—The tradition of Buddhism prominent in Thailand.

Tom yam soup (also known as tom yum soup)—A hot and sour soup often cooked with shrimp.

Toot—Derogatory slang for homosexual.

Tuk-tuk—Similar to a rickshaw in India, a small, three-wheeled taxi.

U-Tapao—Now a Thai Navy Airfield, it was once a base of US military operations during the Vietnam War.

Wai—Similar to a namaste in India, a wai is a Thai greeting where the giver holds their palms together and bows.

Wat Pho—Buddhist temple complex to the south of the Grand Palace in Bangkok.

Wittayayon—Slang for Khon Kaen Wittayayon School, which is a public middle/high school in Khon Kaen, Thailand.

Ya ba—Tablets that include a combination of methamphetamine and caffeine.

Yellow Shirts—Slang for a Thai political movement called the People's Alliance for Democracy that initially opposed the policies and government of former Prime Minister Thaksin Shinawatra.

Glossary of Terms: Australian

Back-door bandit—A male homosexual.

Bloke—A dude, a general term for a man or friend, usually with positive connotation.

Bogan—An unsophisticated person, a hick.

Bogged in—To eat heartily.

Boys in blue—The police.

Brass razoo—An antiquated coin, but usually used in the phrase "I haven't got a brass razoo," which means the speaker is out of money.

Bugger—To sodomize, to have intercourse anally. It could also be used to refer to someone who is annoying, in a derogatory or affectionate way, or as a general expletive.

Bugger buddies—Homosexuals.

Busy boy—Someone who is very active or is going to be very busy.

Chunder—Vomit.

Chunder-fuck—Someone who vomits and can't hold their liquor.

Coit—Asshole, someone's asshole.

Coit dumpster— Promiscuous homosexual.

Cooee—A call or shout used to find people. When used in a phrase "within cooee" it means within manageable distance.

Cum dumpster—Slut, a promiscuous woman.

Cunt—Literally the female vagina. While it is typically a derogatory word used for a woman, and usually is used this way, in Australian slang it could also be neutral or positive, especially when used with a modifying adjective ("sick cunt," for example).

Dipstick—An idiot.

Dob in—To inform on someone.

Donger—Penis.

Dosh—Money.

Fair go—Generally a term that connotes someone is being given a fair chance. It could also imply that something is done fairly or without discrimination.

Fart knocker—A male homosexual, or generally a stupid or heinous person.

Fit—Good for something.

G'day—Good day, hello. Often used in the phrase "G'day mate!" meaning "Hello friend!"

Gab—To talk.

Gammin—Joking, lying, deceiving.

Growler—A hairy and unkempt vagina.

Heaps—A lot.

Heifer—A heavy, fat woman.

How ya going?—How are you doing?

Hezza—Slang for heroin.

Jack—Police officer.

Johnson—Penis.

Mate—A friend, an amicable form of address to another person.

Moolah—Money.

Mut—Vagina.

Pimp—A man who prostitutes a woman or makes money off of a prostitute's earnings.

Poofter—Homosexual.

Reckon—Think; I think.

Randy—Showing sexual attraction or arousal.

Rennie—A heartburn medicine similar to Tums, used more often in Commonwealth countries.

Root—To fuck, sexual intercourse.

Rubbish—Bullshit, nonsense.

Shonky—Shoddy or fraudulent.

Sweetie—Darling, sweetheart.

Swipe—Steal.

Tucker—Food.

Wanker—Literally meaning "one who masturbates." It is used as a common and general insult for people meaning they are a jerk-off. Sometimes, it is combined with a hand gesture mimicking male masturbation.

Wog—An ethnic slur, usually someone of Mediterranean origin, but can also be used on people of southern European or Middle Eastern origin.

Yabber—To talk a lot.

GLOSSARY OF TERMS: INDIAN

Ahimsa—Nonviolence in the Hindu tradition.

Amba (also known as Ambamata and Ambika)—Hindu goddess, usually a form of Durga.

Arjuna—Character in the Indian epic *Mahabharata*, and the character to whom Krishna narrates the *Bhagavad Gita*. Arjuna is the third of the five Pandava brothers, who are the rightful heirs to the throne of the Hastinapura kingdom. Krishna is his cousin, and his doubts about fighting the Kurukshetra war against his family members is the basis for the *Bhagavad Gita*.

Artha—In Hinduism, one of the four major aims in life, dealing with wealth, status, and career. The others are Kama (pleasure), Dharma (duty), and Moksha (renunciation).

Atman (also known as Brahman, although in some definitions they are different. See definition)—God, the divine life force, as well as one's true self or inner soul, which is part of the divine life force and becomes one with it once the individual attains enlightenment. It is the combination of the three main Gods (or the Trimurti): Brahma (The Generator), Vishnu (The Operator), and Shiva (The Destroyer). Atman can be obtained through enlightenment in successive reincarnations, though beliefs vary. In some beliefs, Atman and Brahman are identical; in others, they are mirrors where Atman is the true self and Brahman is the metaphysical self.

Aunti (also known **as** Auntie)—A respectful Anglo-Indian term for an elder woman.

Avatar—The form a God, usually Vishnu, takes when he or she incarnates on earth. This being, including humans like Krishna and animals like Matsya (a fish), profoundly alters world events. Most Hindus count ten avatars for Vishnu, but these beliefs vary. Some Hindus believe that Moses, Jesus, and Muhammad, among others, were also avatars.

Ayodhya—City in India where the epic *Ramayana* is based and also where there has been much conflict between Hindus and Muslims, especially over the Babri Mosque, or Babri Masjid, which was allegedly built over a temple of Rama and was destroyed in 1992 by Hindu nationalists, leading to riots.

Batata poha—Gujarati snack made with potatoes and beaten rice flakes, known as poha.

Bhagvan—Gujarati word for God.

Bhagavad Gita (also known as the *Gita*)—The text of the dialogue that Arjuna, the third of the Pandava brothers, and his cousin Krishna had on the battlefield of Kurukshetra in the epic *Mahabharata*. It is considered one of the holiest texts in Hinduism.

Bhai—Respectful term for brother.

Bhajan—Holy Hindu songs, usually sung by groups of worshippers.

Bhajiya—A fried snack, also called pakora. Could contain a number of ingredients including onions, potato, and cauliflower, then dipped into a gram flour and fried.

Bharat natyam—A type of Indian dance performed by one dancer.

Bhat—Boiled rice, often eaten with dal (dal-bhat).

Bhen (also known as Ben)—Respectful term for sister.

Bhima—The second eldest of the Pandava brothers in the Indian epic *Mahabharata*, and the fiercest rival of Duryodhana.

Bhinda shak—Okra cooked in oil and with spices, often eaten with rotli.

Bhishma—One of the central characters in the *Mahabharata*, a relative of both Pandavas and Kauravas, who takes a vow of celibacy and is given the ability to end his life whenever he wishes. He fights in the Kurukshetra War on the side of the Kauravas and dies on a bed of arrows at his wish.

Bollywood—The large, popular contemporary Indian film industry.

Brahma—One of the three major Gods in Hinduism, known as the "Generator" because he is thought to have created the world.

Brahman—See "Atman."

Brahmacharya—Of the four stages of life in Hinduism, this is the first, the bachelor stage. It is from childhood to twenty-five years of age. In ancient times, a brahmacharya would attend an ashram where he would learn from a guru/teacher and maintain celibacy until marriage and the householder (grihastha) stage of life. The other two stages are forest dweller (vanaprastha) and sannyasa (renunciation). Those priests who practice celibacy and/or worship the god Brahma can also be referred to as Brahmacharya.

Brahmin—One of the four major castes in Hinduism. Brahmins are the priests and scholars. If ranked hierarchically, they are the highest caste in terms of status and respect, though ideally, they are supposed to have little material wealth or power.

Chaas—A drink made from yogurt and water.

Chai—Black tea with milk, herbs, and spices.

Chandlo (also known as a tilak)—A red dot or smudge placed on a forehead using kum kum powder. Usually applied when worshipping God in the temple or at home, during religious ceremonies, or on auspicious days. Signifies, among other things, the worship of intelligence.

Chaniya choli—A colorful, ornately embroidered and mirrored dress for women featuring a short top and skirt, including a decorative scarf called an odhni.

Chutney—A sauce used as a condiment for Indian snacks and cuisines.

Dabbawalla—A lunch box and/or the lunch box delivery system or deliverer for the lunch boxes in India.

Dal—A soup made from split peas and lentils, a staple of a Gujarati meal. Often eaten with bhat (dal-bhat) or boiled rice.

Dalit—Descendants of the "untouchable" caste in India. This "untouchable" caste did laborer jobs often considered unclean. Although, traditionally the Indian caste system has four castes, the "untouchables" were a submerged fifth caste.

Deddy—Short or affectionate Gujarati (see below) term for Father.

Desi—Slang for people of Indian descent or diaspora.

Desi daru (also known as daru)—An alcoholic beverage often prepared in India's rural and impoverished areas, what would be referred to in the US as "moonshine."

Dharma—One's righteous duty or the right way. Contrasts with adharma, which is the wrong way or immorality.

Dhokla—Snack made from chickpeas and rice. It is similar to Khaman but usually whiter, thicker, and not as sweet.

Dhoti—A cloth that is wrapped around the groin and thighs.

Dikra—Dear child.

Divo—A hand-created candle made of ghee.

Dosa—A fried crepe of rice and lentil batter that serves as a wrap for potatoes and other fillings. There are different types of dosas, depending on the flavor and content of rice batter, fillings, and spiciness. The most popular is masala dosa, which contains spicy potatoes. Mysore masala dosa includes a red chutney filling. Pondicherry dosa is similar but sometimes includes vegetables. In a rava masala dosa, the crepe is made from wheat and rice flour.

Dubla (also known as Halpati)—A caste of laborers in Gujarat, India.

Durga—Hindu goddess of war.

Duryodhana—In the *Mahabharata*, he is the son of Dhritarashtra and crown prince of the kingdom Hastinapura, who fights the Pandava brothers for the throne in the Kurukhetra war.

Dwarka—Ancient Indian city in Gujarat that was Krishna's kingdom.

Faliya—A housing cluster in Gujarat that links people of a similar caste.

Gandhari—In the *Mahabharata*, she is the mother of Duryodhana and wife of Dhritarashtra. She is also the mother of all the Kauravas, meaning Duryodhana and his 99 siblings. She conceives these children with the assistance of Veda Vyasa, who incidentally is also credited as the author of the epic.

Ganesh (also known as Ganapati)—An elephant-headed god, son of Shiva and Parvati, often worshipped as the God of intelligence, knowledge, wisdom, the arts and sciences, and the remover of obstacles.

Gayatri—Hindu goddess, personification of the Gayatri mantra from the *Rigveda*, one of the four canonical Vedic texts.

Gayatri mantra—A widely recited and revered mantra in both Hindu and Buddhist traditions.

Ghee—Clarified butter.

Godhra—City in Gujarat, India where a train was burned in 2002, followed by communal riots.

Gopi—A female cowherder. In ancient times, they were devoted to the avatar Krishna.

Grihastha—The second stage of life in Hinduism, the householder stage dealing with marriage and fulfillment of social duty.

Gujarat—A state in northwest India where the major language spoken is Gujarati.

Gujarati—People from the Northwestern state of Gujarat in India and the language they speak.

Guru—Sage or teacher.

Guru dakshina—In ancient India, a gift given to a teacher after a period of service.

Halpati (also known as Dubla)—A caste in Gujarat of laborers.

Hanuman—Devotee of Rama and one of the central characters in the Indian *Ramayana* and Thai *Ramakien*, Hanuman is often depicted as a monkey-man and is considered a master of celibacy, an ideal brahmacharya and yogi, has mastery of over his senses, performs selfless work, and achieves devotion to God. In the *Ramakien*, he is considered God-king of the apes.

Hastinapura—In the *Mahabharata*, the kingdom fought over by the Pandavas and the Kauravas.

Hijra—In India, the transgendered and eunuchs. Hijra often live in communities and come around during weddings to demand money. Not giving to them is considered a sin and can have bad consequences and omens. Some believe hijra have divine powers.

Hindustani—Technically related to Hindi language or Hindu people, generally used to refer to having a Hindu cultural aura.

Hindutva—A form of Hindu nationalism emphasizing that a Hindu way of life should be central to Indian national identity.

Hiranyakashipu—Corrupt king who received divine powers by praying to Brahma. He was not able to be killed, day or night, by man or beast, in earth or space, inside or outside, by animate or inanimate objects. Seeing Vishnu as his enemy, he became upset by his son Prahlad's unswerving devotion to Vishnu. After various methods of killing Prahlad failed, Vishnu incarnated himself as Narasimha, a half-man half-lion, and killed Hiranyakashipu with his claws at twilight, in the middle of a doorway, on his lap.

Holi—A spring festival inspired by Prahlad's triumph over Holika (see below). Participants usually throw colors at each other and dance around a huge bonfire.

Holika—Hiranyakashipu's sister, who had the gift of not being burned by fire. Hiranyakashipu had her sit on a lit pyre with his son, Prahlad, on her lap, hoping to burn him to death, but when Prahlad prayed to Lord Vishnu, Holika died and Prahlad survived. It is the mythological inspiration for the Hindu holiday/spring festival Holi.

Idli sambar—A meal combination of a rice cake (idli) and a lentil stew (sambar).

Indra—Hindu God, and the king of heaven.

Janoi—A simple, multi-threaded string that is worn across the chest, over the left shoulder. and under the right arm. It is received by brahmin and kshatriya (see below) boys after a janoi ceremony, usually when they are teenagers. It represents their passage into their rightful role in society and their knowledge of prayers expected of their caste. Today, it is often merely given as a symbolic passage into manhood.

Kadhi—A drink made from yogurt and gram flour. Often eaten with khichdi, a kind of rice made with lentils or pulao.

Kafni pajama (also known as a kurta pajama)—A male dress featuring loose pajama bottoms and a long pullover shirt. The female version is called a salwar kameez or panjabi.

Kafir—An Arabic term used by many Muslims meaning infidel or unbeliever of Islam.

Kaka—Respectful Gujarati term for blood uncle, though sometimes it is used for respected non-relatives in place of "Uncle."

Kali Yuga—In Hinduism, the last of the four eras of time the world goes through. During Kali Yuga, humanity degenerates spiritually and morally. The other three yugas are Satya Yuga, Treta Yuga, and Dvapara Yuga.

Kama—Desire, pleasure in life.

Kama Sutra—An ancient Sanskrit text on the pleasure aspects of life, including desire, love, sexuality, and marriage.

Kamwali—A maid.

Karma—A complex Hindu concept regarding one's actions and their cause and effect relationship to one's fate and reincarnation.

Kartikeya—Hindu god of war, son of Shiva and Parvati, and brother of Ganesha.

Kauravas—In the *Mahabharata*, the one hundred children of King Dhritarashtra who claim the throne of the kingdom Hastinapura.

Khaman—A Gujarati snack similar to dhokla but softer and often sweeter, made from chickpeas and gram flour.

Khichdi—A kind of rice made with lentils. Often eaten with Kadhi, a yogurt-based drink, and together called Khichdi Kadhi.

Kohl—A black powder used as eye-makeup by Indians.

Kshatriya—One of the four major castes in Hinduism. Kshatriyas are the warrior and kingly caste. If ranked hierarchically, they are considered the second highest caste after Brahmins.

Krishna—One of the incarnations of Vishnu and a major character in the *Mahabharata*. A cousin of the Pandavas, he recites the *Bhagavad Gita* to Arjuna and serves as his charioteer during the battle of Kurukshetra.

Kum kum powder—A red powder used by Hindus for chandlos and other religious markings.

Kurukshetra—Battlefield where the major battle in the *Mahabharata* occurs.

Kurukshetra war—The major battle in the *Mahabharata* where the Pandava brothers and their allies fight the descendants of Dhritarashtra and their allies for the crown of the kingdom Hastinapura.

Laddu—A round sweet made of flour, sugar, and ghee.

Lakshmana—In the epic *Ramayana*, the younger brother of Rama.

Lakshmi (also written Laxmi)—Hindu goddess of prosperity. She is the wife of Vishnu and also, along with Parvati and Saraswati, part of the Tridevi.

Lila—In Hindu philosophy, the divine play of all reality, the human and cosmic drama of life.

Lingam—A phallic symbol usually associated with the god Shiva.

Mahabharata—The longest epic written in human history. It was authored by Veda Vyasa, who is also a minor character in it. Scholars differ on when it was written, but it was probably passed down orally by generations for thousands of years. The epic concerns the fate of the Kuru dynasty, from King Bharat to the death of Krishna. It features the *Bhagavad Gita* and the Kurukshetra war.

Mama—Uncle on the mother's side of the family.

Mandir—A Hindu temple.

Mantra—Words or phrases uttered that have sacred value.

Masala—A mixture of spices.

Masi—Aunt on the mother's side of the family.

Masjid—Mosque or worship hall for Muslims in India.

Mata—Respective term for mother or female goddess in Gujarati.

Mehndi—Body art, usually applied to the hands using paste derived from the henna plant.

Methi—Fenugreek seeds, often used as an ingredient when cooking Indian food.

Moksha—In Hinduism, liberation, perfection of consciousness, or becoming one with God. Can be obtained by human beings through four different methods: jnana-yoga (knowledge), bhakti-yoga (love, devotion), raja-yoga (meditation), and karma-yoga (action).

Mosal—In Gujarati, a person's mother's village.

Motimasi—Oldest aunt on the mother's side of the family. Moti means oldest and masi means aunt on the mother's side.

Motobhai—Big brother.

Mummy—Short or affectionate term for mother used by Gujarati people.

Namaste—A Hindu action used for both greeting someone and taking their leave, similar to the Thai wai. Usually, it is performed with palms together and a slight bow.

Nasta—Snack.

Odhni—A scarf worn with many Indian dresses, including a chaniya choli, sari, and punjabi.

Om—An Indian holy symbol, meaning, among other things, God.

Other Backwards Class (also known as Backwards Class)—The socially disadvantaged castes as defined by the Indian government. Public schools and government positions often will have a certain quota of this caste to fill. They also receive other benefits, sometimes colloquially described as OBC benefits. Another classification is Schedule Castes or Scheduled Tribes, which usually refers to Dalits, or the former untouchables.

Paan—An areca nut snack that is wrapped in a betel leaf, with tobacco and other substances often added. It is often placed in the mouth whole and then the juices are spat out during chewing.

Palathi—Sitting position with legs crossed and feet either sticking out or under the thighs (butterfly-style).

Pandavas—Five brothers who are primary characters in the *Mahabharata*.

Pandu—A character in the *Mahabharata*, descendent of the Kuru dynasty and father of Arjuna and the Pandavas.

Panjabi—See "salwar kameez."

Pappa—Short or affectionate Gujarati term for Father.

Parashurama—The sixth avatar of Vishnu, considered to be the first warrior saint.

Parvati—Hindu goddess of marriage, children, fertility, and love. Part of the Tridevi with Sarasvati and Laxmi, and wife of Shiva.

Patra—An Indian dish made of crushed chickpeas wrapped in big Taro leaves.

Perfect man—A person who has reached moksha after successive births and whose soul is thus ready to rejoin Atman upon death. This person sees the universe as God's lila, or playground, and is mentally detached from all things.

Phalguna Purnima—The last full moon day of the lunar month Phalguna, usually in February or March, when Holi is celebrated.

Prahlad—Son of Hiranyakashipu and a devotee of Vishnu. His father tries to have him killed, but he survives due to his devotion.

Pulao—A rice dish usually mixed with lentils and vegetables.

Puri—Small, round, thin, and puffy deep-fried bread often eaten on special occasions with shak (see below).

Rakshasa—A demon in Hindu mythology.

Rama—Seventh avatar of Vishnu in Hinduism and the hero of the Indian epic the *Ramayana* and the Thai epic *Ramakien*.

Ramayana—Indian epic authored by the sage Valmiki. It narrates the adventures of Lord Rama and his family, including Lakshmana, Sita, and his disciple Hanuman.

Rickshaw—Similar to a tuk-tuk in Thailand, a three-wheeled taxi.

Rigveda—One of the four canonical texts of the *Vedas*, called Samhitas, or collections of mantras. *Rigveda* is primarily filled with hymns. The other Samhitas are *Yajurveda, Samaveda,* and *Atharvaveda*.

Rishi—A Hindu sage.

Rosary—A ring of beads used to assist in praying.

Rotli—A thin, round, flat, unleavened bread made of flour that is rolled, then heated.

Sadhu—A Hindu ascetic.

Salwar kameez (also known as a panjabi)—A combination of pants and long shirt worn by women. The male version is the kafni pajama.

Sambar—A lentil and vegetable soup.

Sanskrit—Ancient Indian written language. Many of the ancient prayers are in this language, and most Indian names derive from it.

Sanyasi—One who renounces worldly desires and concentrates on a spiritual life of detachment.

Saraswati—Hindu goddess of art, knowledge, and education. Along with the wives of Vishnu and Shiva, Lakshmi and Parvati, she is part of the female trinity of gods, or Tridevi.

Sari (also known as saree or shari)—A traditional Indian dress for women consisting of a blouse, or choli, a petticoat, or lehenga, and a single cloth wrapped around the body.

Sev—Thin, crunchy noodles made of chickpeas and eaten as a snack.

Shak (also spelled shaak)—The main staple of Gujarati meals. It consists of a single or multiple vegetables cooked in oil. It is usually eaten with a rotli or other type of bread.

Sherwani—A long, decorative coat worn in India.

Shiva—One of the three major gods in Hinduism. Known as the "Destroyer" because he has the power to destroy the world when it has become too corrupt.

Shiva Sena—A Hindu nationalist political organization in India.

Shloka—Indian epic poetry, usually rehearsed or chanted at Hindu functions.

Shrikhand—Sweet made of strained yogurt.

Siddhartha (also known as Siddhartha Gautama)—Original name of the Buddha, an Indian prince from the 6th or 5th century BC who gave up his royal lifestyle and escaped society to become a monk and reach enlightenment. From his life and teachings, his followers created Buddhism, one of the major religions of the world and the primary religion of Thailand and other Asian countries.

Sikh—A devotee of the religion Sikhism, an offshoot of Hinduism started in the 15th century.

Sita—The wife of Rama in the Indian epic *Ramayana*.

Sudarshana chakra—A spinning disk with 108 sharp edges that is spun on a finger and flung to cut off heads and limbs. One of Vishnu and Krishna's weapons. Vishnu is often depicted with one in pictures and statutes. It also represents the wheel of time.

Swastika—An ancient symbol of spirituality and godliness, often found around doorways in Hindu homes and other places to be blessed. Unfortunately, after its usage by the Nazi Party in Germany, it has a negative and antisemitic connotation in the West.

Sudra—One of the four major castes in Hinduism. Sudras are the labor caste. If ranked hierarchically, they are the lowest caste but theoretically carry the least responsibility.

Thali—A round dish usually made of steel, with many pockets for different types of Gujarati food.

Topi—Hat.

Trinity of Gods (also known as Trimurti for the male gods, and Tridevi for the female goddesses)—The trinity in Hinduism are the forces that generate, operate and destroy the world, as represented by Brahma, Vishnu, and Shiva among the male gods, and Saraswati, Lakshmi, and Parvati among the female goddesses.

Uncle—A respectful term for an adult male.

Uttapam—A type of dosa with toppings.

Vada—A fried snack, usually made of potatoes or legumes, often eaten with chutney.

Vaishya—One of the four major castes in Hinduism. Vaishyas are the tradesmen, artisans, and merchants of society. If ranked hierarchically, they are the third highest caste.

Vedas—The ancient Hindu texts written in Sanskrit that are often cited as the oldest scriptures of Hinduism.

Vedic—Related to the teachings and traditions stemming from the *Vedas*.

Veena—An ancient musical instrument shaped similar to a violin or guitar.

Veg—A sign posted in India indicating an establishment serves vegetarian food.

Vishnu—One of the three major Gods in Hinduism. Known as the "Operator" because he keeps the world running and steps in through incarnation when things are not going right.

Wadi—An orchard.

Yagna (also spelled Yagya or Yajya)—A Hindu ritual with fire, normally officiated by a guru or rishi who leads the singing of prayers, or mantras.

Yoga—Physical exercises from ancient Hindu scriptures.

Yudhishthira—Eldest brother of the Pandavas, rightful heir to the throne who ascends it after the Kurukshetra War.

Acknowledgments

Who else to thank but the usual suspects of beta readers: Matthew Allison, Panth Naik, Robert Ballard, Anasuya Desai. My ever-wonderful and tireless cover designer, Fena Lee; my focused copyeditor, Christine Keleny; and meticulous proofreader, Ashley Evans. Jaymi Grullon, new to my team and eager to learn, worked hard as the publicist for *The Run and Hide*.

To my parents and my amazing core of friends (you know who you are), you've given me the valuable support network and life balance without which I could not produce or disseminate my works. To my countless acquaintances around the world, in real life and on social media, and to my extended family, you've engaged, challenged, and helped me, and I could not be more grateful. To all my readers, whatever your opinions about my writings. I'm so happy that you bother to peruse these pages. My many teachers, whether they be professors or plumbers, who I have learned from throughout the years. Queens Public Library, that has given me employment for twelve years and counting.

No author, particularly independent ones, can produce their works without support, and everyone above and countless others have aided in the writing and publication of *The Brotherhood Chronicle* series, and I thank you.

Tejas Desai
September 2019

Made in the USA
Las Vegas, NV
26 June 2021

25459150R10207